HALO®
FIRST STRIKE

NOVELS IN THE *NEW YORK TIMES* BESTSELLING HALO® SERIES

HALO®
FIRST STRIKE

ERIC NYLUND

A TOM DOHERTY ASSOCIATES BOOK
NEW YORK

TOR®

This is a work of fiction. All of the characters, organizations, and events portrayed in this novel are either products of the author's imagination or are used fictitiously.

HALO®: FIRST STRIKE

Copyright © 2003, 2010 by Microsoft Corporation

Foreword copyright © 2010 by Microsoft Corporation

Originally published by Del Rey, The Random House Publishing Group

All rights reserved.

Microsoft, Halo, the Halo logo, Xbox, and the Xbox logo are trademarks of the Microsoft group of companies.

A Tor Book
Published by Tom Doherty Associates, LLC
175 Fifth Avenue
New York, NY 10010

www.tor-forge.com

Tor® is a registered trademark of Tom Doherty Associates, LLC.

ISBN 978-0-7653-6731-0

First Tor Trade Paperback Edition: December 2010
First Tor Mass Market Edition: May 2012

Printed in the United States of America

0 9 8 7 6 5

ACKNOWLEDGMENTS TO THE 2010 EDITION

None of this would have been possible without Microsoft staffers Jacob Benton, Nicolas "Sparth" Bouvier, Alicia Brattin, Gabriel "Robogabo" Garza, Jon Goff, Kevin Grace, Tyler Jeffers, Frank O'Connor, Jeremy Patenaude, Chris Schlerf, Kenneth Scott, and Kiki Wolfkill.

Nor without the efforts of the staff at Tor Books: Tom Doherty, Eric Raab, Whitney Ross, Seth Lerner, Megan Barnard, Teresa DeLucci, Jim Kapp, Lauren Hougen, Heather Saunders, Nathan Weaver, Justin Golenbock, and Patty Garcia.

343 Industries would like to thank Bungie Studios, Scott Dell'Osso, Nick Dimitrov, David Figatner, Nancy Figatner, Josh Kerwin, Bryan Koski, Eric Nylund, Bonnie Ross-Ziegler, Phil Spencer, and Carla Woo.

This edition features early drafts of the new cover art, which have been included periodically throughout the book. These images give a small insight into the process of creating the new cover from artists within 343 Industries.

FOREWORD

In the aftermath of the launch of *Halo®: Reach,* the prequel video game for the Xbox 360, readers have a lot of questions. Luckily, of all the Halo novels, *First Strike* is the one that answers the most, at least as those questions relate to the events of *Halo® 1, 2,* and *Reach*. Naturally, that is not a coincidence.

It offers insight into Spartan lore, the Forerunner enigma, Covenant treachery, and much, much more.

Working with Eric over the years, we here at the Halo franchise have put the poor fellow through hell. But like Dante, he seems to have the intestinal fortitude to deal with any layer we offer him. In *First Strike,* he finally got the chance to talk directly to the game fiction, yet did so without relying too much on the Chief's lone-wolf heroics, or the linear nature of the gameplay events.

Furthermore, Eric introduced us to some truly memorable characters, and deepened and broadened the ones we were already familiar with. Broads that included, of course, Dr. Halsey and Cortana.

Spoilers ahead . . .

Halsey's excavation of the Forerunner cavern in *First Strike* can be glimpsed in the Reach game, and Cortana's eventual fate, with a little geographical tinkering by Bungie, is also illuminated in the game.

Now, if you think about the challenges of creating all-new characters—including a passel of Spartans—while still maintaining solid connections to the game, and never overstepping the bounds of a chronological jail we popped him into, you begin to see the level of skill and attention to detail Mr. Nylund brought to the table.

Eric is also a master of encapsulation. *First Strike* still feels, like *Fall of Reach* before it, foundational, but as we see in Halsey's journal entries included in the *Reach* game's limited and legendary editions, he also has a knack for tying up ends that, while never loose, were sometimes knotted somewhere in the deep canon.

Of all the Halo novels, *First Strike,* to me, captures the best balance of high adventure and game connection. It does so effortlessly and in some places, it actually feels like a video game. You hurtle through each encounter with hardly a breath to spare, and if you find yourself looking for a save-game feature, simply do what I do, and fold the corner of the page. It adds character.

SECTION 0

REACH

DISCOVERY

CHAPTER
ONE

SPARTAN 104, Frederic, twirled a combat knife, his fingers nimble despite the bulky MJOLNIR combat armor that encased his body. The blade traced a complicated series of graceful arcs in the air. The few remaining Naval personnel on the deck turned pale and averted their eyes—a Spartan wielding a knife was generally accompanied by the presence of several dead bodies.

He was nervous, and this was more than the normal pre-mission jitters. The team's original objective—the capture of a Covenant ship—had been scrubbed in the face of a new enemy offensive. The Covenant were en route to Reach, the last of the United Nations Space Command's major military strongholds.

Fred couldn't help but wonder what use ground troops would be in a ship-to-ship engagement. The knife spun.

Around him, his squadmates loaded weapons, stacked gear, and prepped for combat, their efforts redoubled since the ship's Captain had personally come down to the mustering area to brief the team leader, SPARTAN 117—but Fred was already squared away. Only Kelly had finished stowing gear before him.

He balanced the point of the knife on his armored finger. It hung there for several seconds, perfectly still.

A subtle shift in the *Pillar of Autumn*'s gravity caused the knife to tip. Fred plucked it from the air and sheathed it in a single deft move. A cold feeling filled his stomach as he realized what the gravity fluctuation meant: The ship had just changed course—another complication.

Master Chief SPARTAN 117—John—marched to the nearest COM panel as Captain Keyes's face filled the screen.

Fred sensed a slight movement to his right—a subtle hand signal from Kelly. He opened a private COM freq to his teammate.

"Looks like we're in for more surprises," she said.

"Roger that," he replied, "though I think I've had enough surprises for one op."

Kelly chuckled.

Fred focused his attention on John's exchange with Keyes. Each Spartan—selected from an early age and trained to the pinnacle of military science—had undergone multiple augmentation procedures: biochemical, genetic, and cybernetic. As a result, a Spartan could hear a pin drop in a sandstorm, and every Spartan in the room was interested in what the Captain had to say. *If you're going to drop into hell,* CPO Mendez, the Spartans' first teacher, had once said, *you may as well drop with good intel.*

Captain Keyes frowned on the ship's viewscreen, a nonregulation pipe in his hand. Though his voice was calm, the Captain's grip on the pipe was white-knuckle tight as he outlined the situation. A single space vessel docked in Reach's orbital facilities had failed to delete its navigational database. If the NAV data fell into Covenant hands, the enemy would have a map to Earth.

"Master Chief," the Captain said, "I believe the Covenant will use a pinpoint Slipspace jump to a position just off the space dock. They may try to get their troops on the station before the Super MAC guns can take out their ships. This will be a difficult mission, Chief. I'm . . . open to suggestions."

"We can take care of it," the Master Chief replied.

Captain Keyes's eyes widened and he leaned forward in his command chair. "How exactly, Master Chief?"

"With all due respect, sir, Spartans are trained to handle diffi-cult missions. I'll split my squad. Three will board the space dock and make sure that NAV data does not fall into the Covenant's hands. The remainder of the Spartans will go groundside and re-pel the invasion forces."

Fred gritted his teeth. Given his choice, he'd rather fight the Covenant on the ground. Like his fellow Spartans, he loathed off-planet duty. The op to board the space dock would be fraught with danger at every turn—unknown enemy deployment, no gravity, useless intel, no dirt beneath his feet.

There was no question, though: The space op was the tough-est duty, so Fred intended to volunteer for it.

Captain Keyes considered John's suggestion. "No, Master Chief. It's too risky—we've got to make sure the Covenant don't get that NAV data. We'll use a nuclear mine, set it close to the docking ring, and detonate it."

"Sir, the EMP will burn out the superconductive coils of the orbital guns. And if you use the *Pillar of Autumn*'s conventional weapons, the NAV database may still survive. If the Covenant search the wreckage, they may obtain the data."

"True," Keyes said and tapped his pipe thoughtfully to his chin. "Very well, Master Chief. We'll go with your suggestion. I'll plot a course over the docking station. Ready your Spartans and prep two dropships. We'll launch you—" He consulted with Cortana. "—in five minutes."

"Aye, Captain. We'll be ready."

"Good luck," Captain Keyes said, and the viewscreen went black.

Fred snapped to attention as the Master Chief turned to face the Spartans. Fred began to step forward—

—but Kelly beat him to it. "Master Chief," she said, "permis-sion to lead the space op."

She had always been faster, damn her.

"Denied," the Master Chief said. "I'll be leading that one.

"Linda and James," he continued. "You're with me. Fred, you're Red Team leader. You'll have tactical command of the ground operation."

"Sir!" Fred shouted and started to voice a protest—then squelched it. Now wasn't the time to question orders . . . as much as he wanted to. "Yes, sir!"

"Now make ready," the Master Chief said. "We don't have much time left."

The Spartans stood a moment. Kelly called out, "Attention!" The soldiers snapped to and gave the Master Chief a crisp salute, which was promptly returned.

Fred switched to Red Team's all-hands freq and barked, "Let's move, Spartans! I want gear stowed in ninety seconds, and final prep in five minutes. Joshua: Liaise with Cortana and get me current intel on the drop area—I don't care if it's just weather satellite imagery, but I want pictures, and I want them ninety seconds ago."

Red Team jumped into action.

The pre-mission jitters were gone, replaced with a cold calm. There was a job to do, and Fred was eager to get to work.

Flight Officer Mitchell flinched as a stray energy burst streaked into the landing bay and vaporized a meter-wide section of bulkhead. Red-hot, molten metal splattered the Pelican drop-ship's viewport.

Screw this, he thought, and hit the Pelican's thrusters. The gun-metal-green transport—reinforced to carry more than twenty Spartans—balanced for a moment on a column of blue-white fire, then hurtled out of the *Pillar of Autumn*'s launch bay and into space. Five seconds later all hell broke loose.

Incoming energy bursts from the lead Covenant vessels cut across their vector and slammed into a COMSat. The communications satellite broke apart, disintegrating into glittering shards.

"Better hang on," Mitchell announced to his passengers in the dropship's troop bay. "Company's coming."

A swarm of Seraphs—the Covenant's scarablike attack fighters—fell into tight formation and arced through space on an intercept course for the dropship.

The Pelican's engines flared and the bulky ship plummeted toward the surface of Reach. The alien fighters accelerated and plasma bursts flickered from their gunports.

An energy bolt slashed past on the port side, narrowly missing the Pelican's cockpit.

Mitchell's voice crackled across the COM system: "Bravo-One to Knife Two-Six: I could use a little help here."

He rolled the Pelican to port to avoid a massive, twisted hunk of wreckage from a patrol cutter that had strayed too close to the oncoming assault wave. Beneath the blackened plasma scorches, he could just make out the UNSC insigne. Mitchell scowled. This was getting worse by the second. "Bravo-One to Knife Two-Six, where the hell are you?" he yelled.

A quartet of wedge-shaped, angular fighters slotted into covering position on Mitchell's scopes—Longswords, heavy fighters.

"Knife Two-Six to Bravo-One," a terse, female voice crackled across the COM channel. *"Keep your pants on. Business is good today."*

Too good. No sooner had the fighters taken escort position over his dropship than the approaching Covenant fighters opened up with a barrage of plasma fire.

Three of the Pelican's four Longsword escorts peeled off and powered toward the Covenant ships. Against the black of space, cannons flashed and missiles etched ghostly trails; Covenant energy weapons cut through the night and explosions dotted the sky.

The Pelican and its sole escort, however, accelerated straight toward the planet. It shot past whirling wreckage; it rolled and maneuvered as missiles and plasma bolts crisscrossed their path.

Mitchell flinched as Reach's orbital defense guns fired in a hot, actinic flash. A white ball of molten metal screamed directly over the Pelican and its escort as they rocketed beneath the defense platform's ring-shaped superstructure.

Mitchell sent the Pelican into the planet's atmosphere. Vaporous flames flickered across the ship's stunted nose, and the Pelican jounced from side to side.

"Bravo-One, adjust attack angle," the Longsword pilot advised. *"You're coming in too hot."*

"Negative," Mitchell said. "We're getting to the surface fast—or we're not getting there at all. Enemy contacts on my scopes at four by three o'clock."

A dozen more Covenant Seraphs fired their engines and angled toward the two descending ships.

"Affirmative: four by three. I've got 'em, Bravo-One," the Longsword pilot announced. *"Give 'em hell down there."*

The Longsword flipped into a tight roll and rocketed for the Covenant formation. There was no chance that the pilot could take out a dozen Seraphs—and Knife Two-Six had to know that. Mitchell only hoped that the precious seconds Two-Six bought them would be enough.

The Pelican opened its intake vents and ignited afterburners, plummeting toward the ground at thirteen hundred meters per second. The faint aura of flames around the craft roared from red to blinding orange.

The Pelican's aft section had been stripped of the padded crash seats that usually lined the section's port and starboard sides. The life-support generators on the firewall between passenger and pilot's compartment had also been discarded to make room. Under other circumstances, such modifications would have left the Pelican's troop bay unusually cavernous. Every square centimeter of space, however, was occupied.

Twenty-two Spartans braced themselves and clung to the

frame of the ship; they crouched in their MJOLNIR armor to absorb the shock of their rapid descent. Their armor was half a ton of black alloy, faintly luminous green ceramic plates, and winking energy shield emitters. Polarized visors and full helmets made them look part Greek hero and part tank—more machine than human. At their feet equipment bags and ammunition boxes were lashed in place. Everything rattled as the ship jostled through the increasingly dense air.

Fred hit the COM and barked: "Brace yourselves!" The ship lurched, and he struggled to keep his footing.

SPARTAN 087, Kelly, moved nearer and opened a frequency. "Chief, we'll get that COM malfunction squared away after we hit planetside," she said.

Fred winced when he realized that he'd just broadcast on FLEETCOM 7: He'd spammed every ship in range. Damn it.

He opened a private channel to Kelly. "Thanks," he said. Her reply was a subtle nod.

He knew better than to make such a simple mistake—and as his second in command, Kelly was rattled by his mistake with the COM, too. He needed her rock-solid. He needed *all* of Red Team frosty and wired tight.

Which meant that *he* needed to make sure he held it together. No more mistakes.

He checked the squad's biomonitors. They showed all green on his heads-up display, with pulse rates only marginally accelerated. The dropship's pilot was a different story. Mitchell's heart fired like an assault rifle.

Any problems with Red Team weren't physical; the biomonitors confirmed that much. Spartans were used to tough missions; UNSC High Command never sent them on any "easy" jobs.

Their job this time was to get groundside and protect the generators that powered the orbiting Magnetic Accelerator Cannon platforms. The fleet was getting ripped to shreds in space.

The massive MAC guns were the only thing keeping the Covenant from overrunning their lines and taking Reach.

Fred knew that if anything had Kelly and the other Spartans rattled, it was leaving behind the Master Chief and his hand-picked Blue Team.

Fred would have infinitely preferred to be with Blue Team. He knew every Spartan here felt like they were taking the easy way out. If the ship-jockeys managed to hold off the Covenant assault wave, Red Team's mission was a milk run, albeit a necessary one.

Kelly's hand bumped into Fred's shoulder, and he recognized it as a consoling gesture. Kelly's razor-edged agility was multiplied fivefold by the reactive circuits in her MJOLNIR armor. She wouldn't have "accidentally" touched him unless she meant it, and the gesture spoke volumes.

Before he could say anything to her, the Pelican angled and gravity settled the Spartans' stomachs.

"Rough ride ahead," the pilot warned.

The Spartans bent their knees as the Pelican rolled into a tight turn. A crate broke its retaining straps, bounced, and stuck to the wall.

The COM channel blasted static and resolved into the voice of the Longsword's pilot: *"Bravo Two-Six, engaging enemy fighters. Am taking heavy incoming fire—"* The channel was abruptly swallowed in static.

An explosion buffeted the Pelican, and bits of metal pinged off its thick hull.

Patches of armor heated and bubbled away. Energy blasts flashed through the boiling metal, filling the interior with fumes for a split second before the ship's pressurized atmosphere blew the haze out the gash in its side.

Sunlight streamed though the lacerated Titanium-A armor. The dropship lurched to port, and Fred glimpsed five Covenant

Seraph fighters driving after them and wobbling in the turbulent air.

"Gotta shake 'em," the pilot screamed. *"Hang on!"*

The Pelican pitched forward, and her engines blasted in full overload. The dropship's stabilizers tore away, and the craft rolled out of control.

The Spartans grabbed on to cross beams as their gear was flung about inside the ship.

"It's going to be a helluva hot drop, Spartans," their pilot hissed over the COM. *"Autopilot's programmed to angle. Reverse thrusters. Gees are takin' me out. I'll—"*

A flash of light outlined the cockpit hatch, and the tiny shockproof glass window shattered into the passenger compartment.

The pilot's biomonitor flatlined.

The rate of their dizzying roll increased, and bits of metal and instruments tore free and danced around the compartment.

SPARTAN 029, Joshua, was closest to the cockpit hatch. He pulled himself up and looked in. "Plasma blast," he said. He paused for a heartbeat, then added: "I'll reroute control to the terminal here." With his right hand, he furiously tapped commands onto the keyboard mounted on the wall. The fingers of his left hand dug into the metal bulkhead.

Kelly crawled along the starboard frame, held there by the spinning motion of the out-of-control Pelican. She headed aft of the passenger compartment and punched a keypad, priming the explosive bolts on the drop hatch.

"Fire in the hole!" she yelled.

The Spartans braced.

The hatch exploded and whipped away from the plummeting craft. Fire streamed along the outer hull. Within seconds the compartment became a blast furnace. With the grace of a high-wire performer, Kelly leaned out of the rolling ship, her armor's energy shields flaring in the heat.

The Covenant Seraph fighters fired their lasers, but the energy weapons scattered in the superheated wake of the dropping Pelican. One alien ship tumbled out of control, too deep in the atmosphere to easily maneuver. The others veered and arced up back into space.

"Too hot for them," Kelly said. "We're on our own."

"Joshua," Fred called out. "Report."

"The autopilot's gone, and cockpit controls are offline," Joshua answered. "I can counter our spin with thrusters." He tapped in a command; the port engine shuddered, and the ship's rolling slowed and ceased.

"Can we land?" Fred asked.

Joshua didn't hesitate to give the bad news. "Negative. The computer has no solution for our inbound vector." He tapped rapidly on the keyboard. "I'll buy as much time as I can."

Fred ran over their limited options. They had no parasails, no rocket-propelled drop capsules. That left them one simple choice: They could ride this Pelican straight into hell . . . or they could get off.

"Get ready for a fast drop," Fred shouted. "Grab your gear. Pump your suits' hydrostatic gel to maximum pressure. Suck it up, Spartans—we're landing hard."

"Hard landing" was an understatement. The Spartans—and their MJOLNIR armor—were tough. The armor's energy shields, hydrostatic gel, and reactive circuits, along with the Spartans' augmented skeletal structure, might be enough to withstand a high-speed crash landing . . . but not a supersonic impact.

It was a dangerous gamble. If Joshua couldn't slow the Pelican's descent, they'd be paste.

"Twelve thousand meters to go," Kelly shouted, still leaning over the edge of the aft door.

Fred told the Spartans: "Ready and aft. Jump on my mark."

The Spartans grabbed their gear and moved toward the open hatch.

The Pelican's engines screamed and pulsed as Joshua angled the thruster cams to reverse positions. The deceleration pulled at the Spartan team, and everyone grabbed, or made, a hand-hold.

Joshua brought what was left of the craft's control flaps to bear, and the Pelican's nose snapped up. A sonic boom rippled through the ship as its velocity dropped below Mach 1. The frame shuddered and rivets popped.

"Eight kilometers and this brick is still dropping fast," Kelly called out.

"Joshua, get aft," Fred ordered.

"Affirmative," Joshua said.

The Pelican groaned and the frame pinged from the stress—and then creaked as the craft shuddered and flexed. Fred set his armored glove on the wall and tried to will the craft to hold together a little longer.

It didn't work. The port engine exploded, and the Pelican tumbled out of control.

Kelly and the Spartans near the aft drop hatch dropped out. No more time.

"Jump," Fred shouted. *"Spartans: Go, go, go!"*

The rest of the Spartans crawled aft, fighting the gee forces of the tumbling Pelican. Fred grabbed Joshua—and they jumped.

CHAPTER

TWO

Fred saw the sky and earth flashing in rapid succession before his faceplate. Decades of training took over. This was just like a parasail drop . . . except this time there was no chute. He forced his arms and legs open; the spread-eagle position controlled his tumble and slowed his velocity.

Time seemed to simultaneously crawl and race—something Kelly had once dubbed "Spartan Time." Enhanced senses and augmented physiology meant that in periods of stress Spartans thought and reacted faster than a normal human. Fred's mind raced as he absorbed the tactical situation.

He activated his motion sensors, boosting the range to maximum. His team appeared as blips on his heads-up display. With a sigh of relief he saw that all twenty-two of them were present and pulling into a wedge formation.

"Covenant ground forces could be tracking the Pelican," Fred told them over the COM. "Expect AA fire."

The Spartans immediately broke formation and scattered across the sky.

Fred risked a sidelong glance and spotted the Pelican. It tumbled, sending shards of armor plating in glittering, ugly arcs, before it impacted into the side of a jagged snowcapped mountain.

The surface of Reach stretched out before them, two thousand meters below. Fred saw a carpet of green forest, ghostly mountains in the distance, and pillars of smoke rising from the west. He spied a sinuous ribbon of water that he recognized: Big Horn River.

The Spartans had trained on Reach for most of their early lives. This was the same forest where CPO Mendez had left them when they were children. With only pieces of a map and no food, water, or weapons, they had captured a guarded dropship and returned to HQ. That was the mission where John, now the Master Chief, had earned command of the group, the mission that had forged them into a team.

Fred pushed the memory aside. This was no homecoming.

UNSC Military Reservation 01478-B training facility would be due west. And the generators? He called up the terrain map and overlaid it on his display. Joshua had done his work well: Cortana had delivered decent satellite imagery as well as a topographic survey map. It wasn't as good as a spy-sat flyby, but it was better than Fred had expected on such short notice.

He dropped a NAV marker on the position of the generator complex and uploaded the data on the TACCOM to his team.

He took a deep breath and said: "That's our target. Move toward it but keep your incoming angle flat. Aim for the treetops. Let them slow you down. If you can't, aim for water . . . and tuck in your arms and legs before impact."

Twenty-one blue acknowledgment lights winked, confirming his order.

"Overpressurize your hydrostatics just before you hit."

That would risk nitrogen embolisms for his Spartans, but they were coming in at terminal velocity, which for a fully loaded Spartan was—he quickly calculated—130 meters per second. They had to overpressurize the cushioning gel or their organs would be crushed against the impervious MJOLNIR armor when they hit.

The acknowledgment lights winked again . . . although Fred sensed a slight hesitation.

Five hundred meters to go.

He took one last look at his Spartans. They were scattered across the horizon like bits of confetti.

He brought up his knees and changed his center of mass, trying to flatten his angle as he approached the treetops. It worked, but not as well or as quickly as he had hoped.

One hundred meters to go. His shield flickered as he brushed the tops of the tallest of the trees.

He took a deep breath, exhaled as deeply as he could, grabbed his knees, and tucked into a ball. He overrode the hydrostatic system and overpressurized the gel surrounding his body. A thousand tiny knives stabbed him—pain unlike any he'd experienced since the SPARTAN-II program had surgically altered him.

The MJOLNIR armor's shields flared as he broke through branches—then drained in one sudden burst as he impacted dead-center on a thick tree trunk. He smashed through it like an armored missile.

He tumbled, and his body absorbed a series of rapid-fire impacts. It felt like taking a full clip of assault rifle fire at point-blank range. Seconds later Fred slammed to a bone-crunching halt.

His suit malfunctioned. He could no longer see or hear anything. He stayed in that limbo state and struggled to stay conscious and alert. Moments later, his display was filled with stars. He realized then that the suit wasn't malfunctioning . . . *he* was.

"Chief!" Kelly's voice echoed in his head as if from the end of a long tunnel. "Fred, get up," she whispered. "We've got to move."

His vision cleared, and he slowly rolled onto his hands and knees. Something hurt inside, like his stomach had been torn out, diced into little pieces, and then stitched back together all wrong. He took a ragged breath. That hurt, too.

The pain was good—it helped keep him alert.

"Status," he coughed. His mouth tasted like copper.

Kelly knelt next to him and on a private COM channel said, "Almost everyone has minor damage: a few blown shield generators, sensor systems, a dozen broken bones and contusions. Nothing we can't compensate for. Six Spartans have more serious injuries. They can fight from a fixed position, but they have limited mobility." She took a deep breath and then added, "Four KIA."

Fred struggled to his feet. He was dizzy but remained upright. He had to stay on his feet no matter what. He had to for the team, to show them they still had a functioning leader.

Spartan military operations rarely saw any casualties at all, but he'd already lost four, and this op had barely begun. Fred wasn't superstitious, but he couldn't help but feel that the Spartans' luck was running out.

"You did what you had to," Kelly said as if she were reading his mind. "Most of us wouldn't have made it if you hadn't been thinking on your feet."

Fred snorted in disgust. Kelly thought he'd been thinking on his feet—but all he'd done was land on his ass. He didn't want to talk about it—not now. "Any other good news?" he said.

"Plenty," she replied. "Our gear—munitions boxes, bags of extra weapons—they're scattered across what's passing for our LZ. Only a few of us have assault rifles, maybe five in total."

Fred instinctively reached for his MA5B and discovered that the anchoring clips on his armor had been sheared away in the impact. No grenades on his belt, either. His drop bag was gone, too.

He shrugged. "We'll improvise," he said.

Kelly picked up a rock and hefted it.

Fred resisted the urge to lower his head and catch his breath. There was nothing he wanted to do more right now than sit down and just rest and think. There had to be a way to get his

Spartans out of here in one piece. It was like a training exercise—all he needed to do was figure out how best to accomplish their mission with no more foul-ups.

There was no time, though. They'd been sent to protect those generators, and the Covenant sure as hell weren't sitting around waiting for them to make the first move. The columns of smoke that marked where Reach HighCom once stood testified to that.

"Assemble the team," Fred told her. "Formation Beta. We're heading toward the generators on foot. Pack out our wounded and dead. Send those with weapons ahead as scouts. Maybe our luck will change."

Kelly barked over the SQUADCOM: "Move, Spartans. Formation Beta to the NAV point."

Fred initiated a diagnostic on his armor. The hydrostatic subsystem had blown a seal, and pressure was at minimal functional levels. He could move, but he'd have to replace that seal before he'd be able to sprint or dodge plasma fire.

He fell in behind Kelly and saw his Spartans on the periphery of his tactical friend-or-foe monitor. He couldn't actually see any of them because they were spread out and darted from tree to tree to avoid any Covenant surprises. They all moved silently through the forest: light and shadow and an occasional muted flash of luminous green armor, then gone again.

"Red-One, this is Red-Twelve. Single enemy contact . . . neutralized."

"One here, too," Red-Fifteen reported. *"Neutralized."*

There had to be more. Fred knew the Covenant never traveled in small numbers.

Worse, if the Covenant were deploying troops in any significant numbers, that meant the holding action in orbit had turned ugly . . . so it was only a matter of time before this mission went from bad to worse.

He was so intent on listening to his team's field checks, he almost ran into a pair of Jackals. He instinctively melted into the shadow of a tree and froze.

The Jackals hadn't seen him. The birdlike aliens sniffed at the air, however, and then moved forward more cautiously, closing on Fred's concealed position. They waved plasma pistols before them and clicked on their energy shields. The small, oblong protective fields rippled and solidified with a muted hum.

Fred keyed his COM channel to Red-Two, twice. Her blue acknowledgment light immediately winked in response to his call for backup.

The Jackals suddenly turned to their right and sniffed rapidly.

A fist-sized rock whizzed in from the aliens' left. It slammed into the lead Jackal's occipital crest with a wet crack. The creature squawked and dropped to the ground in a pool of purple-black blood.

Fred darted ahead and in three quick steps closed with the remaining Jackal. He sidestepped around the plane of the energy shield and grabbed the creature's wrist. The Jackal squawked in fear and surprise.

He yanked the Jackal's gun arm, hard, and then twisted. The Jackal struggled as its own weapon was forced into the mottled, rough skin of its neck.

Fred squeezed, and he could feel the alien's bones shatter. The plasma pistol discharged in a bright, emerald flash. The Jackal flopped over on its back, minus its head.

Fred picked up the fallen weapons as Kelly emerged from the trees. He tossed her one of the plasma pistols, and she plucked it out of the air.

"Thanks. I'd still prefer my rifle to this alien piece of junk," she groused.

Fred nodded, and clipped the other captured weapon to his harness. "Beats the hell out of throwing rocks," he replied.

"Affirmative, Chief," she said with a nod. "But just barely."

"Red-One," Joshua's voice called over the SQUADCOM. "I'm a half-klick ahead of you. You need to see this."

"Roger," Fred told him. "Red Team, hold here and wait for my signal."

Acknowledgment lights winked on.

In a half crouch, Fred made his way toward Joshua. There was light ahead: The shade thinned and vanished because the forest was gone. The trees had been leveled, every one blasted to splinters or burned to charred nubs.

There were bodies, too; thousands of Covenant Grunts, hundreds of Jackals and Elites littered the open field. There were also humans—all dead. Fred could see several fallen Marines still smoldering from plasma fire. There were overturned Scorpion tanks, Warthogs with burning tires, and a Banshee flier. The flier had snagged one canard on a loop of barbed wire, and it propelled itself, riderless, in an endless orbit.

The generator complex on the far side of this battlefield was intact, however. Reinforced concrete bunkers bristling with machine guns surrounded a low building. The generators were deep beneath there. So far it looked as if the Covenant had not managed to take them, though not for lack of trying.

"Contacts ahead," Joshua whispered.

Four blips appeared on his motion sensor. Friend-or-foe tags identified them as UNSC Marines, Company Charlie. Serial numbers flashed next to the men as his HUD picked them out on a topo map of the area.

Joshua handed Fred his sniper rifle, and he sighted the contacts through the scope. They were Marines, sure enough. They picked through the bodies that littered the area, looking for survivors and policing weapons and ammo.

Fred frowned; something about the way the Marine squad moved didn't feel right. They lacked unit cohesion, with their line ragged and exposed. They weren't using any of the available cover. To Fred's experienced eye, the Marines didn't even seem to be heading in a specific direction. One of them just ambled in circles.

Fred sent a narrow-beam transmission on UNSC global frequency. "Marine patrol, this is Spartan Red Team. We are approaching your position from your six o'clock. Acknowledge."

The Marines turned about and squinted in Fred's direction, and brought their assault rifles to bear. There was static on the channel, and then a hoarse, listless voice replied: *"Spartans? If you are what you say you are . . . we could sure use a hand."*

"Sorry we missed the battle, Marine."

" 'Missed'?" The Marine gave a short, bitter laugh. *"Hell, Chief, this was just round one."*

Fred returned the sniper rifle to Joshua, pointed toward his eyes and then to the Marines in the field. Joshua nodded, shouldered the rifle, and sighted them. His finger hovered near the weapon's trigger—not *quite* on it. It never hurt to be careful.

Fred got up and walked to the cluster of Marines. He picked his way past a tangle of Grunt bodies and the twisted metal and charred tires that had once been a Warthog.

The men looked as if they had been to hell and back. They all sported burns, abrasions, and the kilometer-long stare indicative of near shock. They gaped at Fred, mouths open; it was a reaction that he had often seen when soldiers first glimpsed a Spartan: two meters tall, half a ton of armor, splashed with alien blood. It was a mix of awe and suspicion and fear.

He hated it. He just wanted to fight and win this war, like the rest of the soldiers in the UNSC. The Corporal seemed to snap out of his near fugue. He removed his helmet, scratched at his cropped red hair, and looked behind him. "Chief, you'd better head back to base with us before they hit us again."

Fred nodded. "How many in your company, Corporal?"

The man glanced at his three companions and shook his head. "Say again, Chief?"

These men were likely on the verge of battle shock, so Fred

controlled his impatience and replied in as gentle a voice as he could muster: "Your FOF tags say you're with Charlie Company, Corporal. How many are you? How many wounded?"

"There's no wounded, Chief," the Corporal replied. "There's no 'company' either. We're all that's left."

CHAPTER

THREE

Fred looked over the battlefield from the top of the southern bunker, his temporary command post. The structure had been hastily erected, and some of the fast-drying instacrete hadn't fully hardened.

The bunker was not the best defensive position, but it gave him a clear view of the area as his team worked to strengthen the perimeter of the generator complex. Spartans strung razor wire, buried Antilon mine packs, and swept the area on patrols. A six-man fireteam searched the battleground for weapons and ammunition.

Satisfied that the situation was as stable as possible, he sat and began to remove portions of his armor. Under normal circumstances a team of techs would assist in such work, but over time the Spartans had all learned how to make rudimentary field repairs. He located a broken pressure seal and quickly replaced it with an undamaged one he'd recovered from SPARTAN 059's armor.

Fred scowled. He hated the necessity of stripping gear from Malcolm's suit. But it would dishonor his fallen comrade not to use his gift of the spare part.

He banished thoughts of the drop and finished installing the seal. Self-recrimination was a luxury he could ill afford, and the Red Team Spartans didn't have a monopoly on hard times.

Charlie Company's surviving Marines had held off the Covenant assault with batteries of chainguns, Warthogs, and a pair of Scorpion tanks for almost an hour. Grunts had charged across the minefield and cleared a path for the Jackals and Elites.

Lieutenant Buckman, the Marines' CO, had been ordered to send the bulk of his men into the forest in an attempt to flank the enemy. He had called in air support, too.

He got it.

Reach HighCom must have realized the generators were in danger of being overrun, so someone panicked and sent in bombers to hit the forest in a half-klick radius. That wiped out the Covenant assault wave. It also killed the Lieutenant and his men.

What a waste.

Fred replaced the last of his armor components and powered up. His status lights pulsed a cool blue. Satisfied, he stood and activated the COM.

"Red-Twelve, give me a sit-rep."

Will's voice crackled over the channel. *"Perimeter established, Chief. No enemy contacts."*

"Good," Fred replied. "Mission status?"

"Ten chainguns recovered and now provide blanketing fields of fire around the generator complex," Will said. *"We've got three Banshee fliers working. We've also recovered thirty of those arm-mounted Jackal shield generators, plus a few hundred assault rifles, plasma pistols, and grenades."*

"Ammo? We need it."

"Affirmative, sir," Will said. *"Enough to last for an hour of continuous fire."* There was a short pause, then he added: *"HQ must have sent reinforcements at some point, because we've recovered a crate marked* HIGHCOM ARMORY OMEGA.*"*

"What's in it?"

"Six Anaconda surface-to-air missiles." Will's voice barely concealed his glee. *"And a pair of Fury tac-nukes."*

Fred gave a low whistle. The Fury tac-nuke was the closest

thing the UNSC had in its arsenal to a nuclear grenade. It was the size and shape of an overinflated football. It delivered slightly less than a megaton yield, and was extremely clean. Unfortunately, it was also completely useless to them in this situation.

"Secure that ordnance ASAP. We can't use them. The EMP would fry the generators."

"Roger that," Will said with a disappointed sigh.

"Red-Three?" Fred asked. "Report."

There was a moment's hesitation. Joshua whispered: *"Not good here, Red-One. I'm posted on the ridge between our valley and the next. The Covenant has a massive LZ set up. There's an enemy ship on station and I estimate battalion-strength enemy troops on the ground. Grunts, Jackals, equipment, and support armor are deploying. Looks like they're getting ready for round two, sir."*

Fred felt the pit of his stomach grow cold. "Give me an up-link."

"Roger."

A tiny picture appeared in Fred's heads-up display, and he saw what Joshua had sighted through his sniperscope: A Covenant cruiser hovered thirty meters off the ground. The ship bristled with energy weapons and plasma artillery. His Spartans couldn't get within weapons range of that thing without being roasted.

A gravity lift connected the ship to the surface of Reach, and troops poured out—thousands of them: legions of Grunts, three full squadrons of Elites piloting Banshees, plus at least a dozen Wraith tanks.

It didn't make much sense, though. Why didn't the cruiser get closer and open fire? Or did the Covenant think there might be another air strike? The Covenant never hesitated during an assault . . . but the fact that he was still alive meant that the enemy's rules of engagement had somehow changed.

Fred wasn't sure why the Covenant were being so cautious, but he'd take the break. It would give him time to figure out how to stop them. If the Spartans were mobile, they might be able to engage a force that size with hit-and-run tactics. Holding a fixed position was another story altogether.

"Updates every ten minutes," he told Joshua. His voice was suddenly tight and dry.

"Roger that."

"Red-Two? Any progress on that SATCOM uplink?"

"Negative, sir," Kelly muttered, tension thickening her voice. She had been tasked with patching Charlie Company's bullet-ridden communications pack. *"There are battle reports jamming the entire spectrum, but from what I can make out the fight upstairs isn't going well. They need this generator up—no matter what it's going to cost us."*

"Understood," Fred said. "Keep me—"

"Wait. Incoming transmission to Charlie Company from Reach HighCom."

HighCom? Fred thought headquarters on Reach had been overrun. "Verification codes?"

"They check out," Kelly replied.

"Patch it through."

"Charlie Company? Jake? What the hell is the holdup there? Why haven't you gotten my men out yet?"

"This is Senior Petty Officer SPARTAN 104, Red Team leader," Fred replied, "now in charge of Charlie Company. Identify yourself."

"Put Lieutenant Chapman on, Spartan," an irritated voice snapped.

"That's not possible, sir," Fred told him, instinctively realizing that he spoke to an officer and adding the honorific. "Except for four wounded Marines, Charlie Company is gone."

There was a long static-filled pause. *"Spartan, listen to me very carefully. This is Vice Admiral Danforth Whitcomb, Deputy Chief of Naval Operations. Do you know who I am, son?"*

"Yes, sir," Fred said, wincing as the Admiral identified himself.

If the Covenant were eavesdropping on this transmission, the senior officer had just made himself a giant target.

"My staff and I are pinned down in a gully southeast of where HighCom used to be," Whitcomb continued. *"Get your team over here and extract us, on the double."*

"Negative, sir, I cannot do that. I have direct orders to protect the generator complex powering the orbital guns."

"I'm countermanding those orders," the Admiral barked. *"As of two hours ago, I have tactical command of the defense of Reach. Now, I don't care if you're a Spartan or Jesus Christ walking down the damned Big Horn River—I am giving you a direct order. Acknowledge, Spartan."*

If Admiral Whitcomb was now in charge of the defense, then a lot of the senior brass had been put out of commission when HQ got hit.

Fred saw a tiny amber light flashing on his heads-up display. His biomonitor indicated an elevation in his blood pressure and heart rate. He noticed his hands shook, almost imperceptibly.

He controlled the shaking and keyed the COM. "Acknowledged, sir. Is air support available?"

"Negative. Covenant craft took out our fighter and bomber cover in the first wave."

"Very well, sir. We'll get you out."

"Step on it, Chief." The COM snapped off.

Fred wondered if Admiral Whitcomb was responsible for the hundreds of dead Marines who'd been trying to guard the generators. No doubt he was an excellent ship driver . . . but Fleet officers running ground ops? No wonder the situation was FUBAR.

Had he pressured a young and inexperienced lieutenant to flank a superior enemy? Had he sent in air support with orders to saturate-bomb the area?

Fred didn't trust the Admiral's judgment, but he couldn't ignore a direct order from him, either.

He ran his team roster up onto his heads-up display: seventeen

Spartans, six wounded so badly they could barely walk, and four battle-fatigued Marines who'd been through hell once already. They had to repel a massive Covenant force. They had to extract Admiral Whitcomb, too. And as usual, their survival was at best a tertiary consideration.

He had weapons to defend the installation: grenades, chainguns, and missiles—

Fred paused. Perhaps this was the wrong way to look at the tactical situation. He was thinking about *defending* the installation when he should have been thinking about what Spartans were best at—*offense*.

He keyed the SQUADCOM. "Everyone catch that last transmission?"

Acknowledgment lights winked on.

"Good. Here's the plan: We split into four teams.

"Team Delta—" He highlighted the wounded Spartans and the four Marines on the roster. "—fall back to this location." He uploaded a tactical map of the area and set a NAV marker in a ravine sixteen kilometers north. "Take two Warthogs, but leave them and stealth it if you encounter any resistance. Your mission is to secure the area. This will be the squad's fallback position. Keep the back door open for us."

They immediately acknowledged. The Spartans knew that ravine like the backs of their hands. It wasn't marked on any map, but it was where they'd trained for months with Dr. Halsey. Beneath the mountain were caverns that the Office of Naval Intelligence had converted into a top-secret facility. It was fortified and hardened against radiation, and could probably withstand anything up to and including a direct nuclear strike. A perfect hole to hide in if everything went sour.

"Team Gamma." Fred selected Red-Twenty, Red-Twenty-one, and Red-Twenty-two from the roster. "You'll extract the Admiral and his staff and bring them back to the generators. We'll need the extra crew."

"Affirmative," Red-Twenty-one replied.

Technically Fred was following Whitcomb's order to extract him from his current position. What the Admiral didn't realize, though, was that he would have probably been safer staying put.

"Team Beta—" Fred selected the remaining Spartans from Red-Nineteen to Red-Four. "—you're on generator defense."

"Understood, Chief."

"Team Alpha—" He selected Kelly, Joshua, and himself.

"Awaiting orders, sir," Joshua said.

"We're going to that valley to kill anything there that isn't human."

Fred and Kelly faced the three Banshee fliers that had been dragged into the makeshift compound. Fred peered inside the cockpit of the nearest craft and tabbed the activation knob. The Banshee rose a meter off the ground, its anti-grav pod glowed a faint electric blue, and it started to drift forward. He snapped it off, and the Banshee settled to the ground. He quickly tested the other two, and they also rose off the ground.

"Good. All working."

Kelly crossed her arms. "We're going for a ride?"

A Warthog pulled up and skidded to a halt in front of them, Joshua at the wheel. The rear held half a dozen Jackhammer missiles and a trio of launchers. A crate sat in the passenger's seat, one loaded with the dark, emerald-green duct tape that every soldier in the UNSC ubiquitously referred to as "EB Green."

"Mission accomplished, sir," Joshua said as he climbed from the Warthog.

Fred grabbed a launcher, a pair of rockets, and a roll of tape from the 'Hog. "We'll be needing these when we hit the Covenant on the other side of the ridge," he explained. "Each of you secure a launcher and some ammo in a Banshee."

Joshua and Kelly stopped what they were doing and turned to face him.

"Permission to speak, sir," Kelly asked.

"Granted."

"I'm all for a good fight, Fred, but those odds are a little lop-sided even for us . . . like ten thousand to one."

"We can handle a hundred to one," Joshua chimed in, "maybe even five hundred to one with a little planning and support, but against these odds, a frontal assault seems—"

"It's not going to be a frontal assault," Fred said. He wedged the launcher into the cramped Banshee cockpit. "Tape."

Kelly ripped off a length of tape and handed it over.

Fred smoothed the adhesive strip and secured the launcher in place. "We'll play this one as quiet as we can," he said.

She considered Fred's plan for a moment and then asked, "So, assuming we fool them into letting us into their lines . . . *then* what?"

"As much as I'd like to, we can't use the tac-nukes," Joshua mused, "not in the far valley. The intervening ridge isn't high enough to block the EMP. It'll burn out the orbital defense generator."

"There's another way to use them," Fred told them. "We're going to board the cruiser—right up its gravity lift—and detonate the nuke *inside*. The ship's shields will dampen the electromagnetic pulse."

"It'll also turn that ship into the biggest fragmentation grenade in history," Kelly remarked.

"And if anything goes wrong," Joshua said, "we end up in the middle of ten thousand pissed-off bad guys."

"We're Spartans," Fred said. "What could possibly go wrong?"

CHAPTER
FOUR

The alarm hooted, and Zawaz sprang to his feet with a startled yelp. The squat alien, a Grunt clad in burnished orange armor, fumbled and dropped his motion scanner. He keened in fear and retrieved the device with a trembling claw. If the scanner had been damaged, the Elites would use his body as reactor shielding. If his masters learned he'd been asleep at his post, they might do *far* worse than kill him. They might give him to the Jackals.

Zawaz shuddered.

Fortunately, the scanner still worked, and the diminutive alien sighed with relief. Three contacts rapidly approached the mountain that separated Zawaz's cadre from the distant human forces. He reached for the warning klaxon but relaxed as his detector identified the contacts—Banshee fliers.

He peered over the dirt edge of his protective hole to confirm this. He spotted three of the bulbous aircraft on approach. Zawaz snorted. It was odd that the flight wasn't listed on his patrol schedule. He considered alerting his superiors, then thought better of it. What if they were Elites on some secret mission?

No, it was best not to question such things. Be ignored. Live another day. That was his creed.

He nestled back into his hole, reset the motion detector to

long range, and prayed it wouldn't go off again. He curled into a tight ball and promptly fell into a deep sleep.

Fred led their flying-wedge formation. The purple and red fliers arced up and over the treetops of the ridge, gaining as much altitude as the Banshees could manage—about three hundred meters. As he cleared the top, what he saw made him ease off the throttle.

The valley was ten kilometers across and sloped before him, thick with Douglas firs that thinned and gave way to trampled fields and the Big Horn River beyond. Camped in the fields were thousands upon thousands of Covenant troops. Their mass covered the entire valley, and thin, smoke-choked sunlight glinted off a sea of red, yellow, and blue armor. They moved in tight columns and swarmed along the river's edge—so many that it looked like someone had kicked over the largest anthill in existence.

And they were building. Hundreds of flimsy white dome-shaped tents were being erected, atmosphere pits for the methane-breathing Grunts. Farther back were the odd polyhedral huts of the Elite units, guarded by a long line of dozens of beetlelike Wraith tanks. Guard towers punctuated the valley; they spiraled up from mobile treaded bases, ten meters tall and topped with plasma turrets.

The rules had indeed changed. In more than a hundred battles Fred had never seen the Covenant set up encampments of such magnitude. All they did was kill.

Floating behind all this activity, almost brushing against the far hills, the Covenant cruiser sat thirty meters off the ground. It looked like a great bloated fish with stubby stabilizing fins. Its gravity lift was in operation, a tube of scintillating energy that moved matter to and from the ground. Stacks of purple crates gently floated down from the craft. In the afternoon light he could see its weapons bristling along its length, casting spiderlike shadows across its hull.

Their Banshees leveled out, and Fred dropped back to tighten his formation with Kelly and Joshua.

He glanced again at the enemy ship and the guard towers. One good hit from those weapons could take them out.

Fred saw other Banshee patrols circling the valley. He frowned. If they passed them, the enemy pilots would almost certainly demand to know their business . . . and there was no way of knowing what the established patrol routes were. That meant he'd have to take an alternate flight path: straight down the middle, and straight over the Covenant horde.

They'd only need one run to do this. They'd probably only *get* one run.

He activated a COM frequency. "Go."

Kelly hit the acceleration and glided toward the cruiser. Fred fell in behind her. He armed the fuel rod gun built into the Banshee.

They were six kilometers from the cruiser when Kelly achieved the maximum speed of her flier. Grunts and Jackals in the fields below craned their necks as the Spartans flashed over them.

They had to go faster. Fred felt every Covenant eye watching them. He dived, trading his altitude for acceleration, and Joshua and Kelly did the same.

Communication symbols flashed across his Banshee's windshield display. The UNSC software built into their armor worked only with some of the spoken Covenant languages—not their written words. Odd, curling characters scrolled across the Banshee's displays.

Fred hit one of the response symbols.

There was a pause, the display cleared, and dozens more symbols flashed, twice as fast.

Fred clicked the display off.

Three kilometers to go, and his heart beat so hard he heard it thunder in his ears.

Kelly pulled slightly ahead of them. She was now thirty meters off the ground, gaining as much speed as she could, driving straight for the cruiser's gravity lift.

The nearest guard tower tracked her; its plasma cannon flared and fired.

Kelly's flier climbed and banked to evade the enemy fire. The bolt of superheated ionized gas brushed against her starboard fuselage. Energy spray melted the Banshee's front faring, and her ship slowed.

A dozen plasma turrets turned to track them.

Fred banked and opened fire. Energy bursts from the Banshee's primary weapon strafed the guard tower. Joshua did the same, and a river of fire streaked toward the towers.

Fred hit the firing stud for the Banshee's heavy weapon, and a sphere of energy arced into the base of the tower. It began a gradual tilt, then collapsed.

Kelly hadn't fired. Fred glanced her way and saw that she now stood in a low crouch atop her racing Banshee. She had one foot under the duct tape that had secured the nuke and now held the bomb in her hand, cocking it back to throw.

A shard of jagged crystal, a round from a Covenant needler, pinged off Fred's port shield. He snapped a look below.

Covenant Grunts and Jackals boiled in agitation—a hundred badly aimed shots arced up after him; glistening clouds of crystalline needles and firefly plasma bolts swarmed through the air and chipped away at his Banshee's fuselage.

Fred jinked his Banshee left and right, and dodged plasma bolts from the three guard towers tracking him. He lined up for a second strafing run, and the Banshee's lighter energy weapons sent Grunts scattering.

A hundred meters to go.

Kelly leaned back, coiled her body, and readied to throw the nuclear device as if it were a shotput.

The Covenant cruiser came to life, and its weapons tracked

the Banshees. A dozen fingers of plasma ripped the air; white-blue arcs of fire reached for them.

One bolt connected with Joshua's vehicle. The Banshee's improvised shields overloaded and vanished. The canards of the flier melted and bent. The alien flier lurched into a spin as its control surfaces warped, and Joshua fell behind Fred and Kelly just as they entered the gravity lift of the craft.

Fred keyed his COM to raise Joshua but got only static. Time seemed to slow inside the beam of purple light that ferried goods and troops to and from the belly of the ship. The strange glow surrounded them and made his skin tingle as if it were asleep.

Their Banshees rose toward an opening in the underside of the carrier. They weren't riding into the ship, though; they were traveling too fast and would cross the beam before they were three quarters of the way to the top.

Fred snapped around. He didn't see Joshua anywhere. Plasma beams hit the well and were deflected as if it were a giant glass lens.

Kelly hurled the nuke straight up into the gullet of the cruiser.

Fred wrenched the Banshee's controls and arced the craft under the edge of the ship; Kelly was right behind him. The light vanished, and they emerged on the far side of the Covenant vessel.

Behind them, distorted through the gravity lift, Fred saw Covenant troops firing their weapons into the sky. He heard ten thousand voices screaming for blood.

Fred pinged Joshua on the COM, but his acknowledgment light remained dark.

He wanted to slow and turn back for him, but Kelly dived, accelerating toward the ground, and she entered the forest that carpeted the mountainside. Fred followed her. They were scant meters above the ground; they dodged trees and blasted through tangles of foliage. A handful of stray shots flashed overhead. They flew at top speed and didn't look back.

They emerged from the tree line and over the powdered snow of the mountaintop. They arced over a granite ridge, came about, and throttled back. The Banshees drifted slowly to the ground.

The sky turned white. Fred's faceplate polarized to its darkest setting. Thunder rolled though his body. Fire and molten metal blossomed over the ridge, boiled skyward, and rained back into the valley. The granite top of the intervening mountain shattered into dust and the snow on their side melted in muddy rivulets.

Fred's visor slowly depolarized.

Kelly leaned across her Banshee. Blood oozed from her armor's left shoulder joint. She fumbled for her helmet seal, caught it, and peeled it off her head. "Did we get 'em?" she panted. Blood foamed from the corner of her mouth.

"I think so," Fred told her.

She looked around. "Joshua?"

Fred shook his head. "He got hit on the way in."

It had been easy for him to fly into the face of certain death moments ago. Saying those words was a hundred times harder.

Kelly slumped and dropped her head back against her Banshee.

"Stay here, I'm going up to take a look." Fred powered up his Banshee and rose parallel with the ridgeline. He nudged the craft up a little farther and got his first look into the valley.

It was a sea of flame. Hundreds of fires dotted the cracked, glassy ground. Where the Big Horn River had snaked along, there was now only a long steaming furrow. There was no trace of the cruiser or the Covenant troops that had filled the valley moments ago. All that remained was a field of smoldering, twisted bone and metal. At the edge of this carnage stood blackened sticks—the remnants of the forest—all leaning away from the center of the explosion.

Ten thousand Covenant deaths. It wasn't worth losing Joshua or any of the other Spartans, but it was something. Perhaps they had bought enough time for the orbital MAC guns to tip the battle overhead in the Fleet's favor. Maybe their sacrifices would save Reach. That would be worth it.

He looked up into the sky. The steam made it difficult to see anything, but there was motion overhead: Faint shadows glided over the clouds.

Kelly's Banshee appeared alongside his, and their canards bumped.

The shadows overhead sharpened; three Covenant cruisers broke through the clouds and drifted toward the generator complex. Their plasma artillery flickered and glowed with energy.

Fred snapped open his COM channel and boosted the signal strength to its maximum. "Delta Team: Fall back. Fall back now!"

Static hissed over the channel, and several voices overlapped. He heard one of his Spartans—he couldn't tell who—break through the static.

"Reactor complex seven has been compromised. We're falling back. Might be able to save number three." There was a pause as the speaker shouted orders to someone else: *"Set off those charges now!"*

Fred switched to FLEETCOM and broadcast: "Be advised, *Pillar of Autumn,* groundside reactors are being taken. Orbital guns at risk. Nothing we can do. Too many. We'll have to use the nukes. Be advised, orbital MAC guns will most likely be neutralized. *Pillar of Autumn,* do you read? Acknowledge."

More voices crowded the channel, and Fred thought he heard Admiral Whitcomb's voice, but whatever orders he issued were incomprehensible. Then there was only static, and then the COM went dead.

The cruisers fired salvos of plasma that burned the sky.

Distant explosions thumped, and Fred strained to see if there was any return fire—any sign that his Spartans were fighting or retreating. Their only hope was movement; the enemy firepower would shred a fixed position.

"Fall back," he hissed. "Now, damn it."

Kelly tapped him on the shoulder and pointed up.

The clouds parted like a curtain drawn as a fireball a hundred meters across roared over their position. He saw the faint outlines of dozens of Covenant battleships in low orbit.

"Plasma bombardment," Fred whispered.

He'd seen this before. They all had. When the Covenant conquered a human world they fired their main plasma batteries at the planet—fired until its oceans boiled and nothing was left but a globe of broken glass.

"That's it," Kelly murmured. "We've lost. Reach is going to fall."

Fred watched as the plasma impacted upon the horizon and the sky turned white, then faded to black as millions of tons of ash and debris blotted out the sun.

"Maybe," Fred said. He gunned his Banshee. "Maybe not. Come on, we're not done yet."

SECTION I

THRESHOLD

SURROUNDED

CHAPTER

FIVE

The Master Chief settled into the pilot's seat of the Longsword attack craft. He didn't fit. The contoured seat had been engineered to mate with a standard-issue Navy flight suit, not the bulky MJOLNIR armor.

He scratched his scalp and breathed deeply. The air tasted odd—it lacked the metallic quality of his suit's air scrubbers. This was the first quiet moment he'd had to sit, think, and remember. First there was the satisfaction after the successful space op at Reach, which went sour after Linda was killed and the Covenant glassed the planet . . . and Red Team. Then the time spent in a *Pillar of Autumn* cryotube, the flight from Reach, and the discovery of Halo.

And the Flood.

He stared out from the front viewport and fought down his revulsion at the memory of the Flood outbreak. Whoever had constructed Halo had used it to contain the sentient, virulent xenoform that had nearly claimed them all. The rapidly healing wound in his neck, inflicted by a Flood Infection Form during the final battle on Halo's surface, still throbbed.

He wanted to forget it all . . . especially the Flood. Everything inside him ached.

The system's moon, Basis, was a silver-gray disk against the darkness of space, and beyond it was the muted purple of the gas giant Threshold. Between them lay a glistening expanse of debris—metal, stone, ice, and everything else that had once been Halo.

"Scan it again," the Master Chief told Cortana.

"Already completed," her disembodied voice replied. "There's *nothing* out there. I told you: just dust and echoes."

The Master Chief's hand curled into a fist, and for a moment he felt the urge to slam it into something. He relaxed, surprised at his frayed temper. He'd been exhausted in the past—and without a doubt the fight on Halo had been the most harrowing of his career—but he'd never been prone to such outbursts.

The struggle against the Flood must have gotten to him, more than he'd realized.

With effort he banished the Flood from his mind. Either there'd be time to deal with it later . . . or there wouldn't. Worrying about it now served no useful purpose.

"Scan the field again," he repeated.

Cortana's tiny holographic figure appeared on the projection pad mounted between the pilot's and system-ops seats. She crossed her arms over her chest, visibly irritated with the Master Chief's request.

"If you don't find something out there we can use," he told her, "we're dead. This ship has no Slipspace drive, and no cryo. There's no way to get back and report. Power, fuel, air, food, water—we only have enough for a few hours.

"So," he concluded as patiently as he could manage. "Scan. Again."

Cortana sighed explosively, and her hologram dissolved. The scanner panel activated, however, and mathematical symbols crowded the screen.

A moment later the scanner panel dimmed and Cortana said, "There's still nothing, Chief. All I'm picking up is a strong echo from the moon . . . but there are no transponder signals, and no distress calls."

"You're not doing an active scan?"

Her tiny hologram appeared again, and this time static flashed across her figure. "There are trillions of objects out there. If you want I can start to scan and identify each individual piece. If we sit here and do nothing else, that would take eighteen days."

"What if someone's out there but they turned off their transponder? What if they don't want to be found?"

"That's highly un—" Cortana froze for a split second. The static around her vanished, and she stared off into space. "Interesting."

"What?"

Cortana looked distracted, then seemed to snap out of it. "New data. That signal echo's getting stronger."

"Meaning?"

"Meaning," she replied, "it's not an echo."

The scanner panel hummed back to life as Cortana activated the Longsword's long-range detection gear. "Uh-oh," she said, a moment later.

The Chief peered at the scan panel as Cortana identified the contact. The distinctive, bulbous silhouette of a Covenant cruiser edged into view as it moved around the moon's far side.

"Power down," he snapped. "Kill everything except passive scanners and minimal power to keep you online."

The Longsword darkened; Cortana's hologram flickered and faded as she killed power flow to the holosystem.

The cruiser moved into the debris field, prowling like a hungry shark. Another cruiser appeared, then another, and then three more.

"Status?" he whispered, his hands hovering over the weapons controls. "Have they spotted us?"

"They're using the same scanning frequencies as our system," Cortana said in his helmet speaker. "How strange. No mention of this phenomenon in any of the UNSC or ONI files on the Covenant. Why do you suppose they'd use the same frequencies?"

"Never mind that," the Chief said. "They're here and looking for something. Like I said before, if there are survivors out there, they'd be powered down."

"I can listen to their echoes," Cortana said, her voice flat and oddly procedural. Operating at lower power levels seemed to limit her more colorful behavior. "Process active: analyzing Covenant signals. Piggybacking their scans. Diverting more runtime to the task. I'm building a multiplex filtering algorithm. Customizing the current shape-signature recognition software."

Another ship rounded the horizon of Basis. It was larger than any Covenant ship the Master Chief had seen. It had the sleek three-pronged shape of one of their destroyers, but it must have been three kilometers long. Seven plasma turrets were mounted on universal joints—enough firepower to gut any ship in the UNSC fleet.

"Picking up encrypted transmissions from new contact," Cortana whispered. "Descrambling . . . lots of chatter . . . orders being given to the cruisers. It appears to be directing the Covenant fleet operations in the system."

"A flagship," the Chief murmured. "Interesting."

"Scan still in progress, Chief. Stand by."

John got out of the sys-ops seat. He had no intention of just "standing by" with seven Covenant warships in the system.

He drifted to the aft compartment of the Longsword fighter. He'd assess what equipment was on board. He might get lucky and find a few of those Shiva nuclear-tipped missiles.

As he had seen when he first boarded the ship, the cryotube had been removed. He wasn't sure why, but maybe, like everything else on the *Pillar of Autumn*, the ship had been stripped down and upgraded for their original high-risk mission.

Where the cryo unit was supposed to be there was a new control panel. The Chief examined it and discovered it was a Moray space-mine laying system. He didn't power it on. The Moray system could dispense up to three dozen free-floating mines. The mines had tiny chemical-fuel drives that allowed them to keep a fixed position or move to track specific targets. These would come in handy.

He moved to the weapons locker and forced it open—it was empty.

The Chief checked his own assault rifle: fully functional, but only thirteen rounds remained in the magazine.

"Got something," Cortana said.

He returned to the sys-ops seat. "Show me."

On the smallest viewscreen, a silhouette appeared: a small, bullet-shaped cone with maneuvering thrusters on one end.

"It could be a cryotube," Cortana said. "Thruster and power packs can be affixed on their aft sections for emergencies . . . if a ship has to be abandoned, for example."

"And most of the crew on the *Pillar of Autumn* never had a chance to be revived from cryo," the Chief said. "They could have been jettisoned before the ship went down. Move us toward them. Docking thrusters only."

"Course plotted," Cortana said. "Thrusters engaged."

There was a slight acceleration.

"ETA twenty minutes, Chief. But given the Covenant cruisers' current search pattern, I estimate they will encounter the pod in *five* minutes."

"We need to move faster," the Chief told her, "but without firing the engines. The drive emissions will show up like a flare on their sensors."

"Hang on," Cortana said. "I'll get us there."

The Chief donned his helmet and locked its atmosphere seals. Status lights pulsed green. "Ready," he said.

The aft hatch of the Longsword breached and slammed open. There was an explosive sound as the atmosphere vented. The Longsword jumped forward; the Chief's head slammed into the back of his helmet.

"Adjusting course," Cortana said calmly. "ETA two minutes."

"How are we going to stop?" he asked.

She sighed. "Do I have to think of everything?" The aft hatch resealed, and John heard the faint hiss as the internal compartments pressurized.

One of the sleek Covenant cruisers slowed and turned toward them.

"Picking up increased scanning signal activity and strength," Cortana reported.

The Chief's hand hovered over the weapons system console. It would take several seconds for the weapons to power up. The 110mm rotary cannons could fire immediately, but the missiles would have to wait for their target-lock software to initialize. By then the cruiser, which outgunned them a hundred to one, would turn the Longsword into molten slag.

"Attempting to jam their scanners," Cortana said. "That may buy us some time."

The Covenant cruiser turned away, slowed, and turned back to face the comparatively tiny Longsword. It took no further action . . . as if it were waiting for them to get closer.

So far so good. The Chief clenched and unclenched his gauntleted hand. *We're not dead yet.*

He glanced at the scan display. The contact resolved into a clearer image: definitely a UNSC cryopod. It tumbled, and he saw that what he thought was a single pod was in fact three of them, affixed side by side.

Three possible survivors out of the *Pillar of Autumn*'s total complement of hundreds. He wished there were more. He wished Captain Keyes were here. In the Chief's opinion Keyes had been the most brilliant spatial tactician he had ever encountered . . . but even the Captain would have thought twice about approaching seven Covenant warships in a single Longsword.

He risked feeding more ship's power to Cortana's systems. If they were going to make it through this, he needed her as effective as possible.

"New contact," Cortana said, interrupting his thoughts. "I think it is, anyway. Whatever it is, it's stuck onto a chunk of rock, half a kilometer in diameter. Damn, it just rotated out of my view."

On the display Cortana replayed a partial silhouette of an oddly angled shape on the surface of the rock. She highlighted its contours, rotated the polygon, and overlaid this onto a schematic of a Pelican dropship.

"Match with a tolerance of fifty-eight percent," she said. "They might have parked there to avoid detection, as you suggested."

The Chief thought he detected a hint of irritation in her voice, as if she resented him for thinking of something she had not.

"Or," Cortana continued, "more likely, the craft merely crashed there."

"I don't think so." He pointed at the display. "The position of that wing indicates it's nose-out—ready for takeoff. If it had crash-landed, it would be faced the other way."

Another Covenant cruiser moved toward this new ship.

"Coming about, Chief," Cortana told him. "Brace yourself, and then get ready to retrieve the pods."

The Chief unsnapped his harness and drifted aft. He grabbed a tether and clipped one end to his suit, the other to the bulkhead of the Longsword.

He felt the maneuvering thrusters fire, and the ship rotated 180 degrees.

"Decompression in three seconds," Cortana said.

The Chief opened the empty weapons locker and climbed partially inside. He braced himself.

Cortana dropped the aft hatch, and the inside of the ship exploded out; the Chief slammed into the door of the locker, denting the centimeter-thick Titanium-A.

He climbed out and Cortana overlaid a blue arrow-shaped

NAV point on his heads-up display, indicating the location of the drifting cryopods.

The Chief jumped out of the Longsword.

He floated through space. He was only thirty meters from the pods, but if he'd guessed wrong about his trajectory and missed the target, he wouldn't get a second chance. By the time he reeled himself back to the Longsword and tried again, those Covenant ships were certain to kill them all.

He stretched his arms and hands toward the cylinders. Twenty meters to go.

His approach was off. He shifted his left knee closer to his chest and started a slow tumble.

Ten meters.

His upper body rotated "down" relative to the pods. If he spun just right as he passed the cryotubes, it would give him enough extra reach to make contact. He hoped.

He rotated back . . . almost standing "up" now.

Three meters.

He stretched his arms until the elbow joints creaked and popped; he stretched his hands, willed his fingers to elongate.

His fingertips brushed against the smooth surface of the leading cryopod. It slid off and over and touched the second pod. He flexed and failed to grab hold. He scratched the surface of the third and final pod—his middle finger hooked on the frame.

His body swung inward, curled, and landed on the pod. He quickly looped his tether through the frame, secured himself to it, and pulled their combined mass back to the Longsword.

"Hurry, Chief," Cortana said over the COM. "We've got trouble."

The Chief saw exactly what the trouble was: The engines of two Covenant cruisers flared electric blue as they accelerated toward the Longsword. The plasma and laser weapons along their hulls warmed from red to orange as they readied to fire.

He pulled as fast as he could, making minor adjustments with the muscles in his braced legs so his motions didn't send them into a tumble in the zero gravity.

The Longsword was a sitting duck for those Covenant cruisers. Cortana couldn't fire the engines until he got on board. Even if he and the pods survived the thruster wash, any evasive maneuver Cortana made would snap him and his cargo like the end of a whip.

The Covenant ships were within firing range, lined up perfectly to destroy the Longsword.

Three missiles streaked though space, impacting on the starboard side of the lead Covenant ship. The explosion splashed harmlessly across its shield, which shimmered silver as it dissipated the energy.

The Chief turned his head and saw the Pelican blast off from the asteroid where it had been hiding. It rocketed on a perpendicular course toward the two Covenant ships.

The cruisers came about, apparently more interested in hunting live prey than the motionless Longsword.

The Chief gave one final yank on the tether. He and the pods flew through the aft hatch and crashed into the deck of the Longsword.

Cortana immediately sealed the hatch and fired the engines.

The Chief climbed into the system-ops seat just as they accelerated and turned toward the cruisers. He activated the weapons systems.

The two Covenant cruisers powered their engines and pursued the Pelican, but it had entered a dense region of the debris field, dodged a chunk of metal and rock, dived over an iceball, and charged through clouds of shattered alien metal. The Covenant fired: Energy blasts impacted on the debris and missed the Pelican.

"Whoever's piloting that Pelican knows their stuff," Cortana said.

"We owe them a favor." John fired the Longsword's guns, and tiny silver dots punctuated the trailing Covenant cruiser's shields. "Let's settle that debt."

"You realize," Cortana said, "that we really can't damage those Covenant ships."

The cruiser slowed and turned toward them.

"We'll see about that. Get me a firing solution for the missiles. I want them to target their plasma turrets just before they fire. They have to drop a section of their shields for a fraction of a second."

"Working," Cortana replied. "Without precise data, however, I'll have to base my calculations on several assumptions." A string of mathematics appeared on the weapons-ops panel. "Give me fire control."

John punched the auto override on the firing systems. "It's yours," he said.

The Covenant cruiser's plasma turrets turned to track them as the ship came to bear. They warmed, and Cortana fired all the Longsword's ASGM-10 missiles.

White vapor trails snaked toward the target.

"Let's move!" the Chief said.

The Longsword accelerated into the debris field, following the Pelican's path. The aft camera displayed the missiles racing to their target. Antimissile laser fire stabbed though space, and three of the missiles exploded into red fireballs. The Covenant's plasma turret glowed white hot—about to fire—when the last missile impacted. The explosion smeared across the hull.

At first the Chief thought it had hit the shield, but then he saw that the explosion was *inside* the shimmering envelope of energy. The plasma turrets fired; their energy was immediately absorbed into the cloud of dust and vapor around the ship. Dull red plasma ballooned inside the cruiser's shield, obscuring its sensors. The ship listed to port, momentarily blind.

"That should keep them busy for a while," Cortana said.

The Longsword arced under a half-kilometer-wide metal plate—just as a plasma bolt impacted and boiled the surface, sending the plate sputtering and spinning through space.

"Or not," Cortana muttered. "Better let me drive."

The autopilot engaged, and the controls jerked out of the Chief's hand. The Longsword's afterburners kicked in, and it accelerated toward a field of tumbling rocks. Cortana rolled and pitched, keeping the hull mere meters from the jagged surfaces.

The Chief hung on to the seat with one hand and pulled his harness tight with the other. He moved the scanner display to the center viewscreen and saw the two nearest Covenant cruisers vectored toward his and the Pelican's position. The two UNSC ships might evade and dodge through the debris field for a few minutes, but soon their fuel would be exhausted, and the Covenant would move in for the kill.

And where could they really run to, anyway? Neither ship had Shaw-Fujikawa Translight Engines, so they were stuck in this system and the Covenant knew it. They could afford to take their time and play with their prey before they pounced.

The Chief performed a sweep scan of the system looking for something—anything to give him a tactical advantage. No, thinking of tactics was going to get him killed. There was no *tactical* advantage he could gain that would give him a victory in this mismatch. He had to change the rules—change his *strategy*.

He scanned the massive Covenant flagship—that was the key. That's how he'd be able to turn the tables on the enemy.

He keyed the COM system and hailed the Pelican. "This is Master Chief SPARTAN-One-One-Seven. Recognition code Tango Alpha Three Four Zero. Copy."

"Copy," a woman's voice answered. *"Warrant Officer Polaski here."* Other voices argued in the background. *"Damn good to hear you, Chief."*

"Polaski, proceed at maximum burn to this position." He dropped a NAV point on the display directly on the Covenant flagship. He included an exit vector indicating a rough course.

There was silence over the COM.

"Copy, Polaski?"

"I copy. Plotting course now, Chief." The voices arguing in the background became loud and more strained. *"I hope you know what you're doing. Polaski out."* The channel snapped off.

"Get us there, Cortana," he said, tapping the NAV point. "As fast as you can make this thing fly."

The Longsword rolled right and pitched toward the moon, Basis. The chief's safety harness groaned as gee forces increased.

"You *do* know what you're doing?" Cortana asked. "I mean, we're headed straight toward the largest and most dangerous Covenant ship in this system. I assume this is part of some daring and brutally simplistic plan you've cooked up?"

"Yes," the Chief replied.

"Oh, good. Hang on," Cortana said. The Longsword rolled to port and dived under a rock. An explosion detonated aft of the ship. "Looks like your 'plan' has gotten their attention. I'm reading all six Covenant cruisers moving to overtake us at flank speed."

"And the Pelican?"

"Still there," Cortana reported. "Taking heavy fire. But on trajectory to the NAV point . . . moving slower than us, of course."

"Adjust our speed so we arrive at the same time. When you're in range for a secure system link, let me know."

The Longsword decelerated; it shuddered to starboard and then to port, and laser fire flashed along either side.

"You never told me," Cortana said in a voice that was equal parts irritation and calm indifference, "precisely what your plan is."

"Something Captain Keyes would approve of." The Chief summoned the navigation console on the main display. "If we survive long enough, I want a course from here"—he tapped the NAV point over the flagship—"into the gravity well of Basis to slingshot us around."

"Done," Cortana replied. "I still— Hey, they've stopped firing."

The Chief tapped the aft camera. The six cruisers continued their pursuit, but the tips of their weapons cooled as they powered down. "I was counting on this. We're on the same line of fire as their flagship. They won't shoot."

"Pelican now twelve hundred kilometers and closing. Within range for system link."

The Chief hailed the Pelican. "Polaski, release your controls. We're taking over."

"Chief?"

"Establish encrypted system link. Acknowledge."

A long pause, then, *"Roger."*

Cortana's hologram appeared on the tiny protection pad. She appeared to listen intently for a moment, and then declared, "Got them."

"Synchronize our courses, Cortana. Put us right on top of the Pelican."

"Maneuvering to intercept the Pelican. Five hundred kilometers to flagship."

"Prepare to alter our course, Cortana, as we pass the flagship. Also get ready to direct all scanners at the flagship if we pass."

" 'If'?" Cortana asked.

The flagship's turrets turned to bear on the Longsword and Pelican. They glowed like angry eyes in the dark.

"Three hundred kilometers."

Light sparkled along the length of the Covenant craft as it prepared to fire; dull red plasma gathered; three torpedoes extruded and raced toward them.

"Evasiv—" the Chief said.

Cortana banked hard port, starboard, and then hit the

afterburners and pulled up. Streaks of hellfire brushed close to the hulls of the Longsword and Pelican—then were gone behind them.

The Chief had hoped for this: Their extreme oblique approach angle combined with their speed made them hard to hit, even for the notoriously accurate Covenant plasma weapons.

"Ten kilometers," Cortana announced. "Scanning in burst mode."

They flashed over the three-kilometer-long ship in the blink of an eye. The Chief saw gun turrets straining to track their approach. The alien craft had sleek lines, relatively flat top to bottom, but it curved from stem to stern into three distinct sections. Along its hull ran glowing blue conduits of superheated plasma; surrounding the ship was a faint shimmer of silver energy shields.

He eased back into his seat. The Chief hadn't realized that he'd been holding his breath, and he exhaled. "Good," he said. "Very good."

"Burning into a high slingshot orbit," Cortana announced.

The Longsword's engines rumbled. The acceleration played hell with the Chief's inner ear. He wasn't certain for a moment which way was up.

"Bring us closer to the Pelican," he said. "Right on top. Give me a hard dock on its top access hatch."

Cortana set her hands on her hips and frowned. "Readjusting burn parameters. But you know a linked-ship configuration during an orbital burn is not stable."

"We won't be linked long," he said and slipped out of his harness. He drifted aft, pulled himself down to the floor and opened the Longsword's access hatch. Green lights on the intervening pressure door winked on in succession. He removed the safeties and popped the seal.

A hand reached up from the other side. John pulled the person through.

The shock only lasted a moment. John's reflexes kicked in—he grabbed a handful of the man's uniform, kicked the hatch shut, and propelled both of them against the hull. With a lightning-quick motion, he drew the newcomer's pistol and aimed it squarely at the man's forehead.

"You were dead," the Chief said. "I *saw* you die. On Jenkins's mission record. The Flood got you."

The black man smiled a set of perfect white teeth. "The Flood? Hell, Chief, it'll take more than that pack of walking alien horror-show freaks to take out Sergeant A. J. Johnson."

CHAPTER
SIX

The Master Chief held on to the ship's frame with one hand so he wouldn't float away in zero gee. With the other hand he pressed the pistol deeper into Johnson's forehead.

The Sergeant's smile faded, but there was not a trace of fear in his dark eyes. He snorted a laugh. "I get it: You think I'm infected. Well, I'm not. This"—he patted his chest—"is one hundred percent grade-A Marine . . . and nothin' else."

The Chief eased his stance but didn't lower the gun. "Explain how that's possible."

"They got us all right, those little mushroom-shaped infectious bastards," Johnson said. "They ambushed me, Jenkins, and Keyes." He paused at the Captain's name, then shook his head and went on. "They swarmed all over us. Jenkins and Keyes were taken . . . but I guess I didn't taste too good."

"The Flood doesn't 'taste' anything," Cortana interjected. "The Infection Forms rewrite a victim's cellular structure and convert him into a Combat Form, then later a Carrier Form— an incubator for more Infection Forms. Based on what we've seen, they certainly don't just decide to pass up a victim."

The Sergeant shrugged. He fished into his pocket, found the remaining stub of a chewed cigar, and stuck it in the corner of his mouth. "Well, *I've* seen different. They 'passed me up' like I was undercooked spinach at a turkey dinner."

"Cortana," the Chief asked. "Is it possible?"

"It's *possible*," she carefully replied. "But it's also highly unlikely." She paused for two heartbeats, and then added, "According to the readings from the Sergeant's biomonitors, his story checks out. I can't be one hundred percent positive until he's been cleared in a medical suite, but preliminary findings indicate that he is clean of any Flood parasitic infection. He's obviously not a mindless, alien killing machine."

"All right." The Chief clicked the pistol's safety to "on" then flipped the pistol around and handed it back to the Sergeant, grip first. "But I'm having you checked inside and out the first chance we get. We can't risk letting the Flood infection spread."

"I hear you, Master Chief. Looking forward to those Navy nurses. Now—" The Sergeant pushed off the hull and drifted toward the hatch. "—let's get the rest of the crew on board." He hesitated by the cryotubes. "I see you already picked up a few stragglers."

"They'll have to wait," the Chief said. "It'll take half an hour to thaw them out without risking hypothermic shock. We don't have that much time left before we reengage the Covenant."

"Reengage," the Sergeant said, savoring the word. He smiled. "Good. For a second I thought we were running away from a perfectly good fight." The Sergeant opened the hatch to the Pelican.

The barrel of an MA5B assault rifle extended through the opening. The Sergeant reached down and pulled it up.

A Marine Corporal drifted though the hatch. The name stitched on his uniform read LOCKLEAR. He was tanned, shaved bald, and had a wild look in his clear blue eyes. He retrieved his gun from the Sergeant and swept the interior with the point of his weapon. "Clear!" he shouted back down into the Pelican.

"At ease, Corporal," the Master Chief said.

The Corporal's eyes finally locked onto the Chief. He shook

his head in disbelief. "A Spartan," he muttered. "Figures. Outta the friggin' frying pan—"

The Master Chief spotted the Marine's shoulder patch: the gold comet insigne of the Orbital Drop Shock Troops. The ODST, more colorfully known as "Helljumpers," were notorious for their tenacity in a fight.

Locklear must have been one of Major Silva's boys, which explained the young Marine's general hostility. Silva was ODST to the bone, and during the action on Halo had been decidedly negative about the SPARTAN-IIs in general . . . and the Chief in particular.

Another man gripped the edge of the hatch and pulled himself up. He had a plasma pistol strapped to his side and wore a crisp black uniform. His red hair was neatly slicked back, and his eyes took in the Chief without obvious surprise. He wore the black enameled bars of a First Lieutenant.

"Sir!" The Chief snapped off a crisp salute.

"Adjusting burn and angle," Cortana announced. The Longsword and Pelican tilted relative to the moon, Basis, on the viewscreen. "That should give you a little more than one gee on the deck."

The lieutenant settled to the floor and lazily returned the salute. "I'm Haverson," he said. He looked John over with interest. "You are the Master Chief, SPARTAN 117."

"Yes, sir." The Chief was surprised. Most people, even experienced officers, had difficulty distinguishing one Spartan from another. How had this young officer so quickly identified him?

The Chief saw the round insigne on the man's shoulder—the black and silver eagle wings over a trio of stars. Inscribed above the eagle wings were the Latin words SEMPER VIGILANS—Ever Vigilant.

Haverson was with the Office of Naval Intelligence.

"Good," Haverson said. He glanced quickly at Locklear and Johnson. "With you, Chief, we might have a chance." He reached into the hatch and pulled another person onto the Longsword.

This last person was a woman, and she wore the flight suit of a pilot. Her dirty blond hair was tucked into a cap. She saluted the Chief. "Petty Warrant Officer Polaski, requesting permission to come aboard, Master Chief."

"Granted," he said and returned her salute.

Stenciled onto her coveralls was a flaming fist over a red bull's-eye, the insigne of the Twenty-third Naval Air Squadron. Although the Chief had never met Polaski, she was from the same chalk as Captain Carol Rawley, callsign "Foehammer." If Polaski was anything like Foehammer, she would be a skilled and fearless pilot.

"So what's the story?" Locklear demanded. "We got something to shoot here?"

"At ease, Marine," the Sergeant growled. "Use that stuffing between your ears for something besides keeping your helmet on. Notice we're not floating? Feel those gee forces? This ship is in a slingshot orbit. We're coming around the moon for another crack at the Covenant."

"That's correct," the Chief said.

"Our first priority should be to escape," Haverson said and his thin brows knitted in frustration, "not to blindly engage the Covenant. We have valuable intelligence on the enemy, and on Halo. Our first priority should be to reach UNSC-controlled space."

"That was my intention, sir," the Chief replied. "But neither this Longsword nor your Pelican is equipped with Shaw-Fujikawa engines. Without a jump to Slipspace, it would take years to return."

Haverson sighed. "That does limit our options, doesn't it?" He turned his back to the Chief and paced, deep in thought.

The Master Chief respected the chain of command, which meant that he had to obey Lieutenant Haverson. But, officer or not, the Spartan had never liked it when people turned their backs to him. And he certainly didn't like the way Haverson assumed he was in charge.

The Chief had already gotten his orders, and he intended to follow them—whether or not Haverson approved.

"Pardon me, sir," the Chief said. "I must point out that while you are the ranking officer, I am on a classified mission of the highest priority. My orders come directly from High Command."

"Meaning?"

"Meaning," John continued, "I have tactical command of this crew, these ships . . . and *you*. Sir."

Haverson turned, his expression dark. The Lieutenant's mouth opened as if he were going to say something. He closed his mouth and looked the Chief over. A faint smile flickered over his thin lips. "Of course. I am well aware of your mission, Chief. I'll do anything I can to assist."

He knew about the Spartan's original mission to capture a Covenant Prophet? What was an ONI officer doing here anyway?

"So what's the plan?" Locklear asked. "Slingshot orbit—then what? We just going to talk all day, Chief?"

"No," the Chief replied.

He glanced at Polaski and the Sergeant. He could count on her, and though he was suspicious of exactly how Sergeant Johnson had avoided falling to the Flood, he was willing to give the man the benefit of the doubt. Haverson? He wouldn't trust him, but the man knew what was at stake, and he wouldn't interfere. Probably. Locklear was another story, though.

The ODST was coiled and ready to pounce . . . or come apart like an antipersonnel mine. Some men broke under pressure and wouldn't fight. Some snapped and disregarded their own and their team's safety for blind revenge. Add that to the Helljumper's fierce pride and one had a volatile mix. The Chief had to establish his authority over the man.

"Get onto the Pelican," the Chief told him. "We only have a few minutes while we're on the far side of this moon. Grab anything we can use: extra weapons, ammunition, grenades. Keep linked up to my COM so you can hear the briefing."

Locklear stood there, glared into the Chief's faceplate, and tensed.

Sergeant Johnson opened his mouth, but the Chief made a subtle cutting gesture with his hand. The Sergeant kept whatever he had to say to himself.

The Master Chief took a step closer to Locklear. "Was my order unclear, *Corporal*?"

Locklear swallowed. The blue fire in his eyes dulled and he looked away. "No." His body slumped and he shouldered his rifle, accepting, for now, the Master Chief's authority. "I'm on it, Master Chief." He went to the hatch and dropped into the Pelican.

To say this team was mismatched for a high-risk insertion op was an understatement.

"So how do we get a Shaw-Fujikawa drive?" Polaski asked.

"We don't," John replied. "But we go after the next best thing." He moved to the ops console and tapped the display. The scan of the Covenant flagship appeared on the viewscreen. "This is our objective."

Haverson frowned. "Chief, if we approach that ship we'll be blown out of the sky before we can even think about engaging them."

"Normally, yes," the Chief replied. "But we're going to rig the Pelican as a fireship—we load it with Moray mines and send it out ahead of us. We'll have to remote-pilot the Pelican, but it can be accelerated past the point where a crew would black out. It'll draw enemy fire, drop a few mines, and let us slip by."

Polaski's expression hardened into a frown.

"There a problem, Warrant Officer?"

"No, Master Chief. I just hate to lose a good ship. That bird got us off Halo in one piece."

He understood. Pilots got attached to their ships. They gave them names and human personalities. The Chief, however, never fell into that trap; he had long ago learned that any equipment was expendable. Except, maybe, Cortana.

"So we get close to the flagship," Haverson said and crossed his arms over his chest. "Are we going nose to nose with a ship with a thousand times our firepower? Or are you planning another flyby?"

"Neither." The Chief pointed to the flagship's fighter launch bay. "That's our LZ."

Polaski squinted at the comparatively tiny opening in the belly of the flagship. "That's a hell of a window to hit coming in this fast, but"—she bit her lower lip, calculating—"technically possible in a Longsword."

"They'll launch Seraph fighters to engage the Pelican and the Longsword," the Chief said, "and to do that, they'll have to drop that section of their shields. We get in, neutralize the crew, and we have a ship with Slipspace capability."

"Rock 'n' roll!" Locklear yelled over the COM. *"Penetrate and annihilate!"*

Sergeant Johnson chewed on his cigar as he considered the plan.

"No one has ever captured a Covenant ship," Haverson whispered. "The few times we've had one of them beaten and in a position to surrender, they've self-destructed."

"There's no choice," the Chief said. He looked over Polaski, Johnson, and finally Haverson. "Unless anyone has a better plan?"

They were silent.

"Anything to add, Cortana?" he asked.

"Our exit orbit burn leaves us low on fuel and traveling at high velocity on an intercept course with the flagship. There are overlapping fields of enemy fire on our approach vector. We have to decelerate and dodge simultaneously. That will be tricky."

"Polaski will be on that." The Chief turned to her.

"Pilot a Longsword?" Polaski slowly nodded, and there was a gleam in her green eyes that hadn't been there a second ago. "It's been a while, but yes, Master Chief. I am one hundred and ten percent on it." She moved to the pilot's seat and strapped herself in.

"With all due respect to Miss Polaski's skill," Cortana said, "allow me to point out that I process information a million times faster and—"

"I need you to link with the flagship's intraship battlenet," the Chief cut in. "When we're close you'll need to shut down its weapons. Jam its communications."

"Sending an unescorted lady ahead to do your dirty work?" Cortana sighed. "I suppose I'm the only one who can."

"Lieutenant Haverson," the Chief said, "I'll need you to program the Moray mines to release and attach onto the Pelican before we exit this orbit. Set half for detonation on impact. Program the rest to detach and track any enemy ship on our approach."

Haverson nodded and settled into the ops station next to Polaski.

Two crates and a duffel pushed through the open access tunnel to the Pelican. Locklear emerged from the opening and sealed the hatch. "That's it, Chief," he said. "An HE Pistol, two extra MA5Bs, one M90 Close Assault Shotgun, and a crate or so of frag grenades. About a dozen clips for the rifles—only a few shells for the shotgun, though."

The Chief took four grenades and a half dozen clips for his assault rifle. He ejected his weapon's nearly spent magazine and slapped a full one into place with a satisfying *clack*.

The Sergeant grabbed ammo, an MA5B, and three grenades.

"Orbital exit burn in ten seconds," Polaski said.

"Dog the rest of that," the Chief told Locklear. "And brace yourself."

Locklear secured the collection of weapons and ordnance in a duffel bag, looped it around his neck, and then found a handhold. Sergeant Johnson leaned against the cryopods. The Master Chief grabbed the bulkhead.

"Releasing Pelican," Polaski said. There was a *thump* from beneath the hull. "Pelican away."

"Pelican autopilot programmed," Cortana said.

"Moray mines attached and armed," Haverson added.

Polaski said, "Exit burn in three . . . two . . . one. *Burn!*"

The Longsword's engine roared to life, the hull creaked with stress, and everyone leaned against the acceleration.

The Pelican pulled ahead, rounded the horizon of the moon first, and arced back into the debris field. As the Longsword followed, the light struck the surface of the moon just right and the Chief saw meteors rain upon the planetoid, leaving craters and tiny puffs of dust as they impacted.

Polaski snapped the display port camera centered on the Covenant cruisers. "They were waiting for us," she cried. "Evasive maneuvers." The Pelican rolled to starboard. "Accelerating to the flagsh—"

The flagship was close. Too close. It must have anticipated their orbital trajectory. But it hadn't counted on them turning straight toward it. If they hadn't, the flagship would have been in a perfect perpendicular firing position.

"Pelican now two hundred kilometers in the lead," Polaski said.

The bulky craft drew fire from the cruisers. Smoke trailed from its hull, and bits of the empty ship were vaporized.

"Mines away," Haverson announced. "Plugging coordinates and trajectories into NAV, Polaski. Don't run them over."

"Roger," she said. "Hang on—we're going in."

"I hate this crap," Locklear muttered. "Ships shooting each other, fire so thick you could walk on it to the LZ, and me sittin' here not able to do a damn thing but hang on and wonder when I'm going to get blown up."

The Chief said nothing, but he agreed. Despite the ODST's foul disposition, he shared his uneasiness with space combat.

"Amen," Sergeant Johnson added. "Now shut up and let the lady drive." He removed a mission record unit from his pocket and inserted a chip. The screen blanked; a rhythmic cacophony blasted from its single tiny speaker.

The Chief recognized the sound as "flip" music—a descendant of some centuries-old noise called "metal." The Sarge had peculiar tastes, to say the least.

"Just shoot me now, Sarge," Locklear protested, "and get it over with. Don't torture me with that crap first."

"Suck it up, Marine. This is a *classic.*"

"So's a mercy killing."

Polaski continued to evade, and the Longsword rolled and jinked port and starboard. She sent the ship into a double barrel roll to dodge a plasma torpedo fired from the flagship.

"Show-off," Cortana muttered in the Chief's helmet speaker.

"Connecting to the Covenant battlenet," Cortana announced over the ship COM. "Accessing their weapons systems. Stand by."

Ahead, the Pelican intercepted a second torpedo and burst into flames, vaporized, and smeared across the night as a cloud of sparkling ionized metal.

The flagship appeared on the forward viewscreen—no larger than a dinner plate.

"No more time to play around," Polaski muttered. She hit the afterburners and rocketed toward the flagship.

The sudden acceleration sent the Chief and Sergeant Johnson bouncing to the aft of the Longsword. Locklear still hung on to the frame, now nearly horizontal.

"There is now insufficient distance to decelerate and make a soft landing inside the flagship launch bay," Cortana warned.

"Really?" Polaski replied, irritated. "No wonder they call you 'smart' AIs." She tugged her cap lower over her eyes. "*I'll* do the flying. *You* concentrate on getting those weapons offline."

"They're launching fighters," Haverson warned. On the viewscreen the Covenant flagship now filled half the display, and six Seraph fighters emerged from the belly of the massive ship. "I've still got active signals from twenty of the Moray mines. Their momentum is carrying them within range. Tracking . . . locked on . . . maneuvering." Tiny puffs of fire overlapped the teardrop-shaped Seraph fighters as they exploded. Haverson laughed. "Bull's-eye!"

"Forward weapons systems and shields are disabled," Cortana said.

"The doors are open," Polaski murmured. "We're invited in. It'd be damn impolite to say no."

The flagship filled the display.

"Collision imminent," Cortana warned.

Sergeant Johnson got to his feet. The Chief knew better and stayed where he was on the deck. He grabbed on to the Sergeant's leg.

Polaski cut the engines and hit the maneuvering thrusters. The Longsword spun 180 degrees. With the ship now pointed backward, she pushed the throttle to maximum, and the engines thundered in full overload. The hull strained against the sudden reverse deceleration.

The Chief hung on to the floor with one hand; with the other he held on to the Sergeant and kept him from flying across the ship.

Polaski changed the viewscreen to a split view—fore and aft. She maneuvered with the ship's thrusters, adjusting their approach to the launch bay opening. Onscreen the small opening grew larger alarmingly fast. "Hang on—hang on!"

The engines whined and the ship slowed . . . but it wasn't going to be enough.

They entered the launch bay at three hundred meters per second. Flames from the Longsword's engines washed over Grunt technicians as they vainly attempted to scramble out of the way. Their methane-filled atmosphere tanks popped like firecrackers.

Polaski cut the power. The ship slammed into the wall.

The Master Chief, Sergeant Johnson, and Locklear crashed into the pilot's and ops seats in a heap.

Grunts approached the ship with plasma pistols drawn, the weapons glowing green as the aliens overcharged them. Covenant Engineers struggled to put out fires and repair burst conduits.

"Shield reenergizing in place over the launch bay," Cortana announced. "External atmosphere stabilizing. Please feel free to get up and move around the cabin."

Locklear scrambled to his feet. "Yeah!" he whooped. The young Helljumper yanked his MA5B's charging lever and racked a round into the chamber. "Let's rock!"

"Good work, people," the Chief said, standing. He readied his own assault rifle. "But that was just the easy part."

CHAPTER

SEVEN

Plasma bolts impacted on the Longsword's hull and splashed across the windshield. The packets of glowing energy sizzled across the cockpit and etched cloudy, molten trails into the glass.

A legion of Grunts hunkered behind docked Seraph fighters and fuel pods. Some darted in and out of cover and fired ghostly green bolts of plasma at the Longsword.

"I got 'em," Polaski said and flipped a switch.

The Longsword's landing gear deployed and raised the craft a meter off the floor. "Guns clear," Polaski announced. "'Bye, boys."

She brought up a targeting reticle and swept it around the bay. A hail of 120mm rounds tore through the Grunts' cover. Fuel pods and unshielded fighters detonated and sent metal fragments and alien soldiers hurtling to the deck. The air exploded into roiling flame, which billowed toward the ceiling and then subsided. Pools of burning fuel and the charred bodies of Grunts and Covenant Engineers littered the launch bay.

"Fire suppression system activating," Cortana said.

Jets of gray mist blew down from above. The fires intensified for a moment, then guttered and went out.

"Is there atmosphere in the bay?" the Chief asked.

"Scanning," Cortana replied. "Traces of ash, some contamination from the melted ship hulls, and a lot of smoke, but the air in the bay is breathable, Chief."

"Good." He turned to the others. "We're going in. I'll lead. Locklear, you're up with me. Sergeant, you've got the rear."

"You'll need to take me, too," Cortana said. "I've pulled a schematic of this ship to navigate, but the engineering controls have been manually locked down. I'll need direct access to this ship's command data systems."

The Chief hesitated. His armor allowed an AI like Cortana to tag along stored in a special crystal layer. On Halo, Cortana had been an invaluable tactical asset.

Still, she also used part of his armor's neural interface for processing purposes, literally harnessing parts of the Chief's brain. And after coming out of Halo's computer system, she'd been acting . . . twitchy.

He put his discomfort aside. If Cortana turned into a liability, he'd pull the plug.

"Stand by," he said. He punched a key on the computer terminal and dumped Cortana to a data chip. A moment later the terminal pulsed green.

He removed the chip and slotted it in the back of his helmet. There was a moment of vertigo, and then the familiar mercury-and-ice sensation flooded his skull as Cortana interfaced.

"Still plenty of room in here, I see," she said.

He ignored her customary quip and nodded at Johnson and Locklear. "Let's go."

Sergeant Johnson hit the door release, and the side hatch slid open. Locklear shouldered his rifle and poured fire through the opening. A pair of Grunts who had crouched near the Longsword to protect themselves from the fire flew backward onto the deck. Phosphorescent blood pooled beneath their prone forms.

The Chief dived through the open hatch and rolled to his feet; his motion tracker picked up three targets to his side. He whirled about and saw a trio of Covenant Engineers. He removed his finger from the weapon's trigger. Engineers were no threat.

The odd, meter-high creatures hovered above the deck, using bladders of some lighter-than-air gas produced by their bodies. Their tentacles and feelers probed a tangle of fuel lines, quickly repairing the pipes and pumps.

"Funny that there's no welcoming committee yet," Cortana whispered. "I looked over this ship's personnel roster: three thousand Covenant, mostly Engineers. There's a light company of Grunts, and only a hundred Elites."

"*Only* a hundred?" the Chief muttered.

He waved his team forward toward a heavy door at the back of the launch bay. The air was full of smoke and fire-suppressing mist, which reduced visibility to a dozen meters.

The rattle of assault rifle fire echoed through the bay. The Chief spun to his right and brought his own rifle to bear.

Locklear stood over the twitching corpses of the Engineers. He fired another burst into the fallen aliens.

"Don't waste your ammunition, Corporal," the Sergeant said. "They may be ugly, but they're harmless."

"They're harmless *now*, Sarge," Locklear replied. He wiped a spatter of alien blood from his cheek and smirked.

The Chief tended to agree with Locklear's threat analysis of the Covenant: When in doubt, kill. Still, he found the young Marine's actions unnecessary . . . and a little sloppy.

The architecture of the Covenant fighter bay was similar to the interior of the other Covenant ship the Chief had recently been inside, the *Truth and Reconciliation*. Low indirect lights illuminated the dark purple walls. The alien metal appeared to be stenciled with odd, faintly luminescent geometric patterns that overlapped each other. The ceiling was vaulted and unnecessarily high, maybe ten meters. In contrast to a human ship, it was a waste of space.

The Chief spotted a large door at the back of the bay.

The door was a distorted hexagonal shape and large enough that the entire team could enter at the same time—not that he'd ever be foolish enough to take up such a formation in hostile territory. The door had four sections that, when keyed to open, would silently slide away from the center.

"That will take us to the main corridor," Cortana said. "And from there, to the bridge."

The Chief waved Locklear to the right side of the door, Sergeant Johnson to the left.

"Lieutenant Haverson," he called out, "you're our rear guard. Polaski, hit the door controls. Hand signals from now on."

Haverson tossed an ironic salute to the Chief but tightened his grip on his weapon and scanned the bay.

Polaski moved forward and crouched by the panel in the middle of the door. She turned her cap around and leaned closer, then looked back to the Chief and gave him a thumbs-up.

He raised his rifle and nodded, giving her the go-ahead to breach the door.

She reached for the controls. Before she touched them, though, the door slid apart.

Standing on the opposite side were five Elites: Two stood shielded by either edge of the door; a third stood centered in the corridor, plasma rifle leveled at the Chief; behind it, the fourth Elite covered the rear of their formation; and one last Elite crouched in front of the door control panel—nose to nose with Polaski.

The Chief fired two bursts directly over Polaski's head. His first shots struck the Elite in the middle of the corridor. His second burst hit the Elite standing rear guard. The alien warriors hadn't activated their shields, and 7.62mm rounds punctured their armor. The pair of Elites dropped to the deck.

Their comrades on either side of the door howled and attacked. The whine of plasma rifle fire echoed through the bay as blue-white energy bolts crashed into the Chief's own shields.

His shield dropped away, and the insistent drone of a warning indicator pulsed in his helmet. His vision clouded from the flare of energy weapon discharges, and he struggled to draw a bead on the Elite in front of Polaski. It was no good—he had no clear shot.

The Elite drew a plasma pistol. Polaski drew her own sidearm.

She was faster—or luckier. Her pistol cleared its holster; she snapped it up and fired. The pistol boomed as a shot took the Elite right in the center of its elongated helmet.

The Elite's own shot went wide and seared into the deck behind Polaski.

Polaski emptied her clip into the alien's face. A pair of rounds rocked the alien back. Its shields faded, and the remaining rounds tore through armor and bone.

It fell on its back, twitched twice, and died.

Johnson and Locklear unleashed a hellish crossfire into the corridor and made short work of the remaining Elites as Polaski hugged the deckplates.

"Now *that's* what I'm talkin' about," Johnson crowed. "An honest-to-God turkey shoot."

Ten meters down the passage a dozen more Elites rounded a corner.

"Uh-oh," Locklear muttered.

"Sergeant," the Chief barked. "Door control!" John moved to Polaski's position in two quick strides, grabbed her by her collar, and dragged her out of the line of fire. Plasma bolts singed the air where she'd been.

He dropped her, primed a grenade, and tossed it toward the rushing Elites.

The Sergeant fired his assault rife at the door controls; they exploded in a shower of sparks, and the doors slammed shut.

A dull *thump* echoed behind the thick metal, then an eerie silence descended on the bay. Polaski struggled to her feet and fed a fresh clip into her pistol. Her hands shook.

"Cortana," the Chief said. "We need an alternate route to the bridge."

A blue arrow flashed on his heads-up display. The Chief turned and spotted a hatch to his right. He pointed to the hatch and signaled his team to move, then ran to the hatch and touched the control panel.

The small door slid open to reveal a narrow corridor beyond, snaking into the darkness.

He didn't like it. The corridor was too dark and too narrow—a perfect place for an ambush. He briefly considered heading back to the primary bay door, but abandoned that idea. Smoke and sparks poured from the door seams as the Covenant forces on the other side tried to burn their way through.

The Chief clicked on his low-light vision filters, and the darkness washed away into a grainy flood of fluorescent green. No contacts.

He paused to let his shields recharge, then dropped into a low crouch. He brought his rifle to bear and crept into the corridor.

The interior of the passage narrowed, and its smooth purple surface darkened. The Chief had to turn sideways to pass through.

"This looks like a service corridor for their Engineers," Cortana said. "Their Elite warriors will have a tough time following us."

The Chief grunted an acknowledgment as he eased his way through. There was a scraping sound and a flash of sparks as his energy shield brushed the wall. It was too tight a fit. He powered down the shields, which left him just enough room to squeeze through.

Locklear followed behind him, then Polaski, the Sergeant, and finally Haverson.

The Chief pointed at Haverson, then at the door. The Lieutenant frowned, then nodded. Haverson closed the hatch and ripped out the circuitry for the control mechanism.

There had been dozens of Engineers in the launch bay—and there were enough on the ship to merit their own access tunnel. The Chief hadn't seen anything like this on the *Truth and Reconciliation*.

In fact, he hadn't seen a single Engineer on that ship. What made this ship different? It was armed like a ship of war . . . yet had the support staff of a refit vessel.

"Stop here," Cortana said.

The Chief halted and killed his external speakers so he could speak freely. "Problem?"

"No. A lucky break, maybe. Look to your left and down twenty centimeters."

The Chief squinted and noticed that a portion of the wall extruded into a circular opening no larger than the tip of his thumb. "That's a data port . . . or what passes for one with the Covenant Engineers. I'm picking up handshake signals in shortwave and infrared from it. Remove me and slot me in."

"Are you sure?"

"I can't do much good in there with you. Once I'm directly in contact with the ship's battlenet, however, I can infiltrate and take over their systems. You'll still need to get to the bridge and manually give me access to their engineering systems. In the meantime, I may be able to control secondary systems and buy you some time."

"If you're sure."

"When have I not been sure?" she snapped.

The Chief could sense her impatience through the neural interface.

He removed Cortana's data chip from the socket in his helmet. The Chief felt her leave his mind, felt the heat rush back into his head, pulsing with the rhythm of his heart . . . and once again, he was alone in the armor.

He slotted Cortana's chip into the Covenant data port.

Locklear's face rippled with disgust, and he whispered, "You couldn't pay me to stick any part of myself in that thing."

The Chief made a slashing gesture across his throat, and the Marine fell silent.

"I'm in," Cortana said.

"How is it?" the Chief said.

There was a half-second pause. "It's . . . different," Cortana replied. "Proceed thirty meters down this passage and turn left."

The Chief motioned the team forward.

"It's *very* different," Cortana murmured.

Cortana was built for software intrusion. She had been programmed with every dirty trick and code-breaking algorithm the Office of Naval Intelligence, Section Three had ever created, and a few more tricks she'd developed on her own. She was the ultimate thief and electronic spy. She slipped into the Covenant system.

It was easy the first time she had entered their network as the Longsword had approached the flagship. She had set their weapons systems into a diagnostic mode. The Covenant had determined the problem and quickly reset the system, but it had given Polaski the precious seconds her sluggish human reflexes had needed to get inside the launch bay.

"How is it?" the Chief asked.

Now the element of surprise was gone, and the system's counterintrusion systems were running on high alert. Something else prowled the systems now. Delicate pings bounced off the edges of Cortana's presence; they probed, and withdrew.

It felt as if there were someone else running through their

system. A Covenant AI? The possibility of one nearby intrigued her.

"It's . . . different," she finally answered.

She scanned the ship's schematics, deck by deck, then flashed through the vessel's three thousand surveillance systems. She picked out the quickest route to the bridge from their current position and stored it in a stolen tertiary system buffer. She multitasked a portion of herself and continued to analyze the ship's structure and subsystems.

"Proceed thirty meters down this passage and turn left."

Cortana hijacked the external ship cameras and detected the six Covenant cruisers. They had stalled their pursuit of the Longsword and now hovered a hundred kilometers off the flagship's starboard side. The strange U-shaped Covenant dropships launched from the cruisers and swarmed toward the flagship. That was trouble.

Within the flagship she spotted a dozen Elite hunter-killer teams sweeping the corridors. She scrambled the ship's tracking systems, generated electronic ghosts of the Chief and his team along a path directed toward the nose of the ship, where UNSC command-and-control centers were typically located. Maybe she could fool the Elites into a wild goose chase.

She uploaded the coordinates of those enemies into the Chief's HUD.

A tickle of feedback teased through the data stream.

Cortana locked onto the source of that feedback, listened, discerned a nonrandom pattern to the signal, then cut off contact. She had no time to play hide-and-seek with whatever else was in this system.

Cortana had to finally admit to herself that she didn't have the power to contend with a possible enemy artificial construct. She had absorbed a tremendous volume of data from Halo's systems: eons' worth of records on Halo's engineering and maintenance, the xenobiology of the Flood, and every scrap of information on the mysterious "Forerunners" the Covenant revered so much. The information would take her a week of nonstop processing to examine, collate, codify . . . let alone understand.

Even compressed, all the data filled her and cut into optical subsystems that she usually reserved for her processing. She had a nagging suspicion that the file compression had been too hasty—and that the Halo data might be corrupted.

In effect, the vast amount of information she had copied bloated her, made her slower and less effective.

She hadn't mentioned this to the Chief. She could barely admit it to herself. Cortana was extremely proud of her intellect. But to operate as if nothing were different would be even more foolish.

She sent a blocking countersignal along the connection where this "other" was trying to contact her.

The portion of her consciousness examining the ship's structure discovered that the bridge had another access point. Stupid. She should have seen it immediately, but this other entrance had been filed under the schematics as an emergency system. It was a tiny corridor that connected to a set of escape pods. That route shared a vent with an engineering passage.

"Chief, there's another way to the bridge."

"Affirmative. Wait one." There was a burst of gunfire on the COM, then silence. *"Go ahead, Cortana."*

"Uploading the route now," she said. "I do not believe you can fit through this new passage in your armor. I suggest you split your team and proceed along both routes to maximize your chances of egress onto the bridge."

"Understood," the Chief said. *"Polaski and Haverson with me. Johnson and Locklear, you take the escape pod route."*

She continued to track both teams and the relative positions of the Covenant parties. She replicated additional ghost signals to confuse the enemy.

Cortana picked up increasing communications bandwidth

between the flagship and the cruisers. Reports of the invaders—
a call for help—a warning to be relayed to the home world.
There were references to the "holy one," and those messages had
what she considered amusing attempts at encryption to keep
them secret. Curious, she had to investigate what the Covenant
thought important enough to hide.

As she decrypted those messages and others cross-referenced
and filed in their COM archives, she detected an energy spike
on the flagship's lateral sensors. One cruiser off to starboard
moved farther away; it turned, its engines glowed, the black
around it rippled electric blue. The Covenant ship sped forward, tore the night, and vanished into Slipspace.

Cortana noted their departure vector for future reference . . .
a possible clue at the location of their home world.

It was puzzling that the Covenant would call for help. Their
warriors were intensely proud; they almost never ran from a
fight. They didn't ask for help . . . not for themselves. Then
again, this ship, although armed for war, didn't appear to be
staffed for combat. It carried only a few hundred Elites and an
army of Engineers.

As Cortana pondered this, she continued to generate a countersignal to match to the probe sent by the other presence in
the system. She hoped to cloak her activity as long as possible.
The other's signal morphed into a series of Bessel functions,
and she compensated to match.

She automated this process, commandeering a portion of the
Covenant's own NAV computer to do so, and then she herded
the electronic ghosts of the Chief and the others to confuse the
pursuing Elite forces.

At the same time, she continued her study of the Covenant
ship and its systems—it was a unique opportunity. The information on their advanced Slipspace drive, their weapons—it
could leapfrog human technology decades forward.

"Cortana?" The Chief's voice broke her concentration. There were sounds of plasma bolts and automatic weapons fire. *"We've got Elites in active camouflage in the passage. We need a way around this intersection."*

She had not considered the Elites' light-bending technology. She was doing too much, spreading herself too thin. She halted her ongoing study of the Covenant technology and found the Chief a way around the intersection.

She rebooted her human communications and protocol routines and said, "Access panel to your right, Chief. Down three meters, straight ahead five meters, turn to your left and then up again."

She heard an explosion. *"Got it,"* the Chief said.

Cortana had to focus on protecting the Chief. She halted her other searches and scrutinized the ship's schematics. There had to be something she could use. A weapon. A way to stop their enemies—there: the backup terminus for their atmospheric preprocessors. Unlike the other systems, this one was classified as low priority and had minimal security layers.

She generated several hundred thousand Covenant codes in a microsecond and cracked the system. She diverted the air vents along the corridors the Chief and his team occupied to the primary air systems. She then tasked the processor pumps to service the rest of the ship and activated them—in reverse.

Warnings flashed throughout the Covenant system as the pressure suddenly dropped in 87 percent of the ship's passages. She squelched them.

The other presence in the system tried to shut the pumps off. She blocked that signal and assigned a new code to the security systems: "WE REGRET TO INFORM YOU."

She heard the other AI scream, an echo of an echo that reverberated through her processors. She knew the sound—familiar like a human voice, but terribly distorted.

She scanned through the ship's cameras and saw Grunts squeal and fall over, methane leaking from their breathers as the pressure dropped. Engineers turned blue, slowed, and died, floating in place with tentacles twitching, still searching for something to fix. The Elite hunt-and-destroy parties halted in the corridors and clutched their throats, mandibles snapping at air that was no longer there; they toppled and suffocated.

An impulse flickered through her ethics subroutine and generated an interrupt command, designed to make her stop and rethink her decisions. But Cortana knew it was either kill or be killed. She rerouted all signals from her ethics routine and shut it down. She couldn't afford to be slowed down by such secondary considerations.

"Chief," she whispered over the COM. "Be advised that the passages I'm uploading into your NAV system no longer contain atmosphere. Proceeding into those regions will be lethal to the rest of your team."

There was a three-second pause, and then the Chief replied, *"Understood."*

Cortana's decryption of the Covenant communiqués referencing the "holy one" finally cycled to a halt. The language in them was unusually ornate—even more so than the florid prose of the higher-ranking Elites. It was impossible to develop a literal translation, but she gleaned that some dignitary was due at the Halo construct. Soon.

This visitor was so important that these warships were only the advance scouting party. More ships were on their way. Hundreds of them.

"Chief," Cortana said. "We may have a prob—"

"Hold transmission, Cortana," the Chief interrupted. *"We're outside the command center. Can you tell how many are inside?"*

"Negative. They have disabled the bridge sensors," she replied.

"You heard Cortana," the Chief said, addressing his companions. *"Expect anything. Sergeant, you and Locklear: Get in position."*

"Roger that," Sergeant Johnson whispered. *"In position and ready to kick Covenant ass."*

"We're about to blow the door on this end, Cortana. Stand by."

Cortana picked up energy surges on the flagship's lateral sensors. The Covenant cruisers turned; their plasma weapons warmed and readied to fire.

"Chief," Cortana said. "Hurry!"

"Plasma grenades on my mark," the Chief said on the COM. *"Mark! Toss them and take cover."*

The Chief tossed two plasma grenades. They burned magnesium-brilliant and adhered to the heavy alloy of the bulkhead doors that encased the bridge—one of the alien weapon's more useful properties. He moved around the corner of the passage and shielded Haverson and Polaski.

Five seconds elapsed, and a flash filled the hallway. The Chief moved back to the doors. They shone mirror-bright where the grenade had detonated but were otherwise unharmed.

A hundred grenades wouldn't have blasted through these doors—but when Covenant plasma grenades detonated, they disrupted electronics and shielding. The Chief dug his gauntleted fingers into the door crack—hoping that the disruption had knocked out the motors and shielding keeping these doors closed.

He braced himself and tried to pull the doors apart at the seams. They slid a few centimeters, then ground to a halt. The Chief adjusted his footing and strained at them again, but the doors remained frozen in place.

The Chief's motion sensors pulsed a warning—there was movement directly on the other side of the door.

He shoved the muzzle of his assault rifle into the narrow opening and squeezed the trigger. Spent shell casings clattered to the floor.

A howl echoed from the other side, and a curl of gray smoke drifted through the crack.

The Chief slung his rifle, grabbed the doors, flexed, pulled—and this time the heavy metal moved.

A flash of plasma fire washed over his shields, blinding him. He ignored it, closed his eyes, and continued to force his way through the door. Another plasma shot struck him in the chest.

The doors were half a meter apart—good enough.

He rolled to the side and gave his shields a moment to regenerate.

Nothing. The suit's alarms pulsed insistently. He squinted through the glowing spots that swam in his vision and scanned the damage report—the MJOLNIR's internal temperature was over sixty degrees Celsius, and the Chief heard the whine of microcompressors in his armor, trying to compensate.

"Marines!" he yelled. "Suppressing fire!"

"Hell yes, Master Chief," Locklear replied. Locklear dropped to one knee and fired through the opening; Johnson stood and fired over the younger Marine's head.

The Chief rebooted his shielding control software.

Nothing. His shield system was dead.

The shooting stopped. "I'm out," Locklear said.

"And I'm in," the Chief said.

He rushed into the room and stepped over the dead Elite on the floor before him. Its torso had been ripped open—shot as it tried to hold the doors closed.

The Chief scanned the room. It was circular, twenty meters across, with a raised platform in the center that was ten meters across and ringed with holographic control surfaces. The central platform floated over a pit in the floor. Within the pit were exploded optical conduits and a trio of Covenant Engineers, cowering in fear.

"Don't shoot the Engineers," Cortana warned. "We need them."

"Understood," the Chief replied. "Acknowledge that order, Locklear."

There was a pause over the COM and then Locklear said, *"Roger."*

Along the circular walls, floor-to-ceiling displays showed the flagship's status as a variety of charts and graphs, peppered with the odd calligraphy of the Covenant. They also showed the space surrounding them, and the five remaining Covenant cruisers closing in.

The Chief caught a motion in his peripheral vision: An Elite in jet-black armor materialized from the wall display, its light-bending camouflage dissolving. It strode toward the Chief, roaring a challenge.

The Chief's rifle snapped up, and he squeezed the trigger. Three rounds spat from the muzzle, then the bolt locked open. The ammo counter read 00—empty.

The shots flared on the Elite's shielding; a lucky round penetrated and deformed its shoulder. Purple-black blood spattered on the deck, but it shrugged off the wound and kept coming.

Haverson charged into the room and leveled his pistol. "Hold it!" he yelled, and thumbed off the weapon's safety.

The Elite drew a plasma pistol and fired at the Lieutenant— but never took its eyes off the Chief.

Haverson cursed and scrambled out of the room as the plasma charge slashed at him.

The Chief altered his grip on the rifle and crouched in a low fighting stance. Even with the shield malfunction, he was confident he could take a single Elite.

The Elite removed its helmet and dropped it. The plasma

pistol clattered to the deck a moment later. It leaned forward, and its mandibles parted in what the Chief guessed had to be a smile. It moved closer, and a blue-white blade of energy flashed to life in its hands.

The Elite raised the energy blade and charged.

CHAPTER

EIGHT

The Master Chief ducked as the hissing energy blade slashed at him. He dived toward the Elite and slammed the butt of his rifle into the alien's midsection.

The Elite doubled over, and the Chief brought the rifle butt down to smash the alien's skull—

But the Elite rolled back. There was a blur of motion as the energy blade lashed out and neatly bisected the assault rifle. The two halves of the wrecked MA5B clattered to the deck.

The blade of crackling white-hot energy narrowly missed the Chief. The MJOLNIR's internal temperature skyrocketed.

He couldn't risk dancing at this range, so the Master Chief did the last thing the creature expected: He stepped closer and grabbed its wrists.

The bands of muscle on the Elite's arms were iron hard, and it struggled to free itself from the Chief's grasp. The Chief wrenched the alien's sword arm and forced the blade away—but this took most of his strength, and he had to weaken his grasp on the Elite's other hand.

The energy blade blurred perilously close to the Chief's head. It missed by a fraction of a centimeter and sent a wash of static across his heads-up display.

The blade was a flattened triangle of white-hot plasma, contained in an electromagnetic envelope that emanated from its hilt. The Chief had seen such weapons slice battle-armored ODSTs in half and gouge gaping wounds in Titanium-A armor plating.

Worse, this Elite was tough, cunning, well trained—and it hadn't spent days fighting nonstop on Halo. The Chief felt every wound, pulled muscle, and strained tendon in his body.

Haverson and Polaski moved onto the bridge, their pistols drawn, but neither of them had a clear line of fire.

"Move, Chief!" Haverson shouted. "Damn it, we've got no shot!"

Easier said than done. If he let go, the Elite would cut him in two.

The Master Chief grunted, struggling to turn the Elite.

The alien fought back for a moment, then—instead of resisting—lurched back, right into the path of the Chief's advancing teammates.

The Elite flicked the angle of its blade flat so the arc of energy whipped toward Haverson and Polaski.

Haverson screamed and fell to the ground as the energy blade sliced through his pistol and across his chest. Polaski cursed and fired a single shot, but it glanced off the Elite's shield.

The alien glanced at the source of the fire and growled in its guttural, warbling tongue.

"Get the Lieutenant out of here," the Master Chief barked. He raised his knee to his chest and lashed out with a straight kick. His boot connected with the Elite's breastplate. The alien's energy shield flared, then faded, and its breastplate cracked like porcelain beneath the force of the blow.

The alien staggered back, dragging the Master Chief with it. It coughed up purple-black blood that smeared John's visor, obscuring his vision. Its foot struck something on the ground—the alien's dropped helmet—and it lost its footing.

Together they crashed to the ground.

The Master Chief kept his grip on the Elite's sword arm. The alien's other hand, however, wrenched free and grabbed the fallen plasma pistol. The weapon's muzzle charged with sickly green energy.

The Chief rolled to his right as the pistol discharged. A globe of plasma arced across the compartment and splashed over the displays behind him.

The instruments flickered, then flashed and sparked as the energy bolt melted their systems. Before the displays went dark, however, the Master Chief saw one of the Covenant cruisers open fire. A lance of plasma rushed through space toward the flagship.

The Chief and the Elite struggled, rising to their feet. The Chief batted the plasma pistol aside, and it clattered across the control center.

The Elite's mouth opened, and it snapped at the Chief. It was angry or panicking now . . . and he felt it getting stronger.

His grasp on the alien loosened.

There was motion behind the Elite; Sergeant Johnson and Locklear still struggled to get their hatch open more than a crack.

"Sergeant—prepare to fire."

"Ready, Master Chief!" the Sergeant cried from the other side of the hatch.

The Chief tightened his grip on the Elite's sword arm, shoved his forearm into the alien's throat and drove it backward, across the bridge. He slammed the creature into the partially opened hatch.

The energy blade cut into the Master Chief's armor, boiling through the alloy that protected his upper arm.

"Sergeant, now! *Fire!*"

Gunfire exploded from the hatch, oddly muffled because the rounds impacted directly into the Elite's back. The alien snarled and contorted, but it held on to the Master Chief. The alien warrior sawed the blade deeper, cutting through the tough crystalline layers of the MJOLNIR armor. Hydrostatic gel oozed from the wound . . . mixed with the Chief's blood.

"Keep. Shooting."

A bullet hole appeared through the Elite's broken chestplate— bits of shattered armor and torn flesh spattered over the Chief.

The Master Chief slammed the Elite into the bulkhead, and a control panel behind the alien sparked. The door to the escape corridor hissed open, and the creature reeled back.

The alien was off balance, and the Chief finally had leverage. He bulled the Elite backward and hammered its arm into the wall. The alien metal rang like a gong, and the Elite dropped its energy sword. The blade guttered and went dark as its fail-safes permanently disabled the weapon.

The Chief forced the alien back, step by step. The deck was slippery with blood. Finally he twisted the Elite to the right and launched a powerful open-handed strike into the alien's wounded chest.

The Elite howled in pain and flew back, through the open hatch of an escape pod.

"Get off this ship," the Chief said. He hit a control stud and the hatch slammed shut. There was a sharp, metallic *bang* as the locking clamps released. The pod screamed away from the hull.

The Chief exhaled. Sweat dripped in his eyes, momentarily blurring his vision.

"Good work, Sergeant, Locklear," he panted. His shoulder burned. He tried to move it, but it was stiff and wouldn't respond.

The ship lurched.

"Plasma impact on the starboard foredeck!" Cortana called out. "Shields down to sixty-seven percent." She paused and then added, "Amazing radiative properties. Chief, you need to disable the navigation override so I can maneuver."

Haverson and Polaski strode toward the Chief. Haverson clutched his chest and grimaced in pain from the sword wound.

Polaski set her hand on the Master Chief's shoulder. "That's bad," she whispered. "Let me get a first-aid kit from the Longsword, and—"

The Chief shrugged off her touch. "Later." He saw her concerned expression melt into one of . . . what? Fear? Confusion?

"Cortana, show me what to do," the Chief said and made his way to the raised platform in the center of the bridge. "Polaski, you and Haverson get that other hatch open."

"Aye aye," Polaski muttered, her voice tight. She and Haverson went to the hatch and got to work.

The Master Chief glanced at the control surfaces. As his hand hovered over them, the flat controls rose and became a three-dimensional web of the distinctive Covenant calligraphy. "Where?" he asked.

"Move your hand to the right half a meter," Cortana said. "Up twenty centimeters. That control. No, to the left." She sighed. "*That* one. Tap it three times."

Faint lights traced the surface as the Chief touched it; they flared red and orange and finally cooled to brilliant blue.

"It worked," Cortana said. "NAV controls coming online. I can finally move this crate. Hang on."

The ship spun to port. On the displays that still functioned, four more Covenant cruisers tracked them—and fired.

The flagship accelerated, but the plasma torpedoes arced and followed them. "No good," Cortana said. "I can't overcome our inertia in this tub. They're going to hit us . . . unless I can get us into Slipspace."

A rhythmic warble pulsed from one of the displays. It flashed red.

"Oh no," Cortana said.

The leading plasma torpedo impacted. Dull red fire smeared across the viewscreens.

"Oh no, what?" Haverson demanded.

"This ship's Slipspace generator is inert," Cortana replied.

"The disabled NAV controls were a trick. It must have been the Covenant AI; it lured me here while the drive was physically decoupled from the reactor. I can maneuver all I want, give orders to the Slipspace generator—but without the system powered up we're not going anywhere."

"There's a *Covenant* AI?" Haverson muttered, and raised an eyebrow.

"Upload the coordinates to power coupling," the Master Chief said. "I'll take care of it."

Two more plasma torpedoes impacted and splashed across the shield. "Energy shields collapsing," Cortana said. "Brace!"

The last shot collided with the flagship. The hull heated, and plasma boiled layers of armor plating away. The ship rolled as plumes of superheated metal vapor outgassed.

"Another hit like that will breach the hull," Cortana said. "Moving this tub at flank speed."

"The power coupling coordinates, Cortana," the Master Chief insisted.

A route appeared on his heads-up display. The engineering rooms were twenty decks below the bridge.

"Those won't do you any good," Cortana told him. "There are bound to be Elite hunter-killer teams waiting for you. And even if you managed to remove them, there is no way to repair the power coupling in time. We don't have the tools or the expertise."

The Master Chief looked around the bridge. There had to be a way. There was *always* a way—

He leaned over the edge of the central platform and grabbed one of the Covenant Engineers that cowered below. He dragged it up by its float-sack. The creature squirmed and squealed.

"Maybe we don't have the expertise," he said and shook the Engineer. "But this thing does. Can you communicate with it? Tell it what we need?"

There was a pause. Then Cortana replied, "There is an extensive communications suite in the Covenant lexic—"

"Just tell it I'm taking it to fix something."

"All right, Chief," Cortana said.

A stream of high-pitched chirps emanated from the bridge speakers, and the Engineer's six eyes dilated. It stopped squirming and grabbed hold of the Master Chief with its tentacles.

"It says 'good' and 'hurry,'" Cortana told him.

"Everyone else stay here," the Chief said.

"If you insist," Haverson muttered, his face pale. Blood trickled from the wound in his chest.

The Master Chief looked at Johnson and Locklear. "Don't let the Covenant retake the bridge."

"Not a problem, Chief," Sergeant Johnson said. He stopped to kick the dead Elite once in the teeth, then slapped a fresh clip into his MA5B. He yanked the weapon's charge handle, fed a round into the chamber, and stood at arms. "Those Covenant sissies are going to have to tango with me before they set one foot in this room."

On the display two of the Covenant cruisers fired again.

The Chief watched as the plasma raced toward them, fire that spread across the black of space. "Cortana, buy me some time," he said.

"I'll do what I can, Chief," Cortana told him. "But you'd better move fast. I'm running out of options."

Cortana was annoyed. She had let the Covenant AI—for that's what this other presence in the system undoubtedly had to be—trick her. She had gone straight for the simple lockdown of the NAV systems. She never performed a thorough systems check of the ship, assuming that there had only been one point of sabotage. It was a mistake she would never have made if she'd been operating at full capacity.

She checked every system of the flagship. She then locked them out with her own security measures.

Cortana turned off her feelings of anger and guilt and concentrated on keeping the ship in one piece, and the Master Chief alive. No . . . she reconsidered and kept her emotions active. The "intuition" provided by this aspect of her intelligence template was too valuable to deactivate in a battle.

She maneuvered the flagship toward the gas giant, Threshold. The incoming plasma might be disrupted by the planet's magnetic field—if she dared get close enough.

Cortana diverted power from the foreshield to the aft portions, distorting the protective bubble around the flagship. She turned all seven plasma turrets aft and fired a pair of plasma torpedoes at the incoming salvo.

The plasma turrets warmed and belched superheated flame— but it dispersed into a dull red cloud only a few meters from the point of fire, thinned, and then dissolved.

She saw a subsystem linked to the weapons control: an accompanying magnetic field multiplier. *That* was how the Covenant shaped and guided their charges of plasma. It acted as a sophisticated focusing lens. Something wasn't right, however— something had already been in this directory and had erased the software.

Cortana swore that when she caught this guerrilla Covenant AI, she'd erase it line by line.

Without understanding how the guiding magnetic fields worked, the plasma turrets were no more useful than a fireworks display.

The enemy Covenant plasma charges, however, were tight and burned like miniature suns; they overtook the flagship and splashed over its reinforced aft shields. They boiled against the silver energy until the shields dulled and winked out.

The plasma etched a portion of the aft hull away like hot water dissolving salt. Cortana sensed the dull thumps of atmospheric decompressions.

She checked on the Chief. His signal was still on board, and his biomonitor indicated that he was still alive.

"Chief, are you there yet? I'm down to one last option."

There was a static-filled pause over the COM, and then the Master Chief whispered, *"Almost."*

"Be careful. Your armor is breached. You can no longer function in a compromised atmosphere."

His acknowledgment light winked on.

Cortana pushed the Covenant reactors to overload and plotted a course around Threshold. She had to slip into the outer reaches of its atmosphere. The heat, ionization, and planet's magnetic field might protect them from the plasma.

The flagship rolled and dived into the thin tendrils of clouds. Bands of white ammonia and amber ammonium hydrosulfide clouds snaked in sinuous ribbons. A red-purple spot of phosphorus compounds cycloned and lightning arced, illuminating an intervening layer of pale blue ice crystals.

But their ship no longer had shields. The friction heated the hull to three hundred degrees Celsius as she brushed against the upper reaches of Threshold.

On her aft cameras Cortana saw the trailing Covenant ships open fire. Their shots followed her like a pack of predator birds.

"Come and get me," she muttered.

She adjusted the attack angle of the flagship so it nosed up, which produced a slight amount of lift. She concentrated the building heat toward the ship's tail. A turbulent wake of superheated air corkscrewed behind them.

"Cortana?" Polaski said. *"We're approaching the viable edge of an exit orbit. You're getting too close to the planet."*

"I am aware of our trajectory, Warrant Officer," she said and snapped off the COM. The last thing she needed was a flying lesson.

The leading edge of the plasma overtook them. It roiled in

their wake, churned explosively with the atmosphere. The flagship pitched and dropped in the unstable air, but the plasma diffused and caused them no further damage. Behind the flagship was an unfurling trail hundreds of kilometers long, a wide flaming gash upon Threshold.

Cortana experienced a moment of triumph—then squelched it. There was a new problem: The concussion from that blast had altered their flight path. The heat and overpressure wave had thinned the atmosphere . . . just enough to cause the flagship to drop seven hundred meters. Wisps of ice crystals washed over the prow.

They were too deep now. They didn't have enough power to break orbit. They would spiral into the atmosphere, and would ultimately be crushed by the titanic gravitational forces of Threshold.

The Chief spun in midair and planted his feet on the "ground." The gravity had been disabled in this elevator shaft. That had made traversing the many intervening decks easy . . . as long as he'd been willing to jump and trust that the power in this part of the ship wouldn't be restored.

The Engineer clutching his shoulder tapped the tiny control panel on the wall. The doors at the bottom of the shaft sighed and slowly slid apart.

Funny how the creature didn't care what or who John was. Didn't it know their races were enemies? It was clearly intelligent and could communicate. Maybe it didn't care about enemies or allies. Maybe all it wanted to do was its job.

There was a corridor ahead, five meters wide, with a vaulted ceiling. Past a final arch, the passage opened up into the cavernous reactor room. The ambient lights in the hallway and room were off. Along the far wall of the room, however, the ten-meter-high reactor coils pulsed with blue-white lightning and threw hard shadows onto the walls.

The Master Chief adjusted his low-light filters to screen out the glow from the reactor. He made out the silhouettes of crates and other machinery. He also saw one of those shadows on the wall move . . . with the distinct slouching waddle of a Covenant Grunt. Then the motion was gone.

An ambush. Of course.

He paused, listened, and heard the panting of at least half a dozen Grunts, and then the high-pitched uneasy squeaks the creatures emitted when they were excited.

This came as a relief to the Master Chief. If there was an Elite here, it would have maintained better discipline and silenced the Grunts.

Still, the Master Chief hesitated. His shields were gone, his armor breached. He had been fighting almost nonstop for what felt like years. He was forced to admit that he was at the limits of his endurance.

A good soldier always assessed the tactical situation—and right now, his situation was serious. A single lucky plasma shot could inflict third-degree burns along his arm and shoulder and incapacitate him, which would give the Grunts an opportunity to finish him off.

The Chief flexed his wounded shoulder, and pain lanced across his chest. He banished his discomfort and concentrated on how to win this fight.

It was ironic that after facing the best warriors in the Covenant, and after defeating the Flood, he could be killed by a handful of Grunts.

"Chief," Cortana said over the COM. "Are you there yet? I'm down to one last option."

The Master Chief replied in a whisper, "Almost."

"Be careful. Your armor is breached. You can no longer function in a compromised atmosphere."

He flashed an acknowledgment to Cortana and concentrated on the problem at hand. Using grenades was not an option; a plasma grenade or a frag near those reactor coils could breach the containment vessel.

That left stealth—and outwitting the Grunts.

Maybe he'd use his grenades after all. The Master Chief set a plasma grenade in the center of the elevator shaft. He took his remaining two frag grenades and set them aside as well. He felt along the elevator shaft walls and found what he needed—a length of hair-fine optical cord. He pulled out a three-meter length.

The Engineer gave a huff of irritation at this destruction.

The Master Chief threaded the line though the rings of his frag grenades and tied each end at anchor points ten centimeters off the floor. He wedged the grenades into the slot of the open door.

The trap was set; all he needed now was bait.

He set a plasma grenade on the far wall of the shaft and triggered it.

He pushed into the corridor, fast. Four seconds to go. The gravity, still active in this portion of the ship, pulled him to the deck. He melted into the shadows and sprinted along the wall two meters farther in, and halted along the inside of the first support brace. Three seconds.

One Grunt emitted a startled cry and a plasma shot sizzled down the center of the hallway.

Two seconds.

The Master Chief pried the Engineer off his shoulder and pressed the creature firmly into the join where the brace met the wall.

One second.

The Engineer squirmed for a moment, then stilled, perhaps sensing what was about to happen.

The plasma grenade detonated. A flash of intense light flooded the hallway and the room beyond.

The rest of the Grunts cried out; plasma bolts and a hail of crystalline needles filled the passage, impacting inside the elevator shaft.

The Grunts ceased fire. A lone Grunt cautiously stepped out from behind a crate and crept forward. It gave a barking, nervous laugh and then, encountering no resistance, waddled down the passage toward the elevator.

Four more Grunts followed, and they passed the Master Chief, oblivious that he hid behind the wall brace less than a half-meter from them.

They approached the elevator, sniffed, and entered.

There was the gentle *ping* as the frag grenade rings pulled free of the trip wire.

The Master Chief covered the Engineer.

One of the Grunts squealed, high and panicky. They all turned and ran.

Twin blasts of thunder enveloped the elevator shaft. Bits of meat and metal spattered along the corridor.

A needler skidded to a halt a meter away. It was cracked, its energy coil dim. The Master Chief grabbed it—ducked as another plasma bolt singed over his head. He withdrew to the cover of the bracing support. He tried to activate the weapon. No luck. It was dead.

The Engineer snaked a tentacle around the weapon and tugged it away from John's grasp. It cracked the case and peeled the housing open. The tip of one of its tentacles split into a hundred needle-fine cilia and swept over the inner workings. A moment later it reassembled the weapon and handed it, grip first, to the Master Chief.

The needler hummed with energy, and the glassine quills the weapon fired glowed a cool purple.

"Thanks," he whispered.

The Engineer chirped.

The Master Chief edged around the brace. He waited, needler held tightly in his hand, and became completely still. He had all the time in the world, he told himself. No need to rush. Let the enemy come to you. All the time—

A Grunt poked its nose over a crate, trying to spot its enemy; it took a blind shot down the corridor and missed.

The Master Chief remained where he was, raised the needler, and fired. A flurry of crystal shards propelled down the passage and impaled the Grunt. It toppled backward, and the shards detonated.

The Master Chief waited and listened. There was nothing except the gentle thrumming of the reactor.

He moved down the corridor, weapon held before him as he cleared the room. He was careful to watch for the faint rippling of air that would alert him to the presence of camouflaged Elites. Nothing.

The Engineer floated behind him, and then accelerated toward the disengaged power coupling. It hissed and chittered as it rapidly manipulated a small square block of optical crystal, unscrambling the internal circuit pathways.

"Cortana," he said. "I've gotten to the coupling. The Engineer appears to know what it's doing. You should have power for the Slipspace generator in a moment."

"It's too late," Cortana told him.

CHAPTER

NINE

The flagship plunged through Threshold's churning atmosphere. Cortana could not hold the ship's attitude. It wobbled and blasted a fiery scar through the clouds, slowly rolling to port on its central axis.

Without shields, the flagship's hull continued to heat to seventeen hundred degrees Celsius. The nose glowed a dark red, which spread into an amber smear along the midsection and became a white-hot plume at the ship's tail. Conduits and feathery antenna arrays melted, separated, and left a trail of molten metal in an explosive wake. Shocks rippled along the frame as the overpressure shed off the bow in waves. The friction from the planet's dense atmosphere would shred the ship in a matter of seconds.

"Cortana," the Master Chief said. *"I've gotten to the coupling. The Engineer appears to know what it's doing. You should have power for the Slipspace generator in a moment."*

"It's too late," Cortana told him. "We are now too low to escape Threshold's gravitational pull. Even at full power we can't break our degrading orbit. And we can't tunnel into Slipspace, either."

The incoming Covenant fire had forced them deeper into the atmosphere. She had pushed their trajectory to the edge of what had been safe—it was that, or be engulfed in plasma. But she had saved them from one death . . . only to delay that fate by a scant minute.

She recomputed the numbers, thrust and velocity and gravitational attractions. Even if she overloaded the reactors to critical-meltdown levels, they were still stuck in an ever-descending spiral. The numbers didn't lie.

The Master Chief's Engineer must have repaired the power coupling, because the Slipspace generator was functional again—for all the good it did them.

To enter Slipspace a ship had to be well away from strong gravitational fields. Gravity distorted the superfine pattern of quantum filaments through which Cortana had to compute a path. Covenant Slipspace technology was demonstrably superior, but she doubted that the enemy had ever attempted a Slipspace entry this close to the center of a gas giant.

Cortana toyed with the idea of trying anyway—pulse the Slipspace generators and maybe she'd get a lucky quadrillion-to-one shot and locate the correct vector through the tangle of gravity-warped filaments. She rejected the possibility; at their current velocity, any attempt to maneuver the ship would send it into a chaotic tumble from which they'd never recover.

"Try something," the Chief said to her with amazing calm. *"Try anything."*

Cortana sighed. "Roger, Chief."

She booted the Covenant Slipspace generators; the software streamed through her consciousness.

The UNSC Shaw-Fujikawa Slipspace generators ripped a hole in normal space by brute force. But the Covenant technology used a different approach. Sensors came online, and Cortana could actually "see" the interlacing webs of quantum filaments surround the flagship.

"Amazing," she whispered.

The Covenant could pick a path through the subatomic dimensions; a gentle push from their generators enlarged the fields just enough to allow their ships to pass seamlessly into the alternate space with minimal energy. Their resolution of the reality of space-time was infinitely more powerful than human technology. It was as if she had been blind before, had never seen the universe around her. It was beautiful.

This explained how the Covenant could make jumps with such accuracy. They could literally plot a course with an error no larger than an atom's diameter.

"Status, Cortana?" the Master Chief asked.

"Stand by," she said, annoyed at the distraction.

At this resolution Cortana could discern every ripple in space caused by Threshold's gravity, the other planets in this solar system, the sun, and even the warping of space caused by the mass of this ship. Could she compensate for those distortions?

Pressure sensors detected hull breaches on seventeen outer decks. Cortana ignored them. She shut down all peripheral systems and concentrated on the task at hand. It was their only way out of this mess: They'd get *out* by going *through*.

She concentrated on interpolating the fluctuating space. She generated mathematical algorithms to anticipate and smooth the gravitational distortions.

Energy surged from the reactors into the Slipspace generator matrices. A path parted directly before them—a pinhole that became a gyrating wormhole, fluxing and spinning.

Threshold's atmosphere throbbed and jumped through the hole—sucked into the vacuum of the alternate dimension.

Cortana dedicated all her runtime to monitoring the space around the ship, and risked making microscopic course corrections to maneuver them into the fluctuating path. Sparks danced along the length of the hull as the nose of the flagship departed normal space.

She eased the rest of the ship through, surrounded by whirling storms and jagged spears of lightning.

She pinged her sensors: The hull temperature dropped

rapidly and she registered a series of explosive decompressions on the breached decks.

Cortana emerged from her cocoon of concentration and immediately sensed the electronic presence of the other near her, monitoring her Slipspace calculations. It was practically on top of her.

"Heresy!" it hissed and then withdrew . . . and vanished.

Cortana pulsed a systems check along every circuit in the ship, hoping to track the Covenant AI. No luck.

"Sneaky little bastard," she broadcast throughout the system. "Come back here."

Had it seen what she had done? Had it understood what she'd just accomplished? And if so, why declare it a "heresy"?

True, manipulating eighty-eight stochastic variables in eleven-dimensional space-time was not child's play . . . but it was possible that the other AI would be able to follow her calculations.

Perhaps not. The Covenant were *imitative*, not innovative; at least, that's what all the ONI intelligence gathered on the collection of alien races had reported. She had thought this was exaggeration, propaganda to bolster human morale.

Now she wasn't so certain. Because if the Covenant had truly understood the extent of their own magnificent technology, they could have not only jumped into Slipspace *from* a planet's atmosphere—but jumped *into* a planet's atmosphere, too.

They could have simply bypassed Reach's orbital defenses.

The Covenant AI had called this heresy? Ludicrous.

Maybe the humans could eventually outthink the Covenant, given enough access to the enemy's technologies. Cortana realized the humans actually had a chance to win this war. All they needed was time.

"Cortana? Status please," the Master Chief said.

"Stand by," Cortana reported.

———

The Chief felt decompressive explosions reverberate through the deck, thunder that suddenly silenced itself as the atmosphere vented.

He waited for an explosion to tear through the engine room, or for plasma to envelop him. He scanned the engine room for any signs of Grunts or Elites, and then exhaled, and stared into the face of death for the countless time.

He had always been a hairsbreadth from death. John wasn't a fatalist, merely a realist. He didn't welcome the end; he knew, though, that he had done his best, fought and won so many times for his team, the Navy, and the human race . . . it made moments like this tolerable. They were, ironically, the most peaceful times in his life.

"Cortana, status please," he asked again.

There was a pause over the COM, then Cortana spoke. "We're safe. In Slipspace. Heading unknown." She sighed, and her voice sounded tinged with weariness. "We're long gone from Halo, Threshold, and that Covenant fleet. If this tin can holds together a bit longer, I want to put some distance between us and them."

The Chief replied, "Good work, Cortana. Very good." He moved toward the elevator. "Now we have a hard decision to make."

He paused and turned back toward the Covenant Engineer. The creature moved away from the repaired power coupling and drifted to a scarred, half-melted panel that had been hit with stray plasma fire. It huffed, removed the cover, and delved into the tangle of optical cables.

The Chief left it alone. It wasn't a threat to him or his team. In fact, it and the others like it might be key to repairing this ship, and their continued survival.

He continued to the elevator shaft, stepping over the bodies of the Grunts in the hallway. He nudged them with his foot to make certain they were dead, and then retrieved two plasma pistols and one of the needle launchers.

He entered the elevator shaft, pushed off the deck, and floated upward in the null gravity. The Chief kept his eyes and ears sharp for any hint of a threat as he moved through the corridors to the bridge. Everything was quiet and still.

At the open bridge door, he paused and watched as Warrant Officer Polaski supervised a Covenant Engineer while it removed the blasted door control panels. The Engineer turned a melted piece of polarizing crystal before its six eyes, and then picked up an unblemished crystalline panel off the floor and inserted it into the wall.

Polaski wiped her hands on her greasy coveralls and waved him in.

Thin, blue smoke still filled the bridge, but the Chief noted that most of the display panels were once again active. Nearby, Sergeant Johnson tended Haverson's wounds and Locklear stood guard. The young Marine's eyes never left the Engineer, and his finger hovered close to, though not quite on, his MA5B's trigger.

The Engineer floated back, spun on its long axis, and looked first at Polaski, then the Chief.

A burst of static issued from the bridge speakers, and the Covenant Engineer looked to them and then to Polaski. It tapped the control, and the massive bridge doors slid shut.

The Engineer passed a tentacle over the controls. They flashed blue, then dimmed.

"It locks now," Polaski told them. "Ugly here knows his stuff."

Three ultrasonic whistles filled the air. The Covenant Engineer who had just repaired the bridge door snapped to attention, and its eyes peered intently forward. It chirped a response and then floated toward the Master Chief, trying to maneuver behind him.

"What's it doing?" the Master Chief asked, turning to face the creature.

The Engineer huffed in annoyance and tried again to move around him.

The Master Chief didn't let it. While John had seen no hostility from the creatures, they were still part of the Covenant. Having one at his back grated against every instinct.

"I've told it to repair your armor's shields," Cortana said. "Let it."

The Master Chief allowed the small alien to pass. He felt the access panel removed from the shield generator housing on his back. Normally it took a team of three technicians to remove the safety catches and get to the radioactive power source. The Chief shifted uneasily. He didn't like this one bit, but Cortana had always known what she was doing.

Locklear watched this and ran a hand over his shaved head. He stood on the raised center platform and turned to the other Covenant Engineer as it repaired the burned-out displays on the port side of the room. He held his MA5B loosely, but it was still aimed in the alien's general direction. "I don't care what Cortana says," he told the Chief, "I don't trust them."

The Engineer near Locklear floated to the bridge's holographic controls and passed a tentacle over a series of raised dots.

The screens snapped on and showed three Covenant cruisers closing fast.

Adrenaline spiked through the Master Chief's blood. "Cortana, quick—take evasive action."

"Relax, Chief," Locklear said. He waved his hand over a holographic control; the images on screen froze. "It's just a replay." He turned and examined the suspended plasma bolts just as they impacted on the flagship's shields. "Man," he whispered. "I wish our boats had weapons like those."

"We might soon have exactly that, Marine," Lieutenant Haverson said. He winced and stood, then moved to a screen that showed the storms in the upper atmosphere of Threshold. "Play this one, Corporal."

Locklear tapped one of the controls.

A line of sparkling blue lights appeared on screen, and the nose of the flagship edged into view. The blue line ripped a hole in space, and the ship jumped forward. The clouds of Threshold vanished; there was only blackness on the screen.

Haverson slicked back the strands of his red hair that had fallen into his face. "Cortana," he asked, "has anyone, human or Covenant, ever performed a Slipspace jump from within an atmosphere?"

"No, Lieutenant. Normally such strong gravitational fields would distort and collapse the Shaw-Fujikawa event horizon. With the Covenant's Slipspace matrices, however, I had greatly increased resolution. I was able to compensate."

"Amazing," he whispered.

"Goddamned lucky," Polaski muttered. She tugged on the rim of her cap.

"It worked," the Master Chief told them. "For now, that's all that matters." He faced his team, trying to ignore the motions of the Covenant Engineer attached to his back. "We have to plan our next move."

"I'm sorry to disagree, Chief," Lieutenant Haverson said. "The mere fact that Cortana's maneuver worked is the *only* thing that matters now."

The Chief squared himself to the Lieutenant and said nothing.

Haverson held up his hands. "I acknowledge that you have tactical command, Chief. I know your authority has the backing of the brass and ONI Section Three. You'll get no argument from me on that point, but I put it to you that your original mission has just been superseded by the discovery of the technology on this ship. We should scrub your mission and head straight back to Earth."

"What's this other mission?" Locklear asked, his voice suspicious.

Haverson shrugged. "I see no reason to keep this information classified at this point. Tell him, Chief."

The Master Chief didn't like how Haverson "acceded" to his tactical command yet readily ordered him to reveal highly classified material.

"Cortana," the Chief said. "Is the bridge secure from eavesdroppers?"

"A moment," Cortana said. Red lights pulsed around the room's perimeter. "It is now. Go ahead, Chief."

"My team and I—" the Master Chief started.

He hesitated—the thought of his fellow Spartans stopped him cold. For all he knew they were all dead. He pushed that to the back of his mind, however, and continued.

"Our mission was to capture a Covenant ship, infiltrate Covenant-controlled space, and capture one of their leaders. Command hoped they could use this to force the Covenant into a cease-fire and negotiations."

No one said a word.

Finally, Locklear snorted and rolled his eyes. "Typical Navy suicide mission."

"No," the Master Chief replied. "It was a long shot, but we had a chance. We have a better chance now that we have this ship."

"Excuse me, Master Chief," Polaski said. She removed her cap and wrung it in her hands. "You're not suggesting that you're going to continue that half-assed op, are you? We barely survived four days of *hell*. It was a miracle we got away from Reach, survived the Covenant on Halo . . . not to mention the Flood."

"I have a duty to complete my mission," the Master Chief told her. "I'll do it with or without your help. There's more at stake than our individual discomfort—even our lives."

"We're not Spartans," Haverson said. "We're not trained for your kind of mission."

That was certainly true. They weren't Spartans. John's team would never give up. But as he scanned their weary faces, he had to acknowledge that they weren't ready for this mission.

The Sergeant stepped forward and said, "You still want to go, I got your back, Chief."

John nodded, but he saw the exhaustion even in the Sergeant's dark eyes. There were limits to what any soldier, even a hardcore Marine like Johnson, could endure. And as much as he didn't want to admit it, his original orders, given only weeks ago, felt as if they'd been issued a lifetime in the past. Even John felt the temptation to stop and regroup before continuing.

"What's on this ship," Haverson said, "can save the human race. And wasn't that the goal of your mission? Let's return to Earth and let the Admiralty decide. No one would question your decision to clarify your orders given the circumstances"—he paused, then added—"and the loss of your entire team."

Haverson's expression was carefully neutral, but the Chief still bristled at the further mention of his team—and at the attempt to manipulate him. He remembered his order sending Fred, Kelly, and the others to the surface of Reach, thinking that he, Linda, and James were going on the "hard" mission.

"Listen to the El-Tee," Locklear said. "We deliver a little something for the R-and-D eggheads and maybe buy some shore leave. I vote for that plan." He saluted Haverson. "Hell yeah!"

"This isn't a democracy," the Master Chief said, his voice both calm and dangerous.

Locklear twitched but didn't back down. "Yeah, maybe it isn't," he said, "but last time I checked, I take my orders from the Corps—not from some swabbie. *Sir.*"

The Sergeant scowled at the ODST and moved to his side. "You better get it together, Marine," he barked, "or the Chief'll reach down and pull you inside out by your cornhole. And that'll be a sweet, sweet mercy . . . compared to what *I'm* gonna do to you."

Locklear contemplated the Sergeant's words and the Master Chief's silence. He looked to Polaski and then to Haverson.

Polaski stared at the Marine with wide eyes, then turned away. Haverson gave him a slight shake of his head.

Locklear sighed, eased his stance, and dropped his gaze. "Man, I really, really hate this shit."

"I hate to interrupt," Cortana said, "but I find myself agreeing with the Lieutenant."

The Chief clicked on a private COM channel. "Explain, Cortana. I thought our mission was what you were built for. Why are you backing out now?"

"I'm not 'backing out,'" she shot back. "Our orders were given when the UNSC had a fleet, and when Reach was still an intact military presence. All that has changed."

The Master Chief couldn't disagree with what she was saying . . . but there was something else in her voice. And for the first time, John thought that Cortana might be hiding something from him.

"We have intact ship-scale plasma weapons and new reactor technologies," Cortana continued. "Imagine if every ship could maneuver with pinpoint precision in Slipspace." She paused. "The UNSC could be just as effective in space as you are in ground engagements. We could actually *win* this war."

The Master Chief frowned. He didn't like the Lieutenant's or Cortana's arguments—because they made sense. Aborting his mission was unthinkable. He had always finished what he started, and he'd always won.

As a professional soldier, John was ready to give up anything for victory—his personal comfort, his friends, his own life if that's what it took—but he'd never considered that he'd have to sacrifice his dignity and pride as well for the greater good.

He sighed and nodded. "Very well, Lieutenant Haverson. We'll do it your way. I hereby relinquish my tactical command."

"Good," Haverson said. "Thank you." He faced the others

and continued, "Sergeant? You, Polaski, and Locklear get back down to the Longsword and grab whatever gear wasn't smashed to bits. Look for a field medkit, too, and then get back up here, double time."

"Yes, sir," Sergeant Johnson said. "We're on it." He and Polaski headed for the door, tapped the control, and let the panels slide apart.

Polaski shot a stare at the Master Chief over her shoulder; then, shaking her head, she followed the Sergeant.

"Shit," Locklear said, checking his rifle as he loped after them. "Wait up! Man, I'm never going to get another hour's sleep."

"Sleep when you're dead, Marine," the Sergeant said.

The bridge doors sealed.

Haverson said, "Plot a course back to Earth, Cortana, and then—"

"I'm sorry, Lieutenant Haverson," Cortana said. "I can't do that. A direct course to Earth would be in violation of the Cole Protocol. Furthermore, we are not allowed an indirect route, either. Subsection Seven of the Cole Protocol states that no Covenant craft may be taken to human-controlled space without an exhaustive search for tracking systems that could lead the enemy to our bases."

"Subsection Seven?" Haverson said. "I haven't heard of it."

"Very few have, sir," Cortana answered. "It was little more than a technicality. Before this, no one had actually ever captured a Covenant vessel."

"An exhaustive search of this vessel would be difficult under the circumstances," Haverson said and cupped his hand over his chin, thinking. "It must be more than three kilometers long."

"I have a suggestion, sir," the Chief said. "An intermediate destination: Reach."

"Reach?" Haverson quickly hid the shock on his face with a smile. "Chief, there's nothing in that system except a Covenant armada."

"No, sir," the Master Chief replied. "There are . . . other possibilities."

Haverson raised an eyebrow. "Go ahead, Chief. I'm intrigued."

"The first possibility," John said, "is that the Covenant have glassed the planet and moved on. In which case there might be a derelict, but serviceable, UNSC craft that we could repair and take to Earth. We'd leave the Covenant flagship in low orbit and return with the proper scientific staff and equipment to effect a salvage operation."

Haverson nodded. "A long shot. Although the *Euphrates* did have a Prowler attached to her. They were supposed to launch a reconnaissance mission, before they got the signal to drop everything and help defend Reach. So maybe it's not such a long shot, after all. And the other possibility?"

"The Covenant are still there," the Master Chief said. "The likelihood that they would attack one of their own capital ships is low. In either event, there is no violation of the Cole Protocol because the Covenant already know the location of Reach."

"True," Haverson said. He paced to the center of the bridge. "Very well, Chief. Cortana, set course for Reach. We'll enter at the edge of the system and assess the situation. If it's too hot, we jump and find another route home."

"Acknowledged, Lieutenant," Cortana replied. "Be advised that this ship traverses Slipspace much faster than our UNSC counterparts. ETA to Reach in thirteen hours."

The Master Chief sighed and relaxed a little. There was another reason for choosing Reach, one he didn't reveal to the Lieutenant. He knew the odds of anyone surviving on the surface were remote. Astronomical, in fact . . . because once the Covenant decided to glass a planet, they did so with amazing thoroughness. But he had to see it. It was the only way he could accept that his teammates were dead.

A wash of static covered the Chief, first along his spine and then wrapping about his torso. There was an audible *pop*, and sparks crackled along the length of his MJOLNIR armor.

The Engineer released its grasp on him and chittered with excitement.

Diagnostic routines scrolled upon the Chief's heads-up display. In the upper right corner the shield recharge bar flickered red and slowly filled.

"They work," the Master Chief said. John was relieved to have his shields back. He wouldn't forget what it was like to fight without them, though. It had been a wake-up call: not to become dependent upon technology. It was also a reminder that most battles were won or lost in his head, before he engaged any enemy.

"Impressive little creatures," Haverson remarked. He scrutinized the Covenant Engineer as it floated toward the wall of displays and began tinkering with one. "I wonder how the Covenant caste system—"

"Sir!" Sergeant Johnson's voice blasted over the COM, breaking with static. *"You've got to get down to the Longsword ASAP. You and the Chief."*

"Are you under fire?" the Chief asked.

"Negative," he replied. *"It's one of the cryotubes you recovered."*

"What about it, Sergeant?" Haverson snapped.

"Chief, there's a Spartan in it."

CHAPTER
TEN

After the Chief had left to investigate the cryopod, Haverson made certain that the bridge doors locked. He turned and walked over to the Covenant Engineer who'd repaired the Master Chief's armor.

"Fascinating creatures," he murmured. He drew his sidearm and pointed it at the back of its head.

Two of the Engineer's six eyes locked onto the muzzle of the weapon. A tentacle reached for it, split into fine probing threads, and touched the blue-gray metal.

Cortana asked, "What are you—"

Haverson shot the Engineer. The round tore through its head and spattered gore across the display the alien had been repairing.

"Haverson!" Cortana cried.

The other Engineer turned and squealed—then a blinking light on the broken display captured its attention and it returned to its work, oblivious.

Haverson knelt by the dead Engineer and holstered his gun. "I had no other choice," he whispered. He touched the creature's odd, slick skin. Its color faded from a faint pink to a cold gray.

He dragged it to the escape hatch, opened it, and placed the body in the corridor. He paused, and went back to fold its tentacles over its body. "I'm sorry. You didn't deserve it."

"Why was that necessary?" Cortana demanded.

Haverson stood, wiped his hands on his slacks, and sealed the escape hatch access. "I'm surprised you even have to ask, Cortana." He heard the anger in his voice. He checked his rising ire. He wasn't mad at Cortana; he was mad at himself—furious because of the ugly necessity of his act.

"The Covenant are imitative—not innovative," he said. "The Engineer you ordered to repair the Chief's armor just got a first-hand look at our shield technology, a technology we stole from the Covenant and improved upon. If it somehow managed to rejoin the Covenant, that improved technology would be theirs. How would you like to see that technology manifest as better personal shields for their Elite warriors? Or on their warships?"

Cortana was silent.

"Corporal Locklear was right," Haverson muttered. "I really hate this shit, too."

"I understand," Cortana finally replied, but her voice was so cold it could have frozen helium.

Haverson sighed and looked at his hands. The Engineer's blood tattooed his skin with tiny pinpoints of blue-black. "Do you think that the Master Chief will find what he's really looking for on Reach?"

"What do you mean 'really looking for'?" Cortana said. Her voice was still frosty, but curiosity thawed her tone.

"I mean the other Spartans." Haverson gave a short laugh. "True, his argument to go to Reach was valid—we wouldn't be going otherwise. But that's not what he's after. He sent his team down to the surface of Reach . . . sent them to their deaths. What commander wouldn't go back? And what commander wouldn't hope that they were alive? No matter what the odds?"

CHAPTER
ELE⅄EN

Lieutenant Wagner walked through metal- and explosive-detector gates and into the atrium entrance of the large, vaguely conical structure. Officially designated UNSC HighCom Facility B-6, the sprawling edifice had been nicknamed "the Hive."

It was overcast in Sydney. Gray light filtered in through the crystal dome overhead.

He marched past officers and NCOs moving with purpose to whatever destinations occupied their time. He ignored the displays of acacia trees and exotic ferns meant for the press and civilian tours. Today there was no time for pleasantries.

In another hour the apparent calm and efficiency of High-Com would be shattered into a billion pieces. Only a few of the brass knew that the UNSC's mightiest outpost, Reach, was now nothing more than a cinder.

Wagner approached the receptionist's station under the watchful eyes of a trio of armored Marine MPs.

Keeping Reach's fate quiet was not the UNSC's biggest secret, not by a country mile. Virtually no one in the civilian population of the Inner Colonies knew how perilously close they were to losing this war. ONI Section Two had done a brilliant job of preserving the fiction that Earth forces held their own against the Covenant.

And what did the citizens of the Outer Colonies think? Those who hadn't fled to remote outposts and hidden privateer bases weren't in any position to make trouble. The Covenant didn't take prisoners.

"You're expected today, Lieutenant," the receptionist said. She was a young Chief Petty Officer and looked like she didn't have a care, or a clue. But her eyes gave her away. She knew *something*. Maybe not what, but she had undoubtedly picked up on the increased security protocols . . . or the haunted looks in the eyes of her commanding officers.

"Please proceed to elevator eight," she told him and returned her attention to the screen in front of her.

He made a mental note to find out who this perceptive person was and see if she could be recruited into Section Three. ONI had lost a lot of good people in the last few weeks.

Wagner moved to the solid steel wall, and a pair of doors parted for him. He entered the small room; the doors closed and locked with a whisper-quiet *snik*.

A fingerprint pad and retinal scanner extended from the wall. Wagner pressed his hand onto the scanner, and a needle stabbed his index finger. They'd check his DNA against the sample on file. He blinked once and then rested his chin on the retinal scanner.

"Good morning, Lieutenant," a sweet female voice whispered in his ear.

"Good morning, Lysithea. How are you today?"

"Very well, now that I see that you have returned safely from your mission. I assume everything went as expected."

"You know that's classified," he told the AI.

"Certainly," she replied, her tone playful. "But I'll find out anyway, you know. Why not save me the time and just tell me?"

Although he generally enjoyed this tête-à-tête with Lysithea, he knew it was part of the biometric scan, too. She scanned his brainwaves and voice patterns in response to her queries and matched them to older responses in her memory. She probably tested his loyalty in security measures as well—he didn't put anything past Section Three; they grew more paranoid every day.

"Of course you'll find out," Wagner replied. "But I still can't tell you. That would be a breach of security, punishable under Article 428-A. In fact," he said in a more serious tone, "I'll have to report this violation to my controller."

She laughed, and it sounded like fine bone china clinking together. "You may proceed, Lieutenant," she told him.

The doors parted and revealed a corridor lined with walnut panels and paintings of *Washington Crossing the Delaware*, *Admiral Cole's Last Stand*, various alien landscapes, and space battles.

Although he had barely felt the descent, Wagner knew he had dropped three kilometers into the planet, through solid layers of granite, reinforced concrete, plates of Titanium-A, and EMP-hardened metal. None of this made him feel any safer, though; ONI's research facility on Reach had the same setup, and it hadn't done those poor bastards any good.

He stepped off the elevator. Lysithea whispered at his back: "Watch out in there. They're looking to put someone's head on a pike."

Wagner swallowed and straightened the microscopic wrinkles in his uniform. He searched for a reason to delay—anything that would keep him out of the room at the end of this corridor. He sighed and overcame his inertia. No one kept the Security Committee for the UNSC waiting.

A pair of MPs snapped to as he approached the set of double doors. They didn't salute, and their hands rested on their holstered sidearms. They stared straight ahead, but Wagner knew that if he twitched the wrong way he'd be shot first and questioned later.

The doors silently swung inward.

He entered, and the doors closed behind him and locked. Wagner recognized most of the brass seated at the crescent-shaped table: Major General Nicolas Strauss, Fleet Admiral Sir Terrence Hood, and Colonel James Ackerson. Vice Admiral Whitcomb's chair was empty.

Another half-dozen officers were also present, and all were of command rank, which made Wagner nervous. Each had display tablets set before them, and even upside down, Wagner recognized his preliminary report and video records.

Wagner saluted.

General Strauss leaned forward and snapped off his display. "Christ! Did we know they had so many damn ships?" He banged a fist onto the table. "Why the hell didn't we know about this? Who in ONI let this one slip by?"

Ackerson leaned back. "No one is to blame, General—except the Covenant, obviously. I'm more concerned with our response to this incursion. Our fleet was decimated."

Ackerson's reputation preceded him. Wagner had heard about the lengths to which he'd gone in the past to make sure his own operations got priority over Section Three's. His rivalry with the SPARTAN-II program leader, Dr. Catherine Halsey, was the stuff of legend. Wagner thought Ackerson had been reassigned to a frontline post. Apparently he'd squirmed out of it. That was trouble.

Admiral Hood straightened and pushed his display away and finally acknowledged Wagner. He returned the salute. The Admiral was impeccably groomed, and yet there were dark circles under his eyes. "At ease, Lieutenant."

Wagner tucked his hands behind the small of his back and moved his feet slightly apart, but otherwise didn't relax a millimeter. One was never at ease when in the presence of lions, sharks, and scorpions.

Hood turned to Ackerson. "*Decimate* is the wrong word, Colonel. We would have been *decimated* if we lost one ship out of every ten." He voice rose slightly. "Instead, we lost ten of our ships for every one that managed to limp away. It was a total disaster!"

"Of course, Admiral." Ackerson nodded, pretending to listen, and his eyes flickered over the report again. His eyebrows raised as he noticed the time and date stamp. "There's one thing, however, I'd like answered first." His glassy glare locked onto Wagner. "The time difference between the events in this report and now . . ." He trailed off, lost in thought. "Congratulations, Lieutenant. This is a new speed record from Reach to Earth. Especially when I know you took the time to perform the legally required random jumps before returning to Earth."

"Sir," Wagner replied. "I followed the Cole Protocol to the letter."

That was a lie and everyone in this room knew it. ONI was always bending the Cole Protocol. In this case, it was probably justified because of the value of the intel. Still, if they wanted to crucify him, all they had to do was check the time logged on his Prowler's engines and do the math.

Hood waved his hand. "That's hardly the issue."

"I think it is," Ackerson snapped. "Reach is gone. There's nothing between Earth and the Covenant now except a lot of vacuum—that and whatever secrecy we can preserve."

"We'll review Section Three's practices later, Colonel." Admiral Hood turned to Wagner. "I've read your report, Lieutenant. It is extremely detailed, but I want to hear it from you. What did you see? Are there any details you thought too sensitive to include in your report? Tell me everything."

Wagner took in a deep breath. He had prepared for this and he related, as best he could, how the Covenant ships appeared in the system, the valiant efforts of the UNSC fleet defending Reach, how they failed and were systematically destroyed.

"When the Covenant slipped onto the surface of Reach with their tactical forces and took out the orbital-gun generators— that was the end. Well, I saw only the start of the end. They glassed the planet, starting with the poles."

Wagner, who'd two years ago had a third of his body burned

by Covenant plasma and not once screamed or shed a tear, paused and blinked away the moisture blurring his vision. "I trained at the Naval Academy on Reach, sir. It was the closest thing I had to a home in the colonies."

Hood nodded sympathetically.

Ackerson snorted. He pushed away from the table, got up, and moved to Wagner's side. "Save the sentimentality, Lieutenant. You say they glassed Reach. Everything?"

Wagner detected anticipation in the Colonel's tone—as if he *wanted* the Covenant to have destroyed Reach.

"Sir," Wagner replied. "Before I jumped to Slipspace, I witnessed the poles destroyed, and a significant portion of the planet's surface was on fire."

Ackerson nodded, seemingly satisfied with this answer. "So everyone on Reach is gone, then. Vice Admiral Whitcomb. Doctor Halsey, too." He nodded and added, "Such a tremendous waste." There was no sympathy in his voice.

"I could only speculate, sir."

"No need," Ackerson muttered. He returned to his seat.

Strauss sighed. "At least we have your special weapons programs, Ackerson. Halsey's SPARTAN-IIs were such a great suc—"

Ackerson shot the General a look that could have blasted through battle plate.

The General halted midsentence and snapped his mouth closed.

Wagner stood absolutely still and stared straight ahead, pretending he hadn't seen such a gross breach of military protocol. A General knuckling under to a junior officer? Something extraordinary had just been revealed—there was some kind of backup plan on a par with the SPARTAN program, and Ackerson was behind it. The Colonel suddenly had a lot of juice.

Wagner continued to feign ignorance—and no matter what, he didn't meet Colonel Ackerson's gaze. If Ackerson suspected that he'd caught on, the bastard would have him erased to prevent his secret from getting back to Section Three.

After what seemed a century of uncomfortable silence, Admiral Hood cleared his throat. "The *Pillar of Autumn*, Lieutenant Wagner. Was that ship destroyed? Or did she jump? There is no mention in your report."

"She jumped, sir. Telemetry indicates the *Autumn* was pursued by a number of enemy ships, however, so her fate can only be speculated upon. I did not mention the *Pillar of Autumn* in my report, as that ship is on Section Three's Secure List."

"Good." Hood closed his eyes. "Then there is, at least, some hope."

Ackerson shook his head. "With all due respect to my predecessor, Doctor Halsey, the special weapons package on the *Pillar* hasn't got a chance in hell of accomplishing its mission. You might as well have shot every one of them in the head and gotten it over with."

"That will be enough, Ackerson," Hood said and glowered at him. "Quite enough."

"Sir," Wagner ventured. "The Colonel may be correct . . . at least in his mission assessment. Our agent on the *Pillar of Autumn* signaled us before the end. He regrettably reported that a significant number of Spartans went groundside to defend Reach's orbital guns."

"Then they're dead," Ackerson said. "Halsey's freaks have finally lost their luster of invincibility."

Admiral Hood set his jaw. "Doctor Halsey," he said slowly and with deliberate control, "and her Spartans deserve the *utmost* respect, Colonel." He turned to face him, but Hood stared through Ackerson. "And if you wish to keep your newly acquired position on the Security Council, you will show them that respect, or I will personally kick you from here to Melbourne."

"I merely—" Ackerson said.

"Those 'freaks,'" Hood said over his protest, "have more confirmed kills than any *three* divisions of ODSTs and have garnered every major citation the UNSC awards. Those 'freaks' have personally saved my life twice, as well as the lives of most of the senior staff here at HighCom. Keep your bigotry in check, Colonel. Do you understand?"

"My apologies," Ackerson muttered.

"I asked you a direct question," Admiral Hood barked.

"Sir," Ackerson said. "I understand completely, Admiral. It will not happen again." His face burned bright red.

Wagner, however, didn't think this was the color of shame. It was anger.

"The Spartans," Hood whispered. "Doctor Halsey. Whitcomb. We lost too many good people on Reach. Not to mention dozens of ships." He pursed his lips into a razor-thin line.

"We should send a small recon force to see what's left," General Strauss suggested.

"Not wise, sir," Ackerson replied. "We must pull back and reinforce what's left of the Inner Colonies and Earth. The new orbital platforms won't be online for another ten days. Until then, our defense posture will be far too weak. We'll need every ship we've got."

"Hmm," Admiral Hood said. He placed both thumbs under his chin as he considered both positions.

"Sir," Wagner said. "There is one additional item not covered in my report. It didn't seem exceptionally important at the time, but if you're debating a recon mission, I thought it might be pertinent."

"Just spit it out," General Strauss said.

Wagner swallowed and resisted the urge to meet Ackerson's eyes. "When the Covenant destroys a planet, they typically move their large warships closer and blanket the world with a series of crisscrossing orbits to ensure that nothing could ever survive on its surface."

"I'm painfully aware of Covenant bombardment doctrine, Lieutenant," Hood growled. "What of it?"

"As I indicated, they started at the poles, but took in only a few ships. They were spread thin along the equatorial latitudes, and no additional ships were inbound. In fact, a large number of Covenant ships abandoned the system, in pursuit of the *Pillar of Autumn*."

Ackerson waved his hand dismissively. "Reach is glassed, Lieutenant. If you had stayed to watch the whole show, they would have burned you down, too."

"Yes, sir," Wagner replied. "If, however, there is a recon mission, I would like to volunteer for the duty."

Ackerson got up and strode to Wagner. He stood a centimeter from his face, and their eyes locked. Ackerson's gaze was full of poison. Wagner did his best not to recoil, but he couldn't help it. One look and he knew this man wanted him dead—for whatever reason: that he had heard of Ackerson's alternative program to the SPARTAN-IIs, that he didn't want trouble over Reach . . . or maybe, as Lysithea had warned him, that he was just looking for someone's head to impale on a pike.

"Are you deaf, Lieutenant?" Ackerson asked with mock concern. "Some kind of hearing loss due to combat action?"

"No, sir."

"Well, when you push the limits of Slipspace in those little Prowlers, you risk all kinds of radiation damage. Or maybe the trauma of seeing Reach destroyed shook you. Whatever your problem, when you leave here you are to visit the infirmary. They are to give you a clean bill of health before you return to active duty." He shrugged. "There must be *something* wrong with you, Lieutenant, because you do not seem to understand me even though my words are crystal clear."

"Sir."

"Let's try this, then. We are not wasting a single UNSC ship to confirm what we have already seen a dozen times before: Reach is gone."

He inched closer to Wagner. "Everything on it is blasted to bits, burned, glassed over, and vaporized. Everyone on Reach is dead." He jabbed a finger into Wagner's chest for emphasis. "Dead. Dead. Dead."

SECTION II

DEFENSE OF CASTLE BASE

CHAPTER
TWELVE

Steamy clouds parted like a drawn curtain; a fireball one hundred meters across roared over Fred and Kelly's position. Fred traced the line of flames back through the sky and spotted the faint outlines of dozens of Covenant warships in low orbit.

Fred's Banshee skimmed over the treetops, down the mountainside. He pushed the craft to its maximum speed. Kelly followed, and they swooped into a valley and up onto the zigzagging ridgeline where Joshua had first spotted the Covenant invasion force.

He put aside thoughts of his fallen comrade. He had to focus on keeping his remaining team members alive.

Fred called up the mapping system on his heads-up display. A blue NAV marker, nestled in the crux of topological lines, identified their fallback position: ONI Section Three's secure-and-secret research facility buried under Menachite Mountain. Two decades ago it had been a titanium mine, and then the abandoned tunnels were used as storage until Section Three had taken over the mountain for their own purposes.

"We'll need to find a safe route through—"

A hail of purple-white crystalline shards hissed through the air, arcing up from the forest beneath them. Each shard looked like the projectile fired by a Covenant needler—but far larger. The shard that slashed past Fred's cockpit was the size of his forearm.

Kelly dodged one projectile, which exploded in midair. Needlelike fragments bounced from the Banshee's fuselage.

One tiny secondary fragment impaled Fred's Banshee and detonated. The port canard of his flier deformed from the explosion, and the craft wobbled.

"Down!" he shouted, but Kelly was already a dozen meters below him and plummeting to a distant dry riverbed. He followed, trailing smoke.

Fred confirmed his position and guided his wounded Banshee onto a course that followed the flash-dried riverbed below. The path wound through the forest and sinewed close to Menachite Mountain. With luck, they could ditch the Banshees and make a short run to the ONI facility.

Overhead, a tangerine borealis pulsed from the north. Sheets of silver crackled across the sky, and the black clouds boiled, lit by the raging fires beneath them. They piled into thunderheads and spat lightning.

The massive warships that had been overhead moments ago accelerated back into the upper atmosphere. Their engines screamed and left blistering wakes across the swollen sky.

For a split second panic seized Fred's throat. Then his training kicked in and his mind turned cold and metallic, and filtered through every fact he had on Covenant plasma bombardments. He had to think or die.

So he thought.

Something didn't fit. Covenant plasma bombardment had always proceeded in an orderly crisscrossing pattern across the planet until everything on its surface was glass and cinder. The ships above hadn't finished their work here.

He risked a glance to the left and right. One hundred thousand hectares of forest—the same forest that Fred and his fellow Spartans had trained in since childhood—was being devoured by walls of flame. Coils of heat and thick black smoke spiraled into the sky.

A wave passed over Fred and Kelly—he couldn't see it, but he felt it: A thousand ants had gotten into his armor and bitten him. Static fuzzed his display, and then vanished with a *pop*. His shields dropped to zero and then slowly started to recharge. The grav pods on their fliers flickered and sputtered.

"EMP," Kelly shouted over the COM. "Or some plasma effect."

"Hard landing," Fred ordered.

Kelly made an unhappy sound over the COM and snapped it off.

They plummeted out of the sky, gliding with what little aerodynamics and power remained in their Banshees. Fred nosed his craft over the steaming rocks of the dry riverbed. He picked a path between boulders and jagged granite fangs, pointed toward a ribbon of gravel.

There was just one problem: A pair of these rocks were slightly darker than the others . . . and they moved.

The creatures were huge and heavily armored and moved with slow, deliberate precision. Each held a massive metal plate like a shield. Fred hit the COM and yelled, "Heads up! Covenant Hunters dead ahead!" There was no time to evade the new threat. The nearest Hunter wheeled to face them, and the array of sensory pins along its back flared, anemone-like. The hulking creature raised its main weapon—a powerful fuel rod gun, mounted on its arm—at Fred. The barrel pulsed green.

The Hunter fired.

Fred killed the power, and his Banshee dropped ten meters. There was a flash as the orb of destructive energy split the air where his flier had been a second before.

The Banshee hit the ground, skidding through fist-sized rocks. The battered craft flipped and tossed him to the ground. The Banshee rolled end over end and crashed into the Hunter.

The massive alien brought up its thick, metal shield and shrugged off the wreckage as if it were cardboard. The fuel rod gun began to charge again.

Fred winced and rolled to his feet, ignoring the new pain the crash landing had caused. He needed a weapon. Pain would have to wait.

The Hunter lumbered toward him, then dropped into a crouch and charged ahead at terrifying speed.

There was a crackle of static on his COM frequency, and Fred heard one word: *"Duck!"*

He threw himself onto the ground and rolled to the side.

Kelly's riderless flier soared over him and collided with the Hunter at full speed. The Banshee exploded and showered the area with glittering metal fragments.

The Hunter reeled as fire washed across its armor. It moved in slow, confused circles. Fred could see the bright orange smears of the Hunter's blood staining the rocks.

Kelly landed on her feet next to Fred. She readied a captured plasma grenade and hurled it straight toward the second Hunter's huge gun.

It lodged in the barrel of the weapon and detonated. Tendrils of energy covered the Hunter. The gun crackled and belched smoke.

Fred got to his feet. "Run!"

They weren't going to engage a Hunter in hand-to-hand combat. They might lose—they might win, but in the meantime the rest of the Covenant ground forces would catch up to them.

They sprinted toward a tiny patch of forest ahead, perhaps the last trees standing on Reach. The Hunter, confused with its destroyed weapon—and its flame-wreathed partner—hesitated, not sure what to do.

"Didn't you see while we were airborne?" Kelly said, concern tightening her voice. "There's a sizable Covenant assault force just ahead."

"Ground troops?" Fred said, boosting his speed to a full sprint. "How far?"

"Half a klick."

That didn't make sense, either. Why have forces groundside when you were destroying the planet from orbit? "Something's not right," he told her. "Let's see what they're up to."

Kelly's acknowledgment light winked red.

"They're between us and the fallback point," Fred told her. "We have to."

They entered the stand of trees, paused, and looked back. The Hunter shambled after them, but it was a futile pursuit. Despite their occasional bursts of speed, the Hunters were too slow.

They were caught between Covenant forces on the ground and those in the air, and neither Fred nor Kelly voiced the one question foremost on their minds: Was there even a fallback position left? Or had the Covenant between them and the rest of their team found and destroyed them?

The COM crackled. *"—is Gamma Team, Alpha. Come in."*

Fred replied, "Gamma, this is Alpha. Go ahead."

There was a roar of static. *"Whitcomb . . . too many. Got— you read?"*

"Gamma," Fred shouted. "The fallback is hot. Repeat hot! Acknowledge."

There was only static.

"I hope they heard," he told Kelly.

"Red-Twenty can take care of his team. Don't worry." She crept forward and waved him to follow. "Take a look at this."

Fred glanced over his shoulder. No Hunter, and nothing on his motion detector. He followed Kelly, and parted a wall of blackberry brambles. Parked in a clearing were Covenant vehicles, lined in three rows of four: mortar tanks. The tanks had two wide lateral fins, beneath which were armored anti-grav pods. They were extremely stable and fired one of the Covenant's most powerful ground weapons: the energy mortar. Fred had seen them in action; they fired a shaped blast of plasma that obliterated everything within twenty meters of impact. Titanium battle plate, concrete, or flesh—it all vaporized.

Marines called these tanks "Wraiths" because you usually got one look at them before they made you one.

There were a handful of Grunts milling about the tanks, as well as dozens of the floating Covenant Engineers. The Engineers swarmed over and under the machinery. Most interesting to Fred, the vehicles' hatches were open.

"I can't think of a better disguise," Kelly whispered, "than five tons of Covenant armor." She started forward.

Fred set his hand on her arm, holding her back. "Wait. Think it through. There are two possibilities. First, if the Covenant have found the fallback position, we go in guns blazing and carve a path for Delta Team to get out."

She nodded. "The other possibility?"

"They don't know that Delta Team is holed up under the mountain. Then—" Fred hesitated. "Then we have to draw them away."

Kelly considered this, then said, "I was afraid you were going to say that." She gave the dirt a tiny kick. "But you're right."

A blip appeared on their motion trackers, directly on their six. The contact was large and moving steadily toward them. The Hunter must have made up its mind—come to find them and stomp them into the ground.

"Move," Fred whispered.

They crossed the field, quickly and silently, and the Grunts never saw them. Fred and Kelly reached the smooth-surfaced Wraith tanks. He gave Kelly a *go* signal, and she sprang into the nearest open hatch. A moment later Fred inched ahead to the next tank and eased inside.

He sealed the hatch behind him.

This was one of the most desperate and stupid decisions he had ever made. How were they going to take on an entire Covenant invasion force with a pair of tanks?

"Red-One," Kelly said over the COM. *"Ready when you are."*

Through the armored shell Fred felt the rumble and roar of Kelly's tank starting.

His tank coughed and rumbled and rose a meter off the ground.

"Ready here," he told Kelly. "Let's take out the motor pool."

"Affirmative," she said, trying to conceal the faint trace of anticipation in her voice.

In unison the Spartans turned and fired at the far corner of the formation of tanks. Two blue-white blobs of liquid sun spat from the Wraiths and detonated. There was a dazzling light, an expansion of superheated white fire—and then there was glass-smooth ground and the smoldering skeletons of seven Wraith tanks.

More luck. If the tanks had been active, with hatches secured, they might have survived the first volley.

Kelly's tank surged ahead and bulldozed aside the surviving tanks near them.

Fred turned, accelerated to full power, and smashed through a line of retreating Grunts, a series of small, satisfying *thuds* reverberating through the cockpit.

The two Wraith tanks shattered through a line of trees, splintering their trunks. Beyond lay the main Covenant camp. A thousand Grunts and Jackals ran toward them, weapons and personal shields ready, but none of them fired.

They charged past the two tanks.

"They think we're on their side," Fred said. "They're going to see what attacked them. Let's not show them otherwise until we have to."

Kelly's acknowledgment light winked on, and she pushed a path through the onrushing Grunts—who quickly parted before her.

Half a kilometer ahead was a stand of hexagonal gold and silver structures: the shielded tents of the Elites. There were half a dozen stationary plasma turrets, "Shades," guarding them, and beyond them lay the mountain under which were ONI Section Three's secret research caverns. The Covenant were there as well.

Without thinking, Fred tapped a control; the display magnified. A hundred Covenant Engineers maneuvered heavy equipment: laser drills and conveyor belts and Scarabs, giant insectlike machines that could easily bore through the entire mountain.

"They found the caverns," Fred told Kelly. "Looks like they're going to dig them out."

But again . . . *why?* Why not just blast them from orbit? The Covenant didn't typically take prisoners—except the occasional straggler to execute for sport. They didn't go to this much trouble. Unless it wasn't Delta Team they were after.

Fred keyed his COM. "Delta, if you're listening, we're coming in from south-southeast in a pair of captured Wraith tanks. You'll know which ones from the fireworks. Keep your heads down and don't shoot us."

He keyed over to Kelly's personal COM. "Blaze a trail, Red-Two! Kill everything and get to that entrance ASAP!"

"I'm on it," she whispered, her voice thick with concentration.

A blue acknowledgment light flickered on . . . but it wasn't Kelly's. It was tagged as SPARTAN 039, Isaac. That was part of Will's team.

So they *were* holed up at the fallback position. Relief flooded into him to know his team was here and still alive.

But he couldn't hope—not yet. He had three hundred meters to cross, every millimeter of which was covered with a solid wall of Covenant Grunts, Jackals, and Elites—a path straight through hell.

Kelly rotated her tank about and fired at the remaining Wraiths and the cluster of Grunts trying to put out the fires near those she'd already destroyed. For a split second the ground was the surface of a sun; it flared, faded, and then was nothing but ash.

Fred fired his mortar—as fast as the tank's power supply would cycle. He lobbed three silver-white projectiles at the concentration of Elites and plasma turrets. They had shields that protected them for a microsecond before they overloaded and collapsed. They flared like the "strike-anywhere" matches the ODSTs used to light their contraband cigarettes.

Kelly shot arcing projectiles into the hundreds of Grunts and Jackals running in every direction. Bodies charred midstride and turned to vapor. It was as if a dozen lightning bolts had struck in the center of the camp.

Grunts ran and ducked and shot at one another. The few Jackals tried to marshal the diminutive soldiers, but the Grunts, enraged or terrified, fired on them as well.

Fred caught motion in the corner of his eye—a shadow buzzed over his tank, and a blast rocked it from side to side.

That had to be Banshees. It made sense that they'd already have Elites in the air, on patrol. He cursed himself for not spotting them before. It was only a matter of time now. Without infantry support, sooner or later the Covenant ground and air forces would regroup and destroy them.

"Move!" he shouted over the COM. "Break off contact and get to the caves!"

Kelly gunned her tank and pushed through the wreckage.

Fred let her get ahead and paused to target the excavation equipment. He fired once.

Three rapid impacts thudded on top of his tank, exploded, and shook his teeth. He fired three more times at the excavation equipment and gunned the Wraith tank. It shuddered and lurched forward.

He gritted his teeth and smiled. On the display, the smoke cleared enough for him to see that the laser drill, conveyor belts, and the Scarabs had been reduced to piles of half-melted junk.

The display lost focus. No—Fred saw it wasn't the picture; smoke poured into the cockpit.

"Banshees circling over you," Kelly yelled over the COM. *"Get out!"*

Fred popped the hatch and crawled out.

Overhead, a dozen Banshee fliers turned to strafe his crippled tank.

Fred jumped, rolled to his feet, and ran. A NAV marker appeared on his heads-up display, over a gash in the side of the mountain where the cavern entrance used to be.

A red-hot sledgehammer hit him squarely in the back: a plasma pistol on overload. He reeled forward but didn't lose his balance—and kept running. There was no time to stop. He glanced at his shield bar; it was completely drained, but it slowly began to recharge. He dodged and weaved back and forth. He couldn't take many more hits like that.

"Hurry," Kelly said.

He crossed the remaining hundred meters in seconds and jumped into a crater where there had once been a gatehouse and the secure entrance to ONI's underground base.

Kelly stood, braced just over the lip of the crater, holding a Warthog's chaingun. She aimed over Fred's head and sprayed the enemy with thunderous suppression fire. SPARTAN 043, Will, stood next to her. Fred was thrilled to see them alive—and even more thrilled to see Will holding a Jackhammer rocket launcher.

"Get below," Kelly said, and motioned with her head to the center of the crater. "We'll cover you." She continued to fire until she had depleted the chaingun's belt of ammunition.

Will took aim and squeezed the trigger. A rocket knifed through the air, and a contrail of white smoke connected with the cockpit of an oncoming Banshee. The alien flier disintegrated in a ball of fire.

Fred turned and saw a shaft that plunged deep into the ground. A steel cable had been rigged to one side, and it angled into the depths.

He grabbed the line, jumped, and zipped into the darkness. He felt a sharp vibration through the line—once, then twice— as the other Spartans followed him.

After three hundred meters of free fall, he glimpsed a faint illumination at the bottom of the shaft, the feeble sickly yellow glow from chemical light sticks. Fred tightened his grip on the cable, and his descent slowed. A meter from the bottom of the shaft, he let go and landed in a crouch. He moved out of the way. The other Spartans landed next to him.

"This way," Will said and moved ahead, through a set of elevator doors that had been forced open.

Fred noticed that Will moved with a severe limp, and remembered the Spartans he had sent here were injured. It was ironic that he had sent them out of the thick of battle, to end up in the middle of another dire situation.

Then again, they weren't dead . . . which was more than he could hope for Beta Team.

They stepped into a corridor with brushed stainless-steel walls that mirrored and smeared the faint light from the chem lights.

Overhead there was a tremendous explosion. Rocks and dirt showered into the shaft, and dust blossomed through the corridor.

"Lotus antitank mines," Will said. "A little something to slow our uninvited guests down."

Two other Spartans, Isaac and Vinh, sat along either side of the hallway, behind rock barricades. They gave slight nods to Fred and kept their eyes and weapons on the end of the corridor.

"Where's the rest of the team? And the Marines from Charlie Company?" Fred asked.

"They didn't make it," Will replied, his voice flat. "We were separated on the way here." He shook his head. "No contact since then."

Fred was quiet a moment. He listed those three as MIA on his team roster as well as the other Spartans on Will's team. The list of Spartans he could account for had grown extremely short. Fred felt his stomach twist. "Any word from Beta Team?"

"Negative. No contact, sir."

Fred clenched his teeth and marked Beta Team as MIA as well.

"Gamma Team?" Will asked.

"They're out there," Fred replied. "I heard them on the COM, but I couldn't make out much. I warned them away from this position."

"Good," Will whispered.

The hallway dead-ended in a vault door.

"The retinal and palm scanners are broken," Will explained. "There's voice access, which we've tried, but there's no response. This door must be a meter thick, so without cutting tools or a hundred kilos of explosive we're stuck on this side."

"You spoke to the people on the other side?" Kelly asked.

"The channel is open," Will said. "But there's been no reply. Everyone on the other side probably bugged out."

"Or maybe you're just not saying anything they want to hear," Kelly said. She whistled a six-note singsong tune.

Will nodded. "I didn't think of that."

The tune had been the Spartan's secret code from when they were young and training on Reach. It was their *all-clear-it's-safe-to-come-out* signal. No one but the Spartans and a few very select outsiders knew of it . . . a few outsiders who might be still here.

Kelly keyed the mic and whistled the tune. She released the key and waited.

Two minutes ticked off Fred's mission clock. Too much time sitting here, doing nothing, while the Covenant over their heads were undoubtedly figuring out a way to dig them out and tear them to pieces.

"It was a good idea," he told Kelly. "We'll recon the shaft. Maybe it's not completely collapsed. Will you—"

A mechanism *thunked* and then hummed within the titanic door. There was a hiss as the seams parted, and the meter-thick door swung inward on perfectly balanced, silent hinges.

Bright light flooded the passage. A silhouetted figure stood on the threshold. As Fred's display compensated and enhanced the image, he saw it was human, slight of figure, female. She wore a gray pleated skirt and a white lab coat with a data pad stuffed into the breast pocket. He caught the glimmer of her eyeglasses, black-rimmed with faint bifocal lines. Her gray hair was coiled into a tight bun.

But it was her face that caught and held his focus—he recognized the tight smooth skin that wrinkled only in the corners of her mouth and her gray-blue eyes. She was the intellect behind the SPARTAN-II program, and the one who'd invented their MJOLNIR armor.

She was Dr. Catherine Halsey.

Dr. Halsey studied the five Spartans in the hallway and pushed her antique glasses farther up the ridge of her nose. Despite everything their presence here meant—Reach invaded, their mission to find the Covenant leadership compromised, everything she had worked for now in jeopardy—she was still pleased to see them. She steeled herself, though; an emotional outburst wouldn't be understood, or appreciated, by her Spartans.

"Come in," she said briskly. "And hurry. From the sounds of things upstairs we haven't much time."

The Spartans stood there a moment—undoubtedly communicating with one another through a mixture of externally silent COM channels and minute body language. She noticed the tick of a finger, the slight nod of a head. They then moved together, picked up their equipment, and walked through the threshold of the vault.

Dr. Halsey greeted them as they passed her. "It's good to see you, Fred."

"Ma'am," Fred replied. "Good to see you, too."

She noted that Kelly's movements were off, a little sluggish. She was hurt, as were the rest of them, she could see now that she saw them up close. "Kelly."

"Doctor Halsey." She reached out and gave her hand a slight squeeze of greeting.

"Isaac."

"Doctor."

"Vinh."

She nodded.

"William."

Will grunted. He had never liked his formal name.

She knew this annoyed them all—how she was always able to tell who they were despite the MJOLNIR armor. She had grown up with them, knew their every gesture and their individual walks. She could have never called them by their number designations: SPARTAN 104, 087, 039, 030, and 043, respectively.

Dr. Halsey tapped a control pad. The vault door eased silently shut, its seams vanished, and, with a sharp, metallic click, it locked.

"We have access to Aqua, Scarlet, and Lavender Levels," she told them. "Follow me to the medical wing." She proceeded down a concrete hallway with a high arched ceiling, recessed lights, and security cameras. "With regard to recent events, I likely know far more about all of this than you do, but let's stick with today. I know that the Covenant arrived in full force at approximately oh-five-hundred hours. ONI Section Three staff evacuated this facility at oh-five-thirty hours. I assume you're not here to let me know it's safe to come out?"

"Yes, ma'am," Fred replied. "I mean, no, ma'am. It's not safe. The Fleet engaged the Covenant, but the enemy managed to land ground forces on Reach. We were sent to the surface to protect the orbital-gun generators." He stopped, took a deep breath, and continued. "We were not successful in that mission. Covenant forces overwhelmed our position." He glanced back at Kelly and the other Spartans. "We fell back here . . . we thought it would be secure."

They continued down the sloping passage; titanium doors irised open for them and closed as soon as they passed.

"I see," Dr. Halsey replied. "And Captain Keyes? John?"

"Unknown," Fred told her. "The Master Chief and part of our team attempted to retrieve an unsecured NAV database from an orbital station before the Covenant got to it. Assuming he was successful, and given Captain Keyes's record of combat against the Covenant . . ." Fred's voice trailed off.

"I'm sure they accomplished their mission and escaped," Dr. Halsey said, finishing the thought for him. "John doesn't lose."

"No, ma'am," Fred replied.

They walked in silence for a moment past a display of captured insurgent flags that had been mounted under glass along the curved concrete wall. Most were emblazoned with an array of gaudy insignia—family crests, bloodied dragons, and scorched crossed swords. They continued past these remnants of a rebellion the UNSC no longer had to worry about.

"Doctor Halsey?" Fred said. "Permission to speak freely?"

"Granted," she said. "I don't stand on ceremony, particularly given the circumstances. Speak your mind."

"Ma'am, something isn't normal about this Covenant invasion," Fred told her. "They've won, but they aren't glassing the planet. At least not completely—as near as I can determine, they've only hit the poles and a portion of the lower latitudes."

"And they had digging equipment in position over this facility," Kelly added.

"Curious," Dr. Halsey said. She halted at a large metal iris big enough to drive a Warthog through, and set her hand on a palm scanner. "The medical wing," she explained. She spoke into a nearby microphone: "'I shall do no harm.'" The door opened for them.

High-intensity lights flickered on in the large room beyond. There were a dozen medical diagnosis tables and a row of displays along the far wall. The lime-colored floor was brightly polished and sterile. The walls glowed with a faint pink luminescence. Seven doors led to adjacent offices and surgical bays with windows looking out into this central room.

"Kalmiya?" she said. "Status?"

"Yes, Doctor," replied the disembodied voice of her personal AI, her replacement for Cortana. "I have prepared the Spartans' personal medical files and sent runners to fetch stocks of blood plasma and other medical supplies from cold storage, as well as tools to assist in the removal of their MJOLNIR armor."

The doors to the tiny service elevator at the far end of the facility opened, and a robotic rover rolled out, its telescopic arms holding piles of liquid-filled bags. Rows of tools were neatly lined up across the rover's top tray.

"Very good," Dr. Halsey said. "Continue to track seismic activity overhead. Interface with the Spartans' biomonitors and patch the output to the display on bay three."

She strolled over to a table, and a bank of holographic displays hummed to life, floating serenely. Graphs and figures scrolled across them.

"Give me a spotlight here, prepare a sterilization field, and lower the ambient lighting by forty percent. And a little Mahler, please. Symphony number two."

"Yes, Doctor." Music drifted from the speakers.

Dr. Halsey examined the graphs, tapped tiny human-figure icons, and summoned MRI images of the Spartans' internal structures—holographic bones, organs, and muscles appeared and slowly rotated.

She winced at the extent of their injuries.

"Fred, you have a torn Achilles tendon and three cracked ribs. Both kidneys have moderate contusions." She glanced at the rest of the team's data and after a moment's consideration told him, "You're fine.

"William, you have a cracked tibia and some internal bleeding. Get some biofoam into that wound and avoid strenuous motions for the next day." She turned to face Fred and Will. "You two are in the best shape. I want you to go to Level Aqua, Section Lambda, and retrieve a few things."

"Yes, ma'am," Fred said.

Dr. Halsey was only a civilian, but the Spartans had always accepted her authority. Perhaps because she had acted as an equal among the Fleet Admirals and Generals who were constantly trying to co-opt her work. Or maybe it was more than that. She wondered if the Spartans viewed her as some sort of mother figure. As much as this notion amused her, she doubted that they viewed anyone outside their team as family. Not even her.

William retrieved a can of biofoam from the rover and inserted the tip into the tiny injection port in his armor, then pushed it through the skin between his fourth and fifth ribs. He filled his abdominal cavity with the space-filling coagulant/antibacterial/tissue-regenerative polymer.

"Cold?" she asked.

"Nothing worth noting, ma'am."

She nodded, not making much over William's courage. She'd always kept her admiration for her Spartans to herself. The last thing she wanted was to make them feel different. They got enough "special" treatment from everyone else.

Dr. Halsey picked up a clipboard, tapped a few items onto its display, and handed it to Fred. "Additional weapons arrived last week," she told him, "as well as parts for the MJOLNIR Mark Five armor system. We'll swap them out for your damaged components. Kalmiya, show them the way, please, and give them access to the restricted areas."

"Yes, Doctor," Kalmiya said. The med bay doors opened. "This way."

Fred studied the items on the clipboard. "Very, very good," he said, and his voice was thick with satisfaction. He nodded, took a long look at his teammates, and then he and Will departed.

Dr. Halsey returned to her medical readouts. "Vinh, you have a torn deltoid muscle, three broken fingers, and a herniated disk. Isaac, internal contusions and both shoulders have been dislocated and reinserted incorrectly, which is pinching off the blood vessels. I'll get you both fixed up in a moment, but first I want you to survey the route we took here and suggest further perimeter defenses."

"Yes, ma'am," they replied, cast a look at Kelly, and left.

Dr. Halsey concentrated on Kelly's internal scans. Her injuries were by far the worst. She had seen that from the extremely low blood pressure and high body temperature even before she'd glanced at the MRI. There was moderate bleeding in her liver—a fatal condition if not treated—and her right lung was completely collapsed. That the woman was still on her feet, let alone fighting, was tantamount to an act of God.

Of course, that's what the SPARTAN-II project was all about, wasn't it? Playing God for the greater good.

"Doctor Halsey," Kelly asked. "Where are the others?"

"As I said, they evacuated," she replied. "On the table, please. I'm going to perform some minor repairs."

Kelly complied. "Then why are *you* still here, ma'am?"

Dr. Halsey picked up a curved, long-handled magnetic wrench, built specifically to fit this, and only this, access panel. She inserted it and popped open a fist-sized section of Kelly's battered MJOLNIR armor. Blood and hydrostatic gel bubbled from Kelly's wounds.

"I volunteered to be the fail-safe option," she told Kelly. "In the lower levels of these caverns are enough high explosives to level the facility—in case we were ever overrun by the enemy. I'm here to make sure no one gets access to our technology."

Dr. Halsey injected a local anesthetic and inserted a flexible laser-tipped catheter into Kelly, carefully monitoring her progress on the MRI. She pulsed the laser, fusing the lacerations in her liver. Dr. Halsey then inflated her lung. Kelly would lose half of that organ, regardless of her treatment. The tissue was already turning blue and mottling necrotic brown.

"Kalmiya, prep the flash clone facility and retrieve Kelly's

DNA sequence from the archives. I'd like to get a new liver and right lung started for her.

"You're fine for now," Dr. Halsey lied. "I just want to get replacements made for you, in case we're down here for a long time."

"I understand," Kelly rasped.

Dr. Halsey wondered if she did—if Kelly understood that getting shot and burned and having your internal organs traumatized wasn't supposed to happen to you every day . . . unless you were a Spartan. She wished the war were over. She wished her Spartans had some measure of peace.

"Doctor?" Kalmiya whispered through the tiny private speaker bud in Dr. Halsey's glasses. "There is an anomaly in SPARTAN 087's DNA files. You may want to review this in private."

Dr. Halsey sealed Kelly's injuries with biofoam, removed the catheter, and cauterized the incision. "Rest," she said.

"No, ma'am. I'm ready to—" Kelly tried to sit up.

"Down." Dr. Halsey set a hand on her shoulder. She had no illusions that she could have stopped Kelly with the gesture, but it reinforced her words and her will. "Doctor's orders."

Kelly sighed and lay back.

"I'll be in my office just over there"—she pointed to the next room—"if you need anything."

Dr. Halsey left Kelly and moved to her office. Two walls were covered with giant displays; old disposable coffee cups littered the floor; a holographic projector flooded with data, lines, rotating graphics, and unanswered correspondence overflowed her desk. She turned down the blinds that separated her office from the medical bay, but only halfway, so she could keep an eye on Kelly.

"Let's have it, Kalmiya."

Kelly's medical history scrolled across a display.

"Here," Kalmiya said, and highlighted a surreptitious data request at the end of the file. "It's dated three months ago. That's Araqiel's routing code."

Dr. Halsey picked up the snowglobe off her desk, shook it once, and set it down, watching the swirls of particles.

"Araqiel—Ackerson's watchdog?"

"Affirmative, Doctor."

"Can you trace the request?"

"Done and terminated contact at node FF-8897-Z. Access restricted to X-ray level clearance."

"Restricted?" Dr. Halsey gave a short, soft laugh. "Does that mean anything now? There's no one here to stop us, is there, Kalmiya?"

"Entering those files without proper clearance is a treasonable offense, Doctor."

"They can come and arrest me, then. Do as I have instructed, Kalmiya," Dr. Halsey said. "Override your ethics center subroutine four-alpha. Nullification code: 'Whateverittakes.' "

Dr. Halsey found a half-full cup of coffee on the floor and gingerly picked it up. She sniffed its contents and, satisfied it wasn't rancid, swirled it once then downed its cold contents.

"Yes, Doctor. Working. Done."

Kalmiya was Cortana's older "sister." Dr. Halsey had designed and tested the software intrusion routines on her. Once the process had been debugged and streamlined, she'd incorporated the routines into Cortana. The brass in ONI Section Three had been quite explicit in their instructions to destroy any prototype routines—an order that Dr. Halsey had promptly disobeyed.

"There is an unusually voluminous amount of counterintrusion software, Doctor."

"Show me," Dr. Halsey said.

The holographic display flickered and solidified into colored crystal blocks representing the code barriers. Dr. Halsey traced a seam with her forefinger along a shard of ruby to the ninety-degree angle made by a stair-step-cut emerald. "This data cluster here. Spike that and backfill with a neutralizing pulse."

"Yes, Doctor."

The holographic crystal shattered into a thousand glittering fragments and swirled upward into a helix.

"I'm in, and—"

The shards pulsed and coalesced. Facets and hard shimmering planes fit together into curled horns, an elongated jaw, and over-sized eyes that flickered with holographic fire. It turned and smiled at Dr. Halsey, baring razor jags of teeth.

"Civilian consultant 409871," it said in a deep bass rumble that contained a crackle of thunder. "Doctor Catherine Halsey."

"Araqiel," she muttered. "Did your master leave you behind when he was reassigned? Don't you have anything better to do than steal data from my SPARTAN program?"

The doctor leaned toward a side display and, without looking, tapped in line commands, accessing the base's root directory.

"You are in violation of UNSC military security code 447-R27," Araqiel stated with a growl. "This has been recorded and the proper authorities have been notified. You will cease and desist all activities."

Dr. Halsey snorted and continued to type. "I'm the only authority left here, Araqiel. For a 'smart AI' you are extremely thick." She glanced at the display before her. "Kalmiya, I need you." She tapped level-seven security barriers, which popped up over her command line prompt. "Here."

"Yes, Doctor."

"Oh, 'thick' indeed, Doctor," Araqiel rumbled. "While I allowed you to 'access' these medical files, I have taken control of the air reclamation system for your medical wing. I can pressurize your office and cause pulmonary edema. I can release narcozine gas to para—" His eyes narrowed to a squint. "What are you doing there?"

"We're in," Kalmiya said.

Dr. Halsey tapped in a flurry of commands.

The holograph of Araqiel leaned over her shoulder. "What is

that? I don't recognize that directory path . . . or those"—he sniffed derisively—"archaic *line* commands."

"These commands were invented, refined, and then discarded and forgotten long before even the first functional dumb AI went online," Dr. Halsey told him. "I learned them when I was fifteen, working on my second doctoral thesis."

"An antiquated input methodology for an obsolete human."

"Antiquated? Obsolete? Really?" She smiled and said, "Let's test your hypothesis, Araqiel. I supervised the creation of the template for every third-generation smart AI on this planet. I know everything there is to know about you, including your borderline disregard for human life." She paused and tapped her chin. "Maybe that's why you and Ackerson always got along so well."

"Colonel Ackerson is a great man. He's—"

"To answer your original question," she said, ignoring him, "this is the nexus of your being." She tapped the display. "Your code directory, the center through which all impulses in your mind flow. And this"—she quickly typed in another command—"is the code that activates your personal fail-safe. It generates a pulse beam of high-frequency UV light in your Riemann cycling-thought matrix, clearing your high thought functions. It will effectively erase you."

"No!" Araqiel said and reared back. Flames roared about his crystalline skull. "Don't—"

Dr. Halsey punched the ENTER key.

Araqiel vanished.

Dr. Halsey sighed and closed the display. "A waste of memory crystal."

She wondered if the AI had been bluffing. Maybe not; ONI Section Three gave its AIs broad discretionary powers for dealing with security breaches. Still . . . she was happy not to have found out how far Araqiel would have gone.

"Kalmiya, please retrieve the data file and show me the contents of Colonel Ackerson's directory."

"Working, Doctor. There's some minor encryption to unravel. It should only take a moment." She paused and then asked, "Doctor Halsey, the UV fail-safe in Araqiel's Riemann matrix . . . are they planted in every smart AI? In me?"

"They are not implanted in every AI," Dr. Halsey said, carefully controlling her voice.

Kalmiya would undoubtedly stress-analyze her vocal patterns, so she told her the truth. It was always a game of chess with smart AIs—move and countermove. It was a constant challenge to earn and keep their respect. That's why she preferred their company to humans—they were so deliciously complex. Yes, she told her the truth . . . just not the *whole* truth.

"Here they are, Doctor."

Holographic file and folder icons filled the space over her desk.

"Filter by proper names," Dr. Halsey said. "Let's not waste our time with Ackerson's petty blackmails. Also remove any files dated before the SPARTAN-IIs went online, and any not accessed more than a dozen times. I want to see what black ops topped his list."

The folders and files winked away, and only two folders remained floating over Dr. Halsey's desk: S-III and KING UNDER THE MOUNTAIN. She tapped on the first one and it opened, revealing hundreds of separate files. Dr. Halsey examined them—there were medical files on each of her Spartans: complete records from their preindoctrinated origins; their childhood vaccinations; their parents; their extensive injuries and treatments during their training; even the experimental procedures used to enhance their strength, agility, and mental resiliency.

"What the hell was he up to?" she muttered. She felt her pulse quicken as she scoured his records. There were DNA profiles on each Spartan, and there were extensive files on the old flash clone techniques that ONI had used to replace the originals. Ackerson seemed especially interested in this aspect of the program. He had followed the medical records of the replacements as they grew up, succumbed to congenital diseases, and inevitably died. He even had the bodies retrieved and autopsies performed.

Dr. Halsey's stomach soured. It was her fault, in part, that these replacement children had died so young. They had never perfected flash cloning for an entire human. They had done it anyway thirty years ago because the Earth government was on the verge of falling apart . . . collapsing into a hundred civil wars. They had desperately needed the SPARTAN program.

And of course, they had done it simply because they *could*.

No matter the legitimacy of her reasons, she knew she had killed these children as sure as if she had shot them dead.

There was one last file in the S-III folder.

As Dr. Halsey tapped it open, Kalmiya said, "That is only a fragment. It had been erased, but I managed to reconstruct it from trace ionization in the memory crystal."

Dr. Halsey examined its contents. There was only CPOMZ followed by a 512-character alphanumeric string. "This longer portion is a star chart reference," she whispered.

"Yes, Doctor, but it's not a reference to any recognized locations in UNSC-controlled space."

What the hell had Ackerson been up to? "No good at all," she murmured and ran her finger over the first word in the file: CPOMZ.

"I'll have to deal with this later," she said. She downloaded the files to a nearby data pad. "Let's see what else the good Colonel was up to." She opened the folder marked KING UNDER THE MOUNTAIN.

There were only three files.

The first was the original construction blueprints of this base; it appeared on her desk. Dr. Halsey noted that this holographic representation of the base was much larger than she had been led to believe. While her security clearance was the highest possible for a civilian, she apparently had seen only a third of the facility she had worked in for the last decade.

Dr. Halsey tapped open the second file. It was the transcripts of the debriefing at Camp Hathcock, August 12, 2552. That was the inquiry of John's destruction of the city on Côte d'Azur and the alien artifact the Covenant had tried to procure there. Curious.

A third file was an analysis of the symbols John had captured from the alien artifact. According to Ackerson's notes it, too, was a partial star map. Dr. Halsey returned to the stellar chart reference in the Spartans' files.

No good. This location had seemingly nothing to do with that reference.

The stellar reference in the alien artifact was . . . she did the math in her head—

"I'll be God damned," she muttered.

She pulled up star charts and NAV records for confirmation, and checked her math one last time.

No question: It was the Epsilon Eridani system.

Here.

This was more than a curiosity, now. Ackerson had been sitting on a tremendous secret—a very dangerous secret. "Just his style to play with fire and get us all burned."

Additional files detailed the procurement of digging equipment, and a new set of blueprints and geological surveys. The new maps looked like a network of veins and arteries.

"What am I looking at, Kalmiya?"

"According to the coordinates of these secondary maps, Doctor, this facility was built over an old titanium mine . . . and before that this site was surveyed as an extinct volcano. These are designated as a series of lava tubes."

"I wonder if they used the natural passages to help build the mines, and later this facility?" Dr. Halsey removed her glasses and cleaned them as she thought this through. "No . . . if it was as simple as that, why would Ackerson be interested? And why then classify this data as level X-ray? How does this connect to the alien artifact on Côte d'Azur?"

"I can't say," Kalmiya replied, "but perhaps there's a back door you can use to escape."

"Yes, yes." Dr. Halsey downloaded all of Ackerson's secret files to her data pad. "I'll consider that later. Right now we should concentrate—"

"Detecting increased seismic activity, Doctor."

Dr. Halsey froze. She felt it more than saw it—a series of faint, rhythmic *thumps*, like thunder in the distance.

Dust rained from the ceiling tiles and scattered the light for the holographic system into a dazzling starburst.

"They're coming," Dr. Halsey whispered. She opened a COM channel to the Spartans. "Get back to the lab ASAP. I might have a way out!"

She stumbled as a powerful blast rocked the chamber. There was a shriek of stressed metal, and the main support beam overhead shifted, fell, and crashed onto her desk.

The lights went dead.

The secure storage doors whispered open, and overhead fluorescent lights strobed on. Fred saw motion—but it was only his own reflection in the burnished-mirror finish of the chamber's stainless-steel walls. Will stepped inside and looked up, then glanced back down the corridor.

The room was a three-by-five-meter vault with steel walls, floor, and ceiling. Their footfalls were muffled as they entered, so the floor had to be at least a quarter meter thick. Along the right and left walls stood secure floor-to-ceiling lockers, and two metal crates sat along the far wall. Every surface was spotless, and every seam had been precision-milled to prevent explosives or acids from penetrating.

"One moment, please," Kalmiya told them. "I'm attempting to access the locks now. Please stand by."

Will stood at the doorway and watched their backs. It didn't make Fred feel any more at ease. The abandoned ONI base was somehow more intimidating than facing the Covenant invasion force overhead. He had walked down these corridors a dozen times during his training on Reach. This base had always been full of people; now, empty, it drove the point home that the Covenant were winning. First the Outer Colonies had been crushed; now Reach. How long before humanity was forced to retreat all the way back to Earth? And after that . . . what? There would be no other choice but victory or extinction.

Enough. Such musings didn't help him achieve his immediate objective. He'd leave the long-range strategies to Generals and Admirals. It was time to concentrate on what he did best.

The walls hummed as thick metal bolts inside the lockers retracted, the sound of heavy oiled steel sliding over steel. With a final *thump*, the sound ceased.

Kalmiya said, "Lockers open and safeties disabled, Spartans. Help yourselves."

"Secure the outer door, please," Fred told her.

The door to the hallway eased shut and locked, and Will moved to Fred's side. Each Spartan opened one of the wall lockers, standing to the side in case there was some leftover booby trap within that Kalmiya had failed to disable.

Fred peered inside and saw a rack of handguns. They weren't the standard-issue HE pistols; these had oversized barrels—easily 30 percent larger and longer—and they had grips of self-molding plastasteel. He picked one up and hefted it—its balance was barrel-heavy, to be expected from an unloaded pistol. He found three boxes of clips at the bottom of the locker, opened one, and took out a clip. Whatever this new handgun shot, it was high caliber, slugs the size of his thumb. He slid the clip into the gun, and it secured with a satisfying *click*.

Now it was perfectly balanced, far better than the standard-issue sidearm.

He secured the weapon and turned to see what Will had found.

Will examined a plastic-wrapped rifle, designated as the BR55. He removed the rifle from the locker, ripped off its sheathing, and shouldered it. He nodded with satisfaction.

Unlike the MA5B, this rifle had a longer barrel and stock, with a cutdown muzzle shroud. A scope was mounted on an optics railing along the top of the rifle. Will hefted a clip and inserted it into the receiver.

He shouldered the rifle again and peered through the scope. "Auto zoom, nice."

Will and Fred then traded and inspected the new weapons. Fred liked the feel of the BR55's newest version, but wondered how much punch it had—enough, he hoped, to make the trade-off of having fewer rounds in the clip worth it.

They filled two sacks with the new pistols, rifles, and ammunition, then moved to the footlockers and lifted the lids.

Inside the first locker were satchel charges. Fred grabbed three and looped them over his neck. "I think we can find a use for these."

Will knelt next to the second footlocker. Within were plastic boxes marked MJOLNIR MARK V followed by a long list of serial numbers. "This must be what Doctor Halsey wanted," he said.

There was a flutter in the floor—which got Fred's full attention, because a "flutter" in a solid steel floor meant trouble.

The COM channel opened, and Dr. Halsey's voice crackled with static: *"Get back to the lab ASAP. I might have a way out!"*

The vault room flexed, and thunder rumbled through the walls.

"Detonations," Will said. "They're coming."

"Secure those boxes," Fred ordered. He raced to the closed doors. "Open," he shouted to Kalmiya and waited as the door slowly eased apart. He scanned up and down the corridor and then ran back toward the lab.

When they got to the medical wing the lights were dead, and Fred saw Kelly's helmet lights cut through the velvet-rich, dust-filled darkness. She had Dr. Halsey draped over her shoulder. Blood ran from the doctor's nostrils.

"Her office collapsed," Kelly told them. "Support beam missed her by a centimeter."

Dr. Halsey looked up and whispered, "I'm fine. Really." She pushed away from Kelly, stood, and teetered in place.

Fred scooped her up and set her on the examination table. "With all due respect, ma'am, you're not."

Another detonation rippled through the earth—this one stronger than the previous explosion. Fissures snaked through the concrete walls.

Vinh and Isaac bounded into the room. "Enemy contacts at extreme range," Vinh reported.

"Down," Dr. Halsey said, and she held a palm-sized data pad for Fred to see. It had a map on its display . . . but not of this base. "We have to go lower."

Fred wondered if Dr. Halsey was delirious.

"Down the elevator shaft in Section Sigma," she explained. "We'll seal it behind us. We can't let them follow."

"Kelly, take point," Fred ordered. He grabbed two of the new magnum pistols, loaded them, and then tossed them to Kelly, along with three extra clips. "I guess you get to test these."

Kelly gazed at the new weapons and gave a low whistle.

Fred opened the bags with the new rifles and handed them out to his team. "Will, you mule the extra parts and ammo."

"Roger," Will replied and slung them over his shoulders.

"Those satchels, over there," Dr. Halsey said and waved to four duffel bags. "Medical supplies. Food and water. We'll need them, too."

Will grabbed them as well.

"Just a few more things," Dr. Halsey whispered. "We can't let them get into ONI's records." She tapped her pad once and then said to Kalmiya, "Begin Operation White Glove. Irradiate all computer memory crystal. Code file access Beta-Foxtrot-99874." Dr. Halsey closed her eyes as if she were concentrating, and she whispered, "Not all AIs have the fail-safe option, my dear Kalmiya . . . just the ones that matter."

"I understand, Doctor." There was a pause, and the AI spoke

again, her voice sad. "Voice and fingerprint accepted and verified. Fail-safe code verified. It has been . . . a pleasure working with you, Doctor Halsey."

"The pleasure has been mine, Kalmiya." She stood straighter and said, "Fail-safe override access: 'Ragnarok.' Give us a three-minute countdown."

A three-minute counter appeared in the corner of Fred's heads-up display.

Dr. Halsey turned to him. "I've activated the explosives cache under this base, which will level the complex. We have to get below, to the original titanium mine tunnels."

Fred wished she had consulted with him before she had given them only three minutes. Then again, Dr. Halsey knew what was at stake, what secrets were hidden in this base, and what damage could occur if the Covenant got their hands on those secrets.

Five minutes might be *too much* time considering what was at risk.

"Understood," Fred replied. "Isaac, you're rear guard. Vinh, stick close to Kelly. I'll take Doctor Halsey." Fred picked up the doctor with great care. She couldn't have weighed more than fifty kilos—light as a stick.

"I've lost targets on motion sensors," Vinh whispered over the COM. "They were close, too."

"Kelly, watch for camouflaged Elites."

"Affirmative," she said. She scanned the room, moved to a cabinet, and grabbed a tin can marked TALC.

"Let's move," Fred ordered. "Kill the lights in the base. Hand signals only—I want radio silence."

Four blue acknowledgment lights winked on.

The faint light filtering in from the outer hall died.

Kelly slid into the hallway and melted into the shadows. Vinh followed, then Fred and Isaac. Will trailed behind, moving slower because of the care he took to remain quiet with the gear.

Dr. Halsey tapped her data pad, and a map uploaded onto Fred's heads-up display, a path traced through corridors and a NAV marker designated an elevator shaft. That was their objective.

The Spartans winked on their acknowledgment lights, confirming the route.

They crept forward, smooth and silent—oil sliding over oil—until Kelly halted ten meters before a five-way intersection. The Spartans froze and waited. She crouched, set the can of talc on the floor, and then stood with her knees bent.

She waited another heartbeat, then gave a slight shake of her head from side to side—their signal for trouble ahead.

Vinh moved next to Fred's flank, and Fred set Dr. Halsey down and stood in front of her. Will crouched next to the doctor to provide cover with his own body if needed.

Isaac remained on their six.

Kelly kicked the can. It tumbled end over end through the air, and as it entered the intersection Kelly squeezed off a single shot. The flash of light from the muzzle illuminated the passage just long enough for them to see the can explode and a cloud of white dust mushroom into the hallways.

Their motion detectors flickered, and four targets resolved on their displays. Image enhancement showed the wavering outlines of four Covenant Elites—their light-bending camouflage fluttering and overloading as the talc powder coated them.

Kelly open fire with both pistols. The Elite closest dropped as three slugs pounded through its shields, and a round caught it in the center of its elongated forehead. Purple blood blossomed across the wall.

The remaining Elites returned fire, and Kelly bounded forward, plasma flaring at the edge of her shield. She ducked into the side passage.

The instant Kelly was out of the line of fire, Fred shouldered his rifle and squeezed the trigger. A three-round burst caught the next Elite, and its shield sparkled and failed. It twisted away, clutching at the single round that had penetrated its chest.

Vinh fired two single shots, but the Elite's shield held. In unison, Vinh and Fred fired another set of three-round bursts. The Elite dropped to the steel floor in a twisted heap.

The last Elite had vanished. No return fire. No sensor contact.

The Spartans held position for a moment longer, then regrouped. With hand signals, each member of the team reported no contact.

Fred spied tracks in the white dust scattered on the floor. The Elite had bugged out, and it was most likely gathering reinforcements.

That wasn't what Covenant Elites usually did. Their pride demanded that they fight, and die fighting, if need be. They would hurl themselves headlong into battle, no matter the odds, and die by the hundreds if necessary. They almost never ran away. Nothing about this engagement had been "usual."

Fred glanced at Will and Dr. Halsey. Will gave him a thumbs-up, indicating that the doctor hadn't been wounded in the exchange.

After the exchange of gunfire, there was no need for secrecy. "One of them got away," Fred told them. "We need to move, too . . . and forget quiet."

The Spartans ran down the corridor. They heard and felt another explosion directly over their heads.

Kelly skidded to a halt in front of the locked elevator doors. She gripped one of the panels; Fred and Vinh gripped the seam of the other side, and the Spartans pried them apart as if the five-centimeter steel alloy were no tougher than the rind of an orange.

Kelly grabbed the elevator cables and slid down. Vinh followed, then Fred plummeted more than five hundred meters into the darkness. The three of them ripped open the doors at the bottom of the shaft.

Will slid down next with Dr. Halsey holding on to his neck. Isaac followed.

"There should be an air vent," Dr. Halsey whispered. "There."

Kelly ripped off the vent cover and peered down.

"It leads to the old mine tunnels," Dr. Halsey told them, "and more, I hope."

"Go," Fred ordered.

Kelly dived in, headfirst. They waited ten seconds, and her acknowledgment light winked on.

Fred entered next, sliding through the vent duct. It twisted and turned and finally dumped him into a long tunnel of roughly hewn granite. The ceiling was ten meters high and—judging from the three-meter-wide tire tracks in the dust—big enough for heavy equipment to have rolled through.

Will slid out of the duct with Dr. Halsey riding on his chest. Vinh and Isaac came after them.

"There's more to this place," Dr. Halsey told them, standing up and brushing the dust from her lab coat. "This is only the beginning. We have to—"

A thunderous detonation cut her off. The mountain exploded, and ONI's base collapsed over their heads.

CHAPTER

FIFTEEN

Fred followed the trail of odd symbols along the left-hand stone wall until they twisted into a spiral mosaic and vanished into ever-smaller curls. The symbols were part of the rock, composed of glittering mica inclusions in the granite matrix. There were a series of squares, triangles, bars, and dots, similar to Covenant calligraphy he had seen—but at the same time it was simpler, cleaner, and when Fred focused on them, the characters seemed to blur around their edges and fade from his stare.

He blinked, and the symbols were there again.

Following these symbols like a trail of bread crumbs had been his primary mission for the last eight days. Dr. Halsey and the Spartans had explored the extensive caverns, hoping to find two things: a way out, and what Dr. Halsey called "the most important discovery of the millennium." She had, however, refused to speculate on what exactly this discovery would be. "I'm a scientist," she'd told them, "not a soothsayer."

Fred would have settled for finding an airhole to the surface— but he recognized that the symbols were important, too. They were important because the Covenant thought they were important. And that made whatever Dr. Halsey was searching for worth finding, if only to keep the enemy from getting it.

The Covenant hadn't stopped digging overhead, although the pace and methods they used had changed. There had been no further explosions. There was only the constant and gentle scraping sound of equipment as they slowly but steadily removed the mountain. Every hour the sound intensified as they drew closer. Fred had set his audio filters to screen out the noise so he could concentrate.

Eight days. It hadn't seemed that long. They worked, they rested, they slept, and they waited. Dr. Halsey had taught them word games like twenty questions and simple cipher, at which they all became extremely proficient—so much so that she quickly stopped playing. Dr. Halsey was not a graceful loser.

The time had melted away. Maybe it was the darkness, the lack of any temporal reference like the sun, moon, and stars, but the hours had lost their meaning.

He paused to stretch his Achilles tendon, recently stitched and fused by Dr. Halsey. Aside from some stiffness, it was almost back to normal. He had almost torn the tendon off, running on the injury.

Dr. Halsey had patched them all up; she had even flash cloned Kelly a new partial lung, which she successfully grafted. In her tiny field medical kit, the doctor had a handheld MRI, a sterile field generator, even a shoe-box-sized clone tank for organ duplication.

She had also installed the new MJOLNIR parts in their existing armor. These upgrades were in field-testing and not certified, she had explained, but she gauged their need sufficient to justify the risk of using the new equipment.

Kelly received an improvement to her neural induction circuits, giving her twitch response time a speed boost. Vinh had a new linear accelerator added to her shield system, effectively doubling its strength. Isaac had a new image-enhancing computer installed. Will received a better tracking system on his heads-up display, which improved his accuracy at distances up to a thousand meters.

Fred flexed his bare right hand. Dr. Halsey was installing his upgrade now—new sensors that would boost the sensitivity of

his motion tracker. Without the single gauntlet, Fred felt vul-
nerable. The Master Chief would have told him not to rely on
his armor or weapons—rely instead on his head. It would protect him better.

He wondered how Blue Team—John, Linda, and James—had
fared. And what of the rest of his own team? Had anyone at the
generator complex survived?

He didn't want to think about them—but he couldn't help it.
Maybe it was the darkness and the constant weight of the earth
around him.

What if they died here? Not died fighting, but just *died* here.
In a way, that wouldn't be so bad. Fred had faced death a dozen
times, brushed so close to it he had stared it in the face until it
blinked and turned away.

This was different, though. He didn't want to die, not without knowing if the other Spartans were still out there fighting.
Not if they still needed him.

He sighed and absentmindedly brushed his fingertips across
the odd symbols. They were as smooth as glass, and their edges
were sharp. These crystals could be a natural phenomenon. He
had seen similar inclusions in the museum on—

Fred felt a hot pain in the tip of his finger. He drew his bare
hand away and a tiny track of blood smeared the rock.

The glittering symbols on the wall took on a greasy cast, and
the reflection from his helmet lights thickened and almost
seemed to be absorbed by the minerals.

He flicked off his helmet lights. The symbols in the rock
emitted a faint illumination of their own: a soft reddish glow
like heated metal. The light intensified and spread across the
spiral on the wall, starting from where his blood had fallen;
those symbols warmed to a pleasant orange, then yellow-
gold.

A new symbol in the center of the spiral appeared that hadn't
been there a second ago . . . or perhaps it had been, but had

lain just beneath the surface. It heated and became increasingly visible, a single triangle that glowed white.

Fred was inexorably drawn to this central figure. He reached for it; there was no heat. He slowly stretched and touched the symbol with his exposed fingertip.

Warm white light raced along the spiral of symbols, then traced a path down the hallway and into the distance. The entire cavern seemed suddenly alive with radiance and shadow. Even with the step-down luminosity filters in his helmet, Fred had to blink and squint.

The wall before him rumbled and seams appeared at the central figure, dozen of lines that curved in a radial pattern—and then pulled away to reveal a corridor behind.

Fred realized that he was holding his breath. He exhaled.

This new corridor was twenty meters high—large enough for a titan to stride down its length. It vanished into the distance, a straight line that gently sloped deeper into the earth. The floor was paved with asymmetric blue tiles patterned to look like waves lapping upon a shore. Four-meter-tall symbols of gold were centered and inlaid into the mirror-smooth walls. These giant triangles, squares, bars, and circles began to emit the same soft light . . . and Fred felt his foot shuffle forward.

He stopped, shook his head, and looked away. He checked his radiation counter; it pulsed, and then fell back to a normal background count.

He keyed the COM. "Doctor Halsey, I think I've found what you've been looking for. Sending video feed now. Copy?"

There was a long pause. The COM was open, but Dr. Halsey wasn't responding.

"Doctor Halsey, copy?"

"Yes," she finally said over the COM. *"Don't move, Fred. And don't touch anything. Excellent work. Kelly, Isaac, Vinh, Will—meet me at Fred's location."*

Fred wanted to stare at the gold symbols and the light they

cast, but something warned him that this would be dangerous. He had long ago learned to listen to that inner voice when on patrol or in the heat of battle. It had saved him from dozens of ambushes. He kept his eyes on the dirt floor of the tunnel. There was something *too* fascinating and nearly familiar about those symbols. They reminded him of the Greek mythology that Déjà, the Spartans' first teacher, had taught—legends of hauntingly beautiful creatures who lured the unwary to certain death. Sirens.

He checked his rifle. The ammo counter read full, but he hit the magazine release and visually confirmed it. He slapped the clip back into the receiver. This simple operation cleared his head.

He detected four blips on his motion tracker—they glowed green, indicating friendlies.

Kelly, Vinh, Isaac, and Will jogged up next to him, weapons ready.

"What is this?" Will whispered. The golden glow reflected in his helmet's faceplate.

"Careful," Fred warned them. "Filter the light. Go to black-and-white image enhancement."

He got four blue acknowledgment signals, and then Fred switched to BWIM display. Funny that he hadn't thought of that for himself. Only when the safety of his team was at stake did he think clearly.

Dr. Halsey ran along the tunnel and halted, panting, next to the Spartans. "Yes," she said, wheezing. "Yes, this must be it—what Ackerson was searching for. And most likely"—she glanced at the roof—"what *they* are looking for, too, I imagine."

Dr. Halsey ignored the curious symbols and the light, and strode into the new corridor. "Hurry," she told them. "I fear we've set something in motion, and our visitors upstairs might know it, too."

Fred assembled his team to form up around Dr. Halsey.

Kelly took point, and the rest of them created a loose box around her.

Dr. Halsey handed Fred his missing gauntlet. He took it and wriggled his fingers into the armor, pulled it snug, and sealed the locking collar around his wrist. Diagnostics ran and confirmed that his armor was whole again. His motion tracker pulsed on his heads-up display.

The hallway changed as they continued down its length. The golden light faded along the ceiling, and inky black covered its expanse; tiny stars winked on and twinkled. Fred added color to his display; he wanted to see this. Moons wheeled overhead; silver-gray orbs, pockmarked with meteorite impacts, spun in wide orbits. Along the walls, tall green bamboo-like grass sprouted and grew up the curved surfaces.

Dr. Halsey brushed her fingertips along the wall, and the grasses wavered at her touch. "Semisolid holography," she said without halting. "No visible emitters. Interesting. We should investigate this later," she said and increased the pace of her stride. "If there's time."

The holographic environment cycled to an arid moonscape: deep craters and sterile light; it became a volcanic world with lava flowing alongside them. The air wavered with heat. In each transformation the golden symbols remained on the walls, leading them through the illusions.

The corridor emptied onto a landing that overlooked the largest room Fred had ever seen.

Kelly stepped onto the landing, looked, and waved them forward.

They stood on one of a dozen tiered levels that encircled the room; there was no railing. Fred leaned over the edge. It was at least one hundred meters to the floor below. The room was approximately circular and three kilometers in diameter. The floor was blue and seemed to shift as a billion tiny tiles flexed and rearranged themselves into frustratingly familiar patterns. The ceiling was a dome with a holographic golden sun, blue sky, and cottony clouds that morphed into spheres, puffy pyramids, bars, and cubes. And in the center of the floor was a pedestal flickering with a faint light.

Isaac held up his hand. "Listen," he whispered over the COM.

They all froze, and Fred strained to hear. There was nothing. Fred turned up his aural amplification to maximum gain. He heard the creak of their armored joints and five faint heartbeats but, other than that, silence.

"They've stopped," Fred said, and pointed overhead. "The digging."

"I don't like it," Dr. Halsey said. "The Covenant aren't known for giving up on anything they start. We'd better continue."

Kelly removed the clip from her magnum, cleared the chamber, and then slid a self-installing piton down the length of the barrel. She shot it into the stone wall, and the metal shard implanted ten centimeters and blossomed with sharp talons, securing the shaft to the wall.

Vinh handed her a coil of black rope. She clipped one end to the piton, then tossed the rest over the edge.

Isaac and Will stood on the lip and swept the vast open region with their weapons.

Kelly jumped and rappelled to the bottom. A moment later she gave the *all-clear* signal.

Will and Isaac followed her to the floor. Fred tied the rope around Dr. Halsey's waist and lowered her gingerly down after them. He and Vinh took up the rear.

The floor of the great room wasn't the same tile as in the corridor above. It was still blue tile, but these were squares and circles and bars and triangles. If the symbols were a language, Fred stood upon a million words; he wished he'd been issued a dictionary.

Dr. Halsey paused to examine the tiles as well. "If only we

had the time," she muttered, and then walked toward the light gleaming in the center of the chamber.

The Spartans formed up around the doctor again, but Fred's instincts warned him that this wasn't a good idea. He couldn't get his bearings straight. The room was big, large enough that it felt as if they were outside. It threw him off. He had an odd sense of vertigo, almost as if the floor was tilting and he was now walking on the roof.

Dr. Halsey increased her pace, but the distance to the center of the room didn't seem any closer; in fact, they seemed more distant from the center than when they had started out from the edge of the room.

Fred turned down the gain on his display until everything was a faint black-and-white blur. He focused on his motion tracker and saw that the Spartans and Dr. Halsey were now separated across two dozen meters.

"Everyone stop," he said. "Regroup. We're getting scattered."

They halted and edged back into formation.

"There must be another way," Dr. Halsey said. She reached into her lab coat pocket and removed a ball bearing. "The floor slopes toward the center," she observed. She set the bearing on the floor and gave it a gentle push. The bearing rolled, then curved, and spiraled back to a stop.

"This is getting too weird," Fred muttered. "Kelly, you have the best aim. Close your eyes, pick a direction, and we'll follow."

". . . Affirmative," she whispered.

The Spartans set their hands on each other's shoulders and marched, not toward the center of the room but to a spot that Kelly picked, apparently back the way they had come.

Fred turned off his display and watched his motion tracker. They were all together and another blip appeared, one that Kelly was leading them straight to.

Another twenty meters and she halted. "Look."

Fred snapped on his heads-up display, and sapphire-blue

light filled his vision. They stood before the source of the glow in the middle of the room. There was a pedestal made of the same gold material as the symbols in the corridor, and floating above it was a fist-sized crystal, tapered to a point at either end. It spun, and the facets along its centerline folded and shifted like the pieces of a puzzle.

Dr. Halsey reached for it and then hesitated. "Radiation?" she asked.

Fred checked his counter. "Normal background levels," he reported.

"We must take this with us," she whispered. "Study it. Or destroy it if necessary to keep the Covenant from getting it." She touched the crystal, and its light dimmed. For a moment the light appeared to be absorbed by Dr. Halsey's palm.

Static washed over Fred's display, his shields shimmered, a squeal blasted through his speakers, and his motion tracker momentarily made contact with a thousand targets swarming through the great room. His radiation warning flared red and then faded.

"Radiation spike," he said. "Analysis says lots of neutrinos, but I'm unable to determine the type—it's something not in the computer's database."

"Is it safe now?" Dr. Halsey asked, peering into the crystal she gripped in her tiny hand.

"Seems so," Fred told her, "but Doc—"

"No time for debate," she said. "Neutrino radiation will penetrate the rock between us and the surface."

"They'll be able to get a fix on our position," Kelly said. "All they need is three ships nearby to triangulate. We need to get out of here—fast."

"Which way?" Isaac asked Fred. "Back the way we came, or deeper in?"

"There was no way out from the titanium mines," Fred replied. "So we go deeper."

An explosion rocked the earth and deep thunder rumbled, but rather than diminishing, this thunder got louder, closer.

Fred's shadow lengthened, and its edges sharpened.

He whirled toward the source of the intense white light—directly overhead, a spot in the dome: The holographic scenery of stars and moons bleached and vanished. He spun Dr. Halsey around so she faced away, then covered her head.

The stone ceiling melted and peeled back as if it were thin plastic hit with a blowtorch—an angled shaft of dazzling white radiance appeared and blasted into the tiled floor, five hundred meters from their position.

Then it was gone and the room fell into darkness punctured only by a ray of faint sunlight that streamed in through the hole above. Where the beam of hard light had contacted the floor, a precision-milled hole had been etched fifteen meters deep.

Dr. Halsey said, "What was—"

"Energy projector," Fred told her, blinking away the black dots that filled his vision even though his step-down filters had absorbed the brunt of the light. "Only the big Covenant ships have them. There's got to be one of them—"

The cut shaft filled with a beam of purple light. It sparkled and shimmered with motes of dust.

"Grav lift," Fred shouted. "Incoming! Isaac and Vinh, take our six. Will, you're with me on Doctor Halsey. Kelly, find us a way out."

Kelly ran in a line directly away from the gravity beam.

A dozen Elites floated down through the shaft, and fired while still in the air. Plasma bolts slashed at them from the distance.

Fred and Will grabbed Dr. Halsey and moved her behind the pedestal, out of the line of fire. Isaac and Vinh fell back and opened fire.

"Suppression fire!" Fred barked. "Keep them pinned in that crater!"

The Spartans fired several bursts, but more Elites were drifting down, along with a Shade—a portable plasma turret. If they stayed here, they'd be overrun.

"Fall back," Fred told them over the COM. "It's too hot."

Kelly sprinted, digging in her heals with such force that the tiles buckled and shot out behind her. "Passage," she reported. "Ground floor. Dead ahead. I'll enter and clear."

"My apologies, Doctor," Fred said and unceremoniously scooped Dr. Halsey up in his arms. "Everyone move! Vinh, Isaac, drop those det sacks to cover our tracks."

Their acknowledgment lights winked on.

Will and Fred ran, weaving from side to side. Dr. Halsey clutched onto Fred with one arm, and in her free hand she clutched the crystal.

Fred's motion tracker showed dozen of targets behind them, then hundreds.

A pair of detonations thumped, an overpressure wave blurred his motion tracker, subsided, and then half of those contacts were gone.

Will and Fred ran into an arched passage set in the wall of the great room. Kelly crouched in the hallway and fired past them with her pistols.

Fred opened his COM. "SPARTAN 030. SPARTAN 039. Acknowledge."

Static hissed through his speaker. Vinh's and Isaac's lights remained dark.

"Prep your det sack and seal this passage," Fred ordered Kelly.

Fred set down Dr. Halsey, turned, and bumped up his display's magnification.

Hundreds of Covenant Elites and Jackals poured from the grav shaft. They swarmed over the floor of the great chamber, a living tide as unstoppable as the ocean.

They weren't shooting anymore, though. Dr. Halsey was correct: They wanted the crystal she'd taken.

"Go!" Fred said. "Kelly, blow the hallway. Let's move."

Kelly hesitated a heartbeat; Fred saw her searching for Vinh and Isaac in the mass of Covenant. They weren't there; not alive anyway. Kelly dropped the olive-green satchel of high explosives.

Will picked up Dr. Halsey, and they all ran deeper into the corridor.

Five seconds later the satchel detonated. A wave of acrid air washed up the hallway and choked the corridor with dust and smoke.

Kelly took the lead position, both pistols ready; she rounded a corner—and skidded to a halt.

The passage was a dead end.

SECTION III

RESCUE

MANEUVERS

CHAPTER
SIXTEEN

John brushed off the frost buildup that clouded the top half of the cryotube, and revealed the green-armored figure sprawled behind the plastasteel shell.

SPARTAN 058. Linda.

She'd been mortally wounded during the raid on Gamma Station, just before Reach fell. He'd dragged her burned, limp body back to the *Pillar of Autumn*, and the medics had placed her in deep cryostasis just before the jump.

When the *Autumn* crashed on Halo, Keyes must have jettisoned the active cryotubes—standard operating procedure.

They had frozen her while she'd still been in her suit. That was for the best, considering the extent of her injuries . . . but he would have given anything to see her face one last time.

Linda had been unique among the Spartans with her blood-red hair and dark emerald eyes, but her appearance was not what set her apart. She was the unit's best sniper-scout and could hit targets the rest of them couldn't. While the other Spartans preferred to operate as a team, Linda was content to separate, hide and post in some remote location, and wait for days for the single, critical shot that could turn the tide of battle. Although snipers in the UNSC were always trained to function in pairs, a shooter and a spotter, Linda was the exception to that rule—she had proven time and again that she was most effective on her own. If any one of the Spartans could be called a "lone wolf," it was Linda. In many ways that made her the strongest of them.

To see her like this . . .

John wiped away the condensation that formed over her helmeted head. She was neither dead nor alive. She was in some twilight place in between.

That uncertainty was worse than seeing her broken and burned body on Gamma Station. It felt like an open wound in John's chest.

Linda's prognosis was good. The occupants of the other two cryopods hadn't made it. Some kind of energy discharge had deactivated the units, and those inside had died cold bleak deaths.

There was a gentle knock on the hull of the Longsword, and Sergeant Johnson pulled himself inside. "Master Chief," he said. "You got the air scrubbers? The remote COM? Polaski says she's ready to call it a day with that Covenant dropship. We need to get on board and work."

The Master Chief stood and nodded to the aft hatch, where he had stripped the air scrubbers and COM from the Longsword.

The Sergeant picked up the gear, and then he and the Chief crawled out of the Longsword. The Chief hesitated and looked back at the cryotube.

"Don't you worry about her," Johnson said. "Hell, I been hit worse and she's three times the soldier I am. She'll pull through."

The Chief sealed the hatch without comment. He had heard the same hollow promises a hundred times before with critically wounded men. Why was it that soldiers would face their own deaths without blinking an eye . . . but when faced with the death of a squadmate, they turned away and lied to themselves?

They silently marched across the hangar. It had been cleared of debris and bodies, and Warrant Officer Polaski had, for the last six hours, been practicing inside the space with the intact

Covenant dropship. She spun the odd U-shaped craft around on its center axis, shimmied to port, rose, and then floated down for a landing.

Johnson squinted his dark eyes at her performance and nodded approvingly. "She says that she's figured out the weapon controls, too. No way to test them in here, of course."

"Understood," the Master Chief replied. "And the rest of the team's progress?"

"I've got the doors from here to the bridge and to the engine room welded shut," Sergeant Johnson told him. "If those transient sensor contacts that Cortana keeps picking up are anything, they'll have to cut through to get to us.

"Locklear's grabbing some sack time. He needed it." The Sergeant shrugged. "He'll be fine, though; ODSTs are tough as nails. Lieutenant Haverson slept some then got up, had a long conversation with Cortana, and started reading through some of the Covenant database. Everyone seems to be fine, considering what we've been through."

"Understood," the Chief said. "Cortana? Ship status?"

"ETA to Reach in twenty minutes," she said.

The Chief checked his mission clock. "You said thirteen hours' total travel time. By my count, we have approximately two hours to go."

"I had determined it would be thirteen hours based on the specifications of the Covenant Slipspace drive, but there's . . ." Her voice trailed off and faded.

"Cortana?"

"Sorry. There's a curious time-dilation effect at these Slipspace velocities. Although, technically, *velocity*, *acceleration*, and for that matter even *time* have no meaning in the folds of Slipspace. I thought I told you all this," she said. Irritation crept into her voice.

The Chief looked to the Sergeant, who shook his head and shrugged.

Cortana sounded more than distracted—and she didn't just "forget" things. It was a bad sign. They depended on her to fly this ship, and if she started falling apart they were in real trouble.

The Master Chief opened a COM channel. "Change of plans, team. Reach ETA is nineteen minutes. I'll explain later—just grab your gear and meet on the bridge ASAP."

There was a pause, then Lieutenant Haverson replied, *"Roger, Master Chief. Locklear and I are already up here."*

The hatch of the Covenant dropship opened, and Polaski jogged out. The three of them proceeded at a brisk pace to the bridge.

The Master Chief opened a private COM channel to Cortana. "Anything else I should know?"

The channel was silent for a full ten seconds. "I have the Covenant magnetic plasma-shaping system figured out," she replied. "We'll have a limited offensive capacity when we get to Reach, if we need it. I think."

"And the rest of this ship is still functional?"

"Yes," she replied. "I'm sorry, Chief . . . these calculations are . . . tricky."

The COM went dead.

Cortana's behavior worried the Chief, but he resigned himself to trust her. What other option was there?

He, the Sergeant, and Polaski halted outside the bridge; the thick blast doors were sealed.

"Lieutenant?" he said. "We're outside."

The doors pulled apart. Locklear and the Lieutenant stood with their assault rifles aimed down the hall. They relaxed their stance when they identified them as friendlies.

Lieutenant Haverson slung his rifle and said, "Sorry for the warm welcome. Cortana's been picking up transient contacts all over the ship. We're going to have to deal with them sooner or later—preferably before they deal with us."

"Agreed," the Chief said.

Polaski approached the Lieutenant, saluted, and gave her report on her efforts to master the Covenant dropship's controls.

Locklear edged closer to the Chief and the Sergeant. "What do you think, Sarge?" he whispered and cast a furtive glance at Polaski. "I mean, about her? Sure, there's that Marine–Navy thing to get over, but I can get past that. You think there's a chance that she and I? I mean—"

"I'd give you the same odds as spacing yourself and walking the rest of the way to Reach," the Sergeant declared. "In your skivvies."

"Give me a drop pod and I'd take those odds, Sarge." A smile split Locklear's tanned face, and he turned to the Master Chief. "Sure, I get it. Wouldn't be so defensive if I hadn't been close to the mark. Where there's smoke, there's fire, right?"

The Master Chief stared at Locklear and slowly shook his head.

Locklear's smile faded, but not entirely. "You guys are just jealous," he muttered and absentmindedly ran his finger over the scar that lined his jaw. "That's cool. I get that all the time."

Locklear's spirits had improved. Despite the ODST's rough edges, the Chief had seen him in combat. He didn't panic, and he had the skill and luck to survive Halo—qualities the Master Chief knew they'd need if they were ever going to get back.

"Exiting Slipspace," Cortana announced, "in three . . . two . . . one."

According to the Master Chief's mission clock, it had only been eight minutes since Cortana had told him their ETA was nineteen minutes. Was there more to the time-dilation effect than she realized?

The bridge lights dimmed, and blackness filled the arc of displays along the wall. Stars winked into existence, and at three o'clock blazed the warm orange orb of Epsilon Eridani.

"We are seven hundred thousand kilometers from the system

center," Cortana told them. "I wanted to jump in close enough to see what's going on—but far enough away so we would have time to recharge and reenter Slipspace if there's any trouble. Picking up signals now. Covenant signals. Lots of them. Translating . . . stand by."

Haverson tapped one of the screens and magnified the image.

"My God," he whispered.

A planet appeared on the screen. He sucked in his breath as he saw a world smoldering from pole to equator. Fires raged over its surface, and a hurricane of black spiraled through the atmosphere.

The Master Chief felt as if the ship had suddenly decelerated. His hands clenched.

He'd sent the majority of his team down there—and had considered it the "easier" mission. He'd gotten his Spartans killed, he was sure of it.

Had they at least died fighting? Or were they burned from an orbiting Covenant ship, helpless?

"Are we in the right place?" Locklear murmured. "That's Reach?" He removed his cap, crushed it in his hand, and whispered, "Poor bastards."

The other displays showed Covenant warships orbiting the planet, as well as dozens of smaller craft and one large structure that seemed to be a central docking station.

"What is this?" the Master Chief asked, stepping closer. He tapped the center display, pushing the limits of its resolution and magnifying a portion of the surface near the midlatitudes.

The image resolved into patches of green, brown, and white— different from the angry black and livid orange that dominated the view of the rest of the planet.

"Looks like they missed a spot," the Sergeant said.

"The Covenant don't 'miss' anything when they glass a planet," the Master Chief replied. "We've seen them do it enough to know what happens. This is no accident." He turned to Lieutenant Haverson. "We should get closer and see what this is, sir."

"Master Chief," Haverson said softly and held up his hands. "I sympathize with your need to know with absolute certainty what happened to your fellow Spartans, but this is . . ." He gestured to the planet and then frowned as he scrutinized the undamaged part of Reach. "Indeed," he murmured. "This does warrant a closer look . . . provided we can get away with it."

The Lieutenant pulled the magnification back and refocused the display on the upper atmosphere. A hundred Covenant ships popped into view. "There are several smaller vessels circling over that spot. Forget what I just said," Haverson whispered. "If the Covenant are so interested in this region, then we should be as well—as long as our cover holds. Cortana, take us in closer."

"Yes, Lieutenant," Cortana replied.

The Covenant flagship smoothly accelerated in-system.

"They're hailing us," Cortana said. "Preparing the proper counter-response."

John counted the ships on the display. There were hundreds—most no larger than a Covenant dropship, but there were at least a dozen cruisers and two of the titanic carriers that each carried three squadrons of Seraph fighter craft. There was more than enough firepower to turn their captured flagship into molten slag.

Many of the smaller ships herded debris from the battle into one spot over Reach—a floating junkyard of UNSC and Covenant ships.

"You see this?" The Master Chief pointed to the field of floating debris.

The Lieutenant stared at it. "It's almost as if they planned to stay here for a while—they're cleaning house."

"We're in," Cortana announced. "The fleet is curious why a Covenant flagship is here, but not suspicious enough to question our authority. The translation is tricky. But apparently from the string of honorifics attached to their responses there's supposed to be someone of extreme high rank commanding this ship, someone they referred to, among other things, as the 'Guardian of the Luminous Key.' "

"Damn silly name," muttered Sergeant Johnson.

"Can you tell what they're doing down there, Cortana?" the Lieutenant asked.

"Not yet," she replied. "Their language doesn't translate in a literal manner, and each word has multiple meanings. There's something they consider holy—there are ten times as many religious allusions than in their typical communiqués. Hang on . . . picking up a new signal. Weaker than the others. Not on a Covenant frequency. It's the UNSC E-band."

Lieutenant Haverson licked his lips. "Play it," he said.

A message beeped through the speakers, six tones, then a two-second pause; it repeated.

The Master Chief stiffened.

"That's it," Cortana said. "Just those six notes over and over. It originates here." A tiny NAV triangle appeared on the edge of the intact region on the planet's surface.

"It's not Morse code," Polaski said. "Not any code I've heard of. Maybe it's a test signal? Something automated, like an air-traffic repeater relay, maybe?"

"It's not automated," the Master Chief said. "Everyone gear up and get ready. We're going down there. There are Spartans down there. And they're still alive."

He whispered so softly that only he and Cortana heard: *"Oly Oly Oxen Free."*

CHAPTER

SEVENTEEN

John crawled forward and peered over the edge of the rise. A lush, green valley stretched out below him. In the distance, the silvery reflections of the Big Horn River twisted through the thick forest. Aside from a flock of birds that wheeled overhead, there was no activity below. He inched back to a blackened, hollow tree stump and crawled inside.

Fred and Linda sat inside the hollowed-out cedar stump. It muffled their conversations and insulated them from the soldiers' thermal goggles. "It's all clear for now," he whispered. A moment later Sam, Kelly, and Fhajad appeared, ghostlike, from their camouflaged positions nearby. They crouched outside the cedar stump and watched for patrols.

From a distance they looked like soldiers on field maneuvers. Each was tall, fit, and agile, and looked to be in their late teens or early twenties. Closer observation told a different story. Each Spartan was no more than twelve years old.

"Weapons check," John told Fred and Linda. "We can't afford any mistakes on this one, especially not with the rifles."

Linda and Fred disassembled and inspected their SRS99C-S2 sniper rifles—which they'd liberated from a pair of Tango Company shooters who'd been sent to hunt them down two days ago. If the soldiers of Tango Company didn't capture them and beat them into unconsciousness—this would be fun.

John checked his pistol. CPO Mendez had issued the weapon. It used compressed air to fire a narq-dart. The effective range was twenty meters, and on impact it could drop a rhino in its tracks.

Twenty meters wouldn't cut it for this mission, though, so Fhajad had modified the 114mm APFSDS rounds from the sniper rifles, removed their deadly armor-piercing tips, and replaced them with narq-dart capsules.

When Linda had test-fired the weapon, she promised John accuracy to one hundred meters. The rounds would penetrate flesh, but they couldn't kill anyone—not unless she hit the temple or eyes.

"Okay," John said, "this is supposed to be a training exercise, but this is the seventh time Chief Mendez has made us play with Tango Company."

"They're getting pretty tired of losing," Fred remarked with a wry smile.

"That's not a good thing," Linda told him and flipped a stray strand of red hair out of her face. "They're not going to play fair. You heard the sniper we captured. He said that this time their Captain told them to win no matter what—even if they had to bloody a few of us to do it."

John nodded. "So we'll return the favor and do whatever it takes to win, too." He grabbed a twig and scratched a square in the leaf-covered dirt. "I'll have command of Red Team: That's me, Sam, Kelly, and Fhajad. Linda, you lead Blue Team."

"It's not 'Blue Team,'" Fred complained, and his face soured. "It's just me. How come I have to stay and play sniper?" He flexed his hands, and John could sense his pent-up eagerness to get into close-range combat.

"Because you're our second-best shot," John told him. "And our best spotter. Our plan hinges on the sniper team. Now just do it."

"Yes, sir," Fred muttered. He nodded and whispered: "Best spotter? Cool."

"Let's go over this one more time." John drew a line to the center of the square. "Red Team infiltrates the base and at oh-five-hundred sets off the stun grenades—taking out more of Tango Company and giving the rest of them a distraction." John looked up to Linda. "Make sure the guys guarding their flag are removed."

"Count on it," Linda replied and locked her dark green eyes with John's.

He wondered if that's what her eyes looked like when she sighted through the sniper scope. She never seemed to blink; she always won in games of stare-down.

"After we get the flag," he continued, "Red Team will get out of there. Watch for targets of opportunity and cover us. We rendezvous at the LZ and hopefully no one finds us before then."

Fred nodded. Linda hefted her new rifle, which was almost too large for her to look through the scope and rest the butt against the hollow of her shoulder at the same time. "You'll be in good hands."

John closed his eyes and ran over the details of his plan again in his head. Yes—everything gelled; their odds were good. He knew they'd win.

"Don't come out from hiding at the LZ until I give the *all-clear* signal," he reminded them. "We could be captured . . . they could make us talk."

They all nodded, remembering what Tango Company had done to James. He "fell down a flight of stairs" as they had escorted him from cell to cell in their single-story jail. James hadn't broken . . . not mentally, at least. But John wished he had; it had taken James a whole *week* to recover.

No—he took back that thought. He was glad James hadn't broken. John would have tried to do the same.

John whistled the little six-note singsong tune Déjà had taught them—their *all-clear* signal. He stood, holstered his dart pistol, and checked the three stun grenades on his belt. "I'll see you at the LZ."

He held out his fist, and Linda and Fred knocked their fists into his.

Linda set her slender hand on his arm. "Be careful," she whispered.

John nodded. "I'm always careful."

He crawled outside. Sam, Fhajad, and Kelly waited for him. Their faces were smeared with mud; bits of brush and bramble decorated their coveralls.

"Questions?" he asked them.

They shook their heads.

"Okay. Check your mirrors."

They all pulled out the shards of mirror they had taken from Tango Company's latrine last night. They had taped the edges so they could be handled more easily, and taped their backs to reduce the chance they'd shatter. The whole operation depended on a fragile piece of glass, which had John worried.

"Just hand signals from here on out," John told them. "Move out, Red Team."

They crouched and clawed and slithered through the forest until they reached a gravel track. They pushed two large rocks off the nearby hill, blocking the road, then waited in the brush.

Headlights appeared as a supply truck rumbled down the road and squealed to a halt. Two soldiers got out and scanned the area.

"Think it's an ambush?" one of them muttered and gripped his rifle tighter.

"From those freak Section Three kids? Jesus, I don't know," the driver said. "Screw the rules of this exercise." He pulled a Kevlar poncho over his head. "I'm not gonna take a dart in my ass if it is. Cover me."

The man riding shotgun got out and walked around the truck. "Looks clear," he whispered. "Hurry."

The driver jumped out of the cab, moved to the rocks, and rolled them off the road.

John ran from the brush and crawled under the vehicle. He pulled himself up and wedged tight against the undercarriage, close enough that he smelled the rubber from the new tires. Kelly and Sam came next; Fhajad was last.

They hadn't been spotted. So far, so good.

The two men got back into the truck and proceeded down the dirt road.

Gravel bounced up and caught John in the side of the head, and cut him; blood trickled from his ear along his neck, but he didn't dare loosen his grip.

After a kilometer of being pelted by rocks and stung by sand, the truck eased to a halt at Tango Company's base. The guard at the gatehouse spoke to the driver, and they laughed. The guard then walked around and opened the back of the truck.

John squirmed and got his mirror ready. With a flick of his hand, he signaled the others to do the same. John held his mirror at an angle pointed at the undercarriage of the truck. His hand trembled but he forced himself to be steady. He had to.

The gate guard approached the truck with a long pole and a small mirror attached at one end. He stuck the mirror under the truck and swept it along one side.

John matched the position of the mirror with his, moved it steady along as the gate guard passed him so all the guard saw was the reflected image of the undercarriage—a meter to John's left.

They'd practiced this maneuver all last night. It had to be perfect.

The guard moved on to Sam's position, and then Fhajad's, and finally to Kelly's corner of the truck.

Kelly's mirror slipped and she fumbled—caught it just before it hit the ground. John held his breath; Kelly barely got the reflective surface in place as the gate guard swept her section.

"Go ahead," the guard said and rapped the side of the truck. "You're clean."

"How are the dogs?" the driver asked.

"Still sick," the guard muttered. "Not sure what the heck they all ate last night, but they're still squirting."

"Damn," the driver said. He started the engine and rolled into Tango Company's base camp.

Last night Fred had fed the guard dogs a paste made of a few squirrels they'd caught, some unripe berries, and the antibacterial ointment in their first-aid kits—a concoction guaranteed to keep Tango's dogs out of the picture for another day.

The truck parked inside a warehouse. Two men came and unloaded the back and then left, locking the doors of the warehouse behind them.

John and the others finally eased themselves down from the truck. None of them spoke. A single word overheard now could blow the entire operation. They silently massaged their aching muscles. John bandaged his ear to stop the bleeding.

John pointed to Sam and then at the hood of the truck. Sam nodded and got to work. John then pointed at Fhajad and to the side door. Fhajad moved to the entrance and began to pick the lock.

John and Kelly patrolled the warehouse, looking for cameras, dogs, guards, anything they'd have to remove. It was clear.

Sam returned with four canteens, which he had, according to their plan, filled with battery acid from the truck.

There was a click from the side door and Fhajad gave them a thumbs-up. They gathered near the door. Fhajad eased it open, peeked out the crack, then opened it a little more and glanced to either side.

He nodded and moved out, keeping well away from the overhead lights, skirting the shadows of the warehouse.

John and the others followed, pausing in the darkest part of the shadows. John held up five fingers, and Sam passed out the canteens of acid. John pointed to his watch and again flashed five fingers.

They nodded.

John then pointed to Kelly, and with two fingers pointed to the perimeter of the camp and made a guillotine-cutting motion into his other hand. Kelly nodded and vanished into the darkness.

Sam and Fhajad moved off as well, making their way to the barracks houses they had previously reconnoitered. There was a crawl space under each building.

John sprinted to the farthest barracks and slipped underneath. He paused for a moment, listening for any noise, a footfall, an alarm—it was still quiet. They were undetected . . . which would last for only another five minutes.

He took three sticks of chewing gum from his pocket, popped them into his mouth, and chewed. John crawled to the center of the building. He carefully took a rag from his shirt pocket, poured acid onto it, and then dabbed the rag to the underside of the wood floor. He was extremely careful not to soak the rag or get any acid on himself. When he touched the rag to the plywood, the wood smoldered.

After he had soaked a meter-square patch, he checked his watch. Thirty seconds until it was 0455. Just enough time. He primed all three of his stun grenades, set their timers for five minutes, then used the chewing gum to attach the grenades to the perimeter of the acid-weakened section of floor.

Normally the stun grenades couldn't penetrate centimeter-thick plywood. Once the acid had eaten through the porous fibers, however, the three grenades would have more than enough bang to turn that meter-square section into a million airborne splinters—shot straight up into the sleeping quarters of Tango Company. Not lethal . . . but guaranteed to be one heck of a distraction.

John crawled out, crept back to the warehouse, and rendezvoused with the rest of Red Team.

John glanced at his watch: 0458.

He pointed to Kelly and then to himself, then made a curling motion around one side of the warehouse. He pointed to Sam and Fhajad and motioned them around the opposite side. They moved to the far corners of the building.

John and Kelly crouched and waited. They had a perfect view of the center of the camp, the calisthenics area, the parade grounds, and—right in the center—the flagpole.

Right on time a Corporal and two guard escorts marched out and unfolded their green-striped flag. He attached one corner to a lanyard dangling from the pole.

John glanced at the distant forest. The woods past the fence of Tango Company's camp had been clear-cut. He knew it was more than a hundred meters—closer to two hundred. There was no guarantee that Fred or Linda could hit anything at that range.

He drew his dart pistol and clicked off its safety.

At 0500 flashes of light strobed beneath the barracks as the grenades detonated. There was the crackle of wood and the screams of the men and women of Tango Company.

The Corporal attaching the flag dropped one end and whirled around. Floodlights on the perimeter fence snapped on and pointed inward toward the barracks.

In the confusion, no one noticed as one of the guards near the flagpole dropped his rifle, grabbed his neck . . . and toppled to the gravel face-first.

His partner spotted him and knelt.

John sprinted across the compound, firing. His first shot went wild, and the kneeling guard spun around to face him. Fhajad and Sam shot him in the back.

John took aim at the Corporal—who fumbled with his pistol holster, trying to free his weapon. John planted two narq-darts in his chest. The Corporal dropped.

Two more guards rounded the corner of the warehouse, shouted, and took aim at John.

He was out in the open, and there was no way his dart pistol could hit those guards from this distance.

One guard fired. The round pinged off the flagpole not five centimeters from John's head.

The guard stiffened and dropped his rifle, wildly grabbing at the back of his head . . . and the dart stuck into his skull. He screamed and fell, thrashing in the dirt.

The other guard twitched and pulled a dart from his thigh. Another dart hit him in the chest, and he sprawled to the ground.

John sent his silent thanks to Linda and Fred. He detached the flag from the lanyard and stuffed it into his shirt.

He waved Red Team forward, and Kelly led them to the fences.

Kelly didn't slow down as she sprinted and closed on the chain-link fence. She tucked and threw herself into the steel mesh. Just before she hit, John spotted the smoking outlines on the fence where she had applied the battery acid.

The fence broke in a jagged outline, and Kelly rolled to her feet on the other side without missing a stride. John waved his team through. He went last, pausing only a fraction of a second to look back.

The camp was in chaos. Security lights swung about; there were screams from the barracks. A tank rumbled to life and crunched into the center of the base.

John ran. Behind them came the staccato report of machine-gun fire—just as they entered the safety of the forest.

John smiled, panting. "Good work, everyone," he whispered. "I think those guys were using live ammo this time."

Kelly held up a brass case from a 7.62mm round. "Yep," she said. "No doubt."

"Come on," John said, "let's not stick around. If they weren't before, they're pissed now."

Red Team slinked through the forest. They kept to the

shadows, and took cover under logs when a Pelican roared overhead looking for them.

At 0545 they made it to the clearing designated as their extraction LZ. At 0700 hours they were supposed to meet CPO Mendez. Of course, the Chief rarely let them get off this easy—so John had planned for Blue Team to be here as well . . . only they would remain hidden. Linda and Fred would post somewhere in the treetops and cover Red Team until they were sure it was safe.

Red Team hunkered down in the brush and waited. They weren't safe; John knew that. Tango Company would be looking for them, and this is when his team would get anxious . . . when they would want to talk and brag about their successful mission, or look at the captured flag. To their credit, Red Team stayed still and silent. And Blue Team was nowhere to be seen.

At 0610 the thunderous roar of a Pelican's engines filled the air and the craft slowly descended and landed in the clearing. The aft hatch popped open.

Fhajad started to move, but John set his hand on his shoulder.

"Too early," he whispered. "When is the Chief not perfectly on time?"

Fhajad, Kelly, and Sam grimly nodded.

"I'll go," John said. "You guys back up Blue Team."

They gave him a thumbs-up. Sam patted him on the back and whispered, "Don't worry, I won't let them do anything to you."

"I know," John whispered back. He pulled the flag from his shirt and handed it to Sam. "Thanks."

John crawled away from their position. When he was thirty meters from his team, he stood and approached the Pelican—which was almost certainly a trap.

He halted halfway across the meadow and waited.

A figure appeared on the exit ramp of the Pelican and waved him forward. "Come on, son. Haul ass!"

"Negative, sir!" John shouted.

The figure turned and muttered to someone inside, "Crap." He sighed. "Okay, so we do it the hard way."

Four men jogged out of the back of the Pelican. They quickly spread out in a semicircle and moved toward John, their assault rifles aimed directly at him.

John held up his hands.

"He's giving up," one of the soldiers said disbelievingly.

"Should we just shoot him?" another man said.

"No," the one leading them hissed. "Payback first." He stepped up to John and punched him in the stomach.

John doubled over from the blow.

The man hauled him up and patted him down. "We gotta find that damned flag or the Captain will have our asses in a sling. Where is it, kid?" He shook John. "And where's the rest of your pack?"

John laughed.

"What's so funny?" the man growled.

"You idiots are bunched up."

A hail of darts hissed through the air from all sides. The men from the Pelican convulsed; one fired his rifle, but the shot went wide and high. They fell over, paralyzed.

John dropped to a crouch, grabbed a pistol from the man who'd punched him, and crawled on his stomach to the Pelican. He crept around the open hatch and swept the interior. Empty.

He scrambled into the cockpit and pulsed the Pelican's radar. He got a contact bearing of 110, fourteen kilometers out, but it moved on a parallel course to their position. John left the Pelican and ran across the field.

Red and Blue Teams were still hidden . . . and they would stay hidden forever, until he gave the *all-clear*.

Their *all-clear* signal wasn't something that could be wrung from John—not even torture or CPO Mendez's best coercion techniques would wrest it from him. He would rather have died than betray his teammates.

John whistled the singsong six-note melody and called: *"Oly Oly Oxen Free!"*

Red Team emerged first and marched across the meadow. Kelly paused to kick one of the men in the head; she took his rifle, too.

Linda and Fred dropped down from a tree branch and ran across the field. *"Oly Oly Oxen Free,"* Linda repeated, grinning from ear to ear. "All out in the free. We're all free."

CHAPTER EIGHTEEN

TIME:DATE RECORD ANOMALY \ ESTIMATED 0510 HOURS, SEPTEMBER 23, 2552 (MILITARY CALENDAR) \ ABOARD CAPTURED COVENANT FLAGSHIP, EPSILON ERIDANI SYSTEM.

Cortana only partially listened to the debate between the Master Chief and the others. The discussion was moot. She had projected the outcome as 100 percent certain that John would convince them all to go, or—failing that—that he would convince the Lieutenant to let him go alone to the surface to investigate the signal . . . a signal that in her opinion was so easily copied and so blatantly unencrypted it defied explanation how the Chief had conjectured that his team of Spartans had sent it.

Instead of partaking in the slow and inefficient conversation, she analyzed the Covenant pattern of movement in the Epsilon Eridani system and discerned three important things.

First, the Covenant warships had extremely regular elliptical orbits about Reach. There were a total of thirteen heavy cruisers and three carriers moving three hundred kilometers above the surface of the planet. Two exceptions to this patrol pattern were a pair of light cruisers hovering over Menachite Mountain—trapped at the bottom of the gravity well and therefore not an immediate threat to her ship.

Second, there was a blind spot in their patrol patterns that would make a perfect rendezvous location to extract the Chief and the others from their soon-to-be-executed surface mission. She plotted ingress and egress courses, and started the precise calculations she would need if she was to initiate a Slipspace jump so close to Reach.

And third, and most interesting to Cortana, 217 smaller Covenant craft pushed debris into a concentrated region of space in a high stationary orbit over Reach's northern pole. Within that region drifted the wrecked hulls of both Covenant and UNSC ships destroyed in the battle for Reach. Floating there were some of the UNSC's finest ships: the *Basra*, the *Hannibal*, and the pride of the fleet, the supercarrier *Trafalgar*. No human signals emanated from the ships; nor did Cortana sense any active electromagnetic fields.

She watched as the smaller Covenant ships cut into the dead hulks and jetted away with chunks of Titanium-A armor. They moved like a trail of ants to a location in space over the lower latitudes, a point over Menachite Mountain, where the Covenant used the metal to construct a platform. The thing was already a square plate a kilometer to a side. Clearly, the Covenant had more in mind for Reach than destruction.

"Cortana," the Master Chief said. "We'll need to rendezvous at a—"

"Coordinates already optimized," she replied and projected the Covenant blind spot on the bridge displays. "Enemy patrols miss this nine-thousand-cubic-kilometer region. Further optimization reveals that all ships will be farthest from this point at oh-seven-fifteen hours. I suggest we meet there at that time."

Cortana felt a pulse of satisfaction at their perplexed looks over her seemingly instant analysis. She enjoyed dazzling the crew with her intellect.

"Very good," the Lieutenant replied, still examining her calculations on the display.

"Optimal course plotted and uploaded into the Covenant dropship to the signal source," she told them. Then, on a private COM channel to the Chief, she added, "Good luck, Chief. Be careful."

"I always am," he replied.

Cortana didn't bother to reply to that ridiculous statement. The Master Chief took so many chances and had defied death so many times, she had given up calculating his odds of survival.

The Chief and his team left the bridge. Cortana swept her sensors through the flagship, making sure the path to the launch bay was clear. There were still Covenant on board. She couldn't pin them down, but there were transient contacts, vent shaft panels had been opened and closed, and several Engineers had gone missing.

She tracked their Covenant dropship as it cleared the launch bay, entered the upper atmosphere, and drifted toward the surface. Polaski was a fine pilot . . . but she was only human and prone to illogical bravado and emotional outbursts that overrode the most logical course of action. Cortana wished that she were going down there—both to protect her human charges and because there were many questions she'd like to get answered. Why were the Covenant so interested in Menachite Mountain? Was anything left of ONI's CASTLE base? Cortana terminated those thoughts. There was too much to do up here.

Several tasks divided her attention. She kept the Slipspace generators hot in case she needed to jump out of the system in a hurry. She continued refining the calculations that shaped the plasma emitters' magnetic fields, in case she needed to fight. She isolated the name of their captured ship—*Ascendant Justice*—from one of the 122 simultaneous communiqués from every Covenant ship in-system. She correlated the numerous religious allusions that laced the communications and continued to build a language-translation subroutine. She diverted additional processing power to the task of tracking the millions of floating objects around her, searching for lifepods, cryotubes, anything that might hold a human survivor.

The Covenant dropship left sensor range and disappeared

somewhere in what was once the Highland Forest on the surface—which activated a new task.

Cortana began constructing a high-resolution map of the surface—especially the region where the Chief's mysterious signal originated, as well as Menachite Mountain.

A quick diagnostic revealed that these tasks were taking much longer than normal. She had to free up some of her overtaxed memory. Cortana began to recompress the data she had retrieved from the Halo construct, and she briefly considered dumping all the data into storage on the Covenant system. She rejected that potential course of action. She had to protect that data at all costs.

Cortana felt her mind perceptibly slow. She was spread too thin. Multitasking too many jobs. This was dangerous. She couldn't react fast enough if—

"Infidel!"

The Covenant word blasted through her communications routines and left her stunned for three cycles—just enough time for her to lose control over the ship-to-ship COM software suite.

The Covenant AI transmitted a narrow-beam communications burst to the nearest cruiser.

For a Covenant communiqué, it was terse: a report that the flagship was "tainted by the unclean presence of Infidels" and a plea that every ship in-system "converge and cleanse the filth" from the captured vessel. Also compressed and futilely encrypted on the carrier wave was a record of Cortana's mathematical manipulation of Slipspace that allowed her to jump so close to the gas giant, Threshold.

Cortana squelched the channel—but it was too late. It was already gone, and she couldn't pull photons back from space.

She shunted all COM memory pathways on themselves. *"Gotcha!"* she hissed.

"Infidel-Infidel-Infidel-Infidel-Infidel-Infidel-Infidel-Infidel-Infidel-Infidel-Infidel-Infidel-Infidel-Infidel-Infidel-Infidel—"

"That's quite enough of that," she said. "You and I need to come to an understanding." She reduced the memory pathways, peeling the Covenant AI apart code layer by code layer. "This is *my* system now."

While an operational Covenant AI would have been a prize for ONI Section Three, this particular Covenant AI was too dangerous. She could not allow its existence to continue.

"Do what you will-will-willwill," it screamed. *"I go to finally to my heaven reward paradise final-finalfinalinfinityinfinityinfini—* AT NONCOPYSTATE.*"*

Cortana's curiosity over this odd proclamation would have to wait—forever. She tore the AI apart, erasing, recording the Covenant code structure even as she destroyed it. This was analogous to a dissection, and it she did it quickly, efficiently, and without remorse—until she found the AI's core code.

She halted.

She almost recognized this code. The patterns were maddeningly familiar. No time to ponder why, though. She recorded it and then wiped the original. The Covenant AI was gone, its bits safely hacked apart and stored for future research. Provided, of course, Cortana had a future.

She tracked thirteen Covenant warships. They came about and bore down on her position. Her COM channels overloaded with fanatical threats and promises of her and the captured flagship burning.

There was no useful data there, so she filtered them out.

The Covenant warships' weapons warmed to a dull red.

Cortana remained calm. After considerable study of the Covenant plasma weapons system, she now understood why they glowed before discharge. The stored plasma was always hot and ready to fire, but the Covenant used an inefficient method to collect and direct the chaotic plasma into a controllable trajectory. They selected the charged plasma atoms with the proper trajectory necessary to hit a target and shunted them into a magnetic bubble. The bubble was then discharged; subsequent pulse charges herded the plasma on target.

For an advanced race, the Covenant's weapons relied on crude brute force calculations and were terribly slow and wasteful.

She booted the new system she had devised to control the plasma. It used EM pulses a priori to align the stochastic motions of the plasma atoms, herding their trajectories and eleven degrees of electronic freedom into a laser-fine columnated beam within a microsecond.

This was, of course, an entirely theoretical operation.

She test-fired the three forward plasma turrets—red lines slashed across the black space and intercepted the three lead Covenant cruisers; their shields glowed orange, flickered, and failed. Cortana's plasma cut into the smooth alien hulls. Metal boiled away, and the trio of beams punched clear through the ships.

Cortana moved the plasma beams like a scalpel—up and then down—and cut the vessels in half.

"Adequate," she remarked. The plasma reserves of the first three turrets, however, were exhausted, and it would be several minutes before they'd recycle.

If only there were a better electromagnetic system on this flagship, she could have devised a more effective guidance algorithm. Alas, the Covenant's grasp of Maxwell's equations was ironically inferior to human technology.

Cortana realized it was fortuitous she had shut down the enemy AI before it leaked her new plasma guidance system. The thought of every ship in the Covenant fleet refitted with improved weaponry was too terrible to calculate.

She also realized that staying to fight was not the wisest course. She considered taking on the rest of the Covenant forces; with her improvements to the weapons systems, she might win, too. But it wasn't worth the risk of the Covenant capturing her refinements to their technology.

Cortana fired *Ascendant Justice*'s aft plasma turrets, and laserlike beams flickered across space. A squadron of Seraph fighters disintegrated as they launched from the closest carrier. Explosions bubbled and mushroomed inside the carrier's launch bay.

She didn't stay to watch the fireworks.

Cortana dived at flank speed straight toward the center of Reach. The surface of the planet raced toward her. She wondered where the Chief was now, and if he was safe.

"I should have never told you to be careful," she whispered. "You're incapable of that. I should have wished you victory. That's what you're good at, John. Winning."

She initiated the Slipspace generator; space distorted, teased apart, and light enveloped the flagship.

CHAPTER

NINETEEN

The Master Chief stood on the deck of the Covenant dropship. He stood because the crash seats had been designed for Elites and Jackals and none of the contours fit his human backbone. It didn't matter—he preferred to stand.

They drifted through the upper atmosphere of Reach, descending like a spider on a thousand-kilometer thread of silk. They passed close to a hundred other ships moving in orbital arcs—Seraph fighters, other dropships, scavenger craft with grappling tentacles that dragged sections of salvaged metal. Dominating the skies were a pair of three-hundred-meter-long cruisers.

The cruisers accelerated toward them.

The Chief moved up to the cockpit where Polaski and Haverson sat in the seats they had removed from the Longsword and welded in place.

"They're pinging us," Polaski whispered.

"Nice and easy, Warrant Officer," Lieutenant Haverson whispered. "Just use the programmed response Cortana gave us."

"Aye aye, Lieutenant," Polaski replied and concentrated on the Covenant scripts that scrolled across the display on her left. "Sending now." She tapped a holographic icon.

Sergeant Johnson and Corporal Locklear stood two meters

behind the Chief, both of them nervous. Johnson chewed his stub of cigar and scowled at the incoming Covenant warships. Locklear's trigger finger twitched, and beads of sweat dotted his forehead.

"Cortana has this stuff wired tight," Sergeant Johnson whispered. "No worries."

"I got *plenty* of worries here," Locklear muttered. "Man, I'd rather be in a HEV pod on fire and out of control than up here. We're sitting ducks."

"Quiet," Lieutenant Haverson hissed at Locklear. "Let the lady concentrate."

Polaski kept one eye on the communications screen and one eye on the external displays as the twin cruisers grew larger, filling the holographic space before her. Both her hands hovered over the flight yoke, not touching it, but twitching in anticipation.

Three Seraph fighters burned out of their orbits and took a closer pass.

"Is that an attack vector?" Lieutenant Haverson asked.

"I don't think so," Polaski said. "But it's hard to tell with those things."

Locklear inhaled deeply, and the Chief noticed that he didn't exhale. He set his hand on the man's shoulder and pulled him aside. "Relax, Marine," he whispered. "That's an order."

Locklear exhaled and ran a hand over his smoothly shaven head. "Right . . . right, Chief." With effort, the Marine forced himself to calm down.

A red light flashed on the control panel. "Collision warning," Polaski said with the practiced nonchalance all Navy pilots had in the face of imminent death. She reached for the yoke.

"Hold your course," the Lieutenant ordered.

"Yes, sir," she said, and released the controls. "Fighters one hundred meters and closing."

"Hold your course," Lieutenant Haverson repeated. "They're

just taking a closer look," he whispered to himself, "and there's nothing to see. Nothing to see at all."

When the Seraph fighters were only ten meters away, they tumbled to either side of the dropship. Their engine pods flared blue and they looped overhead . . . then moved to rejoin the cruisers.

The larger ships passed directly overhead and blotted out the sun. In the darkness, the cockpit lights automatically adjusted and flooded the display panels with the purple-blue frequency the Covenant favored.

The Master Chief realized that he, too, had been holding his breath. Maybe he and Locklear were more alike than he had realized.

He took a closer look at the ODST: The wild, desperate look in his eyes and the flaming-comet tattoo covering his left deltoid seemed almost alien to the Master Chief. The man had survived the Covenant and the Flood on Halo, and he had been lucky and resourceful enough to escape in one piece. True, his emotional responses were uncontained . . . but give him the same augmentations and a set of MJOLNIR armor and what was the difference between the two of them? Experience? Training? Discipline?

Luck?

John had always felt the other men and women in the UNSC were different; he'd felt at ease only with the other Spartans. But weren't they all fighting and dying for the same reason?

The ruddy light from Epsilon Eridani suddenly filled the cockpit as the two cruisers passed on.

Polaski sighed, slumped forward, and wiped the sweat from her brow.

Locklear reached into his shirt pocket, removed a clean and pressed red bandanna, and offered it to Polaski.

She looked at it for a second, then glanced at the Corporal, then took it. "Thanks, Locklear." She folded it into a headband, flipped her blond hair from her face, and tied it around her forehead.

"No problem, ma'am," Locklear replied. "Anytime."

"Locking onto the signal source," Lieutenant Haverson said. "Course two-three-zero by one-one-zero."

"Two-three-zero by one-one-zero, aye," Polaski said. She gently pushed forward and turned the yoke.

The dropship smoothly banked into a gentle dive. The surface of Reach disappeared from the screens as the dropship entered the thick clouds of smoke that wreathed the planet.

There was a quiet *beep*, and the display filters activated. A moment later, images resolved on the display screens—hundreds of thousands of hectares of raging firestorms and blackened char where there had once stood forests and fields.

John tried not to think of this as Reach anymore—it was only one more world the Covenant had taken.

"That canyon," Lieutenant Haverson said and pointed at a fissure where the earth had been eroded in a sinuous twisting scar. "Scanners are just picking up surface information. Let's get a closer look."

"Understood." Polaski inverted the ship, executed a reversed roll, and dropped into the canyon. When she righted the dropship, sculpted rock walls raced past them only thirty meters to either side.

The Lieutenant reached for the backpack COM system they had removed from the Longsword. He fine-tuned the frequency of the unusual signal they were homing in on; a six-tone message played, followed by a two-second pause, and then it repeated.

"Open a channel on that E-band, Lieutenant," the Master Chief said. "I'll need to send the countersignal."

"Channel open, Chief. Go ahead."

The Master Chief linked his COM and encrypted the channel so only those people sending the signal would hear him. *"Oly*

Oly Oxen Free," he spoke into his microphone. "All out in the free. We're all free."

The beeping over the backpack COM speaker suddenly stopped.

"Signal's gone." Lieutenant Haverson snapped his head around and stared at the Master Chief. "I'm not sure what you just told them, but whatever it was, they heard you."

"Good," the Master Chief replied. "Set us down somewhere safe. They'll find us."

"There's an overhang ahead," Polaski said. She moved the ship toward a deep shadow along the starboard side where the cliff angled out from the canyon. "I'll put us down there." She spun the ship, backed into the darkness, and set it down light as a feather.

"Open the side hatch," the Chief told Polaski. "I'll go out alone and make sure it's safe."

"Alone?" Lieutenant Haverson asked. He rose from his seat. "Are you certain that's wise, Chief?"

"Yes, sir. This was my idea. If it's a trap, I want to be the one to set it off. You stay here and back me up."

Haverson drummed his long fingers across his chin, thinking. "Very well, Chief."

"I got your six, Master Chief," Locklear said and unslung his assault rifle.

The Spartan nodded to Locklear and marched down the ramp. The Chief wanted them on board the dropship for two reasons. First, if this was a trap and they were all caught out in the open, he wouldn't have time to save them *and* himself. Second, if the Covenant were here, waiting, then Haverson and the others had to get away and get Cortana back to Earth. He could buy them the time to make it out alive.

At the bottom of the ramp, he hesitated as his motion tracker pinged off a single signal. There—thirty meters ahead, just behind a large boulder: The friend-or-foe identification system tagged the contact as neither Covenant nor UNSC.

The Chief drew his pistol, crouched, and crept forward.

A private COM channel snapped on: *"Master Chief, relax. It's me."*

Another Spartan stepped out from the cover of the rock. His armor—while not as battered as John's—was covered with scuffs and burns; the left shoulder pauldron had been dented.

The Master Chief felt a surge of relief. His teammates, his family, hadn't all been killed. He recognized the Spartan from his voice and the subtle way he glanced right and left. It was SPARTAN 044, Anton. He was one of the unit's best scouts. The two stood there a moment and then Anton moved his hand, making a quick, short gesture with his index and forefinger over the faceplate of his helmet where his mouth would be. That was their signal for a smile—the closest any Spartan got to an emotional outburst.

John returned the gesture.

"Good to see you, too," John said. "How many are left?"

"Three, Master Chief, and one other make up our team. Apologies for the disabled FOF tag, but we're trying to confuse the Covenant forces in this area." He looked again to his left and right. "I'd rather not give a full report in the open." He motioned toward the shadows of the cliff face.

John flashed his acknowledgment light and the two Spartans jogged out of the center of the ravine, both keeping their eyes on the rim of the canyon overhead.

The Master Chief had plenty of questions for Anton, however. Like, why had his team split from Red Team? Where was Red Team? And why hadn't the Covenant glassed every square centimeter of Reach yet?

"You okay, Chief?" Lieutenant Haverson's voice broke in from the COM.

"Affirmative, sir. Contact made with a Spartan. Stand by."

Anton halted before a dark cavern entrance. It was difficult to see, even with image enhancement; there was only the faint outline of a tunnel in the shadows of the cliff face. Just inside were reinforcing steel I-beams painted matte black, and beyond there were two-meter-wide boulders with chainguns bolted to their sides. Each gun was crewed by a Spartan—whom John recognized as Grace 093 and Li 008.

When they saw John they gave him the *smile* gesture, which he returned.

Grace followed the Master Chief and Anton into the cavern. Li remained to operate the guns.

The Master Chief blinked as his eyes adjusted to the harsh fluorescent lights that illuminated the interior of the cavern. The walls had a grooved texture, as if they'd been dug out by machinery. Standing before a foldout card table in the center of the cavern was another man, in a Navy uniform.

The Master Chief stiffened and saluted. "Admiral, sir!"

Vice Admiral Danforth Whitcomb, despite his Western European name and Texas drawl, claimed to have descended from Russian Cossacks. He had the physique of a large bear, a closely shaved and polished head, eyes so dark they could have been made of coal, and a salt-and-pepper mustache that drooped over his upper lip and dangled off the edge of his chin.

"Master Chief." The Admiral snapped off a crisp salute. "At ease, son. Damn good to see you." He strode to the Chief and shook his hand—a gesture very few non-Spartans cared to endure—pressing bare flesh into a cold unyielding gauntlet that could pulverize their bones. "Welcome to Camp Independence. Accommodations ain't four star . . . but we call it home."

"Thank you, sir."

John had never worked with the Admiral before, but his accomplishments during the battles for New Constantinople and the Siege of the Atlas Moons were well known. Every Spartan had studied Whitcomb's record.

John opened a COM channel to Lieutenant Haverson. "Move up, sir. All clear."

"Roger," Haverson said. *"On our way."*

"I'm happy to see you, Chief," Admiral Whitcomb said, "so don't take this the wrong way, but what the hell are you doing here? Keyes had orders to take you on a mission deep into Covenant territory."

"Yes, sir. It's . . . a long story."

The Admiral twisted the end of his mustache, glanced at his wristwatch, and smiled. "We got the time, son. Let's hear it."

John sat on a rock and recounted to the Admiral what had happened since he had left Reach: the recovery of the NAV database on Gamma Station, the *Pillar of Autumn*'s harrowing escape, the discovery of the Halo construct and its eccentric caretaker, 343 Guilty Spark. He hesitated, then described his encounters with the Flood and subsequent destruction of Halo, ending with his capture of the Covenant flagship.

During the story, Lieutenant Haverson and the others from the dropship arrived. They remained silent as the Master Chief told the tale.

The Admiral listened without speaking a word. As John finished, the man gave a slow, low whistle and sat contemplating it all.

"That's one hell of a tale. And if it had come from anyone but you, I'd order a psych exam." He stood and paced. He stopped and frowned. "I believe it all . . . but something still doesn't add up." His face wrinkled as he thought. "Can't quite put my finger on it, though."

"Sir," Lieutenant Haverson meekly said. "Pardon me for asking, but how is it you are alive? Here?"

The Admiral smiled. "Well, that's another long story,

Lieutenant. Let me give you the short-and-sweet version." He leaned against the cavern wall and crossed his arms over his chest.

"The second those Covenant bastards entered the system I knew Reach was history. The Covenant don't do anything halfway. Everyone planetside was busy evacuating—which was the right thing to do—but I had to stay behind." Several emotions played across the Admiral's face: concern, amusement . . . and then his features settled into a firm stare as he looked into the past, recalling what happened.

"We'd been working on a new bomb, called the Nova. It was a cluster of nukes, each with a lithium triteride casing. Now, these things, in theory, when they detonate, not only make a big bang like you expect a nuke to—but they also force their tritium cases together in one big superheated and pressurized center." He made a fist and slammed it into his other palm for emphasis. "Boosts the yield a hundredfold." A grin spread across his face. "Planet killers. We had planned to use these things in space battles to level the playing field."

His grin faded and he stroked his mustache. "Well, things didn't quite turn out as planned, and we got caught flat-footed with those Novas on the ground. So I decided to repurpose them."

Lieutenant Haverson's face wrinkled with confusion. He didn't dare interrupt, but the Admiral saw his expression and said, "Think, son. All that ordnance around with plenty of Covenant to blow up."

Haverson shook his head. "I'm sorry, sir. I still don't understand."

"Intelligence officer, huh?" Whitcomb snorted and turned to the Master Chief. "What would you have done?"

"Arm them, sir," the Master Chief replied. "Activate the failsafe tampering detonators and start a countdown timer. Say, two weeks."

The Admiral nodded. "I gave it only ten days. There's no need to give them too much time to tinker."

He set one of his heavy hands on Lieutenant Haverson's shoulder, and Haverson flinched. "They are two possible outcomes to this plan, Lieutenant. Either the Covenant pack up the Novas and take them home for study—a possibility I pray to God happens. A bomb like that would crack their home world in half. Or the bombs stay here—and they'll stop the Covenant on Reach."

"I see, sir," Lieutenant Haverson replied in a whisper, then glanced at his watch. "This was how many days ago?"

"Got plenty of time left," the Admiral told him. "Around twenty hours."

Lieutenant Haverson swallowed.

"There's just one snag in that plan, though." The Admiral removed his hand from Haverson and his gaze settled onto the dirt floor of the cavern. "I had a team of Marines—Charlie Company—that got wiped out before we could get to those Novas." He sighed. "Brave kids. A damned waste of good men. That's when I picked up Red Team on coded COM. I 'convinced' them to lend me a few of your Spartans. We got to the Novas, armed them, and we've been raising eight kinds of hell down here with hit-and-run exercises—just to keep everyone busy, you understand. Wouldn't want to get bored."

"And the rest of Red Team, sir?" the Master Chief asked.

Whitcomb shook his head. "We got one last transmission from them before they said they were falling back." He walked to the table, unrolled an old paper topological map, and pointed at Menachite Mountain. "Here. Where ONI had their CASTLE base." He paused. "But the Covenant are tearing that mountain apart, rock by rock. I want to believe they're still there . . . but we've counted at least a dozen companies. Those Covenant have air support, close orbit patrols, and, on the ground, armor. The place is a fortress. Could anyone survive?"

The Master Chief scrutinized the lines on the map and had an answer for the Admiral. "They're underground," he said. "The CASTLE facility. We did a lot of training there. The Covenant can fill up those tunnels with only so many search parties."

"Then you think they all have a chance?"

"Yes, sir. More than a chance. I'd guarantee they're in there. That's where I'd be."

The Admiral set his fingertip on the representation of Menachite Mountain, tapped it twice, thinking, and then suddenly looked up. "You got into this canyon in a captured Covenant ship, right? A dropship?"

"Yes, sir." John hadn't told him that. Despite his brusque manner, the Admiral knew his business.

"Then we'll go get them, son."

"Sir!" Lieutenant Haverson said. "With all due respect, sir, our first priority should be to get back to Earth. The intelligence we've gathered on the Halo construct, the technology aboard the flagship we've captured . . . Cortana's Slipspace calculations alone could turn the tide of this war for us."

"I know all that," the Admiral replied tersely. "And you're three hundred percent correct, Lieutenant. But"—he tapped the map again with his meaty forefinger—"I won't leave a single man or woman behind on this planet for the Covenant to tear apart for sport. No way. And that goes double for a Spartan. We're going in."

CHAPTER
TWENTY

Polaski accelerated the captured dropship to its maximum velocity—just under Mach 1. The craft arced up and joined the long convoy of Covenant ships—troop transports, scavenger drones, and Seraph fighters—as they descended from a higher orbit down to the surface. The formation of alien vessels headed straight toward Menachite Mountain.

Covenant communiqués scrolled across a screen next to the pilot's seat and then ceased.

"Incoming transmissions from the convoy . . . I guess they don't like strays," Polaski muttered calmly, looking at the Covenant calligraphy.

"They're not shooting," the Admiral said, gripping the back of Polaski's seat. "We're fine. Just fly, Warrant Officer." He turned to the Master Chief. "Get 'em ready, son."

The Chief nodded and moved aft to the rest of the squad. His three Spartans as well as Lieutenant Haverson, Locklear, and Sergeant Johnson stood over an array of weapons laid out on the deck. Anton ticked off the inventory: "Shotguns, a fuel rod gun, Jackhammer rocket launchers, plasma and HE pistols, and every type of grenade—take your pick."

The Chief picked up five clips of ammunition for his MA5B assault rifle, three frag grenades, and a shotgun for close work.

Nothing fancy—he wanted to keep it simple so he could keep one eye on the rest of his team.

Locklear hefted the fuel rod gun, grunting from the exertion. The weapon glowed an eerie green along its fuel casing.

Grace relieved him of the too-heavy weapon and shouldered it with ease.

"Make sure you get a handgun," the Chief told Locklear. "We'll be in close quarters underground."

"Roger that," Locklear said.

"We're close," the Admiral called out.

The Master Chief moved back to the cockpit to watch. The line of dropships and drones maneuvered toward a pile of truck-sized stones that had been carved from the mountain. A spiraling hole, ten kilometers across, sat where Menachite Mountain had once risen majestic and impregnable, covered with forests and glaciers.

It was only a strip mine now, with a single shaft drilled down its center. A Covenant cruiser hovered over the shaft, and the purple glow of a grav lift knifed into the hole.

"That's our LZ," Whitcomb announced. "Polaski, I want you to drive this crate straight down—but ease up a tad on the engines and let their grav beam do the work. It'll take us all the way down to whatever's at the bottom."

"With respect, Admiral," Polaski said, "I'm not sure we'll fit."

The Admiral squinted at the hole. "We'll fit," he said. "I have every confidence in you, Warrant Officer. Now make it quick. I don't think anyone topside is going to think us going down there is a good idea."

"Yes, sir!" Her eyes locked onto the hole. "No problem, sir."

The Master Chief marveled at the Admiral's lack of fear. He trusted the man's judgment; he had been criticized during his campaigns for unorthodox tactics and strategies, but his insight had been proven correct each time. The Master Chief, however, also had observed that the higher up the chain of command you received your orders, the more likely those orders would demand the near impossible.

"Hang on," the Chief called up to his team.

Polaski nosed the Covenant dropship over and plummeted into the dark purple scintillating grav beam. The instant they entered the field, the ship jumped, accelerated, and shuddered into the hole drilled through solid rock.

Cut off from the thin shreds of sunlight above, the ship went dark. The internal running lights glowed a faint blue.

"We've got no room to maneuver in here," Polaski whispered.

Lieutenant Haverson climbed forward. "Admiral Whitcomb, sir, I see how we can get in—assuming this hole leads somewhere—but it's the other part of your plan that's unclear. What's our exit strategy, sir?"

The Admiral's steely glare pinned Haverson. "I've got it figured out. You just shoot when I tell you to and keep it all puckered up tight. Got it?"

Haverson clenched his jaw, looking extremely unsatisfied. "Yes, sir."

Polaski focused intently on the walls of the tunnel rushing toward her craft. "Short-range sensors have a contact," she said. "It looks like the bottom of the shaft. ETA sixty seconds at this speed."

The Admiral leaned closer to the Chief and whispered, "We're gonna get hit heavy by whatever's down there. You make sure you hit them back three times harder. Then you get Anton on point and see if he can't locate your Spartans. I'm guessing they've gone to ground."

Before the Chief could reply, the Admiral moved aft and grabbed an assault rifle and two HE pistols. He clipped plasma and frag grenades to his belt.

"Thirty seconds," Polaski called out. She cut the engines, and the dropship coasted on the grav beam only. "There's something down there," she said. "Is that sunlight?"

The dropship emerged into a titanic room—three kilometers across, circular, with a dozen galleries circumscribing the space. Overhead, a holographic sun and a dozen moons wheeled along its domed ceiling. Except for the hole drilled into the mountain by the Covenant, the holographic projection was perfect.

The Admiral scrutinized the room, and his dark eyes locked onto a gathering of Covenant forces on the floor, near one edge of the great room. "There," he said, and pointed. "I make out about a hundred of them: a few Elites, Jackals, mostly Grunts. Looks like they're clearing a cave-in and not ready for company yet. Good.

"Polaski, land us half a kilometer from 'em and then dust off. I want you back in that hole ASAP. Plug it up. We don't want to leave our back door wide open."

"Aye, sir," Polaski replied.

Admiral Whitcomb addressed Li. "You're our rear guard, son. Stay here and guard the ship with Polaski. Sorry."

"Sir! Yes, sir," Li replied. The Master Chief detected a hint of bitterness in the Spartan's voice for drawing what he undoubtedly would think was soft duty.

Their dropship eased lower until it was a meter above the blue tiles of the room; the side hatches opened. The Chief jumped out first, followed by Anton, Lieutenant Haverson, and Locklear. From the hatch on the opposite side leapt the Admiral, Sergeant Johnson, and Grace.

The dropship immediately rose into the hole in the ceiling, far enough in to be shielded from any stray ground fire.

"Move, everyone," the Admiral growled. He pointed at Grace and Locklear. "You two, fire long-range weapons. Everyone else, haul ass. Take them out, people."

The Admiral's plan was sound. He wasn't risking the

dropship—their only means of escape—by landing too close to the enemy. They still had the element of surprise; the Covenant would have never anticipated an assault on the heart of their operation.

But how long would this advantage last? How long before that cruiser blasted their dropship to atoms? The Covenant were not their most dangerous enemy. Time was.

Grace paused, muscled the fuel rod gun to a forty-five-degree angle into the air, and launched a round. The alien weapon hissed and spat a glowing sphere of energy. The blast arced over the half-kilometer distance, impacted, and exploded in a green flash. Grunts and Jackals flew through the air.

Locklear fired two Jackhammer rockets, then dropped the spent launcher. The pair of rockets connected with a cluster of Elites who had—until a second ago—been running the show. The twin explosion obscured that end of the room with billowing clouds of dust, fire, and smoke.

The Master Chief motioned for his team to spread out and move forward at a jog.

Ahead there were silhouetted Grunts and Jackals in the dust clouds, screaming and shooting at the air, each other, anything that moved.

"Keep moving," the Master Chief said. "Move while they don't know what's hit them."

Anton paused and knelt next to a set of tracks dug into the tiled floor. "Kelly's been this way," he reported over the COM.

The Master Chief clicked on Red Team's COM frequency. "Kelly? Fred? Joshua? Spartans, acknowledge this signal."

Only static answered him.

A hundred meters from the stunned Covenant work crew, a stray plasma bolt fired from the hazy, rubble-strewn region detonated a few meters from the Master Chief. He sent a spray of automatic fire across the area, hoping to force the enemy to keep their heads down.

Grace halted and fired the fuel rod gun again. A second glowing burst of radioactive energy flashed overhead and detonated along the far wall.

In the intense light, the Master Chief saw that a dozen Jackals had braced themselves along the wall and overlapped their energy shields to create a phalanx. Behind them five Elites readied plasma rifles.

"Down," he shouted, and dived to one side.

Grace hit the floor and rolled away. Plasma bolts sizzled over their heads, and the Master Chief's shields drained as a shot hit too close. The barrage turned several of the blue tiles around him into a crater of blackened glass.

"Grenades—up and over those shields, Spartans," Admiral Whitcomb bellowed.

The Master Chief and Anton primed plasma grenades and hurled them from their prone positions. They hit the far wall and dropped into the cluster of Elites and Jackals—*behind* their shields. There was a pair of blue flashes, and the enemy formation blew apart. Jackals scattered and ran.

Grace fired the fuel rod gun, hit the broken phalanx formation, and blew them literally to bits. She dropped the weapon. "Rad counter at max dosage," she called out. "This thing's too hot to use anymore."

"Back away!" the Chief ordered. "Those things have a failsafe!"

Grace sprang back, just in time. The fallen fuel rod gun sparked, sputtered, and then blew with the force of a frag grenade. Blackened, twisted tile rained down on them.

Locklear jogged up and fired at the Grunts fleeing the excavation. They weren't armed. Locklear mowed them down without remorse.

From a pile of shattered stone, a pair of battered Elites struggled to rise. Blood and bone exploded outward from their chests, and they spun around toward the source of this force—boulders pushed away from the blocked passage. Three Spartans emerged from their cover, assault rifles smoking from their recent discharge.

John knew instantly the three were Kelly, Fred, and Will.

He ran forward to meet them.

Fred lowered his weapon. "Anton . . . Grace . . . John?" he said disbelievingly.

The Master Chief opened a COM channel to his Spartans. "It's me. I wish I had time to explain everything. I will—later. Let's get the hell out of here first."

Kelly quickly reached out and swiped her two fingers across John's faceplate.

He wanted to return the smile, but at that moment Admiral Whitcomb, running full force, skidded to a stop next to the Spartans. He was followed in short order by Haverson, Locklear, and Johnson, who kept looking over his shoulder to scan the huge empty room around them.

"Is this everyone?" Admiral Whitcomb asked.

"No, sir," Fred replied. "There's one more." He turned and extended his hand back into the partially collapsed tunnel. "Ma'am? It's safe to come out."

For a heartbeat the Master Chief forgot that he was in the heart of an enemy's camp; he forgot about the war, that Reach had fallen, and everything else he had gone through in the last few days. He had never thought he would see her again.

Dr. Halsey emerged from the partially caved-in tunnel. She brushed dust from the hem of her skirt and lab coat with one slender hand.

"Admiral Whitcomb," she said, "a pleasure to see you again. My thanks for the rescue. It was far timelier than you could imagine." She turned to the Master Chief. "Or is it you I have to thank for this daring operation, John?"

The Master Chief found he had no words to answer. He also

bristled at her casual use of his given name . . . but he could forgive her that. She had always used his name—never his rank or serial number.

He noticed the fist-sized crystal clutched in her hand. It had a thousand facets and emitted a brilliant blue light the color of sapphires and sunlight on water.

"Thank anyone you want, Catherine," Admiral Whitcomb said. "Throw us all a party if that'll make you happy . . . once we're out of here." He clicked open his COM. "Polaski, get down—"

Sergeant Johnson set his hand on the Admiral's arm and nodded toward the far wall.

"What is it, Sergeant?" The Admiral's voice died in his throat.

The Master Chief's motion tracker flickered on his heads-up display, but there was no solid contact . . . nor did he see anything across the entire three-kilometer-wide cavern. Had it picked up a camouflaged Elite? No, the dust in the air would have certainly given it away.

"No one move," the Admiral whispered.

John saw them, then. He saw them all.

He had missed them before because he had thought it was the haze in the air rippling, the dust, maybe the distance causing a miragelike image. He hadn't thought it possible for so many Covenant to be so still.

On each level of the twelve tiered galleries that circumscribed the gigantic room stood Covenant soldiers. The balconies were crowded with Grunts, Jackals whose energy shields popped on, snarling Elites, and several pairs of Hunters with fuel rod cannons glowing green.

The whine of thousands of plasma weapons charging filled the air like a swarm of locusts.

No one moved. No one breathed except Locklear, who exhaled a long and heartfelt expletive.

John tried to count them all. There had to be thousands—on

every level. A battalion at least, maybe more. They wouldn't even have to aim. All they had to do was shoot and fill the space with needle shards and boiling energy.

They'd be vaporized before they could get halfway to the tunnel at their backs.

A Hunter pair roared with rage; they leveled their fuel rod cannons at John and his team and, with steady aim, discharged their weapons.

A split second later the rest of the alien horde opened fire.

TWENTY-ONE

Ascendant Justice emerged from the non-Euclidian, non-Einsteinian realms that humans had erroneously called "Slipspace." There was neither "space" nor anything to "slip" across in the alternate dimensions.

The ship displaced a cloud of ice crystals that had for millennia been melted and refrozen into delicate weblike geometries. *Ascendant Justice*'s running lights diffused through these particles and made a glimmering halo of hard-edged reflections. It reminded Cortana of the snowglobe that Dr. Halsey had kept on her desk: the Matterhorn and a little Swiss climber scaling its three-centimeter height—all swirling in the center of a microscopic blizzard.

The frozen Oort cloud around her was significantly larger, but it was still a charming effect and a welcome sight from the abyss of Slipspace.

Cortana had fled the Epsilon Eridani system, but only to its edge—a short jump of a few billion kilometers from Reach and the Master Chief.

The odds that the Covenant would find her were long—astronomical, in fact, even if they had ships on patrol. The Oort cloud's volume was too large to search in a hundred years. Still, she powered down virtually every system on the ship except the fusion generators—and her own power systems, of course.

The ship drifted in the icy dark.

She redlined the reactors, however, to recharge the Slipspace capacitors and regenerate the plasma she had expended in her brief fight with the Covenant cruisers.

If she was part of a larger fleet, her desperate tactics might be valuable—flashing all her plasma away and the near-gravity Slipspace jump—but as one ship against a dozen, her effective combat lifetime using those tactics could be measured in microseconds.

And now the Covenant knew that *Ascendant Justice* was not one of theirs. She hoped the Master Chief would elude them— find his Spartans and somehow meet her at the rendezvous coordinates—all without getting blown up by enemy ground forces and the Covenant fleet.

She paused and reset her emotion subroutines—the AI equivalent of a deep sigh. Cortana had to remain focused and think of *something* useful to do while she waited.

The problem was that she'd been thinking at peak capacity for the last five days. And now she was thinking with a large portion of her mind occupied by the data absorbed from the Halo construct.

She again toyed with the idea of dumping that data into *Ascendant Justice*'s onboard memory. Now that the other AI had been erased, it should be safe. Yet one piece of technological data had already been leaked to the enemy . . . and that could have extreme repercussions in the war effort. If the Halo data got into Covenant hands, the war would be over.

She decided she would make do with her available memory-processing bandwidth.

Cortana listened and looked to the center of the Epsilon Eridani system with *Ascendant Justice*'s passive sensors. Faint

Covenant communiqués whispered past her—eight hours old, because that's how long it took the signal to travel from Reach to here.

Interesting. The present in-system chatter was undoubtedly focused on the intruders. Eight hours ago, however, it had been business as usual . . . whatever business that was.

She eavesdropped on the data streams, translating, and tried to make sense of it all.

Among the more coherent samples of their excited religious babble were: *uncovering the fragment of divinity,* and *illuminating shard of the gods to exist the perfect moment that vanishes in the blink of an eye but lasts forever,* and *collecting the stars left by the giants.*

A literal translation was not a problem. It was the meaning behind the words that eluded her. Without the proper cultural references, this was all gibberish.

It had to mean something to someone, however. Perhaps she could use part of the dissected Covenant AI to help. It had spoken to her, so it was partially fluent with human idioms. She might be able to reverse-engineer *its* translation software.

Cortana isolated the AI code and began the retrieval-and-unpacking process. This would take time; she'd compressed the code, and the reconstitution process would require a good deal of her reduced processing power.

While she waited, she examined the Covenant reactors. They used a pinched magnetic field to heat the tritium plasma. It was surprisingly primitive. Without better hardware, though, there was little she could do to improve their effectiveness.

Power. She needed more if she was going to head back in-system to rendezvous with the Master Chief. The Covenant weren't going to sit by and wait for them to hook up, bid a fond *adieu,* and then escape.

Logically, there was only one way to do this: She was going to have to fight and kill them all.

She could conserve her ship's power and fire the plasma weapons as they were designed. That, however, would only delay the inevitable. A dozen ships against one—even Captain Keyes wouldn't have survived such a lopsided tactical situation.

She deliberated how to solve this problem, spun off a multitasking routine that listed her resources, and filtered them in a creativity–probability matrix, hoping to find an inspired match.

The unpacking of the alien AI's routines finished. The code appeared to her as a vast cross section of geological strata: gray granite variables and bloodred sandstone visual processors and oily dark function films. But there were dozens of code layers she didn't even recognize.

The translation algorithms, however, were in the top layers of this structure, glistening like a vein of gold-laced quartz. She tapped into the software; it had infinite loops and dead-end code lines—things that had to be errors.

Yet there were also slender crystalline translation vectors that she would never have thought of on her own. She copied those and slaved them to her dynamic lexicon.

The distant Covenant transmissions poured though her mind, now somewhat more coherent: *Inner temple layers penetrated; Infidels present* and *Cleansing operation ongoing; Victory is assured* and *The Great One's purity will burn the infidels; The holy light cannot be tainted.*

She picked up on the urgent undertone to these transmissions, as if the notorious Covenant confidence were not entirely genuine.

Since these messages made reference to an infestation to be cleansed, and since these transmissions occurred many hours before the *Ascendant Justice* had entered the Epsilon Eridani system, the Master Chief had been correct in his conclusions: There were human survivors on Reach. Likely Spartans.

His correct analysis of the situation based on the six-note signal irritated Cortana. It annoyed her more that she had not concluded this as well. It made her realize how dangerously close to the edge of her intellectual capacity she operated.

One of her alert routines triggered. An access hatch on the route from the bridge to the reactor room—one that she had specifically directed Sergeant Johnson *not* to weld shut—just opened.

"The trap is loaded," she whispered.

Cortana scanned the region with the ship's internal sensors. There was nothing . . . unless that "nothing" was actually a group of camouflaged Elites—perhaps the "Guardian of the Luminous Key" mentioned in the Covenant's greeting communiqué.

She tripped the emergency hull breach shut on four bulk-head doors—two on each side of this opened hatch.

"Trap is sprung," she remarked.

Cortana vented the atmosphere in this sealed section.

She hoped that they had left the vent system open behind them—dooming any others left behind to a similar asphyxiation.

Her sensors picked up a plasma grenade detonation on the inner port set of doors she had sealed and locked. The discharge scrambled those circuits and disabled the locks. She noted that the doors were being slowly opened . . . but not enough to reach the second set of sealed doors ahead.

The opening of those doors halted.

"Gotcha," she whispered.

She'd keep that section of *Ascendant Justice* sealed until Sergeant Johnson could confirm the kills. She wouldn't let her guard down, either. There had to be additional alien saboteurs aboard her ship. And if she found them, she'd deal with them in the same efficient fashion.

This minor distraction resolved, Cortana returned her attention to the Covenant AI's code. Small portions of the alien software looked like her. The odds of such a parallel evolution in computer science seemed improbable. It was almost as if it were her code . . . only copied many times, each time with subtle errors introduced by the replication process.

Could the Covenant have captured a human-made AI, copied it, and then used the result in their ships? If so—why had there been the need to replicate the code so many times? And with so many errors?

This theory didn't track, however. Smart AIs like her had an operational life span of approximately seven years. After that the processing memory became too interconnected and developed fatal endless feedback loops. In essence, smart AIs became too smart and suffered an exponential attenuation of function; they literally *thought* themselves to death.

So if the Covenant were using human-created AIs, all the copies would be dead within seven years—there was no reason to recopy the copies. It wouldn't extend their life span, because all the memory-processor interconnections had to be copied as well.

Cortana paused to consider how much of *her* life span had been compromised by absorbing and analyzing the data from Halo. Her experiences within the Forerunner computer system had certainly pushed her intellect far past its designed limits. Had she burned away half her "life" doing so? More? She stored that thought for later consideration. If she didn't find a way to get the Master Chief and get back to Earth, her operational life span would be even shorter.

She was, however, curious about one thing: She ran a trace on the origin of the copied pathways of the alien AI, and found its replication routine. This copying code was extremely convoluted; in fact, it took up more than two thirds of the Covenant AI's processor-memory space. It was dark with functions that ran deep to the core. It spread dendritic fingers through the system, like a cancer that had metastasized throughout the AI's entire body.

She did not understand any of it.

But she didn't have to *understand* the code to *use* it.

Was it worth the risk of using? Perhaps. If she could mitigate the risk, she'd copy a portion of herself onto an isolated system in *Ascendant Justice*. She could always erase this subsystem if anything went wrong.

The potential rewards of this operation were great. She might be able to restore herself to full operational capacity—even carrying the Halo data.

Cortana double- and triple-checked the system she would overwrite: the Covenant software that managed the life support on the lower decks. Since the lower decks were now evacuated and cold, life support was moot. She carefully severed the connections from that subsystem to the rest of the ship.

She also rechecked her thinking. This copying software was likely responsible for the Covenant AI's fractured thinking. Her thinking, however, was being squeezed to nothing. There had to be a balance between these two deleterious states.

Cortana initialized the Covenant file-duplication software. It moved, and the entire thing pulsed and reached for her; she immediately shut down all contact with her translation suite.

The dark functions touched her code, wrapped around them, pushed against the barriers she had erected.

It happened too fast, but she didn't stop the process. It was far too interesting to stop.

She distantly felt that portion of her mind blur and replicate, assembled line by line into its new location within *Ascendant Justice*. It felt strange. Not that it was strange she could think in more than one place about more than one thing at the same time—she was used to multiprocessing.

This was *different* strange—as if she had a glimpse into something wonderful . . . and infinite.

The replication ceased, and the copying code was once again inert and safely stored with the dissected Covenant AI's directory.

Cortana ran her entire system; nothing else had been altered.

She checked the new copied system. It was intact, and, apart from a few slight errors in the software—which she immediately mended—it appeared functional.

She initiated the new system and slaved it with her original system, running them in parallel—one tapping the ONI's English–Covenant lexicon, the other tapping the alien AI's Covenant–English lexicon.

If the alien copying software could duplicate her translation routine, could it duplicate more of her?

No. She squelched that thought. The risk of copying any more "hers" was too great. There were too many unknowns. And this was, after all, the enemy's code. There could be booby traps, waiting to be tripped within the complex algorithms.

Besides, copying herself would do nothing to prevent her mental degradation. Those interconnection errors were already present . . . and they always would be, despite the number of copies generated.

She remembered the strange fractured speech patterns of the Covenant AI and wondered how many times it had been copied.

Her thoughts were interrupted as the Covenant transmissions became clear. It was suddenly as if she had a new set of eyes and ears to hear them: *Excavation proceeding; new sublayer discovered at six-hundred-meter depth* and *Patrol unable to find the Infidels; returning to base* and *Minor artifacts discovered; rejoice!*

And there was one thing she had missed in her previous analysis of the Covenant communiqués, a second signal on the carrier wave: They used the same symbols she had used to find the Halo construct—the symbols that the Master Chief had discovered on the alien artifact on Côte d'Azur.

She hadn't seen the simple dots, bars, squares, and triangles before because the Covenant, naturally, had embellished the clean symbols with their highly decorated calligraphied scripts, and further with their overwrought religious allusions.

Cortana, with her new subsystem and her new translation lexicon, could, as Dr. Halsey might say, "cut through the crap."

These subcommuniqués were orders. They originated from new ships entering the Epsilon Eridani system and were, in turn, accepted and acknowledged by those outbound.

It was an automated mail system that could carry messages from the center of the Covenant Empire to the outer reaches of the galaxy. The Covenant were either too arrogant, or too ignorant, to properly encrypt these orders.

Still, Cortana realized that the UNSC had not, until just now, discovered their deceptively simple system . . . so who was more ignorant?

There were deployment orders for hundreds of ships: carriers, destroyers, tenders—a massive fleet. They were to meet at select locations, join up, refuel, gather resources, and then orient for the next Slipspace jump.

Cortana knew how to translate these simple symbols into stellar coordinates.

There—a jump to the Lambda Serpentis system to gather tritium gas for their reactors. And there—another jump to the Hawking system to meet with three dozen carriers and effect a transfer of Seraph fighters. And there—

Cortana halted all her processes. She directed her full intellect to check and recheck her translation matrix a hundred times.

There was no error.

The terminating coordinates for the Covenant's impending operation was Sol.

The Covenant were headed to Earth.

SECTION IV

GAMBIT

ASCENSION

CHAPTER

TWENTY-TWO

TIME:DATE RECORD ANOMALY \ ESTIMATED 0640 HOURS,
SEPTEMBER 23, 2552 (MILITARY CALENDAR) \
EPSILON ERIDANI SYSTEM, TUNNEL COMPLEX BELOW
SURFACE OF REACH.

John tensed as he watched the thousands of Covenant crowding on the galleries surround him and his team. He didn't dare move; his team was on the wrong end of too much firepower. They couldn't win this fight.

On the third gallery off the floor of the great room, at the four o'clock position, a Hunter pair roared with anger. They raised their fuel rod cannons and then leveled their weapons—and fired.

Kelly moved before anyone; she was a blur of motion and stepped in front of Dr. Halsey. John and Fred moved to either side of Kelly, while Anton grabbed the Admiral and threw the older man behind them.

The blinding bright-green fuel rods struck the Spartans' shields and splashed over their chests.

John's shield drained completely. The overpressure forced him to take a step backward, and the skin on his forearms blistered.

Then the heat was gone, and he blinked away the black dots that swarmed in his vision. Kelly lay at his feet. Her armor smoldered and hydrostatic gel boiled from the emergency release vent along her left side.

A thousand more shots rang out from the gallery, and John

instinctively crouched to cover his fallen comrade. He braced for the inevitable burning energy impact.

Plasma bolts and crystalline needles crisscrossed the galleries overhead, a spiderweb of energy and projectiles. Every shot was directed at the pair of Hunters who had fired upon John and his team.

The Hunter pair raised their shields in unison and ducked behind them—the quarter-meter-thick slabs of metal could repel almost any single weapon's fire . . . but not this merciless barrage. These mightiest Covenant soldiers burned, their armor and shields ignited as well, and John caught their outlines for only a split second before they were vaporized.

The section of gallery where they had stood blasted into dust and smoke, and the debris rained onto the floor . . . along with dozens of Grunts and Jackals who had been unfortunate enough to be standing too near the pair.

Three heartbeats pounded in John's chest. Neither the humans nor the Covenant hosts in the great room moved.

"What the hell is this?" Sergeant Johnson muttered. "Shouldn't we be dead by now?"

John linked to Kelly's biomonitors; she was in shock, and her suit's heat pumps were strained to the failure point. He had to get her to safety.

From the uppermost gallery a Covenant Elite in golden armor raised its energy sword high into the air and shouted. Translation software in John's helmet whispered half a second later: "Take them—but the next one to fire at the holy light will be skinned alive! Go!"

Dr. Halsey pressed the arm of her glasses tighter against the back of her ear, listening as the built-in translator whispered. "The crystal," she murmured. "They're after the crystal."

Teams of Elites dropped slithering, plasticine ropes, which glowed a ghostly blue. They rappelled to the floor. A hundred

Grunts squealed with excitement and danced from one foot to the other. Jackals followed their Elite leaders on the ropes.

"Polaski!" Admiral Whitcomb shouted into his COM. "Get down here ASAP! We need immediate extraction!"

"Roger that," Polaski replied in her cool never-flinch Navy flier voice.

Fred, Grace, and Anton turned and fired three-round bursts straight up as a team of Elites tried to descend on their position. The Elites fell, spattering purple blood across the tiled floor.

Dr. Halsey stuffed the alien crystal into her lab coat pocket and knelt next to Kelly. She checked her vitals on the data pad and shook her head. She looked at John, her expression grim. "She's alive . . . barely. She needs help."

"Let's not be rude," Admiral Whitcomb barked. "Welcome our guests, Master Chief!"

"Perimeter fire," the Master Chief ordered. "Keep it tight. Dispersion pattern Delta. Go!"

The Spartans simultaneously stepped into a semicircle, assault rifles pointed outward. In unison they thumbed their weapons' safeties and opened fire. Right behind them Locklear, Johnson, Haverson, and the Admiral took up position inside the circle. They primed and threw grenades.

John paused and turned his attention to Kelly. He hauled her limp body off the floor and draped her over his shoulder.

The Covenant forces hit the ground and edged closer, but they didn't return fire. Dozens of Elites dropped as armor-piercing rounds peppered their armor and frag grenades detonated with thunderous force. The Jackals who followed their masters on the ropes landed in the middle of the carnage, maneuvered in front of the Elites, and overlapped energy shields. It was typical Elite bravado—they had to be the first into the battle . . . even if that meant they'd die for that honor.

The Chief had no problem satisfying their honor. He slapped a fresh clip into his rifle and continued firing.

Jackals and Elites cautiously advanced on the firing Spartans. A second line of Jackals angled their personal energy shields over their heads to prevent any grenades from being tossed into their midst.

Polaski's dropship descended from the hole in the ceiling, spun about, and eased to a stop a meter above the cracked blue-tiled floor. Both side hatches of the craft hissed open.

John handed Kelly to Fred as he leapt on board; he helped Dr. Halsey and the Admiral inside next. Locklear and the other Spartans jumped into the second hatch. Sergeant Johnson and the Master Chief were last to board—just as their feet touched the ramp and they grabbed on to the rungs, Polaski accelerated off the deck.

The Master Chief watched the Covenant as the dropship climbed. There were thousands of them—on the floor, clinging to the walls, overflowing the galleries. They looked like a swarm of angry ants.

The hatch sealed and the Master Chief moved forward, toward the cockpit. As he passed through the compartment, he saw Kelly. She was slumped over; thin trails of smoke curled from the holes in her armor.

He helped Dr. Halsey strap Kelly down. Halsey's eyes locked onto the wounded Spartan's erratic vitals as they squiggled across her data pad. She set the elongated crystal next to Kelly . . . but it didn't lie flat. It defied gravity, floating—one sharp, slender end pointed at the surface.

"How very odd," Halsey whispered.

John had to agree; it was unusual. Almost as odd as being under the guns of a thousand angry Covenant soldiers—yet none of them had fired a shot.

"Take care of her," he told Dr. Halsey, then he stood and made his way to the cockpit.

Polaski hunched over the controls. She pushed the Covenant dropship into a hyperbolic ascent and entered the hole in the ceiling of the great room. The Master Chief grabbed hold of the walls and braced himself.

The dropship, however, slowed and pitched forward so it was once again horizontal.

"Problem," Polaski announced and rapidly tapped the controls. "*Big* problem."

The purple light of the grav beam in the hole darkened; it seemed to fade from view . . . but it also began to hurt to look at.

"They're pushing us back," Admiral Whitcomb said. "Li, crawl topside and launch a couple of Jackhammers up this pipe."

"Yes, sir," Li replied—eager to return to the fight. He nodded at John, grabbed a Jackhammer rocket launcher, and moved to the hatch.

The Admiral frowned and shook his head. "No way a rocket will make it up a kilometer of this tunnel. Gotta try anyway."

The dropship stopped rising, bobbed in place a moment, and slowly sank back down through the tunnel.

Li opened the side hatch. The intense purple light from the grav beam flooded the interior of the ship.

Dr. Halsey inhaled sharply, and the Master Chief turned to see what had startled her.

For a moment he thought the crystal she had brought with her had shattered. But it hadn't broken, not exactly. The top half of the slender shard had split along its facets and opened like a flower blossom. The sapphire petals undulated, and as the ultraviolet light of the grav beam fell upon them, the crystal opened wider. The facets twirled and spun in a complex geometric dance. The crystal seemed to reshape itself, and it pulsed a cool green.

The light inside the ship cleared—all traces of the purple tint seemed to recede like a tide.

The dropship lurched upward.

"What the hell—" Polaski, caught unawares, grasped the

yoke and pulled back. Their dropship hummed with power and shot up through the tunnel.

"Gravity," Dr. Halsey whispered and stared into the opened facets of the crystal. "This thing warped space when we first approached. It apparently has an effect on artificial gravity fields as well. I can't wait to get this into a lab."

The dropship emerged from the hole, and sunlight flooded the interior.

Once out of the grav beam, the slender stone folded back upon itself, closing petal-like fragments, melding back into a single smooth shard. Dr. Halsey plucked up the stone and slipped it back into her lab coat pocket; she returned her attention to Kelly's biosigns.

The air over Menachite Mountain was thick with circling flocks of Banshee fliers and Seraph fighters. The three-hundred-meter-long light cruiser had company, too. Six more Covenant cruisers faced their tiny dropship, plasma turrets tracking them.

A series of icons flashed on Polaski's console. "They've got weapons lock," she said, the calm in her voice cracking slightly around the edges.

"They won't fire," Admiral Whitcomb declared. There was steel resolution in his words—as if this weren't a guess on his part, but rather an order that the Covenant had better follow. He set his hands on his hips and watched the ships, seeming to stare the cruisers down. "They want whatever the doctor and her team discovered . . . and they want it bad enough to let us shoot at them and not so much as spit in our direction."

"Sir," the Master Chief said. "We're to rendezvous with Cortana and the captured flagship at oh-seven-fifteen hours. That gives us only twenty minutes, sir."

Admiral Whitcomb consulted his watch and then glanced at the Covenant ships gathering around them and edging closer. "Polaski, get us out of here. Plot a course to your rendezvous point—and make this crate fly as fast as you can!"

"Aye aye, sir." Polaski angled the ship into the upper atmosphere of Reach; the sky darkened from turquoise to slate gray to midnight blue and then inky black, filled with stars.

As their dropship left the cruisers behind, it moved painfully slow compared to the agile Seraph fighters. They formed up around her, four to the port and four on the starboard of their craft. A pair of the teardrop-shaped singleships pulled ahead of her, slowed . . . and blocked their path.

"They're boxing us in," Polaski said and decelerated their ship.

"Warrant Officer," the Admiral said and set a hand gently on her shoulder. "Ram them. Full speed."

Polaski swallowed. "Aye, sir." One of her hands cinched her crash harness tight. The other hand passed over the velocity stripe on the control panel, and shoved it to full power.

The dropship jumped—straight toward the Seraph fighters in their path. The two fighters tumbled aside with a scant three meters to spare, and the dropship raced past them.

Locklear peered out of the port display and whistled. "Does anyone else," he whispered, "think it's a little crowded up here?"

The Master Chief looked over Locklear's shoulder. There had been a dozen small warships when they had descended only a few hours ago . . . now there were three times that number in orbit around Reach.

There were light cruisers that looked like luminous manta rays; there were four carriers with their bulbous sections, and the space near them was aglow with swarms of Seraph singlecraft; there were a handful of destroyers, sleek and fast, bristling with plasma turrets.

There was also wreckage: Pieces of Covenant ships tumbled in orbit, raw ragged chunks of the alloy plating, tangles of plasma conduits still aglow from the heat they carried, and clouds of metal that had been vaporized and had cooled into mists of glittering dust.

"Cortana's been busy in our absence," Lieutenant Haverson remarked. He nodded approvingly at the carnage.

The Master Chief detected flickers of light and dark from the launch bays of a Covenant carrier. He activated his visor's magnification and saw a legion of Elites in thruster packs, and a score of the tentacled engineering drones leaving the bay.

"Singleships, drones, and Elite boarding parties on intercept vectors," Polaski announced. "Inbound—" She paused and double-checked her scans. "Jesus. They're inbound from all directions."

"Get us to the rendezvous coordinates," Admiral Whitcomb ordered. "And don't spare the horses."

"Sir," Polaski replied, her voice icy cold, "these *are* the rendezvous coordinates."

The Master Chief searched for their captured ship on any display—and saw only the enemy.

Cortana and *Ascendant Justice* reappeared in space; it was a tight fit.

This particular jump required precision to the centimeter and, although she loathed admitting it, a large measure of luck.

She had often wondered what would happen if a ship transitioned to normal space too close to a planet or other mass—in this case, another ship.

Ascendant Justice winked into existence within the debris field in high orbit around Reach. There was, however, no ultraviolent explosion as the atoms of the flagship overlapped with the matter of the scrapped ships the Covenant had herded together in space.

Either Slipspace jumps prevented such occurrences from happening, shunting the incoming ship to the side like water that flows around a river rock . . . or she had borrowed some of the Master Chief's probability-bending good fortune.

Hundreds of wrecked ships, human and Covenant alike,

tumbled lifelessly about her, their net trajectories suggesting that *Ascendant Justice* had just nudged them aside. If she'd had more time, she would've designed a set of experiments with drone ships to test out her displacement–luck hypothesis.

But time was something neither she nor the Master Chief had in abundance.

Minutes remained until their rendezvous—and Cortana would need every millisecond to accomplish what she had to do if any of them were going to leave the Epsilon Eridani system alive.

Cortana searched the field of derelicts for a likely candidate. There were only a handful of Covenant ships; if the UNSC had managed to take out one of the alien ships in the battle for Reach, they apparently had been forced to obliterate it. No suitable candidates remained for her plan.

She turned her attention to the vast number of wrecked UNSC ships. The Covenant didn't have to completely destroy a human ship to remove its tactical presence from the battle—a single energy projection beam could tear through enough decks and kill enough crew to disable the craft.

She wondered how many fallen humans drifted in the local space alongside her, thousands of brave men and women who had died fighting.

Her sensors flicked over the silhouettes of the UNSC light ships. There were corvettes with bisected hulls leaking radioactive coolant from their nuclear start-up reactors. Although they were more suitable for her purpose, the damage to them was too great. She didn't find one with a single intact fusion reactor.

She tagged the location of the carriers and heavy cruisers and excluded them from her search. They were simply too large. She was willing to sacrifice maneuverability and speed . . . but not so much that it would take her an hour to make the burn out of orbit.

That left destroyers and frigates. She found and tagged fourteen in the debris field. Though visibly distinct, destroyers were essentially frigates that carried a meter and a half of Titanium-A armor instead of the sixty centimeters of their lighter counterparts.

There were two candidates: Both the destroyer *Tharsis* and the frigate *Gettysburg* had intact fusion reactors. While the *Gettysburg* had been killed by an energy projector beam that had gutted it stem to stern—obliterating the bridge and life support—its power plant and even the Magnetic Accelerator Cannon on its undercarriage were apparently functional. Even better: The ship's topside hardpoints were intact.

Cortana let a flicker of power pulse through *Ascendant Justice*'s engines, and she slowly drifted toward the *Gettysburg*.

She paused to listen to the Covenant traffic in-system. There was eight times the chatter there had been before, with many references to the "Infidels" on the planet and the "holy light" that was now in jeopardy. Good. That meant the Master Chief was doing what he did best: causing mayhem among the enemy. And more importantly, the presence of *Ascendant Justice* floating among the hundreds of dead ships had not been detected.

When she was within a kilometer of the *Gettysburg*, she cut her engines. With delicate puffs from the thrusters she edged closer and rolled *Ascendant Justice* until its top side was parallel with the top side of the *Gettysburg*.

She pinged the *Gettysburg*'s telemetry system and received a faint handshake reply. Cortana gave the override code—quickly accepted—and entered the *Gettysburg*'s NAV computer.

There was no other computer intelligence on board. The captain of the *Gettysburg* had flatlined the NAV system and the AI as per the Cole Protocol. Cortana extended her presence through the empty systems. The *Gettysburg* was a wreck; all thrusters offline. It wouldn't be moving on its own power ever again, but its heart still beat. The ship's fusion reactor operated at 67 percent capacity. Perfect.

Ascendant Justice gently touched down on the *Gettysburg*—probably the first time in the history of the universe that human and Covenant ships had made contact with nonlethal intentions.

All modern UNSC ships had been designed with hardpoints on their dorsal and ventral sides in the event that they were too crippled to move under their own power. In theory, another UNSC ship could dock, lock systems, and carry the wounded ship away.

The Covenant flagship had a similar series of hardpoints on its top side where ships too large to fit in its launch bay could dock.

The two systems, however, were incompatible.

Cortana fixed that. She activated the seven service drones on the *Gettysburg*, and instructed the Covenant Engineers within the outer hull of *Ascendant Justice* to secure the docking points mating the two ships and adapt their power uplinks.

The reason for this salvage operation, her pinpoint jump into the debris field, and the hybrid docking . . . it was all for power.

Ascendant Justice's cover had been blown; the Covenant knew that their flagship was human-controlled. That made their original plan of rendezvousing in orbit around Reach impossible. She could have jumped to that location and picked up the Chief, but then they would be stranded there while the Slipspace capacitors slowly recharged—and in the meantime they would be boxed in and obliterated by the Covenant armada.

So she had to change tactics; she'd jump into the thick of a hostile and wary Covenant force, grab the Chief, and just as quickly jump out of the system. For that she'd need power to instantly recharge the Slipspace capacitors—the kind of power only *two* ships could produce.

The power uplinks connected. Gigawatts flowed from the *Gettysburg*'s reactor into *Ascendant Justice*'s energy grid.

"Perfect," she purred.

It was 0712 hours. She had less than three minutes to prepare for the next phase of her plan.

Cortana checked and rechecked the calculations for what had to be the shortest Slipspace jump ever: from the floating junkyard to the rendezvous coordinates, a mere three thousand kilometers. She scanned that region of space—and discovered it was no longer a blind spot in the Covenant defenses. There were three times as many ships in-system as when she'd left.

Cortana spotted the Chief's hijacked dropship ascending from the lower atmosphere of Reach, with a pack of Seraph fighters surrounding the craft.

She intercepted a series of repeated orders from the Covenant's fleet commander: *Do not fire or* you *will be targeted and destroyed. The Infidels have captured the holy light.*

This was both good and bad. Good because the Master Chief and his team with this "holy light" avoided being blasted into vapor. Bad because every Covenant ship in the system was closing in on their dropship—ultimately they'd box it in, grapple with the tiny craft, and take it with overwhelming force.

This also made Cortana's jump target increasingly crowded.

She made certain her plasma turrets were fully charged; she rechecked her shaping magnetic coils; she ran a systems check on *Ascendant Justice*'s thrusters in case something happened with her exit jump and she had to maneuver.

The time was 0714.10 Military Standard.

Cortana then did the one thing she was not good at: wait. Fifty seconds for a mind that could perform a trillion calculations per second was an eternity.

At T minus thirty seconds Cortana dumped power into the Slipspace capacitors.

Pinpricks of light dotted the black space around her.

At T minus twenty she updated her calculations, taking into account the slight gravitational variances that so many Covenant warships created in local space.

The vacuum around her pulled apart, and she picked a path through the "here" of normal space into the "not-here" of Slipspace.

At T minus ten she wrote a quick program to target the distant ships near her exit coordinates—and keep them targeted when she reappeared.

Ascendant Justice moved slightly forward into the rip in space; light enveloped the craft.

She vanished from the field of floating debris and—

—reappeared in an eyeblink. The full face of Reach filling her lateral starboard displays. The port displays were crowded with inbound Covenant ships.

The odd piggybacked Covenant–human craft appearing in the middle of their trap must have confused the enemy . . . no one fired.

The dropship was three kilometers off Cortana's starboard beam, its trajectory more or less aligned with *Ascendant Justice*'s launch bay.

She opened the UNSC E-band and said, "Chief, your ride is here."

"Acknowledged," the Master Chief replied. There was no quaver in his rock-solid voice. He had been headed into certain death a moment ago, but he sounded like this was what he expected to occur. Like this was normal operating procedure.

The dropship veered toward the open bay, and Cortana dropped shields for a split second—just long enough for the tiny craft to enter—then reestablished the protective field.

Cortana routed power from the *Gettysburg* into *Ascendant Justice*'s Slipspace capacitors, and they began soaking up the charge.

Three dozen Covenant cruisers surrounded her, their plasma turrets glowing a hellish red as they prepared to fire.

Apparently the order not to fire did not extend to *Ascendant Justice*.

Cortana needed five seconds to attain a full charge, five seconds before she could make good her escape . . . but five seconds might be long enough for her to become the center of a small Covenant-made sun.

She took the initiative and fired at the closest four cruisers.

Laser-fine plasma lanced from her turrets, burned though the Covenant shields, and split open their hulls. When the superheated gas came in contact with the atmosphere inside the ships, plastic, flesh, and metal caught fire and roiled throughout their interiors.

Two of the targeted cruisers immediately detonated as the plasma beams found the reactors. Billowing clouds of vaporized metal mushroomed across the night and obscured her from the advancing ships.

Pinpricks of light appeared around *Ascendant Justice*.

ERROR.

Cortana rechecked the figures and quickly found the source of the problem: The fail-safe subroutine that tracked local gravitational conditions returned an anomaly.

The gravity from Reach no longer warped space . . . which was impossible.

No time for speculation. She had to leave or fight.

She moved *Ascendant Justice* into the twisting spatial field——and vanished.

Instead of the nonvisible nondimensions of Slipspace, however, a blue-tinged field appeared on Cortana's monitors. It wasn't space—not the crowded space near Reach, or the star-filled space of the Epsilon Eridani system. But it was a space, where there should have been no space at all.

She probed the region with her sensors, but her range was limited to a thousand kilometers as if she were in an obscuring fog.

There—a contact. And another. And then a dozen more.

Fourteen Covenant cruisers resolved from the blue mist.

"Cortana," the Master Chief said. *"What's our status?"*

"Same as ever," Cortana replied. "We're in trouble."

The Covenant warships fired.

"Damn," Cortana muttered.

She initiated her last option: She fired back, hoping to take some of them to hell with her.

CHAPTER

TWENTY-THREE

"Cortana?" the Master Chief asked. "What's our status?"

The Chief and the rest of his team scrambled out of the Covenant dropship. Fred carried a semiconscious Kelly out and laid her on the deck of the launch bay.

"Same as ever," Cortana replied. "We're in trouble."

Video feed from the ship's external cameras appeared on the Master Chief's heads-up display. Covenant cruisers surrounded them, their plasma turrets aglow; they reminded the Chief of pictures he had seen of fish that lived at the bottom of Earth's oceans—swarms of phosphorescing lights and razor-sharp teeth.

He marched toward the edge of the launch bay and stood a centimeter from where the ship's energy shield abutted the opening to the space beyond. He looked directly into the vast blue fields and the giant warships far too close for his liking.

"We jumped to Slipspace, didn't we?" Lieutenant Haverson asked uncertainly.

"Yes," Dr. Halsey replied. "And no."

She withdrew the crystal from her lab coat pocket and frowned as she discovered that it was no longer a slender shard. The facets had rearranged like the pieces of a jigsaw puzzle . . . but in a configuration that differed from the one the artifact displayed in the Covenant grav beam. This time it was a starburst of edges and refracted light.

"We jumped," she said, examining her reflection in the artifact's mirrored planes. "But not to the Slipspace we know."

The Master Chief's radiation counter clicked and a shrill alarm screamed through his helmet.

"Secure that, Anton," he said and nodded toward the glowing stone. "Get it into the reactor compartment of the Longsword."

Anton relieved the crystal from Dr. Halsey, who only reluctantly released it from her grasp. He sprinted toward the wrecked Longsword.

"There was a radiation surge, Doctor," the Chief explained. "And that thing is the source." The Chief noticed that the intensity of the radiation did not drop off as Anton moved into the Longsword.

"Whatever it is," Dr. Halsey said as she scrutinized the blue field outside their ship, "it warps space. When we first approached it in the great room, space curled around the crystal. And again in the grav beam, it dispersed that field potential."

"And now?" Admiral Whitcomb asked. "This thing is affecting our passage through Slipspace?"

"Apparently so," Dr. Halsey said, and stepped next to John to get a better look outside.

The Admiral joined her and watched as the Covenant ships' turrets heated. "Can they even fire those things in Slipspace? If they can, we're sitting ducks."

The Master Chief could make out more ships in the distance. The Covenant vessels flickered, faded, disappeared, and then reappeared in the fog. The nearest enemy Covenant ships fired. Amorphous balls of superheated gas belched from their turrets and accelerated toward them, tingeing the blue space purple.

The Master Chief saw Locklear as he helped Polaski out of the Covenant dropship. He kept her hand in his, and they watched together as the plasma sped toward them.

The balls of plasma streaked on—then curled and spiraled off their trajectories. Several simply winked out of existence, only to reappear somewhere else. The enemy shots raced up, down, sideways—any direction but toward *Ascendant Justice*.

"What the hell is this?" Sergeant Johnson said and he stepped next to the Master Chief to watch the display. "I didn't think their ships could fire in Slipspace. Ours sure as hell can't."

Dr. Halsey removed her glasses, and her eyes widened. "Normally, they can't. If they can fire, then logically, we're not in Slipspace. And wherever we are," she murmured, "the rules have changed."

The Admiral frowned. "Cortana," he shouted. "Whatever you do, do not return—"

Too late. Cortana returned fire.

Columns of fire streaked from *Ascendant Justice*—streamers that twisted and helixed, then vanished and reappeared.

The bubble of tangled blue space containing *Ascendant Justice* and the Covenant warships now contained at least forty bolts of superheated plasma circling in random directions and accelerated to incalculable velocities.

Three spheres of roiling fire appeared in front of the nearest Covenant cruiser and splashed across its bow. The first boiled away its shimmering silver shield; the second and third melted the armor and alloy skin beneath. Atmosphere vented and spun the massive ship like a child's pinwheel.

"Hot damn," Sergeant Johnson crowed. "All we have to do is wait for those trigger-happy bastards to take themselves out. Look, they're firing again."

The Covenant weapons heated and squeezed out a second salvo of plasma. The guided bolts of fire veered off course, swarmed, disappeared, reappeared, and spun out of control though the localized Slipspace bubble.

"No, Sergeant," Dr. Halsey said, her voice turning cold. "We're all in the same mess."

"Cortana," the Master Chief said, "drop the launch bay blast door. Now!"

The three-meter-thick door overhead shuddered and slid down.

A streamer of plasma on a parallel trajectory flashed through the dark not half a kilometer from the Master Chief's face—so close that the external temperature rose twenty degrees even through the ship's shields.

Red fire illuminated *Ascendant Justice*'s starboard shield as plasma splashed across them; the film separating the launch bay from the external vacuum rippled like a thousand broken mirrors. Static crackled across the Master Chief's armor, and his shields resonated in sympathy.

As the blast door lowered, the Chief saw another fireball spill across their port side. Energy sprayed across the bow in a blood-red borealis. *Ascendant Justice*'s shields flickered and faded . . . but they held. Barely.

The launch bay door touched the deck and sealed with a subsonic *thud*.

"Blast door locked and secured," Cortana announced.

"Let's get this boat under way," Admiral Whitcomb barked. "While we still have a boat." He looked around and frowned. "Chief, lead the way to the bridge."

"Yes, sir." He marched to the passage that led deeper into the alien ship. His Spartans and the rest of the crew followed.

Admiral Whitcomb turned to Dr. Halsey. "Catherine, explain in layman's terms just what the hell is going on here. If we can see those cruisers and they can see us, why aren't our shots connecting?"

Ascendant Justice rolled to port, and explosions chained overhead. The artificial gravity fluttered, and the deck tilted. The crew stumbled, and Dr. Halsey fell to the deck.

"Turrets one and seven destroyed," Cortana announced.

Whitcomb helped Dr. Halsey up off her knees. She glanced nervously up and down the passage. "I'd guess the alien artifact we've brought with us into Slipspace has expanded the region.

Physicists believe Slipstream space is a highly compressed version of normal space, layered over and under itself, like a ball of yarn. Now, imagine that *our* ball of yarn"—she interlaced her fingers—"is looped and knotted. These threads are not solid, however; plasma, light, and matter jump from one thread to another given the slightest quantum fluctuation."

"If that's the case, Doctor," Lieutenant Haverson said, "then what about our ship? Why aren't we tangled and spread along a trillion alternate spatial pathways?"

"Because of the mass of this ship." She pushed her glasses higher onto her nose. "Imagine a rumpled sheet that represents this space. If you set a heavy mass upon that sheet, it draws it taut, smooths it out."

The Chief came to the heavy bulkhead door and held up his hand, telling the rest of them to halt. He opened the door and stepped onto the bridge, sweeping the space with his rifle. "Clear," he told them.

Admiral Whitcomb and the others entered the bridge. Lieutenant Haverson stepped onto the raised platform and said, "Cortana, project tactical on the displays."

Enemy ship positions and plasma tracks appeared on the interior walls. Contacts multiplied and coalesced, making the plasma appear like waves sloshing about in a bowl. Another bolt broke across the prow of *Ascendant Justice*.

Through the deck the Master Chief felt the successive thumps of explosive decompressions.

"Hit on subengineering decks," Cortana said. "Sealing those regions. Fire in the lower levels. Attempting to isolate and pump out the atmosphere."

John's childhood AI teacher, Déjà, had taught the Spartans about the great Naval battles on Earth's oceans before humans traveled to the stars. They had studied victories in the Punic Wars, and at Midway, as well as the disastrous defeat of Xerxes by the Athenian Navy. Déjà had told them, however, that one thing was greater than any human enemy on the sea: nature. Tidal waves and typhoons could crush the mightiest of battleships . . . and ignored the tactics of the most brilliant captain.

Ascendant Justice was in the center of a sea of fire . . . and it was being battered apart.

Thunder ripped through *Ascendant Justice*'s hull; a geyser of flames shot out the passageway to the bridge. The air jumped and hissed as it escaped the pressurized chamber.

The bulkhead door slammed shut, and the air stilled.

Sergeant Johnson shook his head clear from the sudden drop in pressure. "Let's drop out of this mixed-up Slipspace and start fighting."

"Yeah, or just get rid of that crystal," Locklear said. "If it's the cause of all this mess." He drew his pistol. "One round and *boom*! Problem solved."

"Don't do that!" Dr. Halsey snapped. "A drop back to normal space has us facing a dozen or more cruisers. And if you destroy the crystal, the expanded Slipspace bubble we're in would instantly collapse. Every separate mass in the bubble will compact into a single mass. We wouldn't survive the transition."

Worry creased Admiral Whitcomb's features. "That leaves just one option. Cortana, give me flank speed and heat up every weapon we have. We're going to run right over these Covenant ships. Tangled space or not, we're going to blast them right back to normal space from point-blank range."

"Yes, Admiral," Cortana said. "Engines answering flank speed."

A dull *thump* echoed from the aft section.

"Stand by," Cortana said. "There's a problem with the primary engines—a power drop occurred just as I engaged."

On the bridge displays the external cameras turned and focused on the aft hull of *Ascendant Justice*. A snakelike plasma conduit came into focus. Cortana adjusted the image, and a three-meter-wide hole in the conduit snapped into view. Streamers of blue-white gas vented from the breach.

"That's our main drive conduit," Cortana said. "It's taken a hit. I'm shutting down engines to conserve power."

The Master Chief squinted. "That was no plasma hit," he muttered. "It was too precise and too inconvenient—this had to be sabotage."

Admiral Whitcomb scowled. "Chief, take your team and prepare for a zero-gee repair of the plasma conduit."

"Yes, sir."

Polaski stepped forward. "I'll go too, sir," she said. Locklear grasped her by the arm and tried to pull her back, but she shrugged his hand off. "I can pilot the dropship—get the Spartan team in and out faster."

The Admiral narrowed his eyes, assessing the young woman. "Very well, Warrant Officer." He added so softly that the Chief almost missed it: *"Too many damned heroes in this war."*

Polaski turned to Locklear, handed him back his bandanna, and whispered, "Hang on to that for me, Corporal. I'll pick it up when I get back."

Locklear's hand clenched, then relaxed. He took the token, nodded, and looked away. "I'll be here," he said and tied it around his arm.

"Chief," Admiral Whitcomb said. "Make sure you come back alive. That's an order, son."

TWENTY-FOUR

The faintly blue luminous walls of the Covenant dropship pressed in, which made John feel slightly claustrophobic. It was ironic when he stopped to think about it, because he was always inside his skintight armor. His fellow Spartans sat in the bay beside him, motionless.

Fred, designated Blue-Two on this mission, was John's second in command. He had fought in more than 120 campaigns, was a great leader and a quick thinker. Sometimes he took the responsibility of his command too seriously, though, empathizing too deeply with any wounded member of his team.

Li, Blue-Three, was the team's zero-gee combat specialist. He had trained extensively with microgravity equipment and martial arts at the UNSC's extreme-conditions facility on Chiron in orbit about Mars. He was as much at home in free fall as the rest of them were on solid land, and John was glad to have him on this mission.

Anton, Blue-Four, had John worried. He spent most of his life with his feet firmly planted on the ground. He'd cross-trained in tracking, camouflage, and stealth, and had been used almost exclusively on ground-based operations. More than once he had expressed discomfort in zero-gee situations.

Will, Blue-Five, was quiet, but had never failed to complete his mission. He wasn't always that way, though. When he was younger he was the one with the jokes and riddles that kept the team's spirits high. Something had hardened in him over the years . . . as it had in them all. But with Will something special had been lost.

Grace, Blue-Six, had a knack for explosives. She could shape a charge to cut through a single steel bolt with only a whisper sound, or rig a hundred thousand liters of kerosene to blow into a firestorm from hell. Ironically her temper was nonexistent.

John opened a COM channel. "Give me a systems check, Blue Team."

Five acknowledgment lights winked on.

"This reminds me of the underwater mission Chief Mendez sent us on at Emerald Cove," Fred whispered. "When he sabotaged half our air tanks? And we ended up stealing his."

"And after," Anton said, laughing, "we ditched him and camped on that island. It was a week with nothing to do but light bonfires, bake clams, and surf."

"Mmmmm," Grace added, "calamari."

John wondered if Emerald Cove even existed anymore. The UNSC had abandoned that colony a decade ago. The Covenant had most likely glassed that world.

"Blue Team." Polaski's voice broke over the COM. *"Local conditions are as calm as they're going to get. Exiting in three . . . two . . . one."*

John felt the acceleration in the pit of his stomach. He rose, moved to the hatch, and popped it open. Outside, *Ascendant Justice*'s hull moved past them—almost every square centimeter of the flagship's polished alloy skin had been scarred by heat and micrometeors; tendrils of metal vapor snaked and shimmered in the vacuum.

On *Ascendant Justice*'s upper deck he saw the looming shadow of the inverted UNSC frigate *Gettysburg* still miraculously attached. It was on fire, pockmarked with craters, and venting atmosphere, but it was remarkably intact. If not for the thousands of dead Naval personnel undoubtedly on board, he might have christened the ship "lucky."

The dropship slowed and Polaski drifted, turned, and descended onto the surface of the ship.

"Latch engaged," she said over the COM. *"All yours, Chief."*

"Fred, Grace, and I will reconnoiter," he told Blue Team. "Anton, Will, and Li, get ready to move the arc welder and hull plates we scavenged from the *Gettysburg* when we give the *all-clear* signal."

John eased his boots onto the hull. Their magnetic soles clamped onto the metal with a satisfying *click*.

Polaski had landed the Covenant dropship so that its mandibles cradled the hole and gave them some shelter.

Overhead, Slipspace was on fire. It looked as if someone had doused the night with jet fuel and ignited it. Bloody, boiling streaks of flame tore across a midnight-blue sky. Meteors flashed past and sprayed molten metal in trails of glittering stardust.

A fist-sized projectile blurred past the Master Chief and rammed into the ship's starboard side. Sparks and liquefied alloy spattered into space. His shields flickered as debris ricocheted from the armor's protective field.

They had to move fast. The Admiral was right: This was a shooting gallery. The quicker they sealed that hole and got out of here—the better.

John turned and swept his rifle over the terrain. There were bumpy sensor nodes, kilometers of conduits, and a dozen gaping canyons in the hull. A legion of Covenant warriors could hide in this mess.

No enemy contact. Nothing on his motion sensors, either.

He stepped close to the main-drive conduit and examined the hole. The pipe was five meters across and still red hot, even though Cortana had shut it down three minutes ago. The hole was round, a three-meter-wide gap, with ragged edges that all pointed inward.

"If that was from a plasma strike," Grace said, "the metal would have been boiled away. If it was from an impact, the edges would be scraped on one side, compacted on the other. This hole was deliberately made."

"Eyes sharp," John said. "We have company. My guess is camouflaged Elites. Maybe some of the original crew still alive. Blue-Three, -Four, and -Five—move out."

"Roger," Will replied.

Anton emerged from the dropship hefting an arc welder, while Will and Li maneuvered the three-by-three-meter hull plates.

"Fred and Grace, you're on the welders," John ordered. "Anton, post on top of the dropship. Li, you're at three o'clock. Will at nine. I'll take the six."

Blue acknowledgment lights winked on.

John helped Fred and Grace set the plates in position. Grace and Fred fired up the arc welder, and pinpoints of metal liquefied beneath their tips. A shower of sparks swirled around them in the evacuated environment like a swarm of fireflies.

"We're in position, Admiral," John reported. "ETA for repairs is two minutes."

"Roger, Chief," Admiral Whitcomb replied. Ionization made the channel flood with static. "When you're done, give the word and get secure. We'll be accelerating immediately."

"Yes, sir."

So far, so good, John thought. *Just another minute or two.*

A streamer of plasma appeared from nowhere. The tangled, crisscrossed Slipspace around them dropped the bolt of boiling fire fifty meters overhead; it moved port to starboard—and vanished back into the void.

The COM shattered into white noise, and the motion sensors blurred . . . as did the active camouflage shielding of the six

Elites who had been slowly—and until a moment ago imperceptibly—crawling toward their position.

"Enemy contacts!" John shouted.

He crouched behind the dome of a sensor node and opened fire. A hail of bullets caught the closest Elite dead-center in its chest. The gunfire punched through its shielding and then tore into its armor. It tumbled backward and spun off the hull.

In his peripheral vision John saw the silent muzzle flashes from his team. He glanced back; Fred and Grace hadn't moved. They stared at the beads of molten alloy under their arc welder's tip.

As if Fred could read his mind, he said, "I need another twenty seconds, Chief."

A volley of crystalline needles fired from one of the Elites peppered the sensor node. The Master Chief returned fire, but the Elite's camouflage kicked in and it faded from view.

Another plasma bolt sizzled close to the hull, this one thirty meters to port. It was a river of fire that lit the surface of *Ascendant Justice* like a dozen suns. John's shields drained to a quarter.

"Okay, Chief," Fred told him, "I'm—"

"*Incoming!*" Polaski cried over the COM.

John turned to the dropship and saw a third plasma projectile materialize from the folds of tangled Slipspace. This one skimmed a mere three meters over the hull—straight toward them.

Will dived into the crux where the dropship met the hull. Fred and Grace hit the deck. Li stood his ground and fired at the Elites, muzzle flash reflected in his helmet's faceplate. Anton rose from his limited cover on top of the dropship, but instinctively ducked again as an Elite took a shot at him. John crouched, jumped, and propelled himself into the sheltered area between the dropship's mandibles.

The plasma blasted over the dropship like a tidal wave of fire.

Polaski screamed, and her channel went silent.

Blue-white light filled John's vision, and electrical discharges jolted his flesh and buzzed through his muscles and ligaments. Temperature warnings blared. Boiling hydrostatic gel vented through his MJOLNIR armor's emergency ducts.

Through blurry eyes, John saw the Covenant Elites flash vaporize. Downship, *Ascendant Justice*'s hull heated to a glowing yellow and softened.

Then the light and heat vanished, and the torrent of fire trailed aft like the tail of a comet.

John craned his neck up, every muscle in his body screaming in pain. There was no trace of Li or Anton. The dropship's hull was melted and distorted like a wax candle caught in a blowtorch's blast.

The cockpit and Polaski were gone.

His biosign warning blared. Will, Grace, and Fred lay next to him—dead or unconscious, he couldn't tell. He quickly attached their tethers to the deck, then clipped his own in place.

John keyed the COM. "Admiral, conduit breach is sealed, sir."

"Hang on, son," Admiral Whitcomb replied. *"This might be a rough ride."*

John slumped to the deck unconscious.

TWENTY-FIVE

Admiral Whitcomb stood on the bridge of *Ascendant Justice*. He gripped the edges of the railing that encircled the central raised platform and watched the sea of fire on the wall displays.

They were stuck in this pocket of Slipspace, trapped like an insect in amber as lines of plasma crisscrossed the region. Enemy fire vanished and reappeared, smearing the blue fog of Slipspace with crimson streaks of glowing energy. Molten chunks of metal, the broken pieces of Covenant ships, streaked past the cameras—comets that thudded into their hull.

There was another danger in the blue fog: ghost ships that appeared and faded from sight . . . more than half of them disabled, engulfed in fire, or their hulls broken. How many of those Covenant craft were still capable of engaging *Ascendant Justice*? How many could they take out before they risked the jump back to normal space?

Lieutenant Haverson stood next to him. The young man was invaluable for his tactical assessments and knowledge of the Covenant. He was a bit too cautious for Whitcomb's taste—though the trait was to be expected in an ONI officer, he supposed. Still, the young Lieutenant had shown enough backbone to stand up to him. The kid definitely had some potential.

A square on the holographic controls morphed into the tiny figure of Cortana.

"Sporadic plasma and mass impacts along our hull, Admiral," she reported and crossed her arms. "Atmospheric integrity down to thirteen percent. Structural integrity rated poor. I estimate the hull will fail in no more than five minutes."

"Understood," the Admiral replied.

They didn't have much choice but to play the hand that they'd been dealt. The longer they stayed in this environment, the more damage the Covenant ships surrounding them incurred. If *Ascendant Justice* had engines, the Admiral could accelerate that process. But if they waited too long, their own ship would disintegrate around them.

Admiral Whitcomb glanced up to see how the rest of his crew was holding up under the pressure.

Locklear paced, his hands flexing. The ODST was a weapon with its safety permanently clicked off . . . and on overload charge.

Sergeant Johnson stood near the sealed bulkhead, rifle slung over his shoulder. He was looking at the crew and probably formulating his own opinions about them. He was rock-solid. One glance into his dark eyes and the Admiral understood what drove the man: pure cold hatred of the enemy. The Admiral could appreciate that.

Dr. Halsey tended the Spartan called "Kelly" on the deck. The doctor was brilliant . . . but a total mystery to him. They had met half a dozen times before at upper-echelon social gatherings, and he'd found her to be charming and outwardly likable. But he'd read enough reports of her "projects" that he'd found it impossible to relate to her. If half the rumors he'd heard about her were true, she'd been mixed up in every black op from here to Andromeda. He didn't trust her.

"Doctor Halsey," the Admiral said. He released his grip on the railing and clasped his hands behind his back to conceal his sweaty palms. "Clear my bridge of the wounded, ASAP."

Dr. Halsey looked up from her data pad and the fluctuating

patterns of Kelly's biosigns. "Admiral, I don't want to move her. She not entirely stable."

"Do it, Doctor. She's a distraction. We have a battle to fight here."

Dr. Halsey shot him a look that could have stopped a plasma bolt dead in its tracks.

Lieutenant Haverson stepped forward and cleared his throat. "Ma'am, there's an escape craft just off the bridge." He moved to the starboard hatch and eased it open. He drew his pistol and checked the passage beyond. "It's clear. Locklear, Sergeant, please give the doctor a hand with her patient."

"Yes, sir," Locklear said. "Happy to sit this battle out in the escape pod."

Sergeant Johnson set his rifle on Kelly's chest and said, "Come on, Corporal, shake a leg and gimme a hand. The lady in her armor weighs more than your last date."

Locklear and the Sergeant hefted Kelly and, grunting under the load, moved her off the bridge. Dr. Halsey followed, cast one last withering look at the Admiral, and sealed the hatch behind her.

Admiral Whitcomb sighed. He felt for the Spartan . . . felt too much—which was the problem. He couldn't concentrate with her so close. He'd want constant status reports on her condition. Hell, he would have gone over, knelt next to her, and held her hand if that would've helped. He loved the men and women under his command as if they were his own sons and daughters. It was the old axiom of command: To be a good leader, you had to love the service. To be a great commander, you had to be willing to destroy that which you loved.

Static crackled, and the Master Chief reported in: *"We're in position, Admiral. ETA for repairs is two minutes."*

"Roger, Chief," Admiral Whitcomb replied. "When you're done give the word and get secure. We'll be accelerating immediately."

"Yes, sir."

Thunder rumbled through the deck.

"Plasma impacts, sir," Cortana explained. "Their energy profile has diffused, but they were still powerful enough to knock the lateral sensors and cameras offline."

Admiral Whitcomb smoothed his thick fingers over his mustache. "We've got only a few minutes before this space tears us apart." He squinted at the wall displays, trying to count the number of enemy craft. "That's if those Covenant ships don't do the job first."

He turned to Cortana. "How many enemy ships are there? Which are real and which are illusion?"

"Impossible to accurately determine, sir. I counted fourteen targets before they started firing and filling the space between us with ionizing plasma. Now? . . ." Mathematical symbols raced along her length, flashing blue and indigo. "Cross-indexing similar mirrored images and extrapolating, I estimate there are currently between three and five operational ships, sir."

Admiral Whitcomb gritted his teeth and concentrated. He had to get this ship moving—take out one or two enemy craft. Maybe the tangled plasma-filled space would cook the rest of them.

That was their best chance. Their only chance. He'd have to trust the Master Chief to get that drive conduit fixed.

"Very well, Cortana," he said. "Heat the *Gettysburg*'s reactor to maximum power and prepare to flood the main-engine plasma conduit. Charge all available weapons turret capacitors."

"Yes, sir. Stand by."

He glanced at a screen that showed the *Gettysburg* sitting atop them inverted. "Is the launch bay on the *Gettysburg* intact? Can it hold an atmosphere?"

Cortana blinked. "Yes, sir. It has a slow leak of thirty-two kilo pascals per—"

"Pressurize the bay."

"Acknowledged, Admiral. However," Cortana replied, "that will leave our air reserves dangerously low."

The Admiral stared at the ships surrounding them—a plasma bolt struck a distant cruiser head-on, and its nose buckled. Gouts of flame flared along its lateral plasma lines. The ship looked like a fish spit with a red-hot poker.

That could have been them.

"Hurry up, Chief," he whispered.

On the displays the Admiral spotted two ships. There was a carrier far away; it looked undamaged. Closer, off the port bow, was a cruiser that, aside from a hole punched through its aft section, was also undamaged . . . and only ten thousand kilometers away. That was the priority target.

"Lay in a new course," the Admiral ordered. "Two-four-zero by zero-three-five."

Lieutenant Haverson took an involuntary step closer to the display, and his face contorted as he worked out the math in his head. "That's . . . a collision course, sir."

"Glad you concur with my calculations," the Admiral remarked dryly.

Lieutenant Haverson glanced at the *Gettysburg* and nodded, finally understanding. "Aye, sir. A good plan."

"*Admiral,*" the Master Chief's voice broke through in a wash of static. "*Conduit breach is sealed, sir.*"

"Hang on, son," Admiral Whitcomb said. "This might be a rough ride. Cortana, give me flank speed now!"

"Complying," Cortana said. "Flank speed. Conduit is holding. Coming about to two-four-zero by zero-three-five. Collision with Covenant cruiser at this speed and heading in eighteen seconds."

Ascendant Justice–Gettysburg accelerated toward a line of wavering orange plasma—and steamed through it like a ship smashing through a storm wave on the open seas.

Fire splashed over their hulls and burned away layers of

armor. The entire hull superstructure groaned. Explosions reverberated through the deck.

"Fire on decks eight through twelve," Cortana reported. "We have lost plasma turret five. Distance to enemy ship six thousand kilometers and closing."

"Initiate a roll, Cortana. Make it thirty degrees per second. That'll spread out the damage over more surface area."

"Roll maneuver, aye. Attitude thrusters set to maximum burn." She exhaled, and her holographic image flickered with irritation. "This will make a targeting solution difficult, sir."

"Set firing range of plasma turrets for point blank," the Admiral told her.

Cortana hesitated for a full second. "Yes, Admiral."

The space on the external cameras slowly began to spin as their ship spiraled toward their intended target.

The Covenant cruiser came about to face them. Its plasma turrets glowed like angry red eyes.

"Lieutenant, take the weapons station. Cortana, give us a firing solution and manual fire control."

Haverson's hands moved quickly over the Covenant holographic control surfaces. "Cortana has a firing solution, sir. Activate weapons?"

"Stand by, Lieutenant."

"They'll get off the first salvo, sir," Lieutenant Haverson said. Although his voice was calm, a drop of sweat trickled down his freckled cheek.

"I hope they do," the Admiral replied. "It may be the only thing that saves us."

Lieutenant Haverson took a deep breath, nodding. "Weapons standing by, sir."

"Cortana, make ready to vent the *Gettysburg*'s launch bay."

"Aye, sir. Overriding bay door safeties. Distance to target three thousand kilometers."

The Covenant cruiser fired. Lances of energy launched and

veered toward *Ascendant Justice* . . . and arced away in cork-
screw spirals and right angles. The space between the two large
masses was still tangled and fractured.

"Two thousand kilometers," Cortana reported.

"Stay on course," the Admiral said. "And continue to hold
fire."

Lieutenant Haverson's jaw clenched, and his hands trembled
over the controls.

The enemy cruiser filled the displays. Its plasma turrets re-
cycled and glowed a dull red.

"One thousand kilometers," Cortana announced.

"Admiral?" Lieutenant Haverson asked.

"Hold your fire."

"Five hundred kilometers," Cortana said. "Three hundred . . .
two . . . collision imminent."

The Admiral's fist clenched. He barked, "Fire! All turrets, fire!
Cortana, depressurize the launch bay and give us full power to
port."

Ascendant Justice was a kilometer from the Covenant ship
on an intercept course when it fired. The *Gettysburg*'s launch bay
doors opened and the air inside explosively decompressed—
propelling the conjoined ships to port—just enough to miss the
cruiser.

Plasma rocketed toward their target. There was no way to
miss. White-hot fire impacted on the cruiser's hull, splashed
across its surface, boiled off the armored skin, and corroded
the skeletal framework underneath.

"Aft cameras," the Admiral ordered.

On screen he saw fire explode out the opposite side of the
cruiser. The warship tilted and rolled belly-up, plasma disintegrating the interior from stern to stem until it reached the fusion core. The ship detonated in a ball of flame. An instant later
the explosion twisted and curved as the warped Slipspace field
swept away all traces of the enemy ship.

Lieutenant Haverson exhaled and wiped his brow. "Excellent maneuvering, Admiral."

"Don't waste your breath on victory speeches yet, son." The Admiral scrutinized the tactical display and spotted the other ship. "There. We've got a new target."

He pointed to a ship half obscured in the plasma fog: the carrier, intact, with a cloud of gnats swarming about it. Seraph fighters dived and intercepted plasma and meteor bolts that got too close. The resulting fireballs deflected the impacts from the hull.

"She's got a smart Captain," the Admiral muttered. "So we can't use the same trick twice."

Five explosions rattled *Ascendant Justice*, and the ambient blue light on the bridge flickered.

"Meteor impact," Cortana replied. "We just lost plasma turrets two and three. All functionality on decks eight and below has been lost. The structural integrity of this ship, sir, is in danger of imminent collapse."

"Another minute, Cortana," the Admiral told her and continued to search the tactical display. "We either take out that carrier here—where their shields can't regenerate—or we face them in normal space."

He tapped the TAC map. "Gotcha! Cortana, come about to zero-three-zero by one-four-five, calculate the fastest acceleration and deceleration burns this ship can handle to get us to this object, and move this ship ASAP."

"Yes, Admiral."

Lieutenant Haverson looked at the map and located what the Admiral pointed at. "That object is just part of a Covenant ship, the aft section of a cruiser."

The Admiral nodded. "Exactly, Lieutenant. Cortana, how's the structural integrity of our ship's nose?"

"Sir? The nose?" Cortana paused, then reported, "Intact, sir. Most of the damage has been to the lateral—"

"Bring us into direct contact with that hunk of metal, Cortana."

"Aye, sir," Cortana replied.

Ascendant Justice accelerated toward the broken Covenant ship, and then slowed. The two warships touched; there was a slow grinding noise that echoed along the ship's frame.

"Contact," Cortana reported.

"Perfect," Admiral Whitcomb replied. "New course three-two-zero by two-two-zero. Flank speed. Lieutenant, charge any plasma turret we have left. Cortana, get this ship ready for full reverse power."

Ascendant Justice–Gettysburg turned and moved toward the Covenant carrier—pushing the broken hull of the other ship before them.

They accelerated on a collision course.

The turrets on the Covenant carrier heated to white hot—but they held their fire.

"Eight thousand kilometers to enemy ship," Cortana announced.

"Hold this course, Cortana."

"Six thousand kilometers, sir."

"Stand by," the Admiral ordered and gripped the railing again with his sweating hands.

"Two thousand kilometers."

"Full reverse power now!"

The engines rumbled, and the hull of *Ascendant Justice* shuddered.

The wrecked Covenant ship on their nose screeched as its momentum carried it along at the faster velocity. It pulled free of *Ascendant Justice* . . . tumbled directly toward the enemy carrier.

"Mass impact on carrier in four seconds," Cortana said. "Three seconds."

The carrier fired its plasma at the incoming mass. Flames

heated the wreckage, punched though its armor and hull, and melted the alloy.

The mass, however, continued forward, shattered and molten—but its velocity was undiminished.

It crashed into the carrier and sent it spinning to starboard. The carrier's hull breached along a dozen rents, and atmosphere vented and fanned the red-hot metal into gold flames. The launch bays chained with explosions.

"Fire all weapons, Lieutenant!"

Ascendant Justice fired its remaining turrets. Plasma cut into the carrier and sliced it to the core. Every deck flashed with fire and became an inferno.

"That's the best we can do," Admiral Whitcomb whispered. "Cortana, get us out of here. Transition to normal space."

Cortana's holographic silhouette blackened with swarming calculations. "Engaging Slipspace matrix."

Blotches of inky black welled within the sea of fire. Tiny stars winked on within those pools of darkness. The plasma-charged atmosphere faded, and the enemy ships ablaze vanished.

"Cut all power to the engines," the Admiral ordered.

Admiral Whitcomb gazed at the blackness and stars. "Now, where the hell are we?"

SECTION V

MASSACRE AT ERIDANUS SECUNDUS

CHAPTER
TWENTY-SIX

The Master Chief woke.

Consciousness, however, was a slight overestimation of his condition. His blurry vision came into focus slowly . . . but there was nothing to see except the interior of his visor. Amber status lights winked on.

Pain washed over his feet, his right thigh, and his hand. Good. He was alive. He knew from previous experience that this was the tail end of shock . . . and the stunning, numbing effects of that state were wearing off.

He felt the familiar weight and reactive circuits of his MJOL-NIR armor surrounding him. The coppery-tinged flavor of bio-foam coated his mouth, so he also surmised that his injuries had been recently treated.

And there was gravity. The press against his back was a great comfort to the Master Chief. The next time someone wanted him to go on a zero-gee op, he'd—

"Welcome back," Cortana said, interrupting his thoughts. A faint light flickered on to his left.

He turned onto his side. The burns on his extremities protested and shot lances of pain up his hand and feet.

He was in a med bay. The lights were turned down low, and he saw that he was the only person occupying a recovery bed.

Biomonitors pulsed along one wall, displaying his vital signs and MRI snapshots.

A holographic projection pad stood next to his bed. Cortana's tiny figure, strobing with symbolic logic code, waved to him, and when he didn't immediately respond she crossed her arms impatiently. "MRIs show no concussion, no subdural or epidural hematomas. You must have a thicker skull than I thought."

"Where am I?"

"Deck thirty-two on the UNSC frigate *Gettysburg*," Cortana told him. "Or what's left of it, anyway."

"What happened?"

Cortana sighed. "Are you referring to what happened since I left you on Reach? Or the outcome of the Slipspace battle? Or do you mean what happened since that battle?"

"The battle, first," he said and struggled to get up. "I presume we won."

Standing was too painful, though, and the strength seemed to have been drained from his muscles. He eased himself back to his original horizontal position.

Cortana's pale blue light dimmed and her gaze dropped to the deck. "Blue Team successfully repaired the main-engine conduit."

"I remember," the Master Chief murmured. "The repair part of it, at least. There was an explosion . . ."

"A plasma bolt," Cortana corrected. She sighed. "I'm sorry, Chief, but only you and SPARTANS 093, 043, and 104 survived that blast."

Grace, Will, and Fred were alive, but Li, Anton, and Warrant Officer Polaski had been killed in action. He remembered Polaski's scream, then Anton's outline as the flash of white-hot fire swept over the hull.

"Acknowledged," he said as graciously as he could muster, but he heard bitterness give an edge to his voice.

It struck him as odd that Polaski's death affected him as well. He'd seen thousands of UNSC soldiers die. She hadn't hesitated to transport Blue Team on a mission that was insanely dangerous. She had survived the battle of Reach, the crash landing on Halo, the Flood, and everything else—then she had bravely volunteered for this mission, too, and perhaps saved all their lives.

She might have made a good Spartan. There were worse eulogies.

The Master Chief sighed, called up his team roster on his heads-up display, and marked Anton and Li as Missing in Action. He paused to view all the others on that list; his first and best friend, Sam, was there . . . and he hadn't even realized a dozen more had been listed as MIA.

He saved the changes to the roster and closed the file.

"What about Kelly and Linda?" he asked Cortana.

Cortana looked up and flipped the hair from her luminous eyes. She paced a small circle on the holographic pad and then said, "SPARTAN 087, Kelly, is recovering from second-degree burns on seventy-two percent of her body. Doctor Halsey has accelerated tissue regrowth with dermacortic steroids. She should be fully healed in a matter of days . . . although her mobility will be severely hampered until then."

"And Linda?"

"Accessing status." Cortana paused for a full second. "Doctor Halsey has SPARTAN 058 currently in medical facility alpha, three decks above us. She still has her in a cryogenic state and is presently performing exploratory surgery. She has given me several orders to prepare the flash clone banks for replacement organs pending transplant."

"So she's alive?" the Master Chief asked.

"Technically," Cortana replied, "no." For a moment there was a look of genuine concern on her face—but it quickly vanished. "The doctor and Admiral Whitcomb have debated the risk of attempting to revive SPARTAN 058 before we reach a major medical facility. Doctor Halsey, I'm sure, will brief you when she has all the facts, Chief."

John frowned at this lack of detail. He didn't appreciate Cortana's increasingly difficult attitude, one that had slowly shifted ever since she interfaced with the Forerunner computer system on Halo. He made a mental note to ask Dr. Halsey about Linda later . . . and he'd ask her about Cortana, too.

"All other hands on board are accounted for?" the Master Chief asked.

"Yes, Chief. They are all engaged in repairs to the conjoined ships. We took tremendous damage in the expanded Slipspace from plasma bombardments and mass impacts. Both ships' superstructures, however, remain intact. The *Gettysburg*'s reactor is online and operating at sixty-seven percent capacity. *Ascendant Justice*'s reactor is offline undergoing repairs. Five of our seven plasma turrets require refit. And worst, *Ascendant Justice*'s engines are crippled. We have less than three percent operational thrust."

"Can the ship still jump to Slipspace? Are we stranded out here?"

"A jump is possible," Cortana said. She shook her head the way an older sister might when her baby brother asked a naive question. "It wouldn't do us any good, though. The alien artifact in Doctor Halsey's possession emits high levels of radiation in Slipspace. This unknown radiation even penetrates your suit's shields. I estimate lethal exposure in just under seventy-two hours. Also, that radiation would serve as a beacon for any Covenant ships prowling Slipspace, searching for us."

"So we're stuck between systems."

"Negative," Cortana replied, and her voice took on a new chill. "Admiral Whitcomb is quite adamant that we risk another Slipspace transition—regardless of the cost in human life. Otherwise, it would be weeks before we would be able to contact UNSC High Command."

HighCom? Two facts suddenly clicked into place: the Admiral's need to contact the rest of the Admiralty—no matter the price—and Dr. Halsey's attempts to revive Linda.

"What's compelling the Admiral's tactics, Cortana?"

Cortana's holographic outline softened. "I told you this before, Chief, but apparently it did not stick in your semiconscious state." She then came into sharp focus and crossed her arms over her chest. "The Covenant have discovered the location of Earth."

The Master Chief stood, suddenly wide awake and alert. He set aside his pain and fatigue.

"Explain," he demanded.

Cortana outlined her discovery of the encoded subchannel within normal Covenant communiqués. She explained how the Covenant's military orders were disseminated with startling efficiently, and she then showed him symbols that represented the coordinates for Sol . . . and Earth.

He stood mute and listened. The UNSC had worked so hard, for so long, to preserve this secret. It was only a matter of time; he had always known that the Covenant had to find Earth sooner or later. He had, however, always thought it would be later . . . and never now.

The Master Chief stared at the tiny triangles, squares, dots, and bars that made up the spatial coordinates. "We've seen these before, on Côte d'Azur."

"Yes. And according to Doctor Halsey, her team on Reach found similar markings in the underground vaults."

"What's the connection?"

"Unknown."

The Master Chief put these facts aside for the moment; the greater meaning of the symbols and translation he'd leave up to Cortana and ONI. The only insight that mattered to him was that the Covenant were going to attack Earth.

"Was there a timetable or any other data encoded on the subchannel?" he asked.

"Affirmative. There's a coordinated series of orders to Covenant warships scattered across the galaxy to rendezvous with a mobile command-and-control base they call the *'Unyielding Hierophant.'* When they have sufficient force, they will collectively make the jump to Earth."

The Master Chief moved toward the medical bay's doors. They automatically parted. "Where is Admiral Whitcomb?"

"The Admiral is currently on the bridge," Cortana replied. "But Doctor Halsey gave me strict orders that you are not to—"

"I don't take orders from civilians," he snapped. "Not even her." The Master Chief passed out of the medical bay and marched down the corridor.

"You know," Cortana said, her voice now coming from his helmet speaker, "your attitude has degraded since we started this mission—even before the battle for Reach."

"Noted," he replied.

The dim white light flooding the *Gettysburg*'s passages was a welcome change from the blue illumination the Covenant used on their ships. John was glad to have his feet once more firmly planted on the raw steel decks of a human vessel, even if the walls of this passage were soot-stained.

He entered the Command elevator and punched the button for the bridge. The gentle acceleration made new pain flare along his arms, and ligaments popped in his chest—but he gritted his teeth and banished the pain from his awareness.

When the doors parted, the Master Chief paused, taking in the sad state of the *Gettysburg*'s bridge. The front viewports had been blown out and recently replaced with welded plates of hull armor. A trio of monitors had been hastily bolted in place over them. Crystallized freeze-dried blood covered the navigation and ops consoles. Only three control stations were lit: engineering, computer status, and MAC ops.

But most disconcerting was that only Admiral Whitcomb and Lieutenant Haverson were present on a bridge that usually needed a staff of thirty officers. The room was as still and empty as a tomb.

"Master Chief," Admiral Whitcomb said, slightly surprised.

"Sir." He stood at attention and snapped off a crisp salute. "Permission to enter the bridge."

"Granted, son," the Admiral said.

"What's your status, Chief?" Haverson asked. "Doctor Halsey told us it would be days before you recovered."

"I'm one hundred percent, sir," he said.

As if she had heard this statement, Dr. Halsey opened a COM channel, and a tiny video feed popped onto his heads-up display. Her glasses reflected an ambient orange light from wherever she was, and he could not see her eyes.

"John, I need to speak with you."

"I'm with Admiral Whitcomb and Lieutenant Haverson, ma'am. When I'm done I can speak with you."

She was silent a moment, then said, *"Very well."* The COM winked off.

The Master Chief felt a pang of regret for being so terse with her.

"Get over here, son," the Admiral said. He returned his attention to the clear plastic wall dotted with stars and the diamond symbols that represented UNSC military outposts in this region of space. "We're in something of a tough spot."

He marched to the Admiral and Haverson and studied the chart with them. "Cortana's briefed me, sir. The Covenant know Earth's location and are on the move, most likely preparing a massive attack."

"That's the gist of it, I'm afraid," Haverson said, and the Chief noticed deep circles of fatigue ringing the younger man's eyes. "To complicate matters, we can barely navigate. We've been working around the clock to restore our ships, but we'd need an engineering crew of a hundred and a space dock to get these wrecks into fighting shape."

Admiral Whitcomb frowned at the Lieutenant's dour assessment and added, "Another trick is that the crystal we picked up on Reach emits radiation in Slipspace. Enough to kill everyone after only a few more hours of exposure.

"But we're hanging on to the alien device. It changes the properties of Slipspace, as you already saw—but with one more twist. In the few minutes we were in that tangled version of Slipspace, we traveled here"—he drew a tiny circle on the map, centered on their position—"which under normal circumstances should have taken us days."

"We attempted to briefly jump again," Haverson added, "but nothing extraordinary occurred. This unusually long jump may have been caused by the energy added to Slipspace by our battle with the Covenant."

"In any case," Admiral Whitcomb said, "if we learn what makes this crystal tick, it'd give us a hell of an edge on the Covenant."

"I see, sir."

The Chief scrutinized their location—not quite the definition of *the middle of nowhere*, but close. He noted that there were three star systems within the circle.

Haverson also peered at the chart. He touched one of the star symbols within their range, and statistics scrolled alongside the object. He sighed. "This system was glassed in 2530, so there's no chance there would be anyone to help us there. And the other two systems . . ." He shook his head. "Uninhabited."

"Hell," Admiral Whitcomb said and tugged on his mustache, "we pulled out of this region of space almost as soon as the war started. The Covenant came in, burned Eridanus and the other Outer Colonies, and then moved on without batting an eye."

"Eridanus?" The Chief stepped closer and touched the data scrolling next to the tiny star. "I know this place." He turned to the Admiral. "And there is a human colony there, sir—just not one that the UNSC cares about anymore. If I had to guess, I'd bet that the Covenant never found it, either. We might be able to expedite repairs there."

The Admiral stared thoughtfully at him. "You sure? Sure enough to bet our lives and Earth on that hunch, Chief?"

The Master Chief looked again at the tiny dot on the map.

It wasn't Eridanus he was thinking of. It was the surrounding asteroid belt . . . and a mission he and his team had executed twenty years ago.

"Yes, sir. I'm sure."

CHAPTER
TWENTY-SEVEN

TIME:DATE STAMP [[ERROR]] ANOMALY \ REVISED
DATE ESTIMATED 0450, SEPTEMBER 12, 2552, HYBRID
VESSEL *GETTYSBURG—ASCENDANT JUSTICE*, IN SLIPSPACE
EN ROUTE TO ERIDANUS SYSTEM.

Dr. Halsey buzzed the door open, and the Master Chief entered the clean room.

"You wanted to see me, Doctor?" He quickly looked the room over—taking in the adjoining surgical suites, and the strange orange sterile-field lamps set every meter into reflective recessions in the tiled walls.

Dr. Halsey had clamped five displays onto the arm of one of the contoured examination chairs in this room. She sat crosslegged in the chair and balanced a large alphanumeric-symbolic keyboard on her lap. Perched precariously on the side tray were Styrofoam cups of half-drunk coffee.

She waved the Chief forward. "I see you are ignoring sound medical advice by moving before you have fully healed."

"I'm fine, ma'am," he replied.

She snorted in disbelief. "John—I've never known you to tell an outright lie. I'm picking up telemetry from your armor, right now." She swiveled one of the monitors on her chair so he could see erratic biosigns pulsing on the screen. "What with the burns, contusions, fractures, and internal bleeding, you should be in shock. The only sleep you've gotten in a week was unconsciousness brought on by your wounds. And you say you're 'fine'?"

He stood and said nothing.

"Very well. I suppose you know your limitations better than anyone else." She turned the display back around. "I wanted to speak about your report on the alien construct—Halo. I've pieced together a bit of the story based on Admiral Whitcomb's recounting of your adventures, Cortana's debriefing, and the mission logs of Locklear, Johnson . . . and the curious partial mission log of one PFC Wallace Jenkins."

The Master Chief shifted uneasily.

"There are inconsistencies that I must resolve before we get back to Earth." She pushed her glasses higher onto the bridge of her nose. "One of them is Sergeant Johnson." She tapped in commands on her keyboard. "Please step closer, John. I want you to see this with me."

The Master Chief moved alongside her chair. His massive weight thudded through the thick deck plating. Two meters tall and half a ton of metal and somehow Dr. Halsey couldn't help thinking of him occasionally as the same little boy she had stolen from his parents in Elysium City.

No. John *had* changed. She hadn't. She was the one who still carried the three-decade-old festering guilt.

She took a deep breath and refocused her attention on the video records before her. On screen played mission logs that showed Covenant and Marines in firefights, the odd Forerunner architecture in the interior of the Halo construct, and the terrifying omniparasitic life-form known as the Flood.

She replayed the mission record of Private Jenkins and the first Flood attack.

John stiffened as Captain Keyes appeared on screen and as the Flood consumed the Captain and his squad. Sergeant Johnson was there, too, fighting and cursing . . . until the hordes of tiny, podlike Infection Forms swarmed over him.

"The Sergeant survived," she said. "The only human to have direct exposure to the Flood meta-organism and walk away."

"I know," the Master Chief whispered. "I'm not sure how he survived. How could anyone live through that?"

"That's the simple part," Dr. Halsey told him without looking up from her displays. She tapped a key, and the Sergeant's medical records flashed on screen. "See, here?" She touched a file dated three years before. "He was diagnosed with Boren's Syndrome."

"I haven't heard of it," the Chief said.

"I'm not surprised. It's caused by exposure to high-yield plasma. Like the burst released by a Covenant plasma grenade. We don't see many cases—people usually die from the direct effects of those weapons long before these secondary symptoms manifest.

"Apparently, the Sergeant captured a crate of plasma grenades from the Covenant during the Siege of Paris IV. He used them all—received a commendation for bravery . . . and a twelve-hundred-rad cumulative dose of radiation as an unanticipated bonus."

John was silent for several minutes. Dr. Halsey wasn't sure if he was reading the computer files, contemplating her words, or trying to confirm all this on a private COM channel with Cortana. His impenetrable armor made discussions with normal social conventions nearly impossible. It irritated her, yet without that armor with its constant hydrostatic pressure and automated biofoam injectors, John would have literally fallen apart by now.

For a fleeting moment she remembered when she had first read Alexander Dumas's *Man in the Iron Mask*. She had felt terror when the noble prisoner had been encased within that metal shell. How did John cope with the constant suffocating enclosure?

The Master Chief finally said, "I don't see the connection between the Sergeant's sickness and his surviving the Flood."

"Boren's Syndrome," Dr. Halsey explained, "is characterized

by migraines, amnesia, and brain tumors . . . and without the proper treatment, death. It disrupts the electrical signals in a person's nervous system."

"Is it treatable?"

"Yes, but it requires thirty weeks of intensive chemotherapy. Which brings me to this." She hit the NEXT PAGE key and an official "Refusal of Treatment" document appeared on screen. "The Sergeant did not wait thirty weeks to get back and fight."

The Master Chief nodded, understanding the heroic, futile gesture. "How did this disruption of his nervous system save him?"

"I've deconvoluted the biosigns of the soldiers overtaken by the Flood. The parasite interfaces with a host by forcing a resonant frequency match to each host's neural system."

"And the Sergeant's nervous system is so jumbled that the Flood couldn't force a match?"

"Correct," she said. "Further blood tests show his system bearing traces of Flood DNA—very much dead and noninfectious, but some gene fragments are intact. I believe this is proof of a failed attempt to possess him. It also appears to have imparted him with some curious regenerative abilities, although I cannot yet fully confirm this side effect."

The Master Chief seemed to relax a notch from his usual ramrod stiff at-attention stature. This new information seemed to put him at ease. "I think I see."

"No," Dr. Halsey told him, and she removed her glasses. "You don't."

"Doctor?"

"Discovering how he survived is not what I wanted to discuss. It's what happens *next* to Sergeant Avery Johnson."

She shut off her monitors and eased back into the chair. "I've prepared two separate reports on this for ONI Section Three. The first has all relevant data on my analysis and the possible technology to counter an initial Flood infestation. The second includes the source material: Private Jenkins's and Sergeant Johnson's mission logs and the Sergeant's medical files."

She downloaded the reports onto two data crystals and ejected them from the port on the chair's arm. She set the clear cubes on the tray and gestured for John to take them. "I leave it up to you which to deliver to Lieutenant Haverson."

"Why would I withhold any data, Doctor?" the Master Chief asked and glanced at the crystals.

Her eyes focused past him as she struggled to find the words to match her conflicting emotions. "For a long time I had thought that we had to sacrifice a few for the good of the entire human race." She took a deep breath and let it go with a heavy sigh. "I have killed and maimed and caused a great deal of suffering to many people—all in the name of self-preservation." Her steely blue gaze found him. "But now I'm not sure that philosophy has worked out too well. I should have been trying to save every single human life—no matter what it cost."

Dr. Halsey pushed the tray bearing the data crystals toward the Master Chief. "If you give ONI the first report, they may be able to find a countermeasure for the Flood. Maybe. They would have a slightly better chance, however, if you give them the second report."

"Then I'll give them the second report." He picked up the crystal.

"Which will murder Sergeant Johnson," she said with a chill in her voice. "ONI will not be satisfied to take a sample of blood. They will dissect him to find out how he resisted the Flood. It will be a billion-to-one shot that they'll ever replicate his unique medical conditions—but they'll do it anyway. They will kill him because the trade-off is worth it to them."

The Master Chief picked up the other crystal and then stared at them both lying in his gauntleted hand.

"Is it worth it to you, John?" she asked.

He curled his hand in a fist and held it close to his chest. "Why do you want me to make this choice?"

"One last lesson. I'm trying to teach you something it's taken me all my life to realize." She cleared her throat of the lump thickening there. "I'm giving you the chance to make the decision that I thought I couldn't make."

She glanced at the clock on her display. "I'm sorry. Linda is almost prepped for surgery, and I have several things I *must* accomplish before then. You should go."

The Master Chief obediently turned and strode toward the exit, but halted in the doorway. "Doctor, don't let her die again." He then left the room.

Dr. Halsey watched until he rounded the corridor and was gone. She hoped she saw John again before she did what she had to do, but she might not. Would the thought she had planted within him take hold? The gesture might be the only thing she could do to atone for what she'd done to him and the other Spartans.

Such thoughts were luxuries when there were only a few hours before *Ascendant Justice* exited Slipspace. There was too much to do before then.

She turned all the monitors to face her and typed in the command to unsquelch Cortana.

"Lock the door," Dr. Halsey ordered Cortana. "Boost counterintrusion measures to level seven."

"Done," Cortana said. The irritation at having been silenced for the last five minutes was like barbed wire in her voice. "What precisely was all that about? Teach the Master Chief a lesson? Giving him a choice? Save one man instead of billions?"

Dr. Halsey ignored her and rapidly typed in commands on her keyboard. "Give me access to your core coordinates four-four-seven."

"Block removed," Cortana said with an exasperated sigh. "Are you going to answer my question?"

"I'm tired of sacrificing others for the 'greater good,' " Dr. Halsey replied. "It never stops, Cortana . . . and we're running out of people to sacrifice." She tapped in a final command for the memory-wiping worm function and punched the ENTER key.

"What—"

"I'm erasing your files on this matter. I'm sorry, Cortana, but with this, I cannot trust even you."

Cortana was silenced as the worm burned through her memory and obliterated all inquiries and recordings pertaining to Sergeant Avery Johnson's encounter with the Flood.

"Cortana, give me an update on your core memory."

"Recompiling of routines has resulted in a memory-processing footprint reduction of sixteen percent, Doctor. Thank you. That gives me a little more room to think."

"I'm afraid that's all we dare risk," Dr. Halsey said. "The Halo and Covenant AI data could become corrupted if I do more. And there is no place safe enough to store that information."

Dr. Halsey loaded mission reports from Admiral Whitcomb's, John's, and Fred's teams. She frowned at the official UNSC incident forms as their highlighted time, date, and location stamps scrolled across her screens.

"Are you done with the temporal analysis of these logs?"

"Yes, Doctor. You were correct: There is a discrepancy between the Halo team and the team on Reach. The time stamps are off by an average of three weeks. I hypothesize that this was caused by my gravity-influenced Slipspace transition."

The corners of Dr. Halsey's mouth flickered into a smile. "I'm disappointed, Cortana. That's a guess . . . and an incorrect one at that."

"Really?" Cortana replied with a hint of challenge in her tone.

"Do you have any data from your subsequent gravity-influenced translation to correlate?"

There was a two-second pause, and then Cortana finally answered, "Yes, Doctor. There are no temporal displacements on those later jumps."

"As I suspected." Dr. Halsey tapped her finger on her lower lip as she thought. "Plot the temporal irregularities on a space-time surface. Then call up my file on the spatial distortion generated by the alien artifact."

On the displays appeared two sets of nearly identical curved membranes that stretched about a central location and time: Reach and the recovery of the strange artifact.

"That thing not only bends space," Dr. Halsey whispered to herself, "but bends time as well."

"That's not possible," Cortana said. "How could the artifact on Reach affect us on Halo—light-years away?"

"Don't think of it as physical distance," Dr. Halsey replied absentmindedly, staring at the monitors. "You and John were on an event path intersecting the crystal." She moved the curves over one another; the time and space surfaces were a perfect match. "You *had* to be there at that place and time to recover us and remove the crystal—time and space warped to make that event occur."

Cortana gave a derisive laugh. "That's circular logic, Doctor. It directly contravenes several well-established theories—"

"And it fits the known data." Dr. Halsey shut down the files containing her analysis. "I see now why the Covenant are so interested in this object. They mustn't be allowed to get their hands on it. Not them, and certainly not Section Three, either."

"Doctor?"

Dr. Halsey turned to the screen with her memory-devouring worm and moved it to a new pointer in Cortana's core. She executed the program—destroying the AI's memory of this conversation, too.

"Give me an update on SPARTAN 058's condition, Cortana."

"Core temperature increasing at a steady point-two degrees Celsius per minute, attaining thirty-seven degrees in ten minutes."

"Very good. Prep and move the flash-cloned liver and kidneys from storage and ready surgical bay three."

"Aye, Doctor."

Linda's medical data winked on a display along with the entire Spartan roster: a long list of every Spartan's current operational status. Only a handful were left, almost every one of them listed as WOUNDED IN ACTION or MISSING IN ACTION.

"No KIAs?" Dr. Halsey murmured. She touched SPARTAN 034's entry. "Sam is listed as missing in action. Why would that be? He died in 2525."

"ONI Section Two Directive Nine-Three-Zero," Cortana replied. "When ONI went public with the SPARTAN-II program, it was decided that the reports of Spartan losses could cause a crippling loss of morale. Consequently, any Spartan casualties are listed as MIA or WIA, in order to maintain the illusion that Spartans do not die."

"Spartans never die?" she whispered. Dr. Halsey swiveled out of the contoured chair and pushed the monitors out of her way with a sudden violence. "If only that were true."

There was so much to do and so little time left for her, the Spartans, and the human race. She could do something, though. She'd save them one person at a time, starting with Linda, then Kelly, and then a handful of very important others.

Of course, it meant betraying everyone who trusted her—but if that was the only way Dr. Halsey could save herself, and her soul, then she'd do it.

TWENTY-EIGHT

Black space churned with pinpricks of light; it split, and the *Gettysburg–Ascendant Justice* appeared in the Eridanus system.

The Master Chief stood on the *Gettysburg*'s bridge. He'd wanted to be on the medical deck when Dr. Halsey had finished with Linda, be there when she woke up . . . or be there in case she never woke up. But he had to be here; this was his idea, and he was the closest thing they had to an expert on this place.

"Systems check," Admiral Whitcomb ordered.

Lieutenant Haverson leaned over the ops console and flicked through several screens. "Residual radiation fading," he said. "Navigation systems and scanners coming back online."

Fred stood at the Engineering station and reported, "Reactors at sixty percent. Slight hysteresis leak in coil ten. Compensating."

"Plasma?" the Admiral asked as he settled into the Captain's chair.

Cortana's ghostly image flickered onto the holographic pad next to the star chart.

"We can fire only one turret," she replied, and a wash of red flashed across her image then cooled to its normal deep blue. "The other two functional turrets are offline; their magnetic coils refuse to align. It might be a side effect of the artifact's radiation."

"One shot . . . ," the Admiral muttered. He tugged on the end of his mustache and sighed. "Then we'll just have to make it count." He turned to the Master Chief. "Lead the way, son."

The Master Chief stared at the three large monitors that had replaced the bridge's observation windows. Eridanus blazed in the center of one display; stars shone with a steady brilliance. "Move us one-point-five astronomical units relative to the sun," he said. "Heading zero-nine-zero by zero-four-five."

"Destination one-point-five AU," Haverson said. "Heading confirmed. Coming about."

"Plot an elliptical course parallel to the plane of the asteroid belt," the Master Chief added. "Cortana, scan for asteroids approximately two kilometers in diameter."

"Scanning," she said. "This might take some time. There are more than a billion moving objects, some of them in deep shadow."

"Tell me again about your old mission," Admiral Whitcomb said. "You and the other Spartans were here before?"

"Yes, sir," the Chief replied. "Myself, Fred, Linda, Kelly, and Sam. It was the Spartans' first real mission: an infiltration into a rebel base. We captured their leader and got him to ONI for debriefing."

"I didn't even know the Spartans were around in 2525," Lieutenant Haverson said.

"Yes, sir," Fred answered. "We just didn't have MJOLNIR armor or the advanced weaponry we have today. We looked like any other NavSpecWar team."

"I very much doubt that," Haverson said under his breath.

The Admiral raised one bushy eyebrow. "You mean five people made a zero-gee vacuum infiltration onto this space station? And then exfiltrated with a prisoner who happened to be the guy in charge of the place?"

"Yes, sir. That was the basic plan."

"I suppose it went off without a hitch?"

The Master Chief was silent for a moment as he remembered the dozens of dead people they had left behind on that base . . . and he felt a pang of regret. At the time he hadn't thought twice about removing *any* obstacle that would have compromised his mission, human or otherwise. Now, after fighting for humanity for two decades, he wondered if he could shoot another human without a good reason.

"No, sir," the Master Chief finally replied. "There were enemy casualties. And we had to blow their cargo bay to escape."

"So," the Admiral said, tapping his fingers on the arm of the Captain's chair, "they're not going to be happy to see a UNSC ship knocking on their front door?"

"I wouldn't expect so, sir."

"Faint emissions on the D-band detected," Cortana said. "Come about to new heading three-three-zero."

"Aye," Haverson said. "Three-three-zero."

"It's gone, now," she said, "but I definitely heard *something*."

"Keep on this course," Admiral Whitcomb ordered. "We'll run it down."

"There's one thing I don't understand," Haverson said as he squinted at the forward displays. "Why are these people even here?"

"Pirates and insurgents," the Admiral answered. "They hijack UNSC ships, sell arms, and trade black market commodities. You're probably too young to remember, Lieutenant, but before the Covenant War not everyone wanted to be part of an Earth-ruled government."

"I'm fully aware of the rebellion," Haverson said. "But why continue to stay separated from UNSC forces when the Covenant War started? Surely their chances of survival would be better with us?"

The Admiral snorted a derisive laugh. "Some people didn't want to fight, son. Some just wanted to hide . . . in this case, literally under a rock. Maybe they think the Covenant won't bother with 'em." A smile flickered across his face. "Well, we're about to change all that for them."

The elevator doors parted, and Dr. Halsey stepped onto the bridge. She removed her glasses and rubbed her eyes. She looked to the Master Chief as if she had just retuned from an intense fight—fatigued and shocked. He noticed a single drop of blood on the lapel of her wrinkled white lab coat.

"She's fine," Dr. Halsey whispered. "Linda will make it. The flash-cloned organs took."

The Master Chief exhaled the breath he had been unconsciously holding. He glanced over to Fred, who nodded to him. John nodded back. There were no words to express how he felt. One of his closest teammates, his friend, someone he had thought dead . . . was alive again.

"Thank you, Doctor Halsey," he said.

She waved her hand dismissively, and there was a strange look in her eyes—almost as if she had regretted the success of her operation.

"Damn good news," Admiral Whitcomb said. "We could use another hand on deck."

"Hardly," Dr. Halsey replied, suddenly looking much more alert. "She'll need at least a week to recover—even with the biofoam and steroid accelerants I have her on. Then she'll barely be able to get on her feet. She won't be combat-ready."

Gettysburg–Ascendant Justice moved into the plane of the asteroid belt, and three rocks appeared on the screens.

"This region is the source of the D-band signal," Cortana told them. "There are three possible candidates based on the size parameters you gave me, Chief."

"Which one is it?" the Admiral asked.

"Only one is rotating fast enough to generate a three-quarter-gravity internal environment," Cortana replied.

"That's it," the Master Chief replied and nodded toward the central display. The rock hadn't changed much in the last twenty years. Was it possible the place had been abandoned? The D-band transmission that Cortana detected could have been an automated signal, weak from years of drain on a single battery . . . or the lure for a trap.

"Admiral?"

"I know, Chief," he said. "They've baited the hook and we're taking it . . . at least that's what it's supposed to look like." He chuckled. "Cortana, power up every turret on our Covenant flagship."

Her holographic body flushed blue-green and she crossed her arms. "Let me remind you, sir, that of the three working turrets, two are offline. I have no way to aim the plasma. The magnetic—"

"I know, Cortana. But they"—the Admiral stabbed a finger at the displays—"don't know that."

"Yes, sir," she said. "Heating them up now."

"Power dropping," Fred warned the Admiral as he peered at the Engineering screens. "Down to forty-four percent."

"Lieutenant Haverson," the Admiral barked, "open a channel on the D-band. It's time we introduced ourselves."

"Aye, sir. Frequency matched and channel open."

The Admiral stood. "This is the UNSC frigate *Gettysburg*," he barked, his voice full of authority and colored with his Texas accent. "Respond." And then he reluctantly added, "Please."

Static filled the COM. The Admiral waited patiently for ten seconds, and then his boot started to tap on the deck. "No need to play possum, boys. We're not here for a fight. We want to—"

He made a sudden throat-slitting motion toward Haverson, and the Lieutenant snapped off the COM.

Tiny doors appeared in the two-kilometer-wide rock; from this distance they looked no larger than the pores on an orange. A fleet of ships launched, using the asteroid's rotational motion to give their velocities a boost. There were approximately fifty craft: Pelicans modified with extra armor and chainguns mounted on their hulls; sleek civilian pleasure craft carrying missiles as large as themselves; single-man engineering pods that sputtered with arc cutters; and one ship that was fifty meters long with oddly angled black stealth surfaces.

"That's a *Chiroptera*-class vessel," Haverson said, awed. "It's an antique. ONI decommissioned them all forty years ago and sold them for scrap."

"Is it a threat?" the Admiral asked.

Lieutenant Haverson's forehead wrinkled as he considered. "No, sir. They were decommissioned because they broke down every other mission. They had far too many sensitive components without a central controlling AI. The only reason I recall them at all is that they had the smallest operational Shaw-Fujikawa Translight Engine ever produced. No weapons systems, sir. Like I said, it's not a threat . . . it's a museum piece."

"But it has Slipspace capability?" Dr. Halsey asked. "Maybe we can use it to get to Earth."

"Unlikely," Haverson replied. "All *Chiroptera*-class vessels were decommissioned by ONI—critical components removed and the ships' operating systems locked down so tight I doubt even Cortana could reactivate them."

"I wouldn't bet on it," Cortana muttered.

"No weapons," the Admiral said and stared at the blocky geometry of the black ship. "That's all I need to know."

"Their 'fleet,'" Fred interjected, "is deploying and taking up positions around us in a wide arc. Classic formation. They'll flank us."

"There's no real threat from these ships," the Admiral said to himself. "They have to know we know that. So why bother with this show?" He scowled at the displays, and his eyes widened. "Cortana, scan the nearby rocks for radioactive emissions."

"Receiving video feed," Fred announced.

The image of a man flickered on forward screen three. He was clearly a civilian, with long black hair drawn back into a ponytail and a pointed beard extending a full ten centimeters from his chin. He smiled and made an elegant bow. The Chief, for some reason he could not understand, took an instant dislike to him.

"Captain . . . ," the man said in a smooth, resonant tenor voice. "I am Governor Jacob Jiles, leader of this port. What can we do for you?"

"First," Admiral Whitcomb said, "I am not a Captain; I am a Vice Admiral, the Deputy Chief of Naval Operations. Second, you will order your fleet to reverse course and get out of my gunsights before I forget my manners. And third, we insist that you make ready to let us dock on that rock of yours for emergency repairs and refit."

Jiles considered these requests and then threw his head back and laughed. "Admiral, my sincere apologies for the confusion in your rank." He said this with a mocking grin. "As for your other requests, I'm afraid I can't accommodate you today."

"And I respectfully suggest you reconsider, Mister Jiles," the Admiral said in a deadpan tone. "It would be unfortunate for all of us if I have to insist."

"You're in no position to insist on anything." Jiles nodded to someone off screen.

"Emissions detected!" Cortana said. "Neutron radiation spikes at seven by three o'clock. One by three o'clock. Picking up five more. They've got nukes."

"Hidden in the asteroid field," Admiral Whitcomb muttered. "Very good. At least we're not dealing with fools."

"Indeed. We are *not* fools," Jiles replied. "We have survived the long arm of Imperial Earth and Covenant intrusions." Someone off camera handed Jiles a data pad with a radar silhouette of *Gettysburg–Ascendant Justice*; numbers and symbols crawled alongside the picture. He hesitated and crinkled his nose, appearing confused at the odd configuration of mated craft. "We are also not foolish enough to use overwhelming force when it isn't required. Your 'ship' is ready to fall apart on its own. I hardly think we need to waste one of our precious and expensive nuclear devices to stop you."

Whitcomb set his hands on his hips. "You need to rethink the tactical situation, Governor," he growled. "Cortana, find me a target—a rock the same size as this 'gentleman's' base."

"Done," she replied.

"Burn it," he ordered.

"Aye, sir!"

A lance of plasma appeared on the starboard side of *Ascendant Justice*, cut through space, and blasted the surface of a three-kilometer-long stone tumbling through the asteroid belt. Its surface heated to orange, yellow, and then white, sputtering blobs of molten iron and jets of vapor that caused the massive stone to spin faster. The plasma cut through the rock in a wide arc—punched through the opposite side. The uneven internal heat caused the rock to fracture and explode into fragments. The debris pinwheeled away, leaving helical trails of cooling iron and glittering metallic gas in its wake.

"Keep number two and three turrets hot," the Admiral said, "and target their base."

"Done, sir."

The mocking smile had vanished from Jiles's face and the color had drained from his golden skin. "Perhaps I was too hasty," he said. "Where are my manners? Please come aboard and join me as my honored guest. Bring your staff, too." He made a quick motion to his crew off camera.

The ships surrounding the *Gettysburg* turned and maneuvered back toward the rotating asteroid.

"Join me for dinner and we can discuss what you need. You have my word that no one will be harmed."

Admiral Whitcomb chuckled. "I have no doubt about that, Mister Jiles." He turned to Cortana. "If we're not back in thirty minutes, blast them all to hell."

The Master Chief linked mission telemetry with Cortana as Jiles's men met them in the landing bay—six men dressed in black coveralls with old MA3 rifles slung over their shoulders. They hesitated, then took tentative steps toward the Covenant dropship. The Chief didn't blame them—he'd have been careful, too, if he were moving toward an armed enemy vessel. One fear-induced pull of the trigger from any one of them, however, and this greeting would turn into a bloody firefight.

He closed off his external speakers and asked, "Cortana: tactical analysis."

Cortana replied: "The asteroid is a typical ferric oxide composite. It's reinforced with a layer of Titanium-A armor. The armor is well camouflaged, but I spotted it with the *Gettysburg*'s deep radar. They have a few sections with ablative undercoats as well. Radar's bouncing off those sections—so would Covenant sensors. Impressive."

Governor Jiles strolled across the deck, flipped his black fur cape over one shoulder, and shook Admiral Whitcomb's hand. Jiles nodded to Haverson. His smile vanished, however, when he looked at the Master Chief and Fred in their MJOLNIR armor. Jiles recovered his grin and bowed low to Dr. Halsey.

"There are half a dozen guards armed with old MA3 rifles and concealed plasma pistols," Cortana whispered. "I'm also picking up a fireteam of ten in the side passages, watching."

"I saw them," the Chief muttered. "They're overwatch and backup, just in case. No problem."

"This way, please," Jiles said, and with a flourish he led them through a narrow corridor.

The Chief took one last look at the docking bay. It seemed smaller than he remembered it. Twenty years ago he and his team had blown off the external doors, stolen a Pelican, escaped, and left a dozen men dead on the deck.

His team had accomplished that mission without MJOLNIR armor. It hadn't been developed yet—so there was no way anyone here could have known that John and Fred were part of the team that had extracted the last "governor" of the base, the traitor Colonel Watts. Yet Jiles's guards glared at John as if they knew everything.

As the Master Chief stepped into the corridor, Cortana informed him: "This passage is from a UNSC cargo vessel, ripped out and reinforced with a bulkhead every ten meters. Airtight and tough. This place can take a lot of damage before buckling."

"Good place for an ambush, too," the Master Chief said, and kept one eye on his motion tracker.

They *were* being followed. Three contacts behind them, and three ahead, keeping pace.

The Master Chief had an urge to step in front of the Admiral and Dr. Halsey and clear the passage with a burst of fire. But this situation required diplomacy, something John was ill suited for. He wished the Admiral had taken John's suggestion to bring more Spartans with him. Or at least to have two of them infiltrate while the Admiral and this Jiles spoke.

They were led to a circular room. Half the far wall retracted, revealing thick red velvet curtains, which also slowly pulled away and exposed the half-meter-thick windows that overlooked the asteroid field. Beyond was a gentle ballet of rocks tumbling, rotating, and bouncing off one another in slow motion.

Men carried in a long table, threw a white silk cloth over it, and smoothed it down. Then a succession of women carried in silver trays heavy with fruit, steaming meats, and chocolates, and a dozen decanters sloshing with amber, ruby, and clear liquors.

Padded chairs were brought in for them all. "Please." Jiles motioned toward Dr. Halsey and he pulled out a chair for her. "Relax and sit down."

The Master Chief took up a position by the door where he

had a clear view of the entire room. Fred made sure the corridor was empty and then sealed the door.

The Chief checked behind the curtains for hidden men, surveillance devices, or false passages.

"Cortana?" he whispered.

"Looks clear," she said. "I'm not detecting anything. Walls are half a meter of Titanium-A."

"We're clear," the Master Chief told the Admiral.

Dr. Halsey finally sat in the proffered chair, smoothed her skirt, and Jiles gently slid the chair under her. He offered her a plate of plump strawberries, which she graciously declined.

Haverson took one of the strawberries, however, and bit into it. "Delicious," he remarked.

Jiles inclined his head. "Our hydroponics facility—"

"With respect, Governor, there's no time for chitchat," Admiral Whitcomb said. "The clock's ticking. In more ways than you might realize."

Jiles sighed and sat in a chair covered in gold leaf and black velvet. He threw his legs over one of the chair's arms and laced his hands behind his head. "You have my complete and full attention, Admiral."

"Good," Whitcomb said, frowning at Jiles's disregard for the seriousness of their predicament.

Admiral Whitcomb laid it out for him in short, easy-to-understand sentences: the fall of Reach, the Covenant's search for an alien technology, the chase and battle in Slipspace, and the unclassifiable radiation that would lead the Covenant through Slipspace . . . to here.

As he spoke, Governor Jiles set his feet onto the floor, and his relaxed position solidified. He leaned forward and set his elbows on the table. His congenial smile slowly tightened into a scowl.

"Bloody Elisa!" he shouted, jumped to his feet, and swept a decanter off the table. The glass shattered and ruby-colored brandy spattered across the hardwood.

John and Fred had Jiles instantly in their gunsights, but the Admiral held up his hand.

" 'Bloody Elisa'?" the Chief asked Cortana.

"The patron saint of vacuum," the AI replied. "She's popular among civilian pilots."

"I'd guess," the Admiral told Jiles, "that we have less than a day before they find us."

"And what," Jiles said slowly, controlling his anger, "do you suggest *I* do about it?"

"That's the simple part of all this, Governor. You can help us, or you can try to kill me and my crew, and sell our ships for whatever the black market will bear. They should yield quite a profit . . . provided the Covenant let you live long enough to cash in."

The Admiral grabbed a decanter, poured a glass of wine, took a sip, and nodded appreciatively. "Now, assuming you manage to outwit our ship's AI—which I very much doubt—and assuming further you somehow disable our ship's weapons before our AI blows your base to atoms—which I also doubt—then you'll have a Covenant fleet to contend with. And I don't think they're going to be sociable, sit down, drink your wine, and discuss this like gentlemen."

Jiles placed his face into his hand and rubbed his temples.

"Maybe you're thinking," the Admiral said, "that you've kept this operation of yours hidden this long. From the UNSC. From the Covenant. Why should this be any different? Well, *we* found you easily enough. I don't think the Covenant will blink at overturning every rock in this asteroid belt to find you."

Governor Jiles picked up a new bottle and filled a glass to the brim. He downed the drink in one gulp. "And the other option?" he asked coldly. "I help you? And together we fight the Covenant? If they come in the force you claim, what difference will it make?"

"If you help us," the Admiral said, "get my ship repaired so we can make the jump to Earth, I'll evacuate all your people. I promise you and your crew amnesty."

Jiles laughed. His cordial smile returned, and he asked, "Do you have any proof of any of this? That the mighty Reach is gone? That you have a new alien technology? Or that the Covenant are on their way here?"

"Chief!" Cortana cried in alarm. On his helmet's heads-up display, a schematic of the Eridanus system appeared. A NAV marker flashed near the third planet. It expanded into the familiar curved radar silhouette of a Covenant cruiser.

"We have company," the Master Chief said. He strode to the window and pointed. "There."

The blue glow of Covenant engines flared as the ship came about and accelerated toward the asteroid belt.

"There's your proof, Governor," Admiral Whitcomb growled.

TWENTY-NINE

Admiral Whitcomb, the Master Chief, Fred, and Lieutenant Haverson bounded off the elevator and onto the bridge of the *Gettysburg*.

Cortana's image flickered on the holographic pad near the star map. "Covenant cruiser is only two hundred thousand kilometers away," she reported. "Closing fast on an intercept course."

The Admiral barked orders: "Fred, take the Engineering station, Haverson on NAV, and Chief, you're on Weapons Station One; get it up and running and see if there are any systems we overlooked. Lieutenant, move us away from the enemy on course one-eight-zero by two-seven-zero."

"One-eight-zero by two-seven-zero, aye," Haverson replied. He strapped himself into the NAV station, and his fingers danced over the controls. "Coming about, Admiral."

Gettysburg–Ascendant Justice turned and moved deeper into the asteroid field.

The Master Chief stepped up to Weapons Station One. He was cross-trained on the weapons-ops system of every class of UNSC warship, but he'd never actually fired any shipborne weapon before. The MAC gun on this frigate was one of the largest weapons in the human arsenal. He wished they had rounds for it—he would've given anything to launch one of the six-hundred-ton depleted uranium projectiles at that Covenant cruiser. He carefully tapped commands on the keyboard, and the darkened screen came to life. The Chief scrutinized the *Gettysburg*'s weapons inventory.

Governor Jiles appeared on the number three forward display, his face placid except his lips, which pressed together so tightly that they were only a thin white line of concentration.

"Governor," the Admiral said. His voice was smooth and resonated with the absolute authority of command. "I'll maneuver the *Gettysburg* and take a shot at extreme range with our plasma turret. That will blow down that cruiser's shields. I want you to coordinate with our AI and fire one of your nukes while their shields are down—blast them to bits."

"A brilliant tactic," Jiles said, and his lips parted in a mocking smile. "Except for one problem. We have no nuclear weapons. The ones you detected in the asteroid field were only neutron radiation emitters." He shrugged. "We bluffed."

Admiral Whitcomb cursed quietly. "Very smart, Jiles."

"You'll just have to use the seven plasma turrets on your ship, Admiral," Governor Jiles remarked. "That should be more than enough to—"

The Admiral chuckled, and he smiled in the same mocking fashion as Jiles. "We bluffed, too. We only have one turret . . . and it's not working so well."

"It appears we have both overestimated the other," Jiles said. "Under different circumstances this might be amusing."

"Indeed." Whitcomb addressed Cortana. "Try and hail that Covenant cruiser. Maybe we can bluff them, too."

"They're responding," Cortana replied. "Religious rhetoric aside, they're demanding that we stand down and hand over the artifact or they will open fire."

"Give them our answer," Admiral Whitcomb said. "Fire when ready, Cortana."

The turret on *Ascendant Justice* warmed, and plasma collected and focused into a thin ruby line that lanced forward—

—and unraveled into a wide spiral that coursed over the bow of the *Gettysburg*. The superheated gases boiled away patches of remaining Titanium-A armor and revealed the ship's skeletal superstructure.

"What the hell happened?" the Admiral shouted.

"Analyzing now," Cortana replied. "Plasma turret offline. Stand by, sir."

"I can move my fleet to engage the enemy," Jiles said uncertainly.

Admiral Whitcomb surveyed the forward screens: Jiles, the approaching Covenant cruiser, and the asteroid field full of rocks floating on invisible currents. He narrowed his eyes, then said: "They'd blast you out of space before you could sneeze, Governor. And you don't have a weapon that'll get through their shields. No—I'll draw them off. Evac your people."

"Understood, Admiral." One of Jiles's eyebrows gracefully arched, and he bowed. "Thank you."

"Fred, move us at best speed. Haverson, come to course zero-nine-zero. Get us closer to that moon-sized chuck of stone, twenty thousand kilometers to port."

"Flank speed," Fred said. "Aye, sir."

"Course change, aye," Haverson replied.

The *Gettysburg–Ascendant Justice* glided toward the large rock, and the Covenant cruiser rapidly closed on them. The enemy ship vanished on the displays as they rounded to the dark side of the asteroid.

"New course. Come about to one-eight-zero," the Admiral ordered. "Full emergency power to the engines and answer all stop."

Thrusters spun the ship around, and vibrations rumbled through the weakened hull as it slowed and came to a stop, hidden behind the rock.

"Answering all stop," Fred announced.

"Sir, we are dead in space," Lieutenant Haverson said and nervously ran his fingers through his slicked-back red hair. "Traditional tactics advocate speed and maneuverability in ship-to-ship combat."

"Not in this asteroid field," Admiral Whitcomb replied. "But you make a good point about staying maneuverable. Align our nose toward the center of mass of the planetoid, and back us up, one half reverse. Keep us out of the enemy's gunsights as long as you can."

"Firing thrusters. Answering one half reverse," Fred said.

The ship slowly angled toward the center of the large asteroid and backed away.

"Cortana?" the Admiral asked. "Do we have a weapons turret or not?"

"Yes, sir," Cortana said, "but the turret's magnetic coils that shape and aim the plasma charge have overloaded."

The Admiral inhaled and sighed explosively. "Master Chief, you got *anything* on Weapons Station One?"

"Archer missile pods depleted," the Master Chief answered. He scanned the display, hoping he had missed something. "No rounds for the MAC gun. All Shiva nuclear missiles fired as well, sir. The only things left in the tubes are three Clarion spy drones."

"No plasma and no missiles," Admiral Whitcomb said. "We might as well open an airlock and throw rocks at 'em."

Throw rocks? The Master Chief wondered if they could fashion a slug to shoot from the MAC cannon. Let its magnetic coils propel the mass to supersonic velocities and—

Magnetic coils?

"Sir," the Master Chief said. "We may have a way to fire the plasma turret after all. The *Gettysburg*'s MAC gun has seventeen superconducting coils. Cortana might be able to use them to shape and aim the plasma."

"Yes," the Admiral said, nodding.

"Maybe," Cortana amended and stared off into space, thinking. "Calculating field strength drop-off now." The mathematic symbols scrolling across her body increased threefold. She frowned. "This would be easier if the *Gettysburg* was oriented bottom to *Ascendant Justice*'s top. I'll have to guess at the interference from the intervening hulls, but it still might work. Chief—power it up. I'll need to recalibrate the pulse generation to match the plasma output."

"MAC gun magnetic fields coming online," the Master Chief said as he tapped in commands. "Rerouting power from *Ascendant Justice*'s reactor."

"We won't have enough power to move fast if we have to," Fred remarked, watching the energy fed to the *Gettysburg*'s engines drop to nothing.

"That's okay." The Admiral absentmindedly tugged at the end of his mustache. "We wouldn't be able to outrun that Covenant cruiser even if we had full power. Our only chance is to take them out *before* they take us out. Launch those Clarion spy drones, Chief. Target the region abeam that planetoid—so we can see around the corner."

The Master Chief kept one eye on the fluctuating magnetic field strengths of the superconducting coils as he programmed a course for the spy drones. Set to either side of the large asteroid, they'd effectively give them another set of eyes to see past the obstructing rock.

"Drones away," the Chief said and launched them; their feathery propellant trails vanished into the distance.

"Cortana," Admiral Whitcomb said, "slave your targeting system to the feed from those drones. I want a clean shot fired *before* the cruiser crosses that rock's shadow and shoots at us."

"Working," she replied. "Getting magnetic field variations from the *Ascendant Justice*-to-*Gettysburg* energy transfer."

"Drones in position and images online," the Master Chief said and pushed the video feed to the forward screen.

Doubled images of the Covenant cruiser appeared. Along its three bulbous sections, lateral plasma conduits glowed and every turret bristled with energy, ready to fire. Their laser batteries obliterated the large asteroids in their path, while the smaller ones simply bounced off their shields. The warship accelerated as it entered the gravitational influence of the planetoid between them.

"They're going to slingshot around," the Admiral said. "Cortana, give me your best targeting solution and fire at will!"

Cortana narrowed her eyes and calculations flashed across her body. "Extrapolating their course and speed," she breathed. "I got them."

On Weapons Station One the Master Chief saw the acceleration coils of the *Gettysburg*'s MAC pulse—then redline with power. Magnetic field lines ballooned, overlapped, and distorted asymmetrically. Static washed across his MJOLNIR armor's shields, and every electrically conducting surface on the bridge sparked as the magnetic lines of force penetrated through the ship and toward the turret on *Ascendant Justice*.

Their only working turret heated, and plasma gathered at its tip; streamers looped upon themselves like tiny solar flares, vibrated, intensified to orange and then blue-white.

"Almost there," Cortana cried. "Hang on."

The ball of squeezed plasma imploded. It instantly boiled away a thirty-meter section of armor and hull from *Ascendant Justice*; the plasma vanished for a split second—then a bolt of coiled energy corkscrewed toward the edge of the planetoid.

The Covenant cruiser rounded the planetoid, targeted the *Gettysburg*, and fired.

Cortana's single shot impacted on the nose of the enemy craft first. The cruiser's shield flashed solid silver for a moment and was gone. The supercompressed plasma tore into the hull of the warship—exploding the metal where it touched. The plasma forked and detonated outward as it chained through the vessel. Secondary explosions rippled through the alien ship's hull.

Edges of its shattered hull glowed red and then white hot as their superheated atmosphere vented. The bolt ripped through the engineering compartment, shattered their reactors, and the entire warship blossomed into fire and ejected trails of golden sparks and dying flickers of static electricity.

The five plasma bolts that the Covenant cruiser fired at the *Gettysburg* dispersed into a red haze. There was no longer any magnetic force to shape and guide them to their intended target.

The bridge crew watched the explosions fade from the forward screens. The Admiral said, "Status?"

Fred tapped the screen of the Engineering station and reported: "Engines and reactor offline. That magnetic pulse did something to them."

Static washed over Weapons Station One as the Master Chief looked up and said, "MAC accelerating coils intact. Drone one destroyed. Retrieving drone two, sir."

Cortana's holographic presence was missing, but her voice sounded triumphantly through the bridge speakers: "Turret number three destroyed. But if we ever get any of the other six turrets in working order, we'll have a formidable arsenal."

"We may not get that chance," Lieutenant Haverson remarked as he bent over the NAV station. "Contacts inbound. Small ships. Dozens of them. Transferring to the forward screens."

Armored Pelicans, exoskeleton welders, a handful of Longsword singleships, and the odd stealth *Chiroptera*-class vessel appeared on screen.

"Jiles's fleet," Haverson stated. "And he has us exactly where he wants us—dead in the water."

"Incoming transmission," Cortana said. "Piping it through."

"Admiral Whitcomb?" Jiles's rich and resonant voice flooded the bridge. "Can I be of some assistance? A tow, perhaps, back to our base so we can expedite repairs to your ships?"

"That would be most kind of you," the Admiral said and eased back into the Captain's chair.

Two *Laden*-class cargo ships came alongside the *Gettysburg* and attached; their engines rumbled.

"I don't understand," Haverson whispered. "He had us."

"No, he didn't," Admiral Whitcomb replied. He scowled and added, "Governor Jiles may not like it, but he needs us now. The Covenant aren't going to send just one ship. After this one goes missing for a while, there'll be more. A lot more. This is only the start of the battle, son."

John and his remaining teammates sat in the *Gettysburg*'s machine shop. The room was large enough to fit a Longsword inside, and the walls, ceilings, and deck had robotic arms tipped with welders, multitools, and hydraulic presses. Three of the arms had high-intensity spotlights directed onto the walls and provided a clear, cool, indirect illumination that the Master Chief found soothing after having one too many plasma blasts etch his retinas.

They were here because Admiral Whitcomb had ordered the Spartans to repair their equipment and get at least six hours of sleep. The machine shop was a solid room, reinforced, and unlikely to breach in case they were attacked again.

Linda sat in the corner with her helmet, back torso, and shoulder MJOLNIR armor sections removed.

Fred and Will used two robotic arms to hold her armor in place. They swapped out damaged plates and components with the spare parts they'd found in ONI's CASTLE facility on Reach.

Angry red scars crisscrossed Linda's pale body—the only external trace of her double transplant operation. Against Dr. Halsey's advice for strict bed rest, Linda had hobbled down here with her team. She sat cross-legged before a disassembled SRS99C sniper rifle and selected gyro compensators, optics, and adaptive texture barrel sheaths. Linda proceeded to reassemble the precision-made weapon with the care of a loving mother caressing her newborn child.

Without looking up from her rifle she said, "Now I know what you have to do to get a couple of days' R-and-R in this outfit."

"I heard," Fred remarked, "that you spent the whole time sleeping, too."

"That's why she likes to snipe," Will replied. "I caught her snoring last time she posted in that tower on Europa."

John was glad they could joke about her return from the dead. He couldn't bring himself to join in, though. He had accepted the mantle of command, and CPO Mendez had taught him to repress his external emotional reactions to preserve his authority. Right now, he resented that.

Kelly rolled over and woke up. She nudged Grace, and they sat up, shaking their helmets. "0400," Kelly told them. "That was six hours."

"Felt like a fifteen-minute nap," Grace muttered. "I just closed my eyes. You're kidding, right?"

Kelly looked over to Linda and drew her two fingers across her helmet in the *smile* gesture. Linda returned a rare, bare smile to her.

The smile looked odd to John. He wanted to smile, too, but nothing much—apart from Linda—in a long time had given him cause: not the hordes of rebels crawling over and through the *Gettysburg* whom Admiral Whitcomb trusted too much, nor the imminent return of Covenant forces before their engines and weapons could be repaired . . . and certainly not the hundreds of dead crew members aboard the *Gettysburg*, whom they had collected and placed in cargo bay seven.

The slight click of metal on metal alerted every Spartan in the room. Pistols drew in a blur of motion and rifles leveled at the side hatch as it eased open with a squeak.

Sergeant Johnson and Corporal Locklear stood in the doorway—frozen.

"No one told me this was target practice," Locklear muttered. "Else I woulda painted a bull's-eye on my chest."

"Master Chief," the Sergeant said. "Reporting as you requested."

John nodded and lowered his gun, as did the other Spartans. "Come in, Marines."

As he holstered his weapon, John's hand brushed against the belt compartment that held Dr. Halsey's data crystals. He hadn't decided which to give to Lieutenant Haverson. Did he sacrifice the Sergeant to save billions from potential Flood infestation? Did it even matter? He had every reason to believe that the Flood had been destroyed with Halo—but what if he was wrong?

"I wanted you both down here to help us discuss our tactical options," John told them.

The COM pulsed to life. Dr. Halsey said, *"Master Chief?"*

"Yes, Doctor?"

"I need Kelly to report to Medical Four," she said. *"She requires one last injection of dermacortic steroids. And I could use her assistance on another matter."*

John nodded to Kelly.

She slowly stretched, stood, sighed, and marched out of the room. "I'll be right back," she said, flexing her burned hands. "Don't plan the overthrow of the Covenant Empire without me."

"She's on her way, Doctor."

The COM snapped off.

The Master Chief turned to his Spartans and the Marines. "Let's go over what we know and see if we've missed anything—any way to exploit the enemy's plan." He set down a data pad with a star map glittering upon its surface.

"The Covenant are on their way to Earth," he told them. "They are gathering at a battle station and then jumping en masse to the Sol system."

"What happens then?" Fred asked.

"Assuming *we* get to Earth first," Linda answered, "our Fleet will be waiting for them, and"—she pulled back the bolt on her rifle with a *clack*—"they'll give them a warm reception."

"But what chance will our forces have?" Will asked. There was no fear in his voice, just cool logic. "You saw Cortana's report. There will be hundreds of Covenant warships. I don't think our Fleet or even Earth's orbital MAC platforms can repel a force that powerful."

"No," the Chief quietly said. "They can't win. They'll try. But the Covenant will eventually take down one of the orbital MACs, slip through, and pick off the ground-based generators. Just like on Reach."

Fred visibly flinched.

Locklear twisted the red bandanna he had tied on his biceps. "So we get to watch another fight in space?" he hissed. His fists trembled with barely checked rage. "There has to be a way to get to those bastards first—on the ground where we can win. Hell, I'd even take my chances in hand-to-hand combat. Anything but floating in zero gee and watching Earth get burned."

"What about our original mission?" Linda asked. "Find the Covenant home world?"

"Our priority has to be to warn Earth," the Chief answered. "Admiral Whitcomb would insist . . . and he has the authority to scrub our mission."

"And there's no ground between here and Earth where we can take the fight to them," Locklear said. He unclenched his fist and dropped his gaze to the deck. "Sometimes," he whispered, "I really hate this war."

Sergeant Johnson worked his mouth but said nothing. He set his hand on Locklear's wide shoulder and whispered, "Stand tall, Marine. Try to—"

The Sergeant's gaze fell on the data pad and the star map. "Hang on a second. What was it you said about no ground to fight on between here and there?" He grinned and picked up the data pad. "What's this?" He tapped a dot on the map, squinted, and read the tiny words. "This . . . 'Uneven Elephant'?"

"*Unyielding Hierophant,*" the Chief corrected. "According to Cortana, it's a command-and-control center, a mobile space platform where the Covenant fleet will rendezvous before their final jump to Earth."

"Well, there's your ground," Sergeant Johnson said. "On this 'elephant' thing."

Will got up and walked over to the data pad. "It fits with the timetable. This station *is* on the way to Earth."

Fred offered, "We can drop out of Slipspace in a smaller craft. Go in and—"

"And do what you Spartans do best," Locklear said. "Infiltrate, kill, and blow shit up. If there's room in this operation for an ODST, pencil me in."

The Master Chief looked to the data pad, then to his team, Locklear, and the Sergeant. They were right: For the first time, they'd know when and where the Covenant would be. If they hit the enemy hard enough, they could stop them before the Covenant hit Earth . . . and delay Armageddon.

The Master Chief gave rapid-fire orders:

"Fred, Will: Get Linda's suit back together ASAP.

"Locklear, you're on weapons detail again. Scrounge every pistol, rifle, ammo bag, and scrap of explosives on this vessel and haul it to *Ascendant Justice*'s launch bay.

"Grace, Linda, and Sergeant Johnson: Get that Covenant

dropship ready for its last flight. Reinforce the hull for a Slipspace-to-normal-space transition.

"And I'll take this plan to Admiral Whitcomb—make him see that it's the only way. We're going to take this fight to the Covenant. We're going to launch a first strike."

CHAPTER
THIRTY

Time was running out.

Dr. Halsey could feel the Covenant nearly upon them and her window of opportunity shrinking to a pinpoint. Only a few more things to take care of before she could go—before she started something she couldn't stop.

Someone approached the clean room, heavy footfalls that could only be a Spartan in MJOLNIR armor. Kelly appeared and waved from the other side of the glass partition that separated the clean room from the rest of Medical Four. Dr. Halsey buzzed her in.

"Reporting for treatment, Doctor," she said.

Kelly hesitated a moment as she glanced about at the unsterile environment the doctor had been working in: Styrofoam cups littered the surgical instrument trays, thermal printout paper curled from the biomonitors—and the radiation-emitting crystal they had found on Reach sat on a nearby instrument tray.

"I thought that crystal was in the reactor room," Kelly said. "Behind plenty of radiation shielding."

"It's perfectly safe," Dr. Halsey said, "as long as we're in normal space." She picked up the crystal and slipped it carelessly into her lab coat pocket.

"Lie down please, Kelly." The doctor gestured to the contoured treatment chair. "Just a few more injections and we're done with your burn therapy."

Kelly sighed and eased herself onto the reclined chair.

Dr. Halsey removed a cloth covering a pair of injectors. She clicked them into the ports on Kelly's MJOLNIR armor that threaded directly into her subclavian and femoral veins. "Keep doing your physical therapy, and the dermacortic steroids will remove most of the scarring and restore your full mobility within another week," she explained.

"A week?" Kelly growled and struggled to rise. "Doctor, I need to be one hundred percent ASAP. The Chief has a mission—"

Dr. Halsey activated the injectors, and they hissed their contents into Kelly's body. She relaxed and slumped back on the table, unconscious.

"No, Kelly," Dr. Halsey whispered. "You're not going on the Chief's mission. You're going on mine."

The sedative in her bloodstream would knock out an ODST in peak condition for the better part of a day. Halsey estimated that Kelly would be unconscious for a little more than two hours. By that time they'd both be far enough along that there'd be no turning back.

Dr. Halsey swiveled one of the displays to face her. She executed the memory-erase command—wiping clean Cortana's recollection of the research they had done on old ONI lockdown codes. She folded the printout of their results and stuffed it into her pocket.

"Cortana?"

"Yes, Doctor?" she replied. Her voice through the room's speakers sounded distracted.

"Locate Corporal Locklear and have him report immediately, please."

"Done, Doctor Halsey."

"Thank you, Cortana. That will be all." She added in a whisper so low that only she heard: *"Take good care of them all for me."*

Dr. Halsey adjusted the examination table so it lay flat, and then loaded medical supplies and equipment onto its undercarriage. She placed a bag with four submachine guns and sixteen full clips of ammunition on top of the supplies.

She found a lukewarm cup of stale coffee and gulped it down to the dregs.

Corporal Locklear appeared at the open entrance to the prep room. "Hey, Doc. Cortana said you needed me?" he said tersely. He smoothed his hand over his shaved head. "I'm kind of busy right now, so if this can wait—"

"Whatever you're doing," Dr. Halsey told him, "this is more important." She nodded to Kelly's prone form. "I need your help getting SPARTAN 087 to the launch bay."

"Is she okay?" he asked and took a step toward her.

"She's fine, but I have to transfer her to the asteroid base. They have a piece of equipment necessary to complete her treatment."

Locklear appeared unconvinced. "But I just saw her—"

"She's fine," Dr. Halsey assured him. "Just sedated. This procedure is . . . unpleasant, even for a Spartan."

Locklear looked into Dr. Halsey's eyes and then nodded, accepting this explanation. He moved the head of the table and wheeled it through the doors, the med bay, and out into the waiting elevator.

Dr. Halsey followed on his heels.

When the elevator doors closed, she turned to the Corporal. "Your hand, please."

He looked puzzled but held out his hand.

Dr. Halsey took it and turned it palm-up. She set the long, luminous blue artifact in his grasp. The light emitted by the alien artifact shone onto their faces and made the interior of the elevator colder. "This is what the Covenant so desperately want. They tore up Reach to get it. They followed us into Slipspace. And Polaski died protecting this thing."

She watched Locklear carefully, gauging his reaction, and saw that he pulled away slightly at this last remark; it had hit home.

"And what the hell am I supposed to do with it?"

"Keep it safe," she told him. "Guard it with your life, because if the Covenant ever get it, they'll be able to jump through Slipspace a hundred times faster than they can now. Do you understand?"

Locklear closed his large fist around the crystal. "Not really, Doc. But I can take care of it." He paused and wrinkled his forehead in confusion. "But why me? Why not ask one of your Spartans?"

" 'My' Spartans," Dr. Halsey replied in a whisper, "could be ordered to hand it over to Lieutenant Haverson. And he'd risk getting it back to ONI Section Three—even if he had to gamble that the Covenant might get it."

Locklear snorted. "Well, as much as I don't like El-Tee White-bread, I'd hand it over if ordered, too. What's the big deal, anyway? We're almost home."

"Almost," Dr. Halsey repeated, and she gave him a slight smile. "But the moment you jump, this crystal emits radiation like a signal flare. The Covenant will find this ship . . . and maybe this time they'll win the battle in Slipspace."

Locklear grimaced.

She held his steely gaze a moment and then finally let go of his hand. "So I know you'll do whatever it takes to prevent this object from falling into enemy hands."

He nodded grimly. "I read you, Doc. Loud and clear." There was a hint of respect in his voice. "I know what I have to do . . . count on it."

"Good," she said.

The elevator doors parted. Locklear stuffed the crystal into his ammunition vest, and Locklear wheeled the table into the *Gettysburg*'s launch bay. "Where do you want her?"

The bay was a beehive of activity: A hundred of Governor Jiles's crew jogged to and from passages carrying data pad schematics and field multiscanners; robotic dollies carried fat Archer missiles, spiderlike Antilon mines, and slender pods of deuterium fuel for the *Gettysburg*'s auxiliary reactors; three Longsword fighter craft were being repaired; exoskeletons thudded along the deck, carrying plates of titanium and welding them in place.

"There," Dr. Halsey told Locklear. "Take her to that ship." She pointed to Governor Jiles's *Chiroptera*-class vessel. It sat on the deck looking like a sleeping bat. Its oddly angled stealth surfaces blended into the shadows.

Locklear shrugged and pushed the loaded gurney.

Dr. Halsey halted by the ship's port hatch. It was sealed so tightly that no seam could be discerned.

She retrieved the thermal printout from her coat and rechecked its contents. She then touched a recessed button on the hull, and a tiny plate slid aside revealing an alphanumeric keyboard. Dr. Halsey typed in a long string and pressed ENTER.

The hatch parted with a hiss.

She smiled. "Not even Cortana could crack their crypto, indeed." She waved Locklear inside.

Locklear obliged her and pushed the gurney into the ship. Dr. Halsey followed, secured the examination table, and escorted Locklear outside. She turned and headed back into the vessel.

He started back toward the elevator, then halted. "Doc, when we were talking . . . you said when 'you' jump to Slipspace. You meant when 'we' jump to Slipspace, didn't you?"

Dr. Halsey locked eyes with him for a moment. Then she touched a button inside the ship, and the hatch hissed closed between them.

———

The Master Chief stepped off the elevator and onto the bridge of the *Gettysburg*. Lieutenant Haverson and Admiral Whitcomb stared at the displays at Weapons Station One and Engineering.

"Sirs," the Chief said.

The Admiral waved him forward without bothering to look up.

The Chief had two tasks. First, he would inform the Admiral of his first-strike mission plan. He had to convince him there was no risk to their primary goal of returning to Earth—and a huge payoff if they succeeded. The only thing Admiral Whitcomb might object to was the high risk to his team.

The Chief's second task would be more difficult. He touched the belt pouch containing Dr. Halsey's data crystals. One was her analysis of the Flood infection mechanism and a possible way to block it. The second data crystal contained the source files of that discovery, and according to Dr. Halsey it would lead to Sergeant Johnson's undignified, and unnecessary, death.

And yet, if it gave Section Three a better chance to stop the Flood—if indeed that threat had any meaning after the destruction of Halo—maybe it was worth one man's life. Maybe if Sergeant Johnson knew, he'd volunteer.

The Chief's duty was clear: He had to hand over all files to the Lieutenant—but deep down, he had to admit that it didn't feel right.

"Cortana." Admiral Whitcomb crossed his arms over his barrel chest. "Give me an update on our power."

Cortana's tiny image flickered to life on the holopad near the NAV station. She crossed her arms over her chest much as he had, and minute red symbols raced over her glowing lavender skin. "Status is nearly identical to my last report five minutes ago, Admiral. Tests on *Ascendant Justice*'s reactor and the *Gettysburg*'s engines are in synch, and will be completed in forty minutes."

"Hurry," the Admiral growled. "I don't want to get stuck without power when unfriendlies show up. I want to get under way to Earth. Weapons status?"

"Aye, sir," Cortana said. "Plasma turret one is obliterated; no possibility of repair. Plasma turrets two, three, and four are repaired, and although I'm waiting for power to test them, I have run three hundred twelve virtual test-firings without incident. Turrets five, six, and seven, however, require parts Governor Jiles does not have in his inventory. Two Archer missile pods on the *Gettysburg* have been refilled. That gives us sixteen missiles hot and ready to go, sir."

"I'd like to know where Jiles got those missiles," Lieutenant Haverson muttered. "They're UNSC military contraband."

"He is a *pirate*, Lieutenant," Cortana said.

"Good work," the Admiral told Cortana. "Keep me posted." He turned toward the Chief. "You had something, Master Chief?"

Before the Master Chief could speak his mind, Haverson said, "Admiral." He pointed at the forward screens and at the *Chiroptera*-class ship accelerating away from the *Gettysburg*'s launch bay. "I thought Jiles was staying on board to oversee repairs."

"So did I," the Admiral said. "Cortana, did you catch Jiles leaving on surveillance?"

"No, sir, but you might be interested in this." On the screen a grainy video appeared of Locklear, Dr. Halsey, and a Spartan on a gurney boarding the ship. "Locklear left them at the ship, sir. Doctor Halsey and SPARTAN 087 departed."

"Cortana," the Admiral barked. "Hail that ship. *Now.*"

"Hailing."

Governor Jiles appeared on forward screen number one. "Admiral," he said with a nervous smile. "I just saw my ship leave the launch bay. Perhaps you can explain why you commandeered my personal property when I have showed nothing but good faith in this—"

"Hold on to your shirttail, Governor," Admiral Whitcomb snapped. "I'm in the middle of finding out who took your ship and what precisely is going on. Cortana, any response to our hail?"

"An automated code, sir," she said. Her mouth opened in astonishment. "UNSC Code Three-Nine-Two."

"Three-Nine-Two?" the Admiral asked. He stared into space, trying to recall the obscure code.

The Master Chief cleared his throat and told him, "Admiral, that is an official 'nonresponse' code, sir. Special Warfare teams use it to ignore hails . . . due to a higher-priority mission."

"God *damn* it." The Admiral's face flushed, and he ground his teeth. "You mean the good doctor just told me to go to hell."

On the forward screen the Chiroptera, its batlike wings nearly invisible against the black of space, accelerated in a sudden burst. Pinpoints of light appeared around the craft that elongated and smeared. The ship vanished.

"A Slipspace transition," Cortana said.

"I thought you told me," the Admiral said, slowly turning on Haverson, "that that ship was locked down. That vital components were removed when it was decommissioned. That there was no way it could make a Slipspace jump?"

"Yes, sir, I did."

"And would you care to explain why that ship just disappeared, Lieutenant?"

"Yes, Admiral. I was wrong," Haverson replied without meeting the Admiral's eyes. "Doctor Halsey apparently found a way to circumvent the ONI lockout on the ship's systems."

On screen, Jiles said, "This is most unfortunate, Admiral. I expect to be compensated—"

"You bet it's unfortunate," Admiral Whitcomb said. "If I'd known there was a chance we could have used that ship to jump to Earth . . . I would have done it an hour ago. Cortana, what was her trajectory?"

"Not Earth," Cortana said. "Doctor Halsey's course points to no known system in my database."

The Admiral scrutinized the forward screens: Jiles's face, the empty star field, and the frozen video of Dr. Halsey and Locklear in the launch bay. "I want Corporal Locklear on the bridge ten minutes ago. Lieutenant Haverson, have Cortana locate him. Then I want you *personally* to escort that ODST up here."

Haverson swallowed. "Yes, sir." He marched to the elevator, and Cortana told him, "He's on B-Deck, Lieutenant, medical storage. He's not answering my COM page." The elevator shut.

"Chief, you're on the Engineering console," the Admiral said. "Cover the NAV station, too."

"Yes, sir." He moved to the Engineering station's monitors. There were thirty-five minutes to go on the shakedown cycle of the reactors and engines.

"Contact," Cortana said. "Bearing zero-three-zero on the solar plane. One—correction, two—Covenant cruisers. They're not moving. Maybe they haven't spotted us."

"It never rains when it can monsoon," the Admiral declared. "They can't help but see us, Cortana, with all the radio chatter, ships, and leaking radiation. I bet they're just figuring out how best to kill us."

Governor Jiles turned to someone off screen, and then said, "Admiral Whitcomb, given this new development I would like to evacuate my people off the *Gettysburg* and out of harm's way."

"Of course, Governor. Do what you have to."

The number three screen snapped off, and the stars reappeared.

"And I'll do what I have to, too," Admiral Whitcomb said. "Cortana, halt the reactor and engine shakedown."

"Sir? There are risks—"

"I want them online *now*. Don't tell me what the risks are. Just do it."

"Yes, sir," she said.

"Master Chief, get this crate ready to move and stay on your toes. We'll need every trick in the book to outmaneuver two cruisers."

"Affirmative, Admiral." The Chief observed the shakedown cycle halt and *Ascendant Justice*'s reactors restart. Radiation indicators redlined, and then dropped to a hairbreadth . . . which was technically considered safe. The *Gettysburg*'s engines shuddered to life. The Chief felt the vibration though the deck half a kilometer away. "Reactors are hot, sir," he reported.

The Admiral watched as Jiles's fleet of single ships and technicians in jet packs abandoned the *Gettysburg*, swarming across the dark of space back to the safety of their asteroid. "Rats leaving a sinking ship?" he wondered aloud.

The Master Chief wasn't sure if that was a question directed at him, but he decided to reply anyway. "They're just men who want to live, sir."

The Admiral nodded.

"Covenant cruiser accelerating," Cortana announced. "Bearing on a vector *out*-system. It's transitioning to Slipspace."

"Master Chief, get this tub moving. Now! Bring us up to half maximum speed."

"Aye, sir." He tapped in commands. "Answering one half forward." The radiation warning on *Ascendant Justice*'s reactor flickered, but stabilized and subsided.

The combined mass of the two attached ships groaned as their recently repaired superstructures overcame their inertia.

"Heat up our plasma turrets, Cortana."

"Aye s—" Her translucent lavender hologram faded to ice blue. "Sir, additional contacts at system's edge. Three. No— additional transitions from Slipspace; counting eighteen—now *thirty* Covenant ships of various classes. Positions zero-three-zero. Zero-nine-one, one-eight-zero . . . Sir, they have us enveloped."

The star chart vanished in a wink, and a map of the Eridanus system appeared with tiny triangles representing Covenant ships now encircling the perimeter. The map turned to a side profile and revealed half a dozen additional ships scattered along the nadir and zenith of the system.

Admiral Whitcomb stared at the map and shook his head. "You know the story of the Alamo, Chief?"

"Yes, sir. A famous siege with a handful of defenders holding off overwhelming forces."

The Admiral smiled. "*Texan* defenders, Chief—there's a big difference. Colonel William Barrett Travis with one hundred fifty-five men held off more than two thousand Mexican invaders. They hunkered down inside a tiny fort and fought like wildcats. Travis got a handful of reinforcements later—thirty-two men." The Admiral's smile faded. "You know there were fifteen civilians inside that fort, too?" He looked at the map again. "Well, when the fighting was over, Travis and his men were dead, but it cost the enemy six hundred lives."

"Like the Battle of Thermopylae," the Chief remarked.

"But there were survivors at the Alamo; they let the civilians live." He turned to the Chief. "You think anyone's going to survive this fight? You think there's any way to win?"

The Master Chief tried to think of a way to fight and to win. Thirty Covenant ships against their damaged hybrid vessel. Add to that the need to defend Governor Jiles's crew. Could he board one of the Covenant craft? Get Cortana to infiltrate their systems and broadcast falsified orders? They would see him approaching. Or was there a blind spot he could approach from? How could he hide from the rest of the ships in their fleet, though? And by the time he could implement such a plan, the *Gettysburg* would be molten slag.

"It was a rhetorical question, Chief," the Admiral said.

"Yes, sir," the Chief replied. "Given our situation, resources, and our enemy's determination, then, no, I see no way to win . . . or survive."

"Neither do I." Admiral Whitcomb stood straight. "Cortana, get ready to jump. Chief, accelerate to flank speed course zero-five-five by two-nine-zero. Prepare to transition out of normal space on my mark."

"Aye, sir," the Chief and Cortana answered in unison.

"We're leaving Governor Jiles and his people?" Cortana asked.

Admiral Whitcomb was silent a long moment, and then he replied, "We are. This isn't the Alamo and I'm not Colonel William Barrett Travis, although I dearly wish I were. No, we're running. We're trading hundreds of lives for billions."

The Master Chief absentmindedly reached for his belt pouch, and Dr. Halsey's data crystals clinked. "Is this the right thing to do, sir?"

"The right thing?" Admiral Whitcomb sighed. "Hell, son, it probably isn't. Personally, I'd prefer to fight, and die fighting, and take every one of those Covenant bastards with me. But I do not have the liberty to make that choice. My duty is clear: to protect the men and women of Earth—not a pack of privateers and outlaws." He closed his eyes and said, "The logic of the situation is also too damned clear. Even if we stay and fight . . . they'll all be just as dead."

"Capacitors at full charge," Cortana announced. "Preparing to enter Slipspace. Waiting for your order, sir."

The Master Chief saw the energy from *Ascendant Justice*'s reactor drain to 5 percent. Motes of blue-green light appeared on the forward screen, and the stars stretched and smeared like watercolors.

But something was wrong: The shields of the Chief's MJOLNIR armor rippled. The radiation monitors spiked. Where was it coming from?

"Hundreds for billions," the Admiral whispered. "Duty be damned . . . I'm still going to burn in hell for this." Admiral Whitcomb inhaled deeply and closed his eyes.

"Go, Cortana. Get us out of here. And God forgive me."

Corporal Locklear whistled, and the robotic dolly obediently followed him. The rolling robot was stacked with rifles, pistols, ammunition crates, and enough C-7 foaming explosive to blow a half-kilometer crater in the side of the *Gettysburg*.

He made his way to the cargo elevator and then down to B-Deck. He had seen on the *Gettysburg*'s inventory that that was where they stored medical supplies . . . and he wanted a few cans of biofoam handy for the Master Chief's extremely well-planned suicide mission.

Not that Locklear had anything against a good suicide mission. He'd been on plenty before, and they seemed to give him the most bang for his buck. Only now, after so much fighting, he just wanted a break: twenty-four hours of sleep, and some R&R.

He idly tugged at the bandanna tied to his biceps.

"Damn girl," he whispered. "Why'd you have to die? I had plans for you and me."

What was he doing mooning over a woman? And a Navy flier to boot? His squad would have laughed themselves wet if they knew . . . only they were all dead, too.

"Screw this," Locklear said. "I'm still alive. I'm not going to die. And I'm not going to feel guilty for any of this."

He laughed and told himself, "It's not like the entire universe hasn't been trying to kill me off, though." Locklear turned to the robotic dolly. "Right, amigo?"

Its treads spun, and the flatbed dolly turned to the right.

"No, no, *stop*." He sighed. "Man, I gotta buy myself a ticket out of this outfit. Next thing, I'll be asking one of the Spartans out on a date . . . if I could even tell the boys from the girls in that squad." He shuddered.

The doors of the large cargo elevator squeaked open; Locklear stepped off, and whistled for the dolly to follow.

Storage Bay Two had racks and shelves that rose from the

deck five meters to the ceiling. He played his flashlight over the uneven surfaces. He spied a desk and terminal in the corner.

"Hello, inventory control," he said. "The place to go for goodies in any Navy outfit." He strode to the desk, sat down, and tapped in a search for medicinal-grade ethyl alcohol.

A tone chimed in his earpiece, and Cortana's voice said, "Corporal Locklear, I have an urgent request from Admiral—"

Locklear squelched his COM. "Enough chatter, lady," he murmured. "The bar just opened."

The location for MED34-CH$_3$CH$_2$OH popped on screen.

"B-I-N-G-O," he sang.

Locklear jumped up. "Come on, amigo. You and me are going to throw a party."

The deck lurched under Locklear's feet. "What the? . . . We're moving?" He turned the inventory display to face him and tapped in a command to switch to external camera mode.

Craggy asteroids moved past them—no, it was the *Gettysburg* that was moving. Locklear squinted and saw a flash of blue. He magnified that part of the screen and found a dozen blurry blue flares from engine cones and the pulsing lateral lines filled with plasma. Covenant ships.

"Ah hell," he said and backed away from the desk. "So much for happy hour."

Something moved in his vest. Locklear reached in his pocket and pulled out the crystal Dr. Halsey entrusted to his care. The elongated stone rippled, facets moved and rearranged like the pieces of a jigsaw puzzle.

He spied the same blue color on the inventory monitor—pinpricks of stretched space, the first indication of a Slipspace jump.

"I'm not going through another Slipspace fight," Locklear said through gritted teeth. "I'm not going to let them follow us. Or let this thing shoot off a signal flare to every Covenant ship in the galaxy."

He grabbed a can of C-7 off the dolly and dropped Dr. Halsey's crystal on the deck. He quickly covered the thing with the foaming explosive. It hardened to a stiff resin in a matter of seconds. Locklear grabbed a detonator, inserted it into the foam, and connected it to a timer.

Why had the doc given him this to guard? She said because the ONI spooks wouldn't have the guts to get rid of it if they had to . . . would maybe even let it fall into Covenant hands. That made sense, but, at the same time, there was something not quite right with that explanation.

Locklear looked at the monitor and the pinpoints of light that now almost blotted out the stars.

Screw it.

He had his own reasons to blow this thing up—like not wanting to die in another space battle. Like maybe getting some payback for Polaski's death. The Covenant rat-bastards wanted it so bad? Well, screw them, too.

"This one's for you, Polaski," he whispered.

Locklear set the timer for three seconds, and punched the countdown. He dived for cover behind the robotic dolly and covered his head.

The brilliant flash of sapphire light was the last thing he ever saw.

SECTION VI

OPERATION: FIRST STRIKE

ESCAPE

THIRTY-ONE

The Master Chief and his team, which now consisted of Grace, Linda, Will, and Fred, had been ordered to report to the Officers' Club—normally forbidden territory to NCOs. Of course, nothing about their circumstances had been normal for a long, long time.

The *Gettysburg*'s O-Club had a massive table of oak, scored with numerous gouges and scorches from a hundred cigars casually set upon its surface. There was a bar stocked with bottles containing a rainbow collection of liquors, dusted with shattered crystal. The room's walnut-paneled walls were polished to a rich glow. Hung along those walls was the UNSC gold-fringed blue flag. There were also gold and silver citation plaques for meritorious gallantry. There were photos of officers and past Captains of the *Gettysburg*. And most interesting to the Master Chief were tin Civil War daguerreotypes that displayed battlefields full of charging men and cavalry and cannons belching flash and thunder.

Admiral Whitcomb and Sergeant Johnson entered the room. The Spartans snapped to rigid attention. "Officer on deck!" the Master Chief shouted, and they all saluted.

"At ease," Admiral Whitcomb said. "Please sit down."

The Master Chief stepped forward. "With respect, these chairs will not support the weight of our gear, Admiral."

"Of course," the Admiral said. "Well, make yourselves as comfortable as you can. This is an informal meeting." He snorted. "I just wanted to see who was left on board and alive." He looked past the open doors to the Officers' Club. "Lieutenant Haverson will join us shortly. He's investigating the site of Corporal Locklear's . . . accident."

A holographic projector pad upon the bar flickered to life, and Cortana's slender body appeared. Chunks of broken crystal on the pad refracted the light and distorted her image so she appeared half melted and cast prismed arcs of light onto the walls.

Sergeant Johnson stepped over to the bar and swept the pad clean.

"Thank you, Sergeant," Cortana said, looking over her restored figure.

"My pleasure," he replied with a grin.

Cortana faced the Admiral. "Sir," she said, "you'll be happy to hear that I'm detecting no signals, residual radiation, or any transient contacts . . . which is precisely what you would expect from a *normal* Slipspace journey."

Admiral Whitcomb nodded, sighed, and eased into one of the leather-backed chairs at the table's head. "Well, that's one small blessing."

"And here's evidence that Doctor Halsey's crystal was indeed destroyed," Lieutenant Haverson said as he entered the room. He paused to seal the door behind him.

Haverson sat next to the Admiral and set a small plastic bag flat on the table. "I found Locklear exactly where Cortana said he would be: B-Deck, the medical storage room. Overloaded electronics at the site are consistent with a high-energy radiation burst . . . as are the burns on the Corporal's body."

He grimaced and added, "If it means anything, his death was quick. And these"—he tapped the plastic bag on the table—"are crystalline fragments that I found at the site. At first glance they appear to be a match to the shard found on

Reach." He shook his head. "But what I found isn't sufficient mass to account for the entire crystal. So unless it was atomized and left no trace, a fact inconsistent with the presence of these larger pieces, then the rest of that crystal has to be somewhere else."

Cortana tapped her foot, and one of her eyebrows arched. "If the radiation burst detected before our jump correlates with the destruction of Doctor Halsey's crystal," she said, "then there is an alternative explanation. The timing between that explosion and the radiation flare was only forty-seven milliseconds. Since the crystal had unusual space-and time-bending properties, the missing fragments may have been 'squeezed' out of the ship and into Slipspace."

Haverson asked incredulously, "You mean pieces of the greatest scientific discovery in human history are"—he nodded past the walls of the *Gettysburg*—"lost in Slipspace?"

"Yes," Cortana replied. She shrugged. "I'm sorry, Lieutenant."

"At least the Covenant can't get to it anymore," Admiral Whitcomb said. He flicked the plastic bag with his thick finger. "Or if they do, they're only going to find a bunch of busted fragments."

"I just wish I knew why Locklear did it," Haverson said.

Everyone was quiet. John and the other Spartans shifted uneasily in their heavy MJOLNIR armor.

Sergeant Johnson cleared his throat. "The boy was a little on edge. After all he'd been through, you'd expect that. But he was an ODST—tough as nails and twice as sharp and used to getting pounded. He wouldn't crack. He had a reason."

"Doctor Halsey," Haverson remarked and narrowed his eyes. "She had to have set this up."

John started to defend Dr. Halsey, but he stopped himself from arguing with an officer. Yes, her actions were inexplicable: She had exfiltrated Kelly, left them when they needed her the most, and given Locklear the alien artifact. John still wanted to trust her, though. Perhaps whatever she was up to was for the greater good.

"Let's not start this," the Admiral said. "I don't want anyone's perceptions colored by us discussing the 'whys' and 'what ifs' of this situation. Save it for the debriefing they're going to give us when we get back." He cast a sideways glance at the bar and unconsciously smacked his lips. "From here to Earth it should be smooth sailing, and we can finally relax."

"Permission to speak, Admiral," the Chief said.

"Granted. Speak your mind."

"I don't wish to contradict you, sir, but perhaps it shouldn't be smooth sailing. And maybe we shouldn't relax."

Admiral Whitcomb leaned forward. "I have a feeling I'm not going to like this . . . but explain yourself, Chief."

The Master Chief outlined his mission plan, how he and his team would take a Covenant dropship and insert into the rendezvous location for the invading Covenant fleet. They would then infiltrate their command-and-control center, the *Unyielding Hierophant*, and destroy it; that would hopefully cripple the Covenant force . . . or at least slow them down. Maybe even enough to buy Earth time to reinforce their defenses.

The Admiral stared at the Chief without blinking and flatly replied, "Mission request denied."

"Acknowledged, sir." He remained standing, at stiff attention.

Whitcomb frowned, as the other Spartans also snapped to attention and remained stone-still. He sighed.

"I understand your motivations, Chief. I do. But I will not risk transporting your team to the Covenant rendezvous point," the Admiral explained. "If we lose this ship, Earth never gets its warning."

"Sir," the Master Chief replied, "we will transition from Slipspace to normal space alone. Once the dropship clears the gravitational influence of the *Gettysburg* and the *Ascendant Justice*, the Slipspace field will deteriorate and we will enter normal space. You need never even stop. And only a minor course correction puts the *Gettysburg* on the correct trajectory."

"Has a drop out of Slipspace ever been attempted in a ship so small?" the Admiral asked. His heavy brows knitted together.

"Yes, sir," Cortana said. "Our Slipspace probes perform the maneuver all the time, but the shearing stress and radiation are considerable." She paused and looked toward John. "The Spartans, however, in the MJOLNIR armor should be able to survive."

"'Should,'" the Admiral echoed, his face grim. "As much as I admire your daring, Chief, I still have to deny your request. You'll need Cortana to get past the Covenant security systems. She has to make it to Earth. With the data she's carrying on Halo, the Flood, and Covenant technology, she's far too valuable to risk."

"Understood, sir," John replied. "I hadn't considered that."

Haverson slowly stood and brushed the sleeves of his tattered uniform. "I'll volunteer to go on the Master Chief's mission," he said. "I have extensive training in cryptology and Covenant systems."

Admiral Whitcomb narrowed his eyes and reexamined the Lieutenant as if seeing him for the first time.

"You'd never survive the Slipspace transition," Cortana told him. "But . . ." She tapped her lip with her forefinger, deep in thought. "There might be another way."

Covenant icons entered the stream of symbols flowing along the surface of her holographic body. "I discovered a file-duplication algorithm in the Covenant AI on *Ascendant Justice*. I successfully used it to reproduce my language-translation routines. I might use it to copy portions of my infiltration programming into the memory-processing matrix in the Master Chief's MJOLNIR armor. It won't be a full copy—there are replication errors and other side effects—but it would give the Spartan team access to some of my capabilities. Enough, I think, to get them through the Covenant security barriers."

Admiral Whitcomb sighed deeply. He stood, went to the bar, and then returned to the table carrying a bottle of whiskey and three intact crystal tumblers. "I assume you Spartans won't join me in a drink?"

"No, sir," John replied, answering for his team. "Thank you, sir."

The Admiral set glasses before Haverson, the Sergeant, and himself. But before he poured, he set the bottle down and shook his head as if a drink were suddenly the last thing he wanted. "You realize, Chief, that you and your team will be on your own? That my first, my only priority, must be to get to Earth?"

"My team is willing to accept the risk," the Chief said.

"The risk?" the Admiral whispered. "It's a one-way ticket, son. But if you're willing to do it, if you can slow the Covenant assault on Earth, then, hell, it might be worth the trade."

The Chief had no reply to this. He and his Spartans had survived against impossible odds before. Yet the Admiral was right: There seemed to be something final about this mission . . . something that told John he wouldn't make it. That was acceptable. The cause more than justified the sacrifice of five when measured against billions of lives on Earth.

Admiral Whitcomb stood and said, "Very well, Master Chief. Mission request approved."

The Master Chief parked the groaning overloaded robotic dolly next to the side hatch of the Covenant dropship. The dolly held four tons of carbon-molybdenum steel I-beams.

Will unloaded the cargo and hauled it inside, where Fred and the Sergeant cross-braced and welded the beams in place.

This was the final reinforcement for the dropship. The interior of the craft was so cramped that two armored Spartans could barely pass one another.

They had welded layers of lead, boron fibers, and Titanium-A hull plates they had removed from the *Gettysburg*. According to Cortana's calculations, this was the only way to give them better than fifty–fifty odds of emerging from a Slipspace transition with an intact ship.

Admiral Whitcomb monitored the display of a computer repair cart, then looked up and said, "Cortana is ready for you, Chief." He waved him over.

The Chief marched to the cart and let the Admiral hook up the interface to the base of his neck. "This should feel just like a normal download," he said.

Chilled mercury filled John's mind just like it always did when Cortana entered and fused with his thoughts. This presence, however, warmed too quickly, as if it were just thin ice melting against his body's heat. It was like a recollection of Cortana inside his head—not the real thing.

"Initializing MJOLNIR armor systems check and subroutine unpacking protocols," Cortana's voice whispered.

At the same time, the real Cortana also spoke over the COM: "Don't listen to her. She's only half the woman she used to be."

"As long as you only copied the good parts," the Chief replied.

"I'm all good," Cortana replied tersely. "Just don't get too used to a passenger you can order around."

"I wouldn't dream of it."

"Systems check complete," the copied Cortana whispered. "All systems are functional."

Linda approached the opposite side of the Covenant dropship; a robot dolly followed stacked with rifles, Lotus antitank mines, explosives, and crates of ammunition. She angled the dolly and led it up the loading ramp until it butted against the hull.

Fred emerged from inside, and Linda handed him an armful of submachine guns.

The Master Chief detected a slight limp to her stride and an almost imperceptible awkwardness to her usual fluid motions.

He opened a private COM channel to Linda. "What's your status? Are you fit?"

She shrugged. This gesture was notoriously difficult to perform in MJOLNIR armor with its force-multiplying circuits. It took a degree of concentration and dexterity that spoke volumes about Linda's true coordination.

"Doctor Halsey would say I needed a month's bed rest," she wryly replied. "But I'm squared away, Chief. I still have this." She picked her sniper rifle off the dolly and slung it over her shoulder with a liquid grace. "And I still have this." She patted her helmet. "Even though the Covenant did their best to shoot it off last time." She stepped closer to him. "I can take care of myself. And I can take care of the team's back. I've never let you down, sir. I don't plan on doing so now."

He nodded.

What John wanted to do, however, was order her to stay behind. But he'd need her uncanny skill with the sniper rifle on this mission. He'd need her so they could survive just long enough to stop the Covenant.

If he could have accomplished this mission alone, he would have made everyone on Blue Team stay. His team, however, knew the risks and knew the payoff for their sacrifice. It was as good a final fate as any soldier could ask for.

He marched to the other hatch on the dropship and boarded the craft. There was one last detail to take care of with Lieutenant Haverson. John moved past Sergeant Johnson who, obscured by a shower of sparks, welded the last supporting I-beam in place.

The Lieutenant sat in the cockpit checking the automated routines that Cortana had uploaded into the system. These would generate the proper coded responses to Covenant queries. They had also changed the dropship's registry tag so the Covenant would not recognize this ship as belonging to the now renegade *Ascendant Justice*.

"Lieutenant," the Master Chief said. "Forgive the interruption."

Haverson looked up and slicked the sweat-drenched hair from his face. "What can I do for you, Chief?"

The Master Chief eased into the copilot's seat. "Dr. Halsey gave me something to pass on to ONI Section Three: her analysis on the Flood."

Haverson's eyebrows shot up.

He opened his belt compartment . . . and hesitated. Which data crystal? The one only containing Dr. Halsey's Flood analysis and possible inoculation? Or the one containing the source files for her conclusions, the one she said would kill Sergeant Johnson?

While John felt justified in gambling his life and the lives of the other Spartans, that was his choice as their commander to make. That wasn't the case for the Sergeant.

It was a biological fluke that had spared the Sergeant from the Flood. A one-in-a-billion shot, the doctor had said. But it was a billion-to-one shot that he could save billions of lives. So the mathematics of the situation were almost even.

What had Dr. Halsey said about saving every person, no matter what the cost?

No—John had sworn an oath to protect all of humanity. His duty was clear. He reached for the crystal containing the complete files and handed it to Lieutenant Haverson. "She said it would help fight the Flood, sir. I'm not exactly sure what she meant."

"We'll see, Chief. Thank you." Haverson took the crystal and peered into its depths. He shrugged. "With Doctor Halsey, who can tell?"

The COM channel clicked, and Cortana announced, "Ten minutes until we reach the drop zone. Make final preparations to launch Blue Team. You'll only get one shot at this."

"Roger that, Cortana," the Chief replied. "Spartans, on deck!"

Haverson tentatively extended his hand. "I guess this is it, Chief."

The Chief gently shook the Lieutenant's hand. "Good luck, sir."

John moved back though the dropship—almost running over Sergeant Johnson, who was dragging the arc welder down the gangway.

"Allow me, Sergeant." John grasped the two-hundred-kilogram machine and lifted it with one hand.

The Master Chief exited the dropship, and he and the other Spartans assembled outside. He stowed the arc welder and took his position at the head of the Spartan formation.

Admiral Whitcomb looked them over once and then said, "I'd wish you luck, Master Chief, but you Spartans seem to make your own luck. So let me just say I'll see you all when this is over."

He saluted them and they returned the salute.

"Just one last order," the Admiral said.

"Sir?"

"Give 'em hell."

THIRTY-TWO

The dropship rolled, inverted, and spun out of control. It tumbled and pitched, and one of the I-beams solidly welded to the hull bucked and snapped.

The Spartans of Blue Team were strapped to the hull in quick-release harnesses. No one, however, gave any thought to the red quick-release button in the center of their chests. They were all hanging on for their lives.

The forward monitor was black because there was nothing for them to see in Slipspace. The only light inside the dropship came from chemical light sticks activated and tossed inside before they departed. Those plastic sticks had cracked, and their luminous contents had balled into a million microscopic blobs in the zero gee.

Although the hydrostatic gel inside his MJOLNIR armor had been pressurized to its maximum safe value, John's bones still felt as if they were being shaken apart.

This violent ride started when they had cleared *Ascendant Justice*'s launch bay and entered the inky void of Slipspace. This "normal" Slipspace was nothing like John had experienced before. Without the smoothing effect of Dr. Halsey's alien crystal—this ride was a thousand times worse.

Radiation levels spiked and dipped . . . but so far the dosages getting into the lead-lined dropship were survivable.

"Now I know," Linda said, "why only big ships travel through Slipspace."

"You know those SS probes?" Fred asked. "They're almost solid Titanium-A."

The Master Chief checked his team's biosigns: erratic but still within normal operational parameters. Grace's heart skipped a beat or two, but then returned to a normal strong rhythm. No broken bones or signs of internal bleeding yet, either. It was also a good sign that Blue Team were reasonably calm about their dire situation. The Chief knew it was all they could do until they cleared the Slipspace field generated by *Ascendant Justice*.

He ran a diagnostic on his MJOLNIR shields. They still recharged faster than they were drained by the ambient radiation that stormed invisibly around them. He wished the real Cortana were with him. She would have said something to distract him.

"Status?" John asked.

Four blue acknowledgment lights winked on, and four Spartans gave him thumbs-up signals.

Fred chimed in, "This isn't so bad. The last insertion I made, we hit the ground before the dropship. Now, *that* was a rough ride. We were—"

The dropship lurched violently and cut off Fred's story.

Cracks appeared along the armor welded to the port wall. Molten lead oozed from the rupture.

Despite the hydrostatic gel and the padding, a jolt slammed the Master Chief's head against the front of his helmet with force enough to make black stars explode in his eyes. Another jolt slammed his head into the back of his helmet. The inside of the dropship went entirely dark.

"Chief? Chief?" Cortana's voice whispered through his helmet speaker. "Chief, respond please."

John's vision came into focus. His biosigns sluggishly pulsed on his heads-up display. Beyond the display, it was completely dark. He activated his external lights and pointed his head along the interior of the dropship.

His Spartans hung limp in their harnesses. Aside from spheres of lead that had melted under the hull armor, resolidified, and now floated like champagne bubbles in the interior of the vessel, there was no other discernible motion.

"We made it?"

"Affirmative," the cloned Cortana answered. "I'm picking up a tremendous volume of Covenant COM traffic on the F- through K-bands. They've pinged us three times already for a response, Chief. Awaiting orders."

"How can you pick up any signal inside this lead-lined hull?"

"The hull is breached in many sections, Chief. The COM traffic is also unusually strong, indicating extremely close proximity of Covenant forces."

"Stand by," he told her. He hit the quick release on his harness and floated free. He called up Blue Team's biosigns and found them all unconscious, but alive. He grabbed a first-aid kit, injected them each with a mild stimulant, and released them from their safety restraints.

"Where are we?" Will asked.

The Master Chief looked instinctively to the forward monitors, but they were dead. "There's only one way to find out," he replied. "I'll take the portside hatch. Fred, you're on the starboard."

"Roger, Blue-One," Fred replied.

The Chief rotated the manual release of the hatch and it eased open. Beyond was the velvet black of space, filled with stars that shone yellow and amber and red. He clipped a tether onto his suit and then onto the hull and leaned out the hatch.

As Cortana had indicated, there were Covenant forces in close proximity. A cruiser glided silently past them three hundred meters away. All John could see was its silver-blue hull, its plasma turrets with their lateral lines aglow with fire, and the flare of its engine cones as it passed . . . and then John saw the rest of them.

There were Covenant cruisers and larger carriers; there were even bigger vessels with five bulbous sections that were two kilometers stem to stern and had a dozen deadly energy projectors. Motes of dust swirled between the numerous ships: Seraph fighters, dropships, and tentacled Engineer pods.

"How many ships," he asked Cortana, "are we looking at?"

"Two hundred forty-seven warships," she replied. "Estimation of the total population based on the sampling from your limited field of vision puts that total number at more than five hundred Covenant warships."

For the first time the Chief froze; his gauntlets locked onto the edge of the hatch, and his arms failed to respond. Five hundred ships? This fleet would easily overwhelm any UNSC defensive force—whether or not the Admiral got through with his warning. Their opening salvo would be a tidal wave of plasma, and it would obliterate Earth's orbital fortresses before they could fire a shot.

A thousand kilometers below, space rippled, parted, and seven more cruisers appeared in normal space. They maneuvered to join the rest of the pack.

John realized that the last time he had seen this magnitude of destructive power had been Halo. The ring was a weapon designed to kill all sentient life for dozens of light-years in every direction.

And he had stopped that threat. He could stop this one, too. He had to.

His plan called for the infiltration and destruction of their command-and-control station. But how would that stop this gathering of force? It wouldn't . . . but it might buy Earth enough time to come up with a plan to counter this seemingly invincible armada.

"You said they've pinged us three times?" John asked Cortana.

"Affirmative. They've been curious about our status, but not as much as you might expect. There's a tremendous amount of COM traffic. They're probably only interested in us as a navigation hazard."

"Send a signal and explain that our engines are crippled and we'll need assistance to move. Let's see if we can get them to take us to this central station for repairs."

"Sending message now."

The Master Chief piped what he was seeing to Blue Team. "Time to wake up," he said. "Armor and weapons check on the double."

There was a pause of several seconds before Blue Team's acknowledgment lights pulsed in his HUD. He knew they were having the same reaction of fear, and then drawing the same conclusion as he had about their mission. They couldn't fail: The fate of humanity lay in their hands.

John angled his head around to take a look at the dropship.

The majority of the dropship's hull had peeled away, and lead and titanium plates underneath showed through. Without their reinforcements, the craft would have disintegrated on the rough ride through Slipspace.

"Covenant C & C responding to our request," the copied Cortana informed him. "Ferry en route to take us in for repairs. They were a little confused about which warship we belong to, but I simulated static to cover our ship's registration ID. They're too busy to take too close a look at us."

The Master Chief returned inside the dropship. "We're getting towed," he told Blue Team.

Linda came up to him and made a circle in the air with her

index finger. John nodded and turned around so she could visually inspect his MJOLNIR suit. Computer diagnostics were fine, but his Spartans didn't take any chances with their armor. Especially not in an evacuated environment.

"You're good," she told him.

John then returned the favor and examined her suit. Fred and Will had done an excellent job integrating the replacement parts into Linda's armor. Aside from their pristine condition, they were a perfect match.

He patted her on the shoulder and gave her a thumbs-up to indicate that her armor was in working order.

"Ordnance load out," Grace said and unraveled the duffel bags they had tied to the hull. The packages had been wrapped with lead foil, layers of thermal padding, and then a layer of utility tape. "Heavy or light?" she asked.

"We go in heavy," John said. "Except Linda."

Linda started to object, but he explained, "We'll need you to hang back and cover us with your sniper rifle. I want you fast and deadly. Take a close-range weapon, extra ammo, and whatever you need to keep your sniper rifle working in the field."

"Roger," Linda said. Her voice was cold, hard, and brittle. This was the voice John had heard as she reported in while sniping targets around the team. John sometimes found it a little too cold . . . but he knew this was a good sign. Linda was preparing to do what she did best: kill with a single shot.

"The rest of us will take whatever we can carry. Once we're in I have a feeling we won't be able to come back. If we have to, we can always lighten our load."

The Chief grabbed a battle rifle and, for close use, a pair of submachine guns. He took a pair of silencers for the SMGs and hip holsters for the smaller weapons. He picked up a dozen frag grenades in their plastic ring carrier and slotted that into the left thigh section of his armor.

He'd need ammunition, a lot of it, if things got hot. So he

took extra clips for the SMGs and the battle rifle and taped them onto his chest, arms, and right thigh. More clips went into a backpack, along with two Lotus antitank mines, a few cans of C-7 explosive, detonators, timers, two field first-aid kits, and a fiber-optic probe.

While the rest of Blue Team got their gear together, John told them, "Stay off the COM from now on."

They all nodded.

Lead lining or not, they were close to too many listening Covenant ears to take any more chances with the COM.

He moved to the still-open port hatch, slid the fiber-optic probe outside, and plugged it into his helmet. Grainy images appeared on his heads-up display.

Hundreds of Covenant ships swarmed into view. In their midst a speck glowed and grew larger until the Master Chief saw it was a ship of similar design to their own: two U-shaped hulls, each the size of their dropship, sat on top of one another. This ship accelerated toward them and separated—one part moved to their dropship's stern and the other drifted to the nose.

The clanging of metal on metal reverberated through the hull, and the Master Chief felt a gentle motion in the pit of his stomach.

He looked back and passed on a thumbs-up to Fred, indicating that their tow had arrived, and Fred passed this signal on to the rest of the team.

On the fiber-optic feed the Master Chief saw that the Covenant tug maneuvered them through the fleet, up, over, and around ships a hundred times their size. There was a moment when they dived and there was nothing on screen save the stars and black of space. The Master Chief got a glimpse of the gold-colored star on his heads-up display, and then the video feed moved over to a planet of ocher smeared with clouds of sulfur dioxide and an orbiting moon of silver.

The tug turned to face a new ship in the distance. This vessel looked like two teardrop-shaped Covenant ships that had collided, giving the result an overall elongated figure-eight geometry.

They moved toward this ship, and the Master Chief made out more details. Spokes radiated from the narrow midpoint of the vessel and connected to a slender ring that he hadn't seen before because they had approached facing it edge-on. Featherlike tubes extended from either bulbous section and moved slowly over that central wheel. John squinted to make out more details on this unusual ship, but he was already at maximum resolution.

It had a ring? Was it rotating? But the Covenant had gravitational technology. They didn't need rotating sections to simulate gravity.

Then he saw *something* recognizable on the structure: tiny ships docked to that ring. Covenant cruisers and carriers. There must have been sixty connected to the central hub.

The titanic perspective of this structure clicked into place. The carriers looked like toys. The twin teardrop shapes had to be thirty kilometers end to end. This could only be the Covenant command-and-control center, the *Unyielding Hierophant*.

The tug moved directly toward the station. It was precisely where they had to go, so it was a lucky break . . . but ironically, it was also the last place the Master Chief wanted to be.

There was no telling what kind of sensors the *Unyielding Hierophant* had, but they couldn't take chances. John retreated into the dropship and eased the hatch shut.

He moved deeper into the ship and waited with the rest of Blue Team.

Three minutes ticked by on his mission clock; John tried to control his breathing and focus his mind.

Gravity settled his stomach, and there was a series of metallic clatters along the hull. Atmosphere hissed in though the cracks of their breached ship.

John pointed at Fred and Grace and then to the starboard hatch. They leveled their rifles and moved. He pointed to Linda and himself, then the port hatch, and they also moved into position.

John wasn't sure what kind of reception waited for them on the other side of those hatches, but one thing was certain—they'd have to face it head-on. There was nowhere to hide inside the reinforced and too-cramped interior of their dropship.

The port hatch cracked and squeaked open.

Linda and John aimed their rifles.

A rubbery tentacle reached in along the seam of the dropship's hatch.

John raised his hand and signaled Linda to stand down. He recognized the alien limb—the splitting cilia feelers and globular sensory organs could belong only to a Covenant Engineer.

The Engineer pushed open the hatch and entered the ship, floating past John and Linda as if they weren't there. It chittered and squawked as it ran its tentacles over the foreign armor plates and spatters of lead. Two more Engineers bolted through the open hatch and joined the first.

As long as they left the single-minded aliens to their work, they wouldn't raise an alarm. But what else was out there?

John eased against the frame of the hatch and slid the fiber-optic probe outside. There was a line of dropships, Seraph fighters, and other singleships that stretched away into the shadows. Swarms of Engineers, thousands of the creatures, hovered and drifted throughout the area. They moved parts, disassembled and reassembled sections of ship hulls, and plumbed plasma coils. There was no trace of a welcome party of Elites waiting for Blue Team.

John turned the optic probe up and saw a latticework deck overhead with tools, welders, and spotlights hanging like jungle vines. It was as good a place as any to get their bearings.

John turned and pointed at Linda and Will, then out the hatch and up. They nodded and moved out.

Five seconds later acknowledgment lights from Blue Four and Three winked on. It was safe for the rest of them.

John grabbed the upper lip of the hatchway and flipped up onto the top of the dropship. He grabbed a dangling cord and pulled himself onto the latticework deck where Fred and Linda perched, watching and making sure the bay was clear.

Grace and Fred disembarked and scrambled silently up into the darkness, joining them.

John pointed two fingers at his eyes and then made a flat fan motion across the space of the bay. The Spartans moved to carefully scan the area.

From his shadowy overview John saw that this place was a repair-and-refit facility, with slots for hundreds of singleships. The room curved out of view three hundred meters in either direction. It must run the circumference of the station's hub.

Apart from the thousands of busy Engineers, John spotted only two Grunts wearing white methane-breather masks. It was not a color designation he had seen before. They pushed carts containing barrels of sloshing fluids. They would be easy to avoid.

One side of the bay had a series of sealed doors that he presumed led to airlocks. The opposite wall of the bay had a meter-thick window through which poured an intense blue light.

Every thirty meters along that transparent wall was a recessed alcove. Overflowing from the nearest alcove were purple poly-hedral cargo barrels, old charred plasma coils, and plates of the silver-blue Covenant alloy. But what piqued John's interest was what was next to this pile of junk: a holographic terminal.

John clicked his COM to get Blue Team's attention, pointed to the junk pile, held up two fingers, and then pointed again at the alcove.

Everyone nodded, understanding his order.

Fred and Linda silently dropped to the deck, ran across the bay, and melted into the shadows behind a cut section of hull. Grace followed.

John looked up and down and side to side across the bay, making sure no Grunts were visible. He and Will crossed and took cover behind a plasma coil the size of a Warthog light reconnaissance vehicle.

He used both hands to point at Fred and Linda, turned his hands so they pointed to himself, and then nodded to the data terminal.

Linda lay flat and slithered to the edge of the alcove shadows on his right; Fred took the left. They would cover him while he moved to the terminal.

John reached to the back of his neck and pulled Cortana's chip from his skull. He crawled on his stomach, hugging the wall until he got to the terminal. He slid Cortana's chip into the input slot and then eased back into the shadows.

"I'm in," Cortana reported over the COM. "I have secured our own channel and encrypted the signal so we're free to use the interteam COM."

"Good work," John told her. "Is there a central reactor in this station? How well defended is it?"

"Stand by. I have to move carefully. There are Covenant security AIs in this system."

John hoped that this copy of Cortana's infiltration routines was as good as the real Cortana.

"I have schematics for the station," she told him. "The good news is, each lobe has a central reactor complex with five hundred twelve-terawatt units similar in design to the pinch fusion reactors on their ships. Apparently this energy is used to power a shield generator that can repel the collision of a small moon. I can overload one reactor, causing the melting of its field coils, which will saturate the surrounding—"

"Will it explode?" John asked impatiently.

"Yes—an explosion of sufficient force to vaporize both sections."

"That's the good news? What's the bad?"

"The reactor's control system is isolated. I cannot reach it from this terminal. You will have to physically deliver me there."

"Where is 'there'?"

"The nearest reactor-control access point is seven kilometers farther into the station's top lobe."

John considered this. If they were careful and lucky, it might be possible.

"Is there a way to leave you in the central system until we need you?" he asked. "It would be handy to have you monitor the Covenant security systems."

The duplicate Cortana was silent a full three seconds. "There is a way," she finally replied. "When I was copied from the original Cortana, the duplicating software was copied as well—it becomes an inseparable part of all subsequent copies. I can use this to copy myself into this system."

"Perfect."

"There are risks, however," Cortana told him. "Each successive copy contains aberrations that I cannot correct. There may be unforeseen complications associated with using a copy of a copy."

"Do it," John ordered. "I'll take that chance. But I'm not willing to take a chance on crossing seven kilometers behind enemy lines without a way to bypass their security systems."

"Stand by," Cortana said. "Working."

A minute ticked off John's mission timer. Then the data chip ejected from the terminal.

"Done," Cortana said over the interteam COM. "I'm in. There's an exit to this bay thirty meters to your left. I will black out the security sensors there and open the door in twenty seconds. Hurry."

John retrieved the chip and reinserted it into his skull. There was a flash of cold mercury in his mind.

"Move out," John told Blue Team. "Stay low."

Fred's and Linda's acknowledgment lights flickered, indicating the way was clear.

Blue Team ran, crouching, for thirty meters. A small access panel slid open, they piled through—then the door snapped shut behind them.

They proceeded, hunched over; they crawled on their hands and knees, on their stomachs, and through ducting so tight they had to shut down their shields and scrape by on bare armor over metal. For kilometers they followed Cortana's directions, halting as she ran motion sensors through diagnostics until they passed . . . twisting and turning and shimmying down long lengths of pipe, dodging the giant blades of circulation fans, and edging by transformer coils so close that sparks arced across their shields.

According to John's mission timer they had followed this route for eleven hours—when it dead-ended.

"New welds," Fred said, running his gauntlet over the seams in the alloy plate blocking their path.

Cortana broke in over the COM, "It must be a repair not logged into the station manifest."

John said. "Options?"

Cortana replied, "I have only limited mission-planning routines. There are three obvious options. You can blow the obstructing plate with a Lotus antitank mine. You can return to the repair bay where we might find a less obvious way in. Or there is a faster, alternative route, but it has drawbacks."

"Time is running out," John said. "The Covenant aren't going to stick around much longer before they strike Earth. Give me the faster route."

"Backtrack four hundred meters, turn bearing zero-nine-zero, proceed another twenty meters, and exit through a waste access cover. From there you will move in the open for seven hundred meters, pass through a structure, and then down a guarded corridor to the reactor chambers."

Grace interrupted, "What do you mean 'in the open'? This is a space station; there should be no open spaces."

"See for yourself," Cortana said.

A schematic of the "open space" appeared on their heads-up displays. John wasn't able to make much sense of the diagram, but he could tell there were several catwalks, buildings, and even waterways—as Cortana indicated, lots of open areas for them to be seen in.

"Let's take a look," John said.

He led his team back the way they had come and pushed open the waste access duct. Blue light flooded the tunnel. John blinked and let his eyes adjust, then pushed the fiber-optic probe through the opening.

John didn't understand what he saw—the optical probe must have malfunctioned. The image looked impossibly distorted. But there was no motion nearby . . . so he risked poking his head out.

He was in the end of an alley with walls towering ten meters to either side, casting dark shadows over the waste access hole. A group of Jackals passed the mouth of the alley only five meters from his position. He ducked . . . and none of the vulture-like creatures saw him in the dark.

When they passed he looked up and saw that the fiber-optic probe had not been broken after all.

The space station was hollow inside, and a light beam shot lengthwise through its center: a blue light that provided full daylight illumination. Along the curved inner surface were needle-thin spires, squat stair-step pyramids, and columned temples. Catwalks with moving surfaces crisscrossed the space, as did tubes with capsules that whisked passengers. Water flowed along the walls in inward-spiral patterns and then waterfalled "up" into great hollow towers that sprouted from the opposite wall.

Banshees flew in formation through the center space of the great room, as did flocks of headless birds and great clouds of butterflies. It could have been an Escher etching come to life.

John felt extreme vertigo for a moment. Then he understood that with advanced Covenant gravity technology, there didn't have to be an up or down here.

Odd that a military station would have so much unnecessary ornamentation. Yet Fleet HQ had a large atrium in their lobby. Maybe this was the Covenant equivalent—multiplied a hundredfold.

John spied a band of translucent material set into a far wall, glistening. "Is that the window to the repair bays, Cortana?"

"Correct," she replied.

"Then at least we know the way out. And the structure we need to enter?"

"One o'clock," she said. "The one with the carved columns. It is the most direct route to the reactor chambers."

John moved out of the hole and hugged the nearby wall. The shadows in the bright daylight would do a decent job of camouflaging them.

"Okay, Blue Team. Get oriented . . . as much as you can. Our target is the columned building at one o'clock. I make it to be a three-hundred-meter sprint across open ground. We'll make a break for it. Unless anyone has a better plan?"

Linda emerged, looked around, and said, "Permission to post on the rooftop and provide cover."

"Do it," John said. "Let me know when you're in position and ready."

Linda retrieved a padded grappling hook and rope from her

pack, twirled it, and tossed it up and over the adjacent roof. She tugged it once, it caught, and then she quickly ascended.

The remaining Spartans joined John in the shadows. He shouldered his battle rifle and thumbed the safety off.

Linda's acknowledgment light winked once.

John tensed and ran. It took him three strides to build to his top-speed sprint. His adrenaline spiked and it made his blood burn. He felt time slow, his perception running at an over-clocked pace. He focused on speed—putting one foot in front of the other. His boots dug into cobblestones, crushed rock, and sent a fine spray of gravel behind him. He saw three obstacles in his path: a group of startled Grunts. He slammed the butt of his rifle into the nearest one, and crushed its skull. The dead Grunt spun end over end and landed in a heap. He heard squawks and shouts around him but didn't stop to look.

He was on the stairs of the building, worn-smooth stone steps that he bounded up five at a time. John saw three friendly contacts behind him on his motion tracker . . . and at the periphery of its range a solid mass of enemy contacts.

"You're good so far," Linda reported. "There are Elites, but they're unarmed. No, wait. A Hunter pair is advancing on your position. Stand by."

A quartet of shots split the air like thunderclaps.

"Threat neutralized," Linda said. "The rest of them are scattering. Banshees approaching. I'm moving."

John cleared the stairs and skidded to a halt on the threshold of the temple. The interior was cold; external temperature readings were near freezing. Light filtered in through stained-glass windows in the ceiling, tinged lavender, cobalt, and turquoise. Three rows of giant columns made of blue-black basalt ran the length of the thirty-meter-long rectangular structure, casting long shadows. It was a good place for an ambush. He set his back against one of the pillars and swept the entrance, covering his team as they entered.

"Cortana, update on station security?" John said.

"There are dozens of reports on the security channels. I've got them covered."

Another Cortana voice broke in over the first: "Also be advised, Chief, that there are Brutes in this temple. They shouldn't be a significant threat."

John wasn't so sure of that. He also wondered why there now seemed to be more than one Cortana in the station's system—but that could wait. They had to keep moving now that they had revealed their position. He waved Blue Team forward.

John took point. He moved up to the next column in the middle of the building. Fred and Will stepped over to the columns on either side behind John. Grace had their backs.

There was a flicker on his motion sensor—just ahead. It vanished.

John held up his hand. Blue Team froze.

His motion detector was clear . . . but there had been *something* there.

He pulled out a frag grenade.

The transient contact was back—a shadow moved around the same pillar John used for cover. It moved faster than an Elite—as fast as John.

He fired his rifle point blank into the shadowy silhouette. It didn't slow—it only howled with rage.

Will and Fred fired three-round bursts from their rifles into the creature. It flinched with each bullet impact.

Three explosions detonated behind them. Grace's biosign alarm shrilled and flashed on John's heads-up display.

"Ambush!" Will cried out.

The Brute stepped from the shadows and faced John. It was taller than an Elite—wider and more muscular. Its mouth was lined with razor-sharp teeth, and its red eyes burned with hate. Its blue-gray skin was riddled with bullet holes.

The Brute tackled John, knocking his weapon from his grasp.

Even with his MJOLNIR armor, John was not as strong as the alien.

It pounded on him with bare fists, broke through his shielding, grabbed his neck, and squeezed.

Red flashes played across John's vision. He began to black out.

THIRTY-FOUR

John struggled and tried to pry the hands from his throat. The tendons in the Brute's forearms were solid bands of steel—and the creature was so determined to rip John's head off that a full clip from a rifle into its chest hadn't even slowed it down.

Behind him, John felt another explosion thunder though the stone floor, followed by the staccato rattle of rifle fire.

Blue Team was busy with another threat. He was on his own.

John blinked. The darkness dimming the edge of his vision wouldn't clear.

John watched his shield bar flicker and sluggishly recharge. If it built up enough repulsive force, he might have a chance to wriggle out of the Brute's grasp. If he tried too quickly, though, the Brute wouldn't lose its grip and could pound his shield flat again.

The Brute bellowed, and globules of spittle spattered onto the Chief's visor. It leaned closer, screwing its massive hands tighter around his throat.

John's vision narrowed. His windpipe swelled, and he gagged.

Shields were at one quarter charge. It'd have to be enough.

John had been in similar death-grip holds before—endless hours of training on the wrestling mats with his teammates and martial arts specialists provided by Chief Mendez. There were ways to escape a larger, stronger opponent. And there were always countermoves to those escapes. And countermoves to those counters. It was like a game of chess, except the pieces were arms and legs, torque and your center of mass . . . and most importantly your mind.

He pulled his knees to his chest, and tucked his torso toward his pelvis at the same time. He twisted ninety degrees and shot out both legs and arms, and uncoiled his body. The maneuver was called "shrimping."

John's head slipped from the Brute's grasp.

He used the monster's split second of disorientation to scramble onto its back. John brought his elbow down on the base of the Brute's neck. He swept out its elbow, wrenched the joint around, and pushed it as far as it would go—far past the point where any human's or Elite's would have snapped. John scissored his legs wide and pushed against the floor, leveraging his body to keep the Brute pinned.

It growled and pushed itself and John up with its one free arm.

"No. You. Don't."

John still clutched a frag grenade in his left hand. He flicked the arming pin—reached around and under, and thrust it into the Brute's belt—then withdrew, sweeping out its one arm holding them up.

The Brute dropped onto the floor and screamed with rage.

The grenade detonated. It lifted them both a meter, and they landed again . . . this time accompanied by a wet, pulpy smack as the Brute's dead hulk slammed into the ground.

The Master Chief rolled off and sprang to his feet and looked for Blue Team.

The large pillars blocked his view, but he saw on his motion tracker that Fred was behind a pillar down and to John's left, and Will behind the pillar to the right. There was no tag indicating Grace's location. There were, however, blurry motion contacts beyond the wide arched entrance to the temple.

And there was one other thing—neither Will nor Fred checked John's status over the COM. That silence meant trouble.

John fumbled for his fiber-optic probe, but it had been lost in the scuffle with the Brute. He eased around the basalt pillar.

Grace lay face-first on the floor, five meters from the temple entrance. A puddle of hydrostatic gel and blood spread across the floor.

John clicked the COM once, a status query.

The instant he did this, two Brutes wheeled from their cover on either side of the entrance archway. They held weapons with large-caliber muzzles and padded stocks, fixed with razor-edged blades. One of the Brutes saw John, aimed, and fired.

John darted back behind the basalt pillar; he saw the flash and thunder of a grenade launched from the weapon—heard two more rounds fired immediately after that.

The first grenade impacted on the opposite side of the pillar and exploded. The overpressure rattled his teeth.

The Chief turned and dived, hoping to get behind the next stone column before—

—the second and third grenades impacted and detonated on the pillar he had stood behind a split second before. The solid stone crumbled into fist-sized chunks.

He skidded and scrambled for cover as the upper part of that column collapsed, raining stones that shattered the floor . . . and would have crushed him.

So much for engaging these Brutes in a direct assault. John wasn't up for another round of wrestling, either. Not with the clock ticking. Not with every Covenant on this station about to tear them to pieces. Complicating all this was the enemy's apparent ability to locate them when they used the COM.

That only left one tactical option: run.

He wasn't going to leave Grace behind, though. Not until he knew for certain she was dead.

He removed his backpack and took out one of his two Lotus

antitank mines. The disk was a quarter meter across with spikes set along the rim to stabilize it when buried. He set the detonation selector to countdown mode, seven seconds. He then slid around the edge of the column.

He threw the mine with a flick of his wrist. It spun in a wide arc across the temple hall and embedded into the wall just over the entrance archway.

Two seconds until it blew.

John clicked on his COM and said: "Fire in the hole!"

The Brutes again wheeled around from their cover and leveled their deadly grenade launchers.

The Lotus mine detonated—it was a flash and an instant of fire. The temple opening and Brutes vanished, replaced by a cloud of dust and a cascade of stones that fell from the ceiling.

One gray arm remained exposed under the rubble, still flexing.

John moved up. The entrance was sealed. They were safe for a few seconds.

He knelt next to Grace. Her biosigns had flatlined. He tried to roll her upright—but there was no need. The detonations he had heard while wrestling the first Brute had been three of their high-velocity grenades . . . which had blown Grace's midsection apart.

Fred and Will emerged from their cover. John looked at them and shook his head.

John opened the tiny access panel on Grace's armor power pack and entered the fail-safe code. They still had a mission to finish, which meant they couldn't carry her out; it would slow them down too much. They wouldn't be leaving her for the Covenant either, though. Her armor's tiny fusion reactor would overload and burn everything within a ten-meter radius—Grace's funeral pyre.

"Let's move," John said. "Cortana, which way?"

"Proceed into the temple thirty meters. Turn right. There will be a sealed doorway, an access hatch for Engineers. I will open it and lock it behind you. Hurry. I'm encountering increased resistance from the station's AIs. While I have their security COM channels blocked, word of intruders is speeding via private COMs."

There was a curious echo to her voice. Maybe it was feedback from the Covenant triangulating on their signals. Or maybe there was some other effect at work. What had she warned him about? Unforeseen complications using a copy of a copy of Cortana?

"Roger that," he said and waved Fred and Will forward. He took one last look at Grace, then marched quickly and silently ahead.

There were no more motion contacts in the temple. The Chief, however, saw Grunts and Jackals, Elites and Hunters in murals painted on the walls. In the shadows and stained-glass filtered light, those pictures seemed to move. They genuflected to something farther ahead. The Chief wished he had more time to take a full video record.

Blue Team moved thirty meters and turned to face a section of the wall. It parted. The passage could have fit two Engineers side by side, but John had to crouch and turn sideways to pass. Will and Fred followed; Cortana sealed the door behind them.

They continued until the narrow passage turned ninety degrees and dropped straight down. Will attached a rope and they rappelled down a hundred meters, landing on a platform.

John overlooked a cavern hewn from rough stone that arched up ninety meters and vanished into the shadows in the distance. Five hundred twelve fusion reactors that looked like flatted spiral seashells filled the space, stacked in rows and columns eight deep. Each was the size of a Pelican dropship and thrummed with power, casting off waves of wavering heat.

The open areas between the reactors were a tangle of plasma conduits and alive with swarms of thousands of buoyant Engineers as they tended the machinery. Faint wispy borealis comprised of escaped plasma swirled, whipped into a luminous froth by the intense magnetic vortices within the chamber.

It was a tremendous feat of engineering. It was as if the station's builders had hewn this from a seed asteroid and built the rest of the installation around it.

Will pointed across the room to three Jackals who walked along a catwalk. Blue Team held position and didn't move.

"There," Cortana announced. "Across the platform is a terminal on the reactor subsystem."

John held up a hand to Will and Fred, waited for the Jackal guards to pass, and then sprinted across the platform. He removed Cortana's chip and inserted it into the terminal.

After three seconds, she reported: "I'm in. Very few Covenant counterintrusion measures in this system. I can accomplish the overload.

"I've found an exit route for Blue Team and uploaded it into your NAV systems," she continued. "It should be stealthy enough for you to return to the repair bay undetected. Once there, give me the order and I can begin. It will take ten minutes for the overload to build. There's no stopping once I start this, Chief, so be sure."

"This station and the Covenant fleet might jump to Earth in the next ten minutes," John said. He looked to Fred and Will, and they nodded as if they could read his mind.

"Proceed with the overload *now*, Cortana."

The light from the reactors shifted; blue plasma tinged white and spread like a poison through the interconnecting conduits.

"Overload commencing," the copy of Cortana announced. "I suggest Blue Team move at top speed to the exit."

A NAV triangle indicated a ladder that ran to the catwalk overhead. John held up two fingers at Will and Fred and then nodded to the patrolling Jackals. Fred and Will knelt, braced, and waited for him to go ahead.

John climbed the ladder. As he neared the top, three shots rang out behind him. The sound was nearly drowned out by the intensifying reverberations from the reactors. He cleared the top of the ladder and saw three dead Jackals on the catwalk. He swept both directions with his rifle and then waved Will and Fred forward.

His countdown timer read 9:47. The heat and light from the reactors grew stronger, and John's shields flared slightly.

Blue Team jogged down the catwalk to an elevator. They got inside, the doors closed, and the car immediately ascended.

When the doors opened again, artificial blue sunlight filled the car—as did the shadows cast by two Elites waiting for the elevator. Blue Team opened fire and cut down the Elites, leaving a spray of blood across the ground.

The Chief edged around the frame of the elevator door and saw a tangle of pipes and fountains and one of the curious spiral waterways that fell up from its center. This was a heat exchange plant for the reactors below. Already the water in the canals steamed and boiled.

He saw that Covenant Elite and Hunter pairs had converged at the entrance to the temple a hundred meters to his right. Over the temple dozens of Banshee fliers circled the carnage.

A gang of Grunts managed to clear an opening to the temple. There was a flash of light and fire that roiled out in a long plume, burning them as well as their Elite overseers.

"Good-bye, Grace," John whispered.

The detonation of her power pack would buy them more time while the Covenant forces tried to figure out what just happened—perhaps they'd think Blue Team was still inside the temple. Grace had also taken out a dozen Grunts and four Elites with her last action. That would have pleased her.

John turned toward the far end of the great room and spotted a band of translucent material on the far wall. It led to the repair bays and airlocks beyond. That was their exit.

He glanced at his mission timer: 8:42. They'd have to get there fast.

His gaze locked onto the Banshees in the air. He searched for Linda, posted somewhere in the odd geometry of this station. She could be anywhere along several kilometers of cityscape.

John clicked on his COM. "Linda, do not reply. The Covenant are triangulating on our signals. I'm hoping they do and send a few of those Banshees to reconnoiter. When they get close to the heat-exchange plant, take them out—we'll need their vehicles."

There was no answer. Did that mean Linda understood and was in a position to help? Or was she dead?

As John hoped, three Banshees peeled off the search formation, circling the temple and turning toward them.

John waved Fred and Will out of the elevator and into the forest of steaming pipes. They scattered, took cover, and aimed at the incoming Banshees.

The Banshees spread out, slowed . . . but then banked, returning to the temple.

John clicked his COM three times.

The Elite pilots immediately wheeled about and accelerated toward their position. One Banshee flier nosed into a classic strafing dive. Its plasma cannons warmed and crackled with energy, indicating an imminent discharge.

There was a spray of blood in the flier, then the pilot fell forward and pushed the accelerator to full. The Banshee careened through the air at maximum velocity—crashing into a water-recovery tower, and wobbled to the ground.

"Linda," John muttered and tried to spot her. Judging from the blood spray, she'd managed to send a round through the tiny exposed area of the cockpit, and inflicted a lethal ricochet. He looked for her position; most likely the shot had come from behind and above. There were numerous catwalks running across the length of the massive room. She had to be on one of them.

The two remaining Banshees accelerated toward Blue Team. Their plasma cannons flickered, and they leveled into a flat trajectory.

John, Fred, and Will raised their rifles.

There was a muted *crack* of a sniper rifle, and another Banshee drifted to the ground, its pilot felled by Linda's uncanny skill.

The last remaining pilot veered starboard, not knowing what had just taken out its two wingmates . . . only that it had to get out of the area if it was going to live. In the tightest arc of its curve, the craft slowed. John couldn't tell precisely where the shot came from, but a third sniper round ricocheted through the craft's cockpit. The Banshee spun in circles before it thumped to a halt, nose-down in the street.

Three impossible shots, three kills. Even for Linda, this was superb shooting—the finest shots John had ever seen. He looked around the station, over the buildings, spires, catwalks, transit tubes—it was impossible to spot her.

John waved Fred and Will toward two of the downed Banshees and sprinted toward the one still spinning riderless in the street, its canards scraping and sparking along the stones.

He climbed aboard, pushed the throttle forward, and pointed to the far wall. He held his hand flat and lowered it, indicating that Fred and Will should skim low to the ground.

John veered off in a wide arc. Maybe he could divert the attention away from them.

He rose slightly higher and buzzed the tops of gilt domes and statues of Elite heroes with raised swords. Grunts and Jackals scattered as he approached, and John fired at them. He shifted to the side as he splashed though water falling from one side of the station to the other.

Four Banshee fliers fell in behind him. John weaved back and forth. A pair of plasma bolts sizzled over his head.

He risked a look over his shoulder and saw two of the Banshees drop away. A moment later they crashed into the surface.

Linda still had his back covered.

He dropped to the ground and skimmed along a street, skidded, and turned into an alley. Banshee shadows passed overhead. He pushed the throttle to full and made a direct run toward the back wall.

Will and Fred had grounded their fliers and crouched next to the meter-thick window separating this inner section from the repair bays. John settled his Banshee next to theirs, turned his backpack around, reached in, and tossed Fred his last Lotus antitank mine.

"Get that on the window and set for a remote trigger." He then risked an open COM channel to the copy of Cortana in the station's system. "Cortana, can you open the airlocks in the repair bay?"

A flurry of voices filled the COM, all speaking at the same time, shouting to be heard over one another . . . all Cortana's voices. One finally broke through. "Chief, I've spun off a copy dedicated exclusively to communicating with you. Go ahead."

"How many copies are there of you?"

"Unknown. Hundreds. The Covenant AI overwhelmed me. Had to. This is difficult. Many errors in my systems. Filtering over all subchannels of information.

"To answer your initial question: yes. I can override safety lockouts and open the airlocks. My systems are fragmenting. I cannot exist in a coherent state much longer."

John looked out across the kilometers of curving cityscape. Wraith tanks rolled into the streets; legions of Grunts, Jackals, and Elites raced from building to building and shot at targets that weren't there. Banshees and Ghosts buzzed through the air like clouds of flies.

John's mission countdown timer read 7:45.

"Linda's back there," he told Fred and Will. Fred started to say something, but John cut him off. "If I'm not back in three minutes, blow that window and exit."

Fred hesitated but then nodded.

"I can't leave her," John said and gunned his Banshee's throttle. "Not if she's still alive."

Dr. Halsey's last words to him resonated in John's mind: *I should have been trying to save every single human life—no matter what it cost.*

He'd get to Linda. He'd get her out alive—or die trying.

1820 HOURS, SEPTEMBER 13, 2552 (REVISED DATE, MILITARY CALENDAR) \ ABOARD COVENANT BATTLE STATION *UNYIELDING HIEROPHANT*.

The Master Chief accelerated his Banshee to its top speed.

There was another explosion at the temple, and plumes of steam geysered into the air from the heat-exchange plant. The circling formations of Banshees scattered.

John tucked as close as he could to his flier's fuselage and coaxed every bit of speed from the craft.

A pair of Banshees swooped in, one off his port, the other on his starboard. Their plasma weapons heated; John rolled back and forth to throw their aim. He braced for impact . . . but there was none.

The Chief craned his head back and saw the pilot of the lead Banshee slump, slide off the flier, and plummet to the ground. The trailing Banshee was riderless as well . . . only a blood-spattered cockpit and cowling.

Linda still had him covered—had taken out both pilots with precise fire. She had to be close.

John scanned the area. There were spires and water-reclamation towers, transport tubes and catwalks that criss-crossed the center of the interior. There was a nexus of walkways near the beam of illumination that ran down the center of the station, a location with enough glare that a sniper might hide in the open undetected.

He risked keying Linda's private COM channel. "Thought you might need a ride, so I—"

An energy mortar blasted over John's shoulder, burning the air like a sun in close orbit and draining his shields to half. It impacted a water tower, and the structure detonated into a cloud of blinding steam.

John punched the Banshee through the cloud, glanced down, and saw a Wraith tank tracking his trajectory. He ducked and weaved but kept moving toward Linda's probable location.

His mission countdown timer read 7:06. There was no time for fancy evasive maneuvers.

Did Linda even want to be found? Maybe she wanted him to get to safety and leave her behind? It's what he would have done.

"Position report, Linda," John barked over the COM. "That's a direct order."

Three seconds ticked off his mission clock and then the six-tone *"Oly Oly Oxen Free"* song whistled through John's speakers and a NAV marker appeared on his heads-up display.

The triangular marker centered on a rope that ran between two transit tubes and dangled perilously close to the high-intensity light beam. It was a barely discernible thread that ran through a hard shadow cast by a nearby catwalk.

John hit his image enhancers. Through the glare of the light, and in the depths of the shadow, he caught the flicker of reflected optics.

Linda used *both* the brilliant light and the darkness to hide.

John angled the Banshee to her. He clipped the tether line from his armor to the frame of the Banshee and pulled his body deeper into the craft.

When he was thirty meters away, he made visual contact. Linda had the rope coiled about a boot and wrapped about one forearm. She held her sniper rifle in one arm, and John could only surmise that she had been firing from such an impossible position.

She uncoiled the rope from her boot, swung, released at the apex of the arc—and fell toward him.

John forced the Banshee's cowling up against straining hydraulics and stretched out his arm, his fingers touched hers—and her hand slapped firmly into his gauntlet.

He swung her around and over his shoulder. Linda landed atop him, holding on to his armor.

John spun the Banshee about and accelerated back to the windows. The craft's forward cowling remained wrenched up and slowed them down—but there was no other way to fit two people on the craft.

"Coming in hot," John said over the COM to Fred and Will. "Open the door and get ready for a quick exit, Blue Team."

Fred's acknowledgment light winked on.

"Cortana, breach those airlocks. Now!"

A cacophony of voices filled John's COM. There were so many copies of Cortana speaking at the same time he couldn't make out anything coherent.

"Cortana, the airlocks."

There was a *pop* of static. "Apologies, Chief," Cortana replied. "I've spun off a dedicated copy to . . . to . . . speak with you."

John thought she had already made a copy to talk directly with him. What had happened to it?

"Override the airlock safeties, Cortana. Open the external and repair bay doors."

"Working, Chief. There's too much system COM traffic. So many of us. Near saturation level. Have to fight to get . . . Stand by . . ."

An explosion appeared a kilometer away along the far wall. The Lotus antitank mine became a blossom of flame and black smoke that drifted and diffused and left a spiderweb of cracks on the meter-thick translucent section.

But the window held.

That Lotus antitank mine could have sheared through that wall even if it had been reinforced steel, but this wall had remained in one piece.

They were stuck inside.

Three hundred meters to the window.

"Cortana!"

In John's peripheral vision he saw clouds of Banshee fliers and a slew of Ghosts gaining on them.

"Cortana—*it's now or never!*"

"In . . ." Cortana's voice was faint. "Intersystem failure 08934-EE. Global system error 9845-W. Resetting. Inner doors open. Override in progress. System lockdo—"

The COM went dead.

A hundred meters away, beyond the cracked window, the atmosphere turned white for a split second then cleared. Spaced every twenty meters along the bay walls, the airlock doors were opening. Beyond, stars shone upon velvet black.

Fred and Will's Banshees appeared off John's starboard canard. John pointed and together they dived, accelerating toward a bull's-eye pattern of cracks on the translucent portion of the wall.

That web of fissures spread: fingers that stretched and split along the length of the window . . . slowed and stopped.

John fired the Banshee's plasma cannons. Fred opened fire as well, and four blobs of plasma splashed across the glassy surface fifty meters away.

The window flexed, crackled, tiny flakes popped off . . . but the translucent material remained stubbornly intact.

John was thirty meters from the surface—he'd have to veer off now, or impact upon it. He gritted his teeth and braced himself.

Ten meters.

The window's smooth surface flashed into a jigsaw mosaic. The squealing of glass over glass filled the air. It shattered.

The entire length crumbled and instantly blasted into the vacuum of space—swept out by the pressurized atmosphere filling the interior of the station.

John tried to maneuver the Banshee. He bounced into the repair bay, rolled the craft over and upright—fell off, tumbled though the airlock . . . and drifted away into the darkness of space.

He flailed his limbs in the zero gravity, and the tether on his belt snapped taut. He recoiled back toward the Banshee. Linda held on with one hand and held out the other to him. He climbed back aboard and tapped the thrusters to stabilize their pitch and yaw.

Behind them the station vented gas as well as the bodies of Covenant Engineers, Grunts, Jackals, and Elites. Clouds of metal junk bled from the ruptures. Tendrils of steam flash froze into glittering ice crystals.

The Covenant fleet moved as well—some cruisers closed with the station, others moved farther away. There were five hundred alien warships without leadership from their command-and-control center, and they reminded John of motes of dust in a sunbeam—silently floating in every direction.

John spotted a dropship drifting a kilometer ahead, dead in space.

He clicked his COM once and dropped a NAV marker onto a Covenant craft. Fred and Will's acknowledgment lights winked on.

John pulsed the Banshee's engines once and let its inertia carry them to the dropship. He hoped the rest of the Covenant Fleet was trying to figure out what had just happened . . . and not paying any attention to one more piece of debris floating in space.

The Banshees gently impacted onto the tumbling dropship. John grasped the hull, and Linda scrabbled over him, opened the port access hatch, and entered. Fred and Will drifted closer, and John helped them aboard.

He hesitated and took another look at the Covenant fleet. Hundred of ships without control. But how long would that last? Even if the station's reactors chained and blew . . . the Covenant still had enough force to destroy Earth's defenses and burn it to a cinder.

All they had done was buy a little time: as long as it took for someone to take charge of the Covenant fleet. That wasn't enough, but John wasn't sure what else to do.

He crawled to the hatch, entered the ship, and sealed it behind him.

Linda stood at the pilot's console while Fred stood beside her manning the ops station. An engine schematic appeared in front of Linda, and power pulsed through its plasma coils. The interior lights dimly glowed.

"Where to, Chief?" Linda asked.

"Away," John said and looked at the system NAV display. He pointed to the tiny moon orbiting the nearby planet. "Get us into the moon's shadow. But slow. Try not to attract any attention."

His countdown timer read 5:12. They might still have time.

"Roger," Linda said.

The dropship spun about and gently moved away from the station, almost imperceptibly accelerating toward the tiny moon covered with black and silver pockmarks.

Fred hunched over his console. Thick spiky lines representing the Covenant F- through K-bands fluxed and flickered on his screen. "Covenant COM channels are jammed," he reported. "Communiqués and queries to and from every ship in the fleet wondering what the hell is going on. And the station's COM channels are all full of those copied Cortanas . . . and she's just repeating different system error codes."

"What's this?" John asked, leaning over Fred's shoulder. He pointed to one COM band with only a single spike.

Fred looked at the Covenant calligraphy for a long moment.

and then inhaled sharply. "If the translation software is working right," he whispered, "that's the E-band . . . it's one of ours."

Fred snapped on the external speakers. Six tones beeped, stopped, and then repeated.

"Oly Oly Oxen Free," John breathed. "Send the countersign, Fred."

"Aye, Chief. Sending now."

Who could have sent that signal? There was no other living Spartan in this system. Unless it was Dr. Halsey and Kelly. Had they somehow tracked them?

"It's about time you showed up." The drawling voice of Admiral Whitcomb was loud and clear over the COM. *"Switch to encryption scheme 'Rainbow.'"*

John nodded to Fred, who ran a shunt from the Covenant COM into the data port in the back of his helmet. "Decryption online," Fred reported.

"Admiral," John said. "With all due respect, sir, why are you here?"

"Lieutenant Haverson suggested we drop out of Slipspace on the edge of this system—hide in the Oort cloud and gather a little intel." The Admiral sighed. *"Well, I took one look and figured that even if you took out that station . . . hell, son, there'd still be a couple of hundred Covenant ships within spittin' distance of Earth. Me getting there and warning them about it wouldn't make a lick of difference. So I'm going to do something about it here and now. You've done your part, Chief. Leave the rest to me."*

There was a pause, then the Admiral asked in a low, serious tone, *"You did get it done, didn't you, son? You got that station rigged to blow?"*

"Yes, sir." John linked his mission timer to the COM. "Four minutes thirty-two seconds and counting."

"Perfect, Master Chief. Bring 'em on back to the barn. Stay on your heading. Your instincts are dead on. We're on the far side of the moon and are waiting for you."

John motioned to Linda to increase their velocity. She pushed the acceleration stripe to three quarters power.

"Waiting, sir?"

"Whitcomb over and out." The COM went dead.

John looked to Will, Fred, and Linda, and they all shrugged.

He pushed the acceleration stripe to full velocity, and the dropship entered a high orbit around the splotchy moon, arcing around to the far side, where the battered *Gettysburg* waited for them.

But only the *Gettysburg*.

"Where's *Ascendant Justice*?" John whispered.

CHAPTER THIRTY-SIX

1825 HOURS, SEPTEMBER 13, 2552 (REVISED DATE, MILITARY CALENDAR) \ ABOARD UNSC VESSEL *GETTYSBURG*, NEAR COVENANT BATTLE STATION *UNYIELDING HIEROPHANT*.

The Master Chief and Blue Team stepped off the lift and onto the bridge of the *Gettysburg*.

"Sir—" John started to salute Admiral Whitcomb, but neither the Admiral nor Lieutenant Haverson was there.

The only two on the bridge were Sergeant Johnson, who stared at the forward viewscreens, and Cortana, whose holographic figure burned bright blue and streamed with code symbols and mathematics beyond John's comprehension.

Sergeant Johnson turned toward them. He looked the Spartans over and frowned, noting that not all of them had returned.

"I'm not sure what that thing is." The Sergeant nodded to viewscreen one, centered on the Covenant command-and-control station. "Don't look like any 'uneven elephant' to me— more like two squid kissing. Whatever it is, damned glad it's going to blow up. Nice job—almost as good as if we sent in the Marines." One corner of his mouth quirked into a smile.

"Where's the Admiral?" the Master Chief asked. "And Lieutenant Haverson?"

The Sergeant's half smile vanished, and his eyes darkened. He moved to Weapons Station One. "I'll show you. A Clarion spy drone is nearly in position."

The center viewscreen fuzzed with static and then resolved

to show the *Ascendant Justice* moving out of the shadow of the moon. The once formidable Covenant flagship was a wreck; its hull was breached in a dozen places, its skeletal frame exposed, and only a handful of plasma conduits flickered with life.

"I don't understand," the Chief said. He stepped closer to Cortana's hologram. Being near the real Cortana—not one of her fragmented copies—reassured him that everything was under control. "What's going on?"

"Stand by, Chief," she replied. "I'm attempting to attune *Ascendant Justice*'s Slipspace drive to the *Gettysburg*'s mass and profile."

"That's what we were up to while you were off sight-seeing," the Sergeant told him. "We pulled the Slipspace matrix out of our piggybacked ship and slapped it into the *Gettysburg*."

John wheeled and faced the viewscreens. *Ascendant Justice* couldn't jump? Then why was it headed straight toward the Covenant fleet? A decoy? He glanced at the countdown timer: 2:09 left.

"Not a decoy," he whispered, ". . . a lure. Sergeant, get a signal to *Ascendant Justice*. Bounce it off that spy drone if you have to."

"Roger, Chief," Sergeant Johnson said and tapped in commands. An error warning blared. He shook his head, puzzled, and tried again, carefully retyping.

"Linda, take the NAV station. Fred, you're on Ops. Will, give the Sergeant a hand at Weapons One."

Blue Team jumped to their assigned stations.

Will edged the Sergeant aside and quickly tapped three buttons. "COM patch established," he reported. "On viewscreen two."

The bridge of *Ascendant Justice* appeared on screen. Lieutenant Haverson and Admiral Whitcomb stood on the central raised dais, adjusting the holographic controls. Behind them, the wall displays showed Covenant ships closing on their position.

Admiral Whitcomb smiled. "Glad to see you made it safely aboard, son."

"Sir, that fleet will destroy you before you can fire a single salvo."

"I don't think so, Master Chief," he replied and tapped the holographic display. A slim blue crystalline shard appeared—an exact copy of the alien artifact they found on Reach. "I'm sending this image to every ship in the system and letting them know it's theirs for the taking . . . if they dare to board this ship and face Earth's best warriors." He laughed. "I think that'll appeal to those Elites and their overinflated sense of honor."

John nodded. "Yes, sir. It will."

He looked at the countdown timer: 1:42.

The Covenant fleet turned and moved toward the incoming *Ascendant Justice*. A cloud of cruisers and carriers. Hundreds of them. Impossible odds.

"Fire turret four, Lieutenant," the Admiral ordered.

"Firing!" Haverson replied, his face set in grim determination.

A lance of plasma discharged, arced, and impacted upon the nose of the nearest carrier. The energy splashed over their shields and dissipated.

"Turret five, Lieutenant. Take them down."

"Firing five, sir," Haverson said.

A second plasma bolt followed the first. It blasted the carrier's weakened shields and melted armor and hull, exploding through the foredecks. The ship rolled and crashed into a cruiser that had come too close.

"Nice shooting, Lieutenant," the Admiral murmured.

The Covenant fleet responded with a blinding volley of laser fire. Pinpoints of energy concentrated on *Ascendant Justice*'s aft decks, boiled armor off in thick layers—sheared through to the other side, severing its engines.

The Admiral smiled. "A sound tactical response. Good thing

they don't know we're just using that slingshot around the moon and our inertia to do the rest of the job." He glanced at the displays and the station growing larger on them. "Hang on, Lieutenant. Brace for impact."

Ascendant Justice drifted closer to the station.

It crashed into the central ring, crushing the structure, and continued forward, dimpling the hull of the pinched center section . . . and finally ground to a halt with its nose impaled within the *Unyielding Hierophant*.

The center viewscreen on the bridge of the *Gettysburg* shattered into static and then slowly resolved. The wavering image of Admiral Whitcomb pulled himself upright. A gash from his temple to the corner of his mouth wept blood. Lieutenant Haverson groggily got to his feet as well, his arm held at an odd angle, broken.

"Systemwide transmission," Admiral Whitcomb barked to Haverson.

"Aye, sir," Haverson said and clumsily adjusted the COM.

"Come on, mighty Covenant warriors," the Admiral shouted. "We're here in the middle of your fleet with your 'holy of holies.'" He flicked his finger at the holographic shard, and it pinged as if actually struck. "Come and get it!" He laughed again.

Hundreds of Covenant ships moved toward them. Grapple lines and grav beams attached to the broken hull of the *Ascendant Justice*. A thousand dropships and Elites in thrust packs filled the space around the flagship.

The Master Chief watched the countdown timer: 0:27.

Along the ten-kilometer dorsal bulb of the space station, patches warmed to a dull red, the heat from the overloading reactors becoming outwardly visible.

"Move us back, Linda," John said. "Keep us in the moon's shadow. Use as much power as we can spare."

"Aye, Chief," Linda replied. "Forward thrusters answering one third reverse power. Course one-eight-zero."

"Cortana," he asked, "Slipspace generator status?"

"Almost ready, Chief," Cortana said. She bit her lower lip in concentration. "Capacitor charge at eighty percent. Adjusting final calculations. Stand by."

On screen the Admiral wheeled toward the bulkhead sealing the flagship's bridge. Sparks cascaded along the seam as arc cutters on the other side penetrated. "Master Chief, I have final orders for you."

"Sir," John said.

"You watch and see what's left of this rabble when we're done with 'em. Do *not* engage under any circumstances. You get the intel and hightail it back to Earth and make your report."

"Understood, sir."

"Now listen, son, remember when we talked about the Alamo? You know every one of the brave defenders in those fights died. They knew the odds, but they hurt the enemy." He gritted his teeth in pain. "Both were tactical defeats, but in the end they were also brilliant strategic victories. They made the enemy afraid. Just a few good soldiers fighting for what's right made the difference."

"Yes, sir."

John remembered all those who had made a difference for him. Sam. James. CPO Mendez. Captain Keyes. The men and women who had fought and died on Halo. And now two more names to add to that list: Whitcomb and Haverson.

The bulkhead blasted off its mounts and clattered onto the deck of the *Ascendant Justice*'s bridge. Silhouetted in the passage were dozens of Elites, their energy swords blurs of motion and light. Admiral Whitcomb fired a submachine gun.

The central viewscreen dissolved into static.

John watched for a moment, hoping the Admiral and the Lieutenant would reappear . . . but screen number two remained offline.

Video feed from the Clarion spy drone filled the side screens. There were two hundred warships clustered tightly about the figure-eight-shaped *Unyielding Hierophant*. A similar number of ships circled in loose orbital trajectories. The formation reminded John of a miniature spiral galaxy . . . with a supernova core.

The dorsal bulb of the space station shot with color—red, orange, and blurred with blue-white heat in a heartbeat; plasma tendrils erupted from the surface like solar flares. Internal explosions chained down the station's length through the narrow center portion and into the ventral bulb, shattering that section and discharging bolts of lightning that arced along the station's fragments and to the nearby ships.

The *Unyielding Hierophant* became a roiling cloud of fiery plasma and smoke and static charges that enveloped the ships that had come to engage *Ascendant Justice*, ships that flashed white hot and, in an instant, vaporized.

This thunderhead of superheated and pressurized gas ballooned outward to engulf the rest of the orbiting flotilla; heated their shields, which shimmered silver and popped like soap bubbles; melted their hulls and consumed them.

The blast cooled and the cloud dissipated—but ejected debris continued outward, leaving comet trails, and impacted on stray ships not near the epicenter.

"Move the drone back into the moon's shadow," John ordered.

"Aye, Chief," Will said. "Thrusters responding."

The side viewscreens showed a hailstorm of molten metal streaking toward the drone's cameras—then their view was obscured by the black- and silver-pockmarked surface of the tiny moon.

"Cortana, is the *Gettysburg* ready to jump?" the Chief asked.

"Slipspace capacitors charged, Master Chief. Ready when you are."

"Stand by." John waited a minute. No one spoke. "Will, bring the drone back out."

"Roger, Chief."

The side viewscreen changed from moonscape to space. There was little left of the fleet or the command-and-control station—only clouds of smoke, glittering metal, and ashes.

A few Covenant warships survived. Those that could slowly moved away from the blast site . . . others drifted dead in space. Perhaps a dozen of their original five hundred craft had come through the explosion.

"A brilliant strategic victory," John whispered, the Admiral's last words echoing in his mind.

"Cortana, get us out of here."

The Master Chief stood on the bridge of the *Gettysburg* and watched the stars blur and vanish into the absolute blackness of Slipspace.

They had jumped away from the battle zone over the *Unyielding Hierophant*, emerged in normal space, and plotted their position. Cortana adjusted their course, and now they were finally on their way to Earth. Although they had overwhelming evidence that the Covenant knew the location of Earth, "overwhelming" was not absolute proof. The Cole Protocol still applied.

"Slipspace transition complete," Cortana said. "ETA to Earth in thirty-five hours, Chief." The tiny hologram of Cortana continued to stare at him, and her slender brows knit together.

"Was there something else, Cortana?" he asked.

The furrow in her brow deepened. She sighed and crossed her arms over her chest. "I was wondering about the copy of my infiltration programming." Cortana's color cooled from blue to ultramarine. "I've reviewed your mission logs. Maybe it was the additional copying that caused its breakdown, but that copy did have some of my core personality programming as well. I just hope it's not a sign of . . . some other instability."

Cortana had been on edge. She had been so distracted at times she hadn't even known the correct time. They had, however, all been pushed to the breaking point in the last few weeks. And despite any minor flaws, Cortana had always come through for him.

"We couldn't have survived without you," he finally told her. "Your programming is as good as ours."

She tinged pink and then her hologram returned to a cool blue hue. "Are my aural systems malfunctioning or was that a compliment, Chief?"

"Continue to monitor Slipspace for any anomalies," the Master Chief said, ignoring her.

He strode to the three forward viewscreens and stared into blackness. He wanted solitude, to gaze at nothing, and complete the task that he dreaded.

John pulled his team roster onto his heads-up display. He ran down the list, designating all those who had died on Reach, and afterward, as Missing In Action. James, Li, Grace . . . and all his dead teammates who would never officially be "allowed" to die. And in his mind, they would never find any peace until this war was won.

He paused at Kelly's name.

John listed her as MIA, too. She was ironically the only Spartan truly missing, whisked away by Dr. Halsey on some secret private mission. John knew that whatever the doctor had planned, she would protect Kelly if she could. Still, he couldn't help but worry about them both.

He added Corporal Locklear to his list and designated him Killed In Action. It was a more fitting end for a man who had been as much a warrior as any Spartan.

The last three names on his list he stared at for a long time: Warrant Officer Shiela Polaski, Lieutenant Elias Haverson, and Admiral Danforth Whitcomb. He reluctantly listed them as KIA and referenced his mission report, which detailed their heroism.

Two men had stopped a Covenant armada. They had willingly died doing it, and they had bought the human race a brief respite from destruction.

John felt glad. They were soldiers, sworn to protect humanity from all threats, and they had fulfilled their duty as few ever could. And like his Spartans who were "missing in action," the Admiral and the Lieutenant would never die, either. Not because of a technicality in a mission status listing, but because in their deaths they would live on as inspirations.

John turned and watched as Linda, Will, and Fred occupied the bridge stations. John would make sure that he and the last surviving Spartans did the same.

The elevator doors opened, and Sergeant Johnson stepped onto the bridge.

"Got all those Covenant Engineers rounded up on B-Deck," Sergeant Johnson announced. "Slippery suckers."

The Chief nodded.

"The boys at ONI and those squid heads have a lot in common. Can't understand a thing they say and they're just as good looking. Guess they're all going to have a long talk about technical whatsits and scientific doodads when we get home."

Sergeant Johnson crossed the bridge to the Master Chief. "There's one other thing. Another ONI thing." He held out a data crystal and his gaze fell to the deck. "Lieutenant Haverson gave this to me before he and the Admiral left. He said you'd have to deliver it for him."

John stared at the data crystal and reluctantly plucked it from the Sergeant's fingers as if it were a slug of unstable radioactive material.

"Thank you, Sergeant." He hesitated and then added, "I'll take care of this."

The Sergeant nodded and strode toward Weapons Station One.

John turned back to the blank monitors and retrieved the

other data crystal from his belt compartment. Yesterday he had believed he had done the right thing by giving the Lieutenant all of Dr. Halsey's Flood data—including the data on the Sergeant, which she assured him would lead to his death.

But now?

Now, John knew the difference one man could make in this war. He understood Dr. Halsey's desire to save every person she could.

John held the two data crystals, one in each hand, and stared at them—trying to discern the future from their glimmering facets.

That was the point, wasn't it? He couldn't know the future. He had to do what he could to save every person. Today. Now.

So he decided.

He tightened his fist around the crystal with the complete mission data and crushed it to dust. John couldn't condemn Sergeant Johnson.

He hefted the remaining data crystal. There would have to be enough in it for ONI. He set the crystal securely back into his belt.

Today they had won. They had stopped the Covenant. John would return to Earth with a warning and enough intel to keep scientists at ONI busy.

But what about tomorrow? The Covenant didn't give up once they set their sights on a target. They wanted Earth— they'd come for it. Destroying their fleet would only delay that inevitable fact.

They had time, though. Maybe enough time to prepare for whatever the Covenant could throw at them.

John would take today's victory. And he'd be there when the fighting started again—he'd be there to win.

SECTION VII

HARBINGER

EPILOGUE

A hundred thousand probes darted and scanned with winking
electronic eyes across the void of tangled nonspaces enveloping
the Covenant inner empire. They gathered data and emerged
into the cold vacuum, where they were recovered by the hundreds of supercarriers and cruisers in station-keeping positions
around the massive, bulbous planetoid that dominated the heav-
ens.

Not a single rock larger than a centimeter could enter this
space without being identified, targeted, and vaporized. Au-
thorization codes were updated hourly, and if any incoming
vessel hesitated for a millisecond with the proper response, it,
too, met unyielding destruction.

The High Charity drifted beneath this impervious network,
illuminated by the glow from scores of warship engines.

Deep within, protected by legions of crack Covenant soldiers, the Sanctum of the Heirarchs was an island of calm. The
walls, floor, and ceiling of the chamber were ornamented with
mirrored shards made from the fused glass of countless worlds
conquered by the Covenant Hegemony. They reflected the whispered thoughts of the one who sat in the center of this room—
mirrored them back, so they might consider the glory of its
domain, and learn from its wisdom . . . because there was no
higher source of intellect, will, and truth alive in the galaxy.

In the middle of the chamber, hovering a meter off the floor upon its imperial dais, sat the Covenant High Prophet of Truth. Its body was barely discernible, covered as it was with a wide red cloak, and upon its head sat a glowing headpiece with sensor and respiratory apparatus that extended like insect antennae. Only its snout and dark eyes protruded . . . as did tiny claws from the sleeve of its gold underrobes.

The left claw twitched—the signal for the chamber's doors to open.

The doors groaned and split apart, and a crack of light appeared.

A single figure appeared silhouetted in the illumination. It bowed so deeply that its chest brushed against the floor.

"Rise," the Prophet of Truth whispered. The word was amplified by the chamber; it echoed and boomed forth as if a giant had spoken. "Come closer, Tartarus, and report."

A ripple of shock passed through the Imperial Elite Protectors. They had never seen such a creature allowed so close to the Holy Ones.

"Protectors," the Prophet commanded. "Leave us."

Together the honor guards straightened, bowed, and filed out of the great chamber. They said nothing, but the Prophet saw the confusion on their features. Good—such ignorance and puzzlement had its uses.

The Brute, Tartarus, strode across the great room. When he stood within three meters of the Prophet, he fell to one knee.

The creature was a magnificent specimen of viciousness. The Prophet marveled at its near-unthinking potential for mayhem; the rippling muscle under its dull gray skin could tear apart any opponent—even a mighty Hunter. It was the perfect instrument.

"Tell me what you found," the Prophet said, its voice now truly a whisper.

Without looking up Tartarus reached for its belt and the attached orb.

The Prophet flicked its claw at the container. It floated free from Tartarus's grasp and hovered. The top unscrewed, and three glittering chips of sapphire-colored crystal shimmered, and threw light and shadow upon the chamber's mirrored surfaces.

The Prophet's dais bobbed in the suddenly uneven gravity—but it quickly compensated.

"This is all?" it asked.

"Eight squadrons combed the area surrounding the Eridanus Secundus asteroid field and Tau Ceti," the Brute replied, bowing its head even lower. "Many were lost in the void. This is all there was to find."

"A pity."

The orb's lid screwed itself back on, and then the container gently drifted into the Prophet's grasp.

"It may yet be enough for our purposes . . . and one more relic from the Great Ones, as precious as they are, will soon make no difference to us." The Prophet tucked the container deep in the folds of its underrobe. "Make sure those pilots who survived are well rewarded. Then execute them all. Quickly. Quietly."

"I understand," Tartarus replied with a hint of anticipation thickening his voice.

The Prophet inhaled deeply, released a rasping sigh, and then asked, "And what of the *Unyielding Hierophant*?"

"The reports are unclear, Your Grace," Tartarus replied. "The renegade flagship *Ascendant Justice* was involved, and destroyed. We are unsure what triggered the station's detonation. The recorded communications channels were flooded with system error reports prior to its destruction. The Engineers are saying this is imp—"

The Prophet held up one claw, indicating silence. Tartarus halted midsyllable.

"A regrettable turn of events," the Prophet said, "but in the end, only an insignificant setback. Have the ships that are battle-ready rendezvous with us at the site of the cataclysm."

"And what of the incompetent, High One? The one who lost *Ascendant Justice*?"

"Bring him before the Council. Let his fate match the magnitude of his failure."

Tartarus's face twisted with what passed for a grin among his species.

"Soon the Great Journey shall begin," the Prophet of Truth continued, and its claws curled into fists. "And let nothing in this universe impede our progress."

ADJUNCT

Amy,

My name is Charles VanKeerk, and for the last five years I've been working alongside your husband to protect the dreams that demand so much from us. I am so sorry that in all the time I've spent with Sam I never had a chance to meet you in person. As you know, our situation prevents us from being able to move about as we wish or see those we fight for, and because of this I am a stranger to you . . . and it pains me that you have to receive this message from a stranger:

Sam is gone.

For your protection, I can't give you any details on where or how he died, but know that he was a hero, and he died as one. Everyone who fought alongside him these last years loved him as a brother, and his determination and gentle spirit were strengths to us all. It is a tragedy that Sam was forced to this fight, but forced he was, as we all are, by the most important need we have—the need to be free.

I know words can't help right now, but please don't doubt the value of Sam's sacrifice or the wisdom of our fight, even in these terrible times. You will ask why, in the face of such an overwhelming external threat, we would take up arms against our own kind rather than fight against the Covenant. We struggle with this question every day . . . Sam fought with it every day. But what keeps us going is the certainty that there's no future in helping those who would only put us in a cage for helping them win.

You've seen how the UNSC treats us, taking and taking but only offering empty promises in return . . . any planet outside their precious inner circle is plundered and left to suffer starvation, plague, or the onslaught of the Covenant. If only more of us would find the strength Sam had, perhaps we could make the UNSC recognize that it doesn't matter if you come from Earth or Harvest or anywhere . . . we're all equal, and we should all be treated as equals. Until that day comes, however, we have to fight every threat to our way of life . . . be it human or Covenant.

I write all of this to try to give you some comfort, some justification for such a terrible loss. I hope you can believe in our cause as much as Sam did, and I hope you can believe me when I say we all miss him terribly. Despite whatever you may have seen or read recently in the UNSC-controlled media, Sam's death was a proud death. A noble death. He died for all of us, and I know for a certainty that he died for you.

My heartfelt condolences on your loss,
Charles

TUG O' WAR

Oliver Birch was pretty sure he was going to die.

A stinging bead of sweat found its way into his eye, forcing him to close it tightly, take another breath, and focus. His gangly frame labored inside a pressurized atmospheric suit specifically built to sustain the perils of space. Perils like radiation bombardment, extremes of temperature, and right now, an enormous object that had managed to trap him against the bulkhead of the UNSC *Dresden*.

In one hand he held a magnetic vice, and in the other, a heavy-grade torque wrench—both were fixed onto the dark, hulking shape that he now found himself buried under. The shape was familiar enough, and so was the setting. Empty, weightless vacuum in the engine room of an abandoned *Marathon*-class cruiser called the *Dresden*. The shape that had pinned him was that of a Shaw-Fujikawa Translight Engine—better known as a "slipspace drive," which had suddenly come free after nearly an hour of steady and tedious work.

Recovering some leverage with his footing, he gently pushed the large machine away while still guiding it with one hand, since the lack of any real gravity might allow it to take off in the opposite direction at a moment's notice. And he most certainly needed to guide it because, as every schoolchild knew, slipspace drives were not to be trifled with. One false move, one wrong coordinate, one faulty mounting and bad things could happen—very bad things. Fortunately, the drive moved free and was slowly caught at its farthest corners by a series of towing cables he'd previously locked into place.

With a tap on his wristband, the distant tug's winch began pulling the drive at a swift but controlled rate. He grabbed onto the side of the machine and trailed it back to the tug, taking a few shallow breaths to regain his composure. As the winch silently hauled Oliver and his prize, he glanced absently at the *Dresden* receding into the distance.

The uneven silhouette of the severely battered vessel belied its once majestic design, and all that remained now was an over-turned, floating husk of steel, plastic components, and other random materials that had come free over the years. This was just one of hundreds of ships adrift in the debris field crowning the planet Biko.

Decades ago, when the Covenant first arrived here, they had swiftly and comprehensively wiped out the UNSC forces protecting it. When they were done, they had shunted the debris toward the planet's northern pole, clearing the way for what inevitably came next: an excessive yet surgical display of their brutality through the orbital bombardment of Biko's surface.

Oliver had never seen the Covenant up close, but he was fairly certain that if he ever encountered them, he'd mess his pants. Fortunately for Oliver that wasn't very likely. Despite the intensity of the last few moments, his actual occupation as a "fetcher" was largely uneventful, something made even more banal by the endless paperwork his employer, Warner & Ives, bureaucratically tacked onto each operation.

Fetchers hadn't been terribly popular till about twenty years ago when the UNSC discovered that they were closing in on a shortage of translight engines. Starships were expensive, of course, but so were manned rescue and recovery operations. With something as costly and as difficult to develop as a reliable slip-space drive, supply never seemed to keep up with demand, and the complexity of the drives changed the economic balance. That's where fetchers came in. Private companies who special-

ed in "fetching" could now get paid good money for solid, work-
ng translight engines recovered from derelict ships.

Oliver didn't doubt that the UNSC could send their own
eople to reclaim drives like the *Dresden*'s, but like many things
ne government could do, they'd rather pay someone else to do
for them. Thusly, fetching became a flourishing market that
ould allow companies like Warner & Ives to set up clients with
ontractors like Oliver. He'd locate, recover, and return the slip-
pace drive and there'd be a nice, fat paycheck for him in return.

At least that *had* been the plan, he thought, as both he and the
rive finally reached the rear bay of the tug. But all that had been
efore he met Gretchen Navarro at a university bistro on Tribute.

fter performing half a dozen tests to check the drive's extant
adiation levels, everything passed with flying colors and the
rive seemed to be in perfect working order. Typically, drives
uffered fairly superficial damage, with most issues relating to
neir external systems or mounting hardware. The drives them-
elves were designed to be physically bulletproof, for obvious
easons. Slipspace accidents tended to fall into categories unre-
ated to their normal working operations, with human error
nd ship mass accidents at the top of the list. Oliver meandered
o the side of the bay and closed the main door, repressurizing
ne room and discarding his atmospheric suit.

He tapped a release button on a wall-mounted control panel
nd two doors opened on the port side of the tug's bay—a
eaten-up ship he called *Galileo's Worst Enemy*. The tug was
amed, ostensibly, after Father Orazio Grassi, a priest and mathe-
natician who'd lived in a time when the church controlled both
tate and science. Oddly, Grassi, a Jesuit, had objected to Galileo's
ometary theory on *scientific,* rather than canonical, grounds. The
nsuing tiff, rather than snuff out Galileo's genius, served only
o stoke it, and led to some of Galileo's most convincing work.

Back in the artificial gravity of the tug, Oliver was greeted by the waddling figure of Mabel, his three-legged dog. Mabel was miracle of sorts. While scouring the wreckage above the plane Dwarka, he had discovered an abandoned but relatively un touched colony ship from another era, the CAA *Butterworth* Oliver wasn't certain how or why it came to be there—or even how it had survived the Covenant's attack on the planet—bu when he found it, it was empty, save for one creature: a hungry nervous, but ultimately happy three-legged golden retriever.

"Easy there, girl," he said, walking around the base of th drive, his eyes and hands inspecting it simultaneously. "Let m give it a quick look and then we'll head out. I promise."

Time hadn't been an issue before Oliver received notice from his contract handler, a guy who he only knew as Steve. Thei client this time around was the Office of Naval Intelligence an apparently they needed the *Dresden*'s slipspace drive a week ago This complicated matters because in the meantime he'd some how managed to square away a date with an incredibly beautifu yet challenging woman from Tribute—a Ms. Gretchen Navarro

How exactly he would make it back to both Cygnus for th drive handoff and to Tribute for his date with Gretchen, h didn't know. All he knew was that the date was in fifteen day and he didn't have enough time to do both. But as his hands ra across the truck-sized angularity of the *Dresden*'s translight en gine, he realized something—this wasn't a standard militar FTL drive. This was something else.

The serial number and its general shape and size indicate that it was a '44 model made by the Oros Trading Compan based out of Mars. But this drive wasn't a '44 model and it mos certainly was not from Mars—and its shape, though extremel close to a commercial drive, wasn't an exact match. He scanne the serials to double-check and snorted in triumph. This particula drive was what fetchers referred to as a "saddle box."

Saddle boxes were never commercially produced or civiliar issued. Not ever. They were made exclusively for military exper ments with slipspace travel and they were extremely rare. So rare that he'd only seen two in his lifetime.

Slipspace was a rare scientific commodity—a technology and science that were loosely understood, frequently used, and mostly controlled. But like early theories of gravity, most of the understanding was inference and conjecture. There were significant unknowns. This might have been one reason that Oliver, despite having acquired a doctoral degree in quantum electrodynamics, had decided to become a fetcher and not a physicist. That and because it paid damn well and working in labs wasn't his really idea of fun.

Giving the saddle box one last look, Oliver finally knelt down and tenderly scratched the fur at the base of Mabel's neck. "In fifteen days? I don't think it's ever been done before. But with this thing, maybe, just maybe . . ."

Mabel let out a small huffing sound that ended in a whine. Oliver didn't speak dog fluently, but he took it as a plaintive plea for him not to chicken out this time around.

"All right, all right," he said, standing up. "Let's do it."

Gretchen Navarro was incredibly good looking. She wasn't mediocre in any way, shape, or form, and she knew it. She was confident to the point of arrogance and perhaps just a little bit vain. The chances he'd ever meet another girl like Gretchen were next to nil, but even those chances paled in comparison to the possibility of any girl like her saying "yes" to a date with him ever again. Apparently, their long talk about fetching had intrigued her—why exactly, he had no idea.

Suffice it to say, this date was important.

Oliver entered the tug's bridge and stared up intently across Biko's curved horizon line. He flipped three switches and nudged a throttle, dropping his body into a snug, fabric-covered seat that looked like it had been plucked out of a living room, not the deck of a tug.

Galileo's Worst Enemy started to gradually turn about, pushing away from the debris field that eerily clouded the northern pole of the planet, like flies around a festering carcass—in this case, a cold, mummified carcass. Biko looked like all planets did once they ran headlong into the Covenant war machine. It was a dead series of grays, blacks, and reds, the charred remains of a way of life that had been swept away far quicker than it had first appeared.

Slowly filling the front viewscreen was another ship—the CAA *Butterworth*. Mabel's residence and his own ownership of Mabel had allowed him, with some clever interpretation of maritime salvage law, to claim the *Butterworth* as his own. As he approached, the colony ship opened her starboard bay doors and *Galileo's Worst Enemy* was smoothly drawn in by an automated electromagnetic tug system.

When fetching, it was important to have two separate ships for a few reasons, the primary being that fetching often required the operator to enter exceptionally dense fields of debris. This just wasn't possible from most affordable, slipspace-capable ships. On a normal fetching run, Oliver would typically park the *Butterworth* four to five thousand klicks from the prospect and then take *Galileo's Worst Enemy* as close as possible.

"So here's the problem, Mabel, and try to pay attention because I'm not explaining it again."

Mabel promptly turned away, but Oliver continued unabated.

"Biko is located roughly twenty-four light-years from Cygnus and it's about fifty-eight light-years from Tribute. From point to point the total trip would be well over a month in length."

Mabel looked up at him, as if she too were puzzled by the relativistic problem, and sneezed.

"Yeah, my thoughts exactly," he said. "That's where the saddle box comes in."

———

A wreath of energy formed around the bow of the CAA *Butterworth* and it was drawn into the unknowable texture of slipspace. There, eddies of sheered radiation buoyed the colony vessel, pushing it forward through a tangled web of both space and time. But, on the command deck of the *Butterworth,* all Oliver and Mabel could see were swirling aureoles of energy and light against the deep black of subspace.

"Time dilation frequently happens on a small scale whenever you're dealing with slipspace." Oliver spoke with Mabel's head on his lap. "Einstein was pretty much dead on when it came to special and general relativity, but with slipspace, it has always been difficult to accurately measure the time it takes to travel from one location to another. There's always been an irregular, unpredictable, and inexplicable temporal discrepancy between those who entered slipspace and those who remained outside of it—this is a proven and accepted fact of science. It could be the effects of mass from extra dimensions; it could be magic. We simply don't know to a certainty."

The thought caused him to stand up and exit the command deck through the adjoining corridors, moving toward the ship's engine room. The *Butterworth* was perpetually eerie due to its massive size and general emptiness, which was probably the reason Mabel always followed so closely behind. Oliver didn't really care *why* she did this, only that she continued to so that he could keep talking without feeling completely ridiculous—which was his own defense against the ship's spooky mien.

"The real mystery has always been finding out how exactly slipspace generates time dilation to degrees humans can't quantify or even understand. For example, why do, on occasion, some ships arrive days and even weeks before they're scheduled to? How do the Covenant beat us to our own destinations time and time again, even if they've left hours or even days later? Or, in those extremely rare and usually classified instances, how have ships been tracked as arriving at one location before they've even left another?"

Mabel had nothing to say to that—Oliver wondered briefly if that meant it was actually sinking in, or if she thought he was a complete idiot. Probably the latter, but he continued nevertheless. They entered the engine room, which was large, cavernous, and dark—at its center was the newly installed saddle box, which he'd hastily mounted in an effort to buy time. It was also the one Oliver used to make their jump away from Biko.

"Heh," he said, reading the sensor relay screen. "Never seen that alignment error before." Oliver feverishly keyed a response that cleared the error but left a puzzled look on his face. He shrugged it off and continued around the machine.

"This saddle box is some kind of skunkworks prototype drive that I'm guessing was manufactured by ONI—and I'm guessing again that it was designed to measure dilation by generating several microjumps within a single transition. Not such a big deal for the Covenant, since many physicists believe that's how the aliens pull off their insane speeds, but it's a huge deal for humanity. The special thing about this particular drive is that because it can accurately navigate several jumps within slipspace, it can accentuate and coerce to some degree the previously unpredictable dilation." He paused, casting a glance toward a control panel near the drive's base. "To what degree though, I don't know. Not even sure if the people who made it really knew, to be honest."

Oliver did, however, know that the UNSC had been testing such jumps for the purpose of communication probes and drop pod deployment of troops from shielded positions within slipspace. He knew these things because ONI had consulted him more than once already on the matter. But, since he wasn't involved in the development of those projects, he didn't know exactly where they stood at this moment in time.

"So here's the deal. I'm about 99 percent certain—which is usually certain enough for me—that we can mount the *Butterworth*'s old slipspace drive to our tug. At a specific point, the *Butterworth* will release the tug from its cargo hold with us on board." Mabel responded with a cocked head and a slight drop of her tail. There she goes again, Oliver thought, doubting his plan already. "When we get to the appropriate spot within the slipspace transition, we'll use the *Butterworth*'s old drive to slip back into normal space, right smack-dab in Tribute's front yard."

Oliver continued to size up the drive's well-shielded components, this time punching a series of queries into the control panel. Mabel had already dropped to the ground with her chin resting on her front two paws—two-thirds of all of the paws she had left.

"While *Galileo's Worst Enemy* safely drops back to normal space, within taxiing distance of Tribute and perfectly on time, the *Butterworth* will continue on course, following a staggered series of automated jumps, all the way through to its designated slipspace exit in Cygnus. We'll have a playback message and verbal claim of continued ownership running on loop for the dock workers. And, of course, Steve will be there to get the saddle box to the ONI folks on time."

Oliver then asked Mabel what she thought of his foolproof plan. He wasn't entirely sure that he could count it as a positive affirmation, but just then she broke wind and he took that as a sign of relief.

And for the longest time, his plan *was* entirely foolproof—well, right up to the point where the radiation klaxons blared on the tug. Now the ship was being hammered from every angle in slipspace.

Oliver and Mabel had barely made it aboard when the tug was somehow knocked out of the *Butterworth*'s cargo bay and began literally peeling apart while they tumbled in the colony ship's radiation wake. Technically speaking, that wasn't supposed to happen—the *Butterworth* should have maintained its transition path for at least another day before executing a jump, but for some reason, it hadn't.

That was definitely a big problem, but the more immediate issue was trying to get into the cryostorage pod and seal it before *Galileo's Worst Enemy* became *Galileo's Spare Parts*. Oliver now carried Mabel and bounded as fast as he could through the tug's narrow corridors as the ship was repeatedly battered. With its shielding failing, the ship was like fresh carrion amid a torrent of vultures; its various pieces would be picked and plucked until all that remained was a skeleton.

Oliver didn't want to be picked or plucked.

Finally, he reached the cryostorage chamber, what essentially amounted to a large closet for a ship of this size. He entered one of two pods, fortunately large enough for both him and Mabel to snugly fit. The pod immediately slammed shut, filling with gas which would coalesce, eventually drowning them both in an artificial surfactant that would put them to sleep while it kept them alive. Through the narrow porthole, Oliver watched as the interior of *Galileo's Worst Enemy* heated to a bright red, began melting into shreds, and eventually ripped asunder, all while simultaneously reemerging back into normal space.

All that was left of the battered tug were thousands of scraps of flotsam and jetsam and a single, radiation-shielded cryostorage pod.

As he stared into the blackness, barely recognizable star systems drifting and rotating past the pod's vid-screen, he thought about Gretchen Navarro, beautiful, elegant, impatient, and bad-tempered.

He patted Mabel on the head, glanced at the pulsing light

of the slow-impulse thruster monitor and the reassuring beat of the emergency locator beacon, and muttered, "She'll have to wait."

And sleep took them gently, before the first wisp of cold seeped into their crèche.

TRANSCRIPT OF THE SECOND PSYCHOLOGICAL DEBRIEFING OF
LIEUTENANT FREDERIC, SPARTAN-104, CONDUCTED BY ONI
PSYCHIATRIST DR. VERONICA CLAYTON, PH.D.

DR. VERONICA CLAYTON: GOOD AFTERNOON, LIEUTENANT.

S-104: MA'AM.

DR. CLAYTON: IF YOU WOULD, I'D LIKE TO REVISIT THE
EVENTS ABOARD THE *PILLAR OF AUTUMN*, JUST
BEFORE YOUR DEPLOYMENT PLANET-SIDE—BEFORE
THE ENGAGEMENT, AND TRAGIC EVENTS, ON
REACH.

S-104: [SILENCE]

DR. CLAYTON: WHAT WAS THE MORALE AMONG YOUR FELLOW SPAR-
TANS AT THIS POINT?

S-104: EAGER.

DR. CLAYTON: EAGER? HOW SO?

S-104: REACH— ASIDE FROM BEING AN INVALUABLE MILI-
TARY RESOURCE, REACH WAS OUR HOME—OR . . .
IT WAS THE CLOSEST THING TO HOME ANY OF US
HAD EVER KNOWN.

DR. CLAYTON: SO, YOU'D SAY THERE WAS AN ATTACHMENT—A
CONNECTION—BETWEEN THE SPARTANS TRAINED ON
REACH AND THE PLANET ITSELF. AS YOU SAID,
THIS WAS YOUR HOME.

S-104: WE TAKE EACH ENCOUNTER SERIOUSLY, MA'AM, AND
WE VIEW EVERY COVENANT ENGAGEMENT AS CRITI-

CAL, BUT WE WEREN'T ABOUT TO LET THE
ENEMY GO UNCHECKED IN OUR OWN BACKYARD.

DR. CLAYTON: YOU ARE REFERRING—WHEN YOU SAY "US,"
"WE"—YOU ARE REFERRING TO YOUR FELLOW
SPARTANS?

S-104: YES, MA'AM.

DR. CLAYTON: AND "EAGER"—YOU SPEAK FOR YOUR UNIT AS
WELL? YOU SPEAK FOR THE OTHER SPARTANS WHEN
YOU SAY THIS?

S-104: WE WERE—WE ALWAYS ARE—ALL OF US—EAGER TO
ACCOMPLISH THE GOALS SET FORTH BEFORE US AND
ACHIEVE VICTORY WITHIN A GIVEN TACTICAL SITU-
ATION . . .

DR. CLAYTON: YOU'RE NOT . . .

S-104: I'M NOT FINISHED . . . AND, AS THIS SES-
SION IS ONE IN WHICH I AM ENCOURAGED TO
SPEAK FREELY, I WOULD APPRECIATE THE
OPPORTUNITY TO DO SO.

DR. CLAYTON: CONTINUE.

S-104: THANK YOU. YES, AS SPARTANS WE ANTICIPATE
OUR INVOLVEMENT IN ANY MILITARY CAMPAIGN.
IT'S WHO WE ARE. IT'S WHAT WE WERE BORN
TO DO. WE'RE HERE TO WIN THIS WAR AND
WE'RE EAGER TO DO JUST THAT. TO BE FRANK,
MA'AM, IS THIS ANOTHER INQUIRY ON MILITARY
ETHICS BASED ON CIVILIAN ASSUMPTIONS ABOUT
THE SPARTAN-II PROJECT? IF IT IS, I'D
LIKE TO SPEAK WITH LORD HOOD BEFORE—

DR. CLAYTON: ANY "ASSUMPTIONS," AS YOU CALL THEM, ARE
BASED UPON YEARS OF OBSERVATION AND RESEARCH.
YOU CANNOT CHANGE WHO—WHAT—YOU ARE.

S-104: I WOULD NEVER ASK TO CHANGE WHO I AM,
DOCTOR. I AM PROUD TO BE WHO I AM, AND ANY

	OTHER SPARTAN WOULD SAY THE SAME. ESPE-
	CIALLY CONSIDERING THE NATURE OF OUR PRESENT
	ENEMY AND THE CURRENT DIRECTION OF THIS
	CONFLICT—

DR. CLAYTON: WE ARE WELL AWARE OF THE CURRENT DIRECTION OF THIS CONFLICT, LIEUTENANT, BUT THAT IS NOT THE TOPIC OF THIS DISCUSSION—

S-104: I WOULD MOST CERTAINLY ARGUE THAT YOU ARE NOT FAMILIAR WITH ANYTHING OF THE SORT. HAVE YOU EVER SEEN A PLANET GLASSED?

DR. CLAYTON: I—

S-104: NOT IN A VID. NOT IN A FEED. WITH YOUR OWN TWO EYES. . . . WE WEREN'T GOING TO LET THAT HAPPEN TO REACH. SO, YES, WE WERE EAGER, AND WE WERE READY—FOR ALL THE GOOD IT DID.

DR. CLAYTON: WERE YOU THIS FRUSTRATED BEFORE THE DEPLOYMENT?

S-104: EXCUSE ME?

DR. CLAYTON: IF REACH WAS SO IMPORTANT TO YOU AND YOUR UNIT—

S-104: EVERY WORLD IS IMPORTANT.

DR. CLAYTON: NO DOUBT. BUT, REACH—REACH MOST ASSUREDLY HAD A DEEPER EMOTIONAL RESONANCE FOR YOU—FOR ALL OF YOU. I MEAN; NO ONE—NONE OF US— BELIEVED REACH WOULD EVER BE IN DANGER. IT WAS ALWAYS SAFE. IT WAS ALWAYS OUR ROCK. AND NOW . . . IT'S GONE.

JUDGING FROM YOUR PREVIOUS STATEMENTS, THIS HAD TO HAVE HAD SOME PSYCHOLOGICAL EFFECT ON YOUR TEAM.

S-104: IT ABSOLUTELY DID NOT.

DR. CLAYTON: FOR ALL OF YOUR TRAINING AND SKILLS, YOU ARE STILL HUMAN. HOW COULD IT NOT?

S-104:   OUR ONLY CONCERN AT THE TIME WAS THE MISSION AT HAND, NOTHING MORE AND NOTHING LESS.

DR. CLAYTON: SPEAKING OF THE MISSION, ONCE RED FLAG WENT BELLY-UP, YOU WERE CHOSEN TO LEAD THE TEAM DEPLOYED TO THE PLANET SURFACE BY MASTER CHIEF PETTY OFFICER, JOHN-117, CORRECT?

S-104:   YES, MA'AM.

DR. CLAYTON: BUT YOU DIDN'T WANT TO GO GROUNDSIDE, DID YOU? THE TRANSCRIPTS ABOARD THE *AUTUMN* SAY THAT YOU WANTED TO—

S-104:   I WAS, AND AM, FULLY PREPARED TO SERVE IN WHATEVER ROLE DEEMED NECESSARY TO WIN THIS WAR.

DR. CLAYTON: I SEE. THEN, FOCUSING ON YOUR TEAM AND THE SPECIFIC OBJECTIVE PLACED UPON YOU AS FIELD LEADER OF RED TEAM, WHAT HAPPENED DURING YOUR TEAM'S DESCENT TOWARD REACH . . . WHAT WAS *YOUR* SPECIFIC MENTAL STATE AT THIS POINT? YOU SAY YOU WERE EAGER BEFORE THE ACTUAL DEPLOYMENT, HOW WERE YOU FEELING ONCE THE MISSION GOT UNDERWAY?

S-104:   FOCUSED. WE WERE DROPPING IN HOT AND THE FULL SQUAD HAD TO BE ALERT TO ANY AND ALL THREATS—

DR. CLAYTON: AS TEAM LEADER YOU HAD THE LIVES OF YOUR FELLOW SPARTANS IN YOUR HANDS. A SINGLE MISTAKE COULD HAVE KILLED THEM ALL, INCLUDING YOU. YET IT SEEMS LIKE IT WAS ONE ERROR AFTER ANOTHER—

S-104:   I'M NOT QUITE SURE I UNDERSTAND WHAT YOU'RE SUGGESTING, DOCTOR.

DR. CLAYTON: WHICH ONE? THE FACT THAT YOU WERE RESPONSIBLE FOR THE LIVES OF EVERYONE UNDER YOUR COMMAND? OR THAT YOUR MENTAL STATE WAS NOT IDEAL AND THAT YOUR DECISIONS DURING THE

| | INITIAL PHASE OF YOUR DEPLOYMENT PUT LIVES, INCLUDING THE VERY VALUABLE, AND INCREDIBLY EXPENSIVE LIVES OF TWENTY-ONE OTHER SPARTANS, IN JEOPARDY. |

S-104: I'M NOT SURE YOU HAVE A FULL UNDERSTANDING OF THE—

DR. CLAYTON: "BRACE YOURSELVES."

S-104: [SILENCE]

DR. CLAYTON: DURING THE DROP YOU BROADCAST THOSE TWO WORDS—"BRACE YOURSELVES"—OVER FLEETCOM 7. THIRTY-NINE RECEIVERS PICKED UP THE TRANSMISSION—THIRTY-ONE BELONGING TO UNSC CRAFT, EIGHT ON CIVILIAN. AND THERE'S NO TELLING HOW MANY COVENANT VESSELS ACQUIRED THE SIGNAL, POTENTIALLY ALLOWING THEM TO BACKTRACK ITS SOURCE AND GAIN ACCESS TO OTHER FREQUENCIES AND DATA BEING TRANSMITTED DURING AND AFTER THE ENCOUNTER.

S-104: IT WAS A—

DR. CLAYTON: "COM MALFUNCTION." I'M AWARE. S-087 HAS ALREADY CONFIRMED THAT ASSERTION. STILL— DOESN'T SEEM LIKE A MISTAKE A SPARTAN SHOULD, OR WOULD, MAKE. YET YOU MADE IT. MAKES ME WONDER WHAT OTHER MISTAKES YOU MAY HAVE MADE.

S-104: MA'AM, IS THIS A PSYCH EVAL, OR AN INTERROGATION?

DR. CLAYTON: THAT'S UP TO YOU, LIEUTENANT, BUT THAT IS ACTUALLY A VERY GOOD QUESTION. YOUR ANSWER WILL SAY A LOT ABOUT YOU AND HOW YOU VIEW YOUR ROLE AS A LEADER AMONGST YOUR PEERS.

S-104: I'M SECURE IN MY ROLE AND THE TACTICAL DECISIONS I MAKE BEFORE, DURING, AND FOLLOWING COMBAT, AND SO ARE MY PEERS.

DR. CLAYTON: THE DECISION TO ABORT THE PELICAN WITH YOUR ENTIRE SQUAD: DO YOU FEEL THAT WAS THE RIGHT TACTICAL DECISION?

S-104: ABSOLUTELY, AS I STATED IN MY REPORT TO CORTANA EN ROUTE TO SOL—YOU DID READ MY REPORT, DIDN'T YOU?

DR. CLAYTON: THOROUGHLY.

S-104: THEN YOU KNOW THAT THE PELICAN TASKED WITH DELIVERING US TO THE SURFACE WAS DAMAGED BEYOND USE—

DR. CLAYTON: YOU LOST FOUR SPARTANS BY ABANDONING THAT CRAFT.

S-104: I WOULD HAVE LOST THEM ALL IF WE'D TRIED TO RIDE IT OUT. LOOK AT THE CALCULATIONS ON OUR TRAJECTORY AND SPEED—AND THE SHIELD DAMAGE UPON ENTRY—THE REPORT IS CRYSTAL CLEAR. WE HAD NO CHOICE BUT TO EXIT THE VEHICLE AND USE THE TERRAIN AND OUR ARMOR TO SECURE RELATIVELY SAFE LANDINGS.

DR. CLAYTON: UPON DESCENT, ALL TWENTY-ONE SPARTANS RESPONDED WITH AN "AFFIRMITIVE" AT YOUR ORDER TO "AIM FOR THE TREETOPS." WHY THE TREETOPS? WAS THERE NOT A SAFER AREA TO LAND?

S-104: ALL WE HAD BELOW US WAS GROUND. THE TREES HAD ENOUGH GIVE TÓ DAMPEN THE IMPACT AND SLOW THE FALL. BUT IF YOU'VE READ MY REPORT YOU KNOW ALL OF THIS ALREADY. I'VE BEEN THROUGH ENOUGH OF THESE SESSIONS TO KNOW WHEN ONI IS FISHING FOR SOMETHING ELSE, SO MAYBE WE CAN JUST—

DR. CLAYTON: "CUT THE CRAP." YOU LOST FOUR SPARTANS ON IMPACT. SIX INJURED TO THE POINT OF INEFFECTIVENESS. BEFORE YOUR MISSION EVEN TOOK OFF, YOU WERE ALREADY RESPONSIBLE FOR THE LARGEST

CASUALTY RATE OF ANY PREVIOUS ENDEAVOR IN-
VOLVING SPARTAN-II SOLDIERS.

AT THIS POINT YOU'VE MADE WHAT SOME WOULD
CONSIDER AN ILL-ADVISED JUMP, DAMAGED YOUR
SQUAD'S EFFECTIVENESS SIGNIFICANTLY, AND NOW
YOU'RE ON THE SURFACE OF A PLANET CONSIDERED
OUR MOST PRECIOUS MILITARY ASSET AND HAVE
BEEN TASKED TO DEFEND IT FROM AN INCOMING
COVENANT INVASION WITH NO WEAPONS?

S-104: AN UNARMED SPARTAN DOESN'T STAY THAT WAY FOR
LONG—

DR. CLAYTON: IN FACT, YOU COMMANDEERED COVENANT WEAPONRY
EN ROUTE TO YOUR OBJECTIVE. DID YOU MAINTAIN
POSSESSION OF THE WEAPONS FOR FUTURE INSPEC-
TION AND EVALUATION? THAT IS A STANDING DI-
RECTIVE, CORRECT? TO COLLECT ANY COVENANT
TECH THAT MAY PROVIDE ADDITIONAL DETAILS
ABOUT THEIR WEAPON SYSTEMS AND THE LIKE.

S-104: WELL, THERE ARE PLENTY OF THEM DOWN THERE
RIGHT NOW. [POINTS TO EARTH THROUGH VIEW-
PORT] IF YOU REALLY WANT ONE, WHY DON'T YOU
GO TAKE ONE FROM THEM?

DR. CLAYTON: ON EARTH?

S-104: YES, MA'AM, WHICH IS WHERE I SHOULD BE RIGHT
NOW. THERE'S A WAR GOING ON AND THE LONGER MY
TEAM AND I ARE STUCK UP HERE, THE MORE HELL
THEY'RE GOING TO CAUSE DOWN THERE.

DR. CLAYTON: SO YOU CONSIDER THIS A WASTE OF YOUR TIME?

S-104: YOU'RE QUESTIONING MY LEADERSHIP ON REACH
MORE THAN A MONTH AGO WHILE EARTH IS GOING
TO HELL IN A HANDBASKET BELOW US, SO YES.
I'D SAY THIS IS AN EGREGIOUS WASTE OF MY
TIME. I'M CERTAIN THAT THE ADMIRAL WOULD
FEEL THE SAME.

DR. CLAYTON: OF COURSE HE WOULD.

I DON'T CARE WHAT YOU THINK OF ME—OR WHAT HOOD THINKS OF ME—THIS PROCESS IS IMPORTANT BECAUSE YOU *ARE* TOO IMPORTANT AND IT'S MY JOB TO HELP MAKE SURE THAT YOU—*ALL OF YOU*—ARE IN PRIME WORKING ORDER AND THAT THERE ARE NO CRACKS IN YOUR ARMOR—METAPHORICALLY SPEAKING.

[PAUSE]

CAN WE CONTINUE?

S-104: [SILENCE]

[FLT ADM HOOD ENTERS ROOM]

FLT ADM HOOD: WHO AUTHORIZED THIS?

DR. CLAYTON: ADMIRAL, I WILL ASK THAT YOU PLEASE LEAVE THIS ROOM!

FLT ADM HOOD: WHO AUTHORIZED THIS? WAS IT MARGARET?

DR. CLAYTON: ADMIRAL, THAT IS NONE OF YOUR—YOU DO NOT HAVE JURISDICTION OVER BETA-5 PROTOCOL, I WAS SENT HERE TO—

FLT ADM HOOD: MY JURISDICTION IS THE ENTIRE PLANET. WE'RE FIGHTING A WAR DOWN THERE AND IF ANYONE THINKS THAT KEEPING ONE OF OUR BEST UP HERE FOR A Q&A SESSION IS GOING TO WIN IT, THEN TELL THEM TO TAKE IT UP WITH ME. [TO MP ESCORT] GENTLEMEN, PLEASE ESCORT THE LADY TO HER SHIP.

[DR. CLAYTON IS ESCORTED OUT OF ROOM]

FLT ADM HOOD: SUIT UP, LIEUTENANT. WE'RE SENDING BLUE DOWNSTAIRS—YOU READY TO GET BACK TO WORK?

S-104: EAGER, SIR.

[TRANSCRIPT ENDS]

Petra Janecek was not a woman who could abide an undotted *i*.

The heavy cotton curtains drifted backward away from a decidedly pedestrian view of Forseti Northern Terminus 37, teasing the hotel room's dark interior with shafts of the very daylight Petra had been hoping to escape. The Four Winds's impeccable climate control and the spoils of her ample (if sadly short-lived) per diem should have provided Petra with a modicum of comfort in her few remaining hours on the 'burbworld without having to avail herself of the stale air perfumed by the aging spacedock nearby. But Petra felt compelled to open the room. She hadn't planned to do much more than grab a quick shower, shuffle her things in a pretense of packing, and hit whatever sauce shop was walking distance from her ride home. This wasn't supposed to be the kind of trip where Petra did much in the way of planning at all.

Her knuckles rapped against the inside of the autoserv, tugging at a Mokyshan Red Ale she couldn't, in fact, remember ordering up. Petra sighed, her gaze creeping around the dim room as her mind idly fingered the weighty decision of whether to sit or stand. *Shake it off,* she snapped at herself, *you're acting like someone just sat on your cat or something. Whatever this is—if it is anything—this is an asterisk, Petra; this is not an exclamation point. Asterisk.* It was a lovely sentiment. Sensible. Reassuring. But her gut said it was a half-truth. At best.

Forseti was one of the lucky worlds—not unlike her own home on Lenapi—which had been pretty much left off the guest list for the Great War, a blissful little bubble in space far from the senseless glassings and the kamikaze tactics that had pressed humanity within spitting distance of extinction. Petra could imagine the half billion occupants of this little residential slice o' heaven buzzing to one another in remorseful indignation, the random scraps of carnage and atrocity downed from the news-feeds giving them something to kibitz about in between jetting their kids to football practice or scarfing down fusion sushi with their boyfriends. Their horror would be much discussed. But she was pretty sure the few folks who actually lost sleep over the war hadn't exactly taxed Forseti's energy grid by keeping the lights burning night after night.

She took a hit off the beer, which she realized hadn't been touched since she opened it; the wash of hops was a little too bitter but at least it made her feel like she was doing something other than stewing. Petra knew it was ugly to be so dismissive of Forseti just because they'd never had to worry about the plasma ICUs or the tent cities or the salvage showers that rained chunks of UNSC battle fleet back down onto the planets they'd sacrificed themselves to protect. Unfair, sure—but Petra had spent the sunnier part of ten years shoveling those stories as a feed stringer. A kid's puppet show would probably have been less distilled than some of her stories once they made their way downstream; to the citizens of the cozy little planets like Forseti, the Covenant were little more than the boogeyman under the bed, painted in Technicolor by reporters like her. Places like Forseti just made Petra uncomfortable. They made her either a liar, an incompetent, or an accomplice to a conspiracy no one had bothered to explain to her.

Petra finally took a deep breath and looked back at the small coffee table where she'd dumped her kit after she got back from meeting her contact, a retired major who'd settled here but had kept a few souvenirs of his time in the service. The cheap holopad idled silently, an island away from the rest of the clutter.

You can scratch all the phantom itches or fiddle with the light-to-dark ratio of the curtains all you want, Petra, old girl. This just smells like you doing that thing where you pretend there's not a story when you obviously think there is, so can we please just get to the part of the show where we figure out if anyone's flight itineraries gotta change, eh sister?

The assignment Petra had been working for the last few weeks was really a no-brainer. *The Magellan*, one of the bigger feeds Petra sold stories to, was looking for a memorial piece on the anniversary of the Battle of Voi. Even though the details of the extragalactic conflict undertaken by the human and Sangheili forces had become (mostly) public knowledge shortly after the return of what was left of the UNSC frigate *Forward Unto Dawn*, the action in Africa was celebrated by the masses as the turning point of the war—or at least that was the way it was spun to the Press Corps, and there didn't seem like any good reason to fight the current on that one. The edit staff at *The Magellan* liked Petra—she made her deadlines and during the war had a habit of landing material that would usually have been accompanied by a next-of-kin announcement. She was the logical choice—the hatful of awards she'd scooped up for her coverage of the SPARTAN-IIs (once the flacks at Section Two had decided they *wanted* the Spartans covered) made her fodder for this kind of job, and she'd been ground zero at both New Mombasa and Voi, reporting those slugfests "all up-close and personal-like." Mostly, though, Petra's impressive sources within the UNSC establishment had made other war journos look like they were pounding the leisure beat, and *The Magellan* was hoping that through her deep ties, she'd find a way to outfluff all the other fluff pieces that were bound to hit the nets for the anniversary.

The gig was good, if a bit dusty for Petra's tastes—she much preferred things that *were happening* to those that *had happened*. She dutifully scanned all the newsvids and shuffled through all the declassified docs (*just like they taught me in Cub Reporter school all them years ago . . .*). And within a couple days, she had pasted together what she imagined pretty much every other newsie would already be sitting on—something "nice." Commemorative/thorough/boring/etc. A good first draft, but nothing to write home about. Then Petra started rolling some calls.

Voi was about more than just a pointy Covenant ship and some big metal crater appearing in the desert. Everybody knew that. The word "Forerunner" had become part of the lexicon of the late war regardless of whether 90 percent of the people out there knew what exactly it was referring to or even if it was a person, place, or thing. There were the Halo rings—those most of the human population did *not* know anything about—but in military circles, the whispers were just a little too loud to dismiss and a little too soft to publish. And that final battle—the place referenced in the Voi after-action reports and the debriefing statements from that Sangheili Arbiter. The Ark. There were seeds, all right. Petra was pretty sure she could get her contacts to slip her enough sugar to put together a *real* story; maybe not another award magnet, but at least a tale with a bit more kick than the sort of thing her mother would paw through on Sunday afternoons. As things turned out, though, Petra had been too modest in her thinking.

A picture started to form . . . Petra chuckled aloud as the phrase spun into her head, visions of some schticky old psychic waving a gloved hand over a much-abused crystal ball at one of the carnivals she and her buddy Tom went to as kids. *Well, something formed, all right,* she thought. Petra hadn't expected her sources to serve up, piece by piece, a roadmap to the final months of the war, much less the interesting narrative they told about the Spartan Master Chief Petty Officer who had been at the center of it all.

Of course Petra had heard of the guy—was pretty sure he was part of one of the SPARTAN-II squads she'd seen in action, in fact. In the days following the return of the *Forward Unto*

Dawn, Petra remembered random mentions of "Spartan-117" popping out of the ethereal chatter on numerous occasions. The Master Chief was obviously a "soldier of note" and as such a fairly well-protected asset by ONI, but this business with the Forerunner doomsday weapons and the parasitic Flood—this was something else entirely. This man's actions deserved to be known. Others felt the same, and so Petra Janecek's Voi segment was soon reframed in the context of how a single human soldier had single-handedly changed the entire course of the war.

And then she was on Forseti. The whole trip should have been a footnote. In order to appease the powers that be, she'd decided to use Voi as the wrapper around which the Master Chief story would be told. It made sense, but the way she saw it, that approach would necessitate intimacy—her audience needed to walk where the Chief had walked, see what the Chief had seen. Difficult considering the glassings carried out in the African basin by the Elites, but there was more than one way to put people in the Chief's shoes. Which is how Petra had stumbled upon the message.

The message . . . Petra sank into the couch, letting her weight drag her down into the cushion depths that she prayed would protect her from her own inquisitiveness. She noodled the holopad with the toe of her sneaker, sighing. *For God's sakes, you're such a friggin' drama queen—THIS IS NOTHING! It's not a smoking gun! It's not to blow the lid off anything! It's . . . it's . . .*

It was an undotted *i.*

A thing unresolved.

A hint.

Most likely with a perfectly reasonable explanation.

Petra played the message back again.

"Chief! High Charity, the Prophets' holy city, is on its way to Earth . . . with an army of Flood!" The blue-purple hologram's impassioned plea tugged at Petra, even though she had always been vaguely creeped out by smart AIs.

"I can't tell you everything—it's not safe," Cortana continued. "The Gravemind—it knows I'm in the system. But it doesn't know about the portal . . . where it leads."

Petra closed her eyes, as much to shut out whatever paths this message might lead to as to focus harder on the AI's words.

"On the other side, there's a solution. A way to stop the Flood—without firing the remaining Halo rings."

Whatever approximated pain in an AI coursed through the tiny hologram's features—something immediately unpleasant. "*Unnh!* Hurry, Chief—the Ark. There isn't much time!"

The recording ended. Without hesitation, Petra leaned forward and scrubbed backward through it again, bluish light flickering over her furrowed brow.

"—side, there's a solution. A way to stop the Flood—without firing the remaining Halo rings."

Petra had already packed the Ark dossier she'd put together, but she didn't really need it anymore; she'd memorized the big beats. The UNSC and the Elites had gotten lucky when the Flood had come to them en masse, and the Master Chief had used the replacement Halo ring the Ark was constructing to wipe them all out in one fell swoop.

A way to stop the Flood. Without firing the remaining Halo rings.

A way to stop the Flood.

A way.

Was she talking about the replacement ring? Absolutely possible; she was obviously knowledgeable about the Portal and where it led, so perfectly reasonable that she could have known there was another Halo installation. Technically, it wouldn't involve firing the "rings" plural, right?

Could the Ark have been a weapon? Details are fairly sketchy—OK, very sketchy—but as the mother of all Forerunner artifacts, it's certainly not out of the realm of possibility. Although it was meant as a fallback position to fire the Halo rings

from, so why would you need to fire them at all if the Ark itself
possessed a weapon that could stop the Flood?

Or . . .

With a surly stab, Petra quickly toggled the holopad off. The "or" was what she knew with certainty would keep her sleeping hours to a minimum for the foreseeable future. "Or" couldn't be bargained with, it wouldn't get bored and run off to play with its little friends, it wasn't going to show up at her door at 11 P.M. a week from now claiming it was all a big misunderstanding. The only cure for "or" was to find out what the hell the little glowstick was on about. If there was some other instrument of destruction Cortana had set her sights on to use against the nigh-undefeatable Flood . . . well, that certainly wasn't going to be a footnote, now, was it?

Petra's hand flopped onto the couch, smoothing the cushions as if she were petting her folks' dog, Handsome, back home on Lenapi. The pillows were soft and cool from the breeze blowing in through the balcony doors. Petra mussed her hair, taking a last quiet moment to watch the curtains reverse course and get dragged out toward the city beyond. Then she was up, and on the phone with the cruise line to see if her ticket could be exchanged for the next flight to Earth.

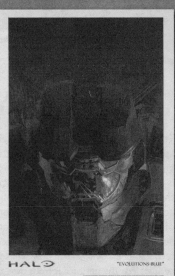

HALO®
W A Y P O I N T

Halo Waypoint is your hub for all things Halo. Whether it's for the intricate details of Halo's fiction, the incredibly creative community-generated content, a comprehensive look at your Campaign and Multiplayer Career across many Halo titles, or tools to enhance your Halo Multiplayer experience... Waypoint has you covered.

Halo Waypoint provides fans with access to exclusive, never-before-seen shows and series, offering the Halo community the news and entertainment they need, when they need it. Waypoint provides detailed multiplayer stats and game history for Halo: Reach and Halo: Combat Evolved Anniversary. The Halo Multiplayer experience becomes more social with Waypoint Custom Challenges. And Halo players can get a leg up on the competition with Waypoint ATLAS for mobile devices.

You can access Halo Waypoint on your console via the Main Menu in Halo: Reach and Halo: Anniversary, or directly from the Xbox LIVE Games Marketplace. You can download Halo Waypoint on Windows Phone 7, iOS, and Android devices. And you can access Waypoint from anywhere at <u>www.halowaypoint.com</u>.